The Beating of His Wings

The Publishers of *The Beating of His Wings* are ordered by the International Court of Archaeological Artefacts to print this judgment on the first page of each copy.

Moderator Breffni Waltz
38th of Messidor AD 143.830

Summary of Preliminary Judgment dated Republican Era 143.710 from the International Court of Archaeological Artefacts concerning the Left Hand of God trilogy and administration of the so-called 'Rubbish Tips of Paradise'. These 'tips', for the avoidance of doubt, constitute the four square miles centred on the first discovery by Paul Fahrenheit of large amounts of printed paper dating from extreme antiquity. My judgement is preliminary and subject to review in the first instance by the Court of Pleas. However, an immediate decision is required because of the claim by UNAS that irreplaceable documents and artefacts are being lost for ever, citing the routine use of the contents of the Rubbish Tips of Paradise as toilet paper by the nomadic tribes that frequently pass through the site.

The facts of this case are not in dispute and are as follows:

This litigation has its origins in the first landing on the moon by Captain Victoria Ung Khanan some thirty years ago. That within days Captain Khanan discovered she had been beaten to this greatest of all firsts by some 165,000 years was as great a shock, perhaps, as has ever been delivered to WoMankind. The fragile remnants of what must have been an even more fragile spacecraft revealed that it had its origins in a vanished terrestrial civilization we knew nothing about, a civilization which soon became known as the Flag People, after the starred and striped insignia planted next to the craft. As a result, The Unified Nations Archaeological Survey was founded with the sole purpose of searching for evidence of the Flag People on earth itself.

So far this search has proved fruitless and for one simple reason: ice. UNAS quickly discovered that 164,000 years ago a period of major glaciation, now known as The Snowball, covered nearly the entire planet in ice, often to a depth of several miles. Ice that brings low vast mountain ranges has little problem removing the veneer of even the most complex civilization – clearly only the smallest rump of the population could have survived. Further investigation, however, revealed a later and significant period of warming during The Snowball, which for fifteen thousand years caused the ice to retreat far enough and long enough for new civilizations to emerge, before they in turn were swallowed up by the returning ice.

It is at this point in this frustrating story that Paul Fahrenheit emerged to criticize, to put it at its mildest, his colleagues for their obsession with technological solutions to this great problem. He pointed out that trying to find such whispery traces of the past was like 'looking for hay in a haystack' unless they used 'some mechanism' to guide the technology. The 'mechanism' likely to prove most effective in narrowing down the haystack, he argued, was that of legend and folk story. He claimed that real historical events from the distant past could become embedded in what were apparently entirely imaginary stories of gods and monsters and other fantastical tales. His ideas were dismissed out of hand and the relationship between Fahrenheit and his colleagues and superiors at UNAS became what could only be called vituperative.

As a result, in the Ventose of Republican Era 139, Paul Fahrenheit left UNAS in pursuit of what to his colleagues was the very definition of a wild goose chase – in search of what the isolated Habiru people called the Rubbish Tips of Paradise. It was here Mr Fahrenheit thought he might be able to find the first terrestrial evidence if not of the Flag People then of the civilizations that briefly followed.

Four years after Paul Fahrenheit's disappearance the first volume of a 'fantasy' fiction trilogy entitled *The Left Hand of God* was published. It was widely translated into some twenty-six languages but its reception by both audiences and critics was highly polarized: it was greatly admired by some but much disliked by others for its peculiar tone and odd approach to the art of storytelling. How are these two apparently unrelated events connected? It turns out that Mr Fahrenheit was behind the publication of *The Left Hand of God* and a subsequent volume, *The Last Four Things*. These books were very far from the contemporary works of escapist fantasy they were presented as. As it happens, Fahrenheit's belief in the potential of the Rubbish Tips of Paradise was entirely on the mark. To cut a long and bitter story short, Fahrenheit took it into his head not to tell his former employer of his discovery, as he was legally bound to do. Instead, he claimed UNAS would, and I quote, 'smother the undoubted brilliance of what I have called the Left Hand of God trilogy in a dreary academic translation worked over by an army of self-serving pedants who would bury its vitality under a layer of high-minded dullness, footnotes and incomprehensible and obscurantist analysis.'

Fahrenheit became obsessed with his belief that the modern world should confront these three books in something of the way their original audience might have confronted them. As a result, he took it upon himself to translate them (a considerable intellectual feat recognized even by his detractors) and have them published under his mother's family name as the above contemporary works of fiction. Who knows how long this curious subterfuge might have worked were it not for Mr Fahrenheit's indiscreet pillow talk with a young woman, who, it turned out, was not as trustworthy as he believed and who promptly sold the story to a news tablet, which in turn led to UNAS applying to this court for an injunction putting the Rubbish Tips of Paradise under their legal control.

The Unified Nations Archaeological Survey is granted, as requested, complete but temporary control over the site.

However, its suit to prevent the publication of the final 'novel' in the Left Hand of God trilogy, *The Beating of His Wings*, in a translation by Paul Fahrenheit, is denied. Publication may proceed under the condition that the summary of this judgement is printed at the beginning of *The Beating of His Wings*. Both UNAS and Paul Fahrenheit are given leave to add an appendix at the conclusion of the work in which they may explain their positions.

The Beating of His Wings

PAUL HOFFMAN

PENGUIN BOOKS

PENGUIN BOOKS

Published by the Penguin Group
Penguin Books Ltd, 80 Strand, London WC2R ORL, England
Penguin Group (USA) Inc., 375 Hudson Street, New York, New York 10014, USA
Penguin Group (Canada), 90 Eglinton Avenue East, Suite 700, Toronto, Ontario, Canada M4P 2Y3
(a division of Pearson Penguin Canada Inc.)
Penguin Ireland, 25 St Stephen's Green, Dublin 2, Ireland (a division of Penguin Books Ltd)
Penguin Group (Australia), 707 Collins Street, Melbourne, Victoria 3008,
Australia (a division of Pearson Australia Group Pty Ltd)
Penguin Books India Pvt Ltd, 11 Community Centre,
Panchsheel Park, New Delhi – 110 017, India
Penguin Group (NZ), 67 Apollo Drive, Rosedale, Auckland 0632, New Zealand
(a division of Pearson New Zealand Ltd)
Penguin Books (South Africa) (Pty) Ltd, Block D, Rosebank Office Park, 181 Jan Smuts Avenue,
Parktown North, Gauteng 2193, South Africa

Penguin Books Ltd, Registered Offices: 80 Strand, London WC2R ORL, England

www.penguin.com

First published 2013
Published in Penguin Books 2014
001

Set in Garamond MT
Typeset by Palimpsest Book Production Ltd, Falkirk, Stirlingshire
Printed in Great Britain by Clays Ltd, St Ives plc

ISBN: 978-0-141-04240-4

www.greenpenguin.co.uk

For my editor, Alex Clarke, who got there first.

There are three fundamental human emotions: fear, rage and love.

J. B. Watson, *Journal of Experimental Psychology*

Give me a dozen healthy infants, well-formed and my own specific world to bring them up in and I'll guarantee to take any one at random and train him to become any type of specialist I might select – a doctor, lawyer, artist, merchant-chief and, yes, even into a beggar-man and thief, regardless of his talents, penchants, tendencies, abilities, vocations and race of his ancestors.

J. B. Watson,
'What the nursery has to say about instincts'
Psychologies of 1925

By the time you are fourteen years old the worst thing that will ever happen to you will probably have already taken place.

Louis Bris, *The Wisdom of Crocodiles*

PART ONE

I came alone and I go as a stranger. I do not know who
I am, or what I have been doing.

Aurangzeb

I

A brief report on Thomas Cale, Lunatic. Three conversations at the Priory on the Island of Cyprus.

(NB This appraisal took place after Mother Superior Allbright's stroke. The notes she filed have been mislaid along with Cale's admission details. This report needs to be read in the light of this absence and so I will not be held liable for any of my conclusions.)

PHYSICAL CHARACTERISTICS
Medium stature, unusually pale. Middle finger of his left hand missing. Depression fracture to the right side of his skull. Severe keloid scar tissue in wound in left shoulder. Patient says he experiences intermittent pain from all injuries.

SYMPTOMS
Severe retching, usually in mid-afternoon. Exhaustion. Suffers insomnia and bad dreams when able to sleep. Loss of weight.

HISTORY
Thomas Cale suffers no hysterical delusions or uncontrolled behaviour beyond that of his sour nature. His mid-afternoon retching leaves him speechless with exhaustion, after which he sleeps. By late evening he is able to talk, although he is the most sarcastic and wounding of persons. He claims to have been bought for sixpence from parents he does not remember by a priest of the Order of the Hanged Redeemer.

Thomas Cale is droll, not his least irritating affectation, and always tries either to make his interlocutor unsure as to whether he is mocking them or, by unpleasant contrast, to make it abundantly clear that he is. He tells the story of his upbringing in the Sanctuary as if daring me to disbelieve the daily cruelties he endured. Recovering from an injury which caused the dent in his head he claims – again it is not possible to tell with what degree of seriousness – that his already great prowess (he seems boastful in hindsight, but not at the time) was greatly increased as a result of the injury and that since this recovery he is always able to anticipate in advance any opponent's movements. This sounds unlikely; I declined his offer of a demonstration. The rest of his story is as improbable as the most far-fetched children's story of derring-do and swashbuckling. He is the worst liar I have ever come across.

His story briefly. His life of deprivation and military training at the Sanctuary came to a dramatic end one night after he accidentally came upon a high-ranking Redeemer in the middle of performing a live dissection upon two young girls, some kind of holy experiment to discover a means to neuter the power of women over mankind. Killing that Redeemer in the ensuing struggle, he escaped from the Sanctuary with the surviving young woman and two of his friends, with more Redeemers in vengeful pursuit. Evading their pursuers, the quartet ended up in Memphis where, plausibly, Thomas Cale made many enemies and (rather less plausibly) a number of powerful allies, including the notorious IdrisPukke and his half-brother, Chancellor Vipond (as he then was). Despite these advantages his violent nature asserted itself in a brutal but unusually non-fatal altercation with (so he says) half a dozen of the youths of Memphis in which (of course) he emerged triumphant but bound for prison. Nevertheless, Lord Vipond again mysteriously intervened on his behalf and he was sent into the countryside with IdrisPukke. The peace of the Materazzi hunting lodge where they were staying was interrupted shortly after he arrived by a woman who attempted to assassinate him, for reasons he was unable to clarify. His murder was prevented not by his own wonderful abilities – he was swimming naked at the time of the attack – but by a mysterious, unseen and insolent stranger who killed his would-be assassin by means of an arrow in the back. His saviour then vanished without explanation or trace.

By now the priests of the Sanctuary had discovered his general whereabouts and attempted to flush him out (he claims) by kidnapping Arbell Materazzi, daughter of the Doge of Memphis. When I asked him why the Redeemers would risk a ruinous war with the greatest of all temporal powers for his sake, he laughed in my face and told me he would reveal his magnificent importance to me in due course. The inflated mad, in my experience, take their importance most seriously but it is a feature of Thomas Cale that his demented state only becomes apparent a few hours after a conversation with him comes to an end. While you are in his company even the most implausible stories he tells cause you to suspend disbelief until several hours later, when a most irritating sensation creeps over you, as if you had been tricked by a marketplace quack into parting with ready money for a bottle of universal remedy. I've seen this before in a lunatic, though rarely, in that some are so powerfully deluded and in such a strange way that their delusions run away with even the most cautious of anomists.

Of course, Thomas Cale rescues the beautiful princess from the wicked Redeemers but, it must be said, not by means of the fair and noble fight against overwhelming odds but by stabbing most of his opponents in their sleep. This is another unusual feature of his delusion – that each one of his endless triumphs is not generally achieved by heroism and noble audacity but through brutal trickery and conscienceless pragmatism. Usually such madmen present themselves as gallant and chivalrous, but Thomas Cale freely admits to poisoning his enemies' water with rotting animals and killing his opponents in their sleep. It's worth recording briefly one of our exchanges in this regard.

ME
Is it a matter of course with you that you always kill unarmed prisoners?

PATIENT
It's easier than killing armed ones.

ME
So you believe the lives of others are a matter for sarcasm?

PATIENT
(NO REPLY)

ME
You never consider showing mercy?

PATIENT
No, I never did.

ME
Why?

PATIENT
They wouldn't have shown it to me. Besides, what would I do but let them go only to find I'd have to

6

fight them again. Then I might become their prisoner
– and be killed myself.

ME
What about women and children?

PATIENT
I never killed them deliberately.

ME
But you've killed them?

PATIENT
Yes. I've killed them.

He claimed to have built a camp to sequester the wives and
children of the Folk insurrection and that because of his
having been removed elsewhere almost the entire cantonment
of five thousand souls died through famine and disease.
When I asked him what he felt about this he replied: 'What
should I feel?'

To return to his story. After his brutal rescue of the beautiful
Arbell Materazzi (are there any merely plain princesses in the
world of the delusional?) he was promoted, along with his
two friends, to guard the young woman towards whom he
maintained throughout our three long conversations a deeply
held resentment as to her ingratitude and disdain for him.
This bitterness seems to hold a great sway over him because
of his belief that when Memphis later fell to the Redeemers,
it did so because the Materazzi failed to execute his plan to
defeat them. (He is, by the way, very insistent that his skill in
generalship is greater even than his talent for personal
savagery.)

Usually sarcastic and matter-of-fact as he boasts of his great
rise to power – again, his droll tone makes it seem not like

boasting until one reflects upon his claims in tranquillity – he became most indignant as he recounted the way in which he was caught by the Redeemers after the Battle of Silbury Hill (certainly a disaster for us all whether or not Thomas Cale was involved). It is possible he was caught up in the battle in a minor way; his description of the events there has the note of real experience. Like all skilled romancers he can use his actual events to make the imagined ones truly plausible. For example, he frequently expresses repentance for any noble or generous actions he has performed. He says that he risked his life to save a Materazzi youth who had bullied and tormented him – an act of sanctity which he says he now bitterly regrets. When I asked whether it was always bad to act generously towards others he said that in his experience it might not be bad but it was always a 'bloody catastrophe'. People thought so well of doing good, he said, that in the end they always decided it should be done at the end of a sword. The Redeemers thought so highly of goodness they wanted to kill everyone including themselves and start again. It turns out that this was the reason his former mentor, Redeemer Bosco, wanted him back at any price. Thomas Cale is (of course) no ordinary boy but the manifestation of God's wrath and destined to wipe his greatest mistake (you and me, for the avoidance of doubt) off the face of the earth. I have treated shopkeepers who thought they were great generals and men who could barely write who thought they were poets of unparalleled genius but I have never encountered an inflation of such magnitude before – let alone in a child. When I asked him how long he'd had such feelings of importance he began to backtrack and – with very bad temper – said that this was what Bosco thought, not what he, Thomas Cale, thought. More circumspectly, I asked him if he believed Redeemer Bosco was mad and he replied he had never met a Redeemer who wasn't and that in his experience a great many people who seemed to be right in the head, once you got to see them 'put under grief', were 'completely barking' – an expression I have not encountered before though its meaning was clear enough.

He is clever, then, at avoiding the implications of his delusions of grandeur: in the opinion of great and powerful men he is mighty enough to destroy all the world but this delusion is not his but theirs. When I asked him if he *would* do such a thing his reply was extremely foul-mouthed but to the effect that he would not. When I asked whether he had the *ability* to do such a thing he smiled – not pleasantly – and said he had been responsible for the deaths of ten thousand men killed in a single day, so it was only a question of how many thousands and how many days.

After his recapture by the Redeemer Bosco, his role of Angel of Death to the world was explained to him in detail and he was put to work by his former mentor. This 'Bosco' (the new Pope is called Bosco but Thomas Cale clearly likes a big lie) is much hated by Cale although, since buying him for sixpence, training him and then elevating him to the power almost of a god, Bosco is paradoxically the source of all his excellence. When I pointed this out he claimed to know this already, though I could see I had scored a hit to his vanity (which is very great).

He then detailed an endless series of battles, which all sounded the same to me, and in which he was, of course, always victorious. When I asked if, during all these successes, he had not suffered even a few setbacks he looked at me as if he would like to cut my throat and then laughed – but very oddly, more like a single bark, as if he could not contain something very far from high spirits or even mockery.

These numerous triumphs led in turn to his being less watched over by Bosco than formerly. And after yet another great battle, in which he overcame the greatest of all opponents, he slipped away in the resulting chaos and ended up in Spanish Leeds, where he suffered the first of the brain attacks that brought him here. I witnessed one of these seizures and they are alarming to watch and clearly distressing to endure – his entire body is wracked by convulsions, as if he is trying to vomit but is unable to do so. He insists he has been sent here by friends of some power and influence in Spanish Leeds. Needless to say, of these important benefactors there is no sign. When I asked why they had not been to see him he explained – as if I were an idiot – that he had only just arrived in Cyprus and that the distance was too great for them to travel to see him regularly. This great distance was a deliberate choice in order to keep him safe. 'From what?' I asked. 'From all those who want me dead,' he replied.

He told me that he had arrived with an attendant doctor and a letter for Mother Superior Allbright. Pressed, he told me that the doctor had returned to Spanish Leeds the next day but that he had spent several hours with the Mother Superior before his departure. Clearly Thomas Cale must have come from somewhere, and there might indeed have been some sort of attendant who arrived with him bearing a letter and who spoke with the Mother Superior prior to her stroke. The loss, as it were, of both letter and Mother Superior leaves this case somewhat in the Limbo in which unbaptized infants are said to wait out eternity. Given the violent nature of his imaginings (though not, to be fair, his behaviour) it seems wisest to place him in the protective ward until the letter can be found or the Mother Superior recovers enough to tell us more about him. As it stands, there is no one to whom I can even write to make enquiries about him. This is an unsatisfactory state of affairs and it is not the first time by a long chalk that records have gone missing. I will discuss the alleviation of his symptoms when the herbalist comes the day after tomorrow. As to his delusions of grandeur – in my opinion, treating those is the work of many years.

Anna Calkins, Anomist

For weeks Cale lay in bed, retching and sleeping, retching and sleeping. He became aware after a few days that the door at the end of the twenty-bed ward was locked at all times, but this was both something he was used to and, in the circumstances, hardly mattered: he was not in a fit state to go anywhere. The food was adequate, the care kindly enough. He did not like sleeping in the same room as other men once again but there were only nineteen of them and they all seemed to live in their own nightmares and were not concerned with him. He was able to stay quiet and endure.

2

The Two Trevors, Lugavoy and Kovtun, had spent a frustrating week in Spanish Leeds trying to discover a way of getting to Thomas Cale. They had been thwarted by the cautious nature of the enquiries forced on them in Kitty the Hare's city (as it had now become). It didn't do to upset Kitty and they didn't want him to know what they were up to. Kitty liked a bung, and the amount of money he'd expect for allowing them to operate in his dominion was not something they were keen to pay: this was to be their last job and they had no intention of sharing the rewards with Kitty the Hare. Questions had to be discreet, which is not easy when fear is usually what you do, when threats are your legal tender. The two were considering more brutal methods when discretion finally paid off. They heard of a young seamstress in the town who had been encouraging a better class of client to come to her by boasting, truthfully, that she had made the elegant suit worn by Thomas Cale at his notoriously bad-tempered appearance at the royal banquet held in honour of Arbell Materazzi and her husband, Conn.

Who knows what helpful information Cale might have let slip while he was having his inside leg measured? Tailors were almost as good a source of information as priests, and easier to manipulate – the tailors' immortal souls were not at risk for blabbing a bit of dropped gossip; there was no such thing as the silence of the changing room. But the young seamstress was not as easily menaced as they'd hoped.

'I don't know anything about Thomas Cale, and I wouldn't tell you if I did. Go away.'

This response meant that one of two things was going to happen. Trevor Kovtun had by now resigned himself to committing an atrocity of some kind, Kitty the Hare or not. He locked the shop door and brought down the shutter on the open window. The seamstress didn't waste her time telling them to stop. They lowered their voices as they worked.

'I'm fed up with what we have to do to this girl,' said Trevor Lugavoy. This was both true and a way of frightening her. 'I really do want this to be our last job.'

'Don't say that. If you say it's our last then something will go wrong.'

'You mean,' said Lugavoy, 'some supernatural power is listening and will thwart our presumption?'

'It doesn't do any harm to act as if there were a God sometimes. Don't tempt providence.'

Trevor Kovtun walked over to the seamstress, who had by now realized something dreadful had come into her life.

'You seem to be a clever little thing – your own shop, a sharp tongue in your head.'

'I'll call the Badiel.'

'Too late for that now, my dear. There are no Badiels in the world we're about to take you to – no defenders or preservers, no one at all to watch over you. Here in the city you believed you were safe, by and large – but being an intelligent girl you must have known there were horrible things out there.'

'We *are* those horrible things.'

'Yes, we are. We are bad news.'

'Very bad news.'

'Will you hurt him?' she said – looking for a way out.

'We will kill him,' said Trevor Kovtun. 'But we've given our word to do it as quickly as we can. There will be no cruelty, just the death. You must make a decision about yourself – live or die.'

But what decision was there?

Later, on leaving the shop, Kovtun pointed out that even a year earlier they would have killed the girl in such an unspeakably vile way that any question of resistance to their investigations would have evaporated like the summer drizzle on the great salt flats of Utah.

'But that was a year ago,' said Trevor Lugavoy. 'Besides, I've a feeling we're running out of deaths. Best be thrifty. Cale should be our last ticket.'

'You've been saying we should stop almost since we started twenty years ago.'

'Now I mean it.'

'Well, you shouldn't have said anything to me about finishing until we were done – then we could just have finished. Now that you've made a thing about this being our last job you've turned it into an event, so. If you want to get God's attention, tell him your plans.'

'If there was a God who was interested in sticking his nose in, don't you think he'd have put a stop to us by now? Either God intervenes in the lives of men or he doesn't. There's no halfway.'

'How do you know? His ends might be mysterious.'

They were experienced men and used to difficulties and they were not especially surprised to discover that Cale had gone somewhere else for reasons the girl was unclear about. But they had the name of Vague Henri, a good description of a boy with a scar on his face, and a convincing assurance that he'd know exactly where Cale had gone. Three days of hanging about followed, asking their unsuspicious questions and trying not to be conspicuous. In the end, patience was all that was required.

Vague Henri liked people but not the kind of people who lived in palaces. It wasn't that he hadn't made an effort. At one banquet at which he'd accompanied IdrisPukke he'd been asked, with a polite lack of attention, how he'd come to be there. Thinking they were interested in his extraordinary experiences he told them, starting with his life in the Sanctuary. But the details of the strange privations of the place did not fascinate, they repelled. Only IdrisPukke overheard the chinless wonder who said, 'My God, the people they're letting in these days.' But the next remark was heard by Vague Henri as well. He'd mentioned something about working in the kitchens in Memphis and some exquisite, intending to be overheard, drawled: '*How banal!*' Vague Henri caught the tone of contempt but couldn't be sure – he didn't know what it meant, perhaps it was an expression of sympathy and he'd misunderstood. Deciding it was time to leave, IdrisPukke claimed he was feeling unwell.

'What does barn owl mean?' asked Vague Henri on the way home. IdrisPukke was reluctant to hurt his feelings but the boy needed to know what the score was with these people.

'It means commonplace – beneath the interest of a cultured person. He was a drawler: it's pronounced *ban-al.*'

'He wasn't being nice, then?'

'No.'

He didn't say anything for a minute.

'I prefer barn owl,' he said at last. But it stung.

Most of the time IdrisPukke was away on business for his brother and so Vague Henri was lonely. He now realized he wasn't acceptable to Spanish Leeds society, not even its lower rungs (who were, if anything, even more snobbish than their betters), so several times a week he took a walk to the local beer cellars and sat in a corner, sometimes striking up a conversation but mostly just eating and drinking and listening to other people enjoying themselves. He was too used to wearing a cassock to be comfortable in anything else and, like Cale, had got the seamstress to run him up a couple in blue birdseye: twelve ounce, peaked lapel and felted pockets, straight, no bezel. He was quite the dandy. But in Spanish Leeds, a fifteen-year-old in a cassock with a fresh scar on his cheek was hard to miss. The Two Trevors watched Vague Henri from the other side of the snug as he enjoyed a pint of Mad Dog, a beer he marginally preferred to Go-By-The-Wall or Lift Leg.

For the next two hours, to the irritation of the Two Trevors, he chatted away to various locals and was cornered for half an hour by an amiable drunk.

'D'yew liked metalled cheese?'

'Sorry?'

'D'yew like metalled cheese?'

'Oh,' said Vague Henri, after a pause. 'Do I like melted cheese?'

'Shwat I shed.'

But he didn't mind. There was something miraculous to him still about the talk, buzz and laughter, the ordinary good times being had by almost everyone except the occasional maudlin boozer or angry bladdered toper. At chucking-out he left with the others, the inebriated and the sober. The Two Trevors followed at a cautious distance.

These experienced men were never careless, they were as prepared for the unexpected event as if one took place daily on the backs of their hands, but their position as they closed on Vague Henri was a little more hazardous than even these careful murderers had reckoned.

Cale's reputation as an epic desperado had not so much overshadowed Vague Henri's as caught it in a general eclipse. To the Two Trevors he was dangerous, no doubt – they knew his background as a Redeemer acolyte and that you would have to be unusually hard-wearing to make it to the age of fifteen – but they were not, in truth, expecting a nasty surprise, even though nasty surprises were something they were used to.

Be clear, two against one is hideous odds, particularly when it's night and the Trevors are the two who want a word with you. But Vague Henri had already improved his chances: he knew he was being followed. They soon realized their mistake and stepped back into the shadows and called out to him.

'Vague Henri, is it?' said Trevor Lugavoy.

Vague Henri turned, letting them see the knife in his right hand and that he was easing a heartless-looking knuckle-duster onto his left.

'Never heard of him. Buzz off.'

'We just want a word.'

Vague Henri opened his mouth as if in joyous surprise and welcome. 'Thank God,' he said, 'you've come with news of my brother, Jonathan.' He moved forward. Had Lugavoy, who was ten yards in front of Kovtun, not been an assassin of a very superior kind he would have had Vague Henri's knife buried in his chest. Unluckily for Vague Henri, Lugavoy instantly backed away, alarmed by the boy's odd-ness as he stepped forward and struck out. The trick that had earned Vague Henri his nickname, the sudden incomprehensible question or answer intended to distract, had failed, if only just. Now they were alert and the balance in their favour once again.

'We want to talk to Thomas Cale.'

'Never heard of him, either.'

Vague Henri backed away. The Two Trevors moved apart and then forward – Lugavoy would make the first jab, Kovtun the second. There would be no more than four.

'Where is he, your friend?'

'No idea what you're talking about, mate.'

'Just tell us and we're on our way.'

'Come a bit closer and I'll whisper it in your ear.'

They wouldn't have killed him right away, of course. The knife driven in three inches deep just above the lowest rib would have taken the fight out of the boy long enough to get some answers. Never before in his life and only once afterwards was Vague Henri rescued – but tonight he was. In the almost silence of the trio's scuffling manoeuvres there was a loud CLICK! from behind the two advancing men. All three knew the sound of the latch of an overstrung crossbow.

'Hello, Trevors,' said a cheerful voice from somewhere in the dark.

There was a moment's silence.

'That you, Cadbury?'

'Oh, indeed it is, Trevor.'

'You wouldn't shoot a man in the back.'

'Oh, indeed I would.'

But this wasn't quite the rescue in the nick of time so loved by magsmen and yarn-spinners and their gullible audiences. In fact, Cadbury had no idea who the young person in the peculiar clothes was. For all he knew, he might entirely deserve the fate the Two Trevors were about to hand out to him – the people they were paid to murder usually did. He had not been watching over him but, only in a manner of speaking, the Two Trevors.

They'd had a change of heart about Kitty after talking to

the seamstress; it was no longer plausible to imagine he wouldn't become aware of their presence. So they'd observed the proper form by paying him a visit and, while declining to say what their business was in Spanish Leeds, assured Kitty that it would not conflict with his own. As he pointed out to Cadbury later, who were these pair of murderers to know what did or did not conflict with Kitty the Hare's multitude of concerns? Kitty invited them to stay as long as they wished. The Two Trevors replied that they would almost certainly be gone by the following Monday. The result was that, at considerable expense and some difficulty, Cadbury had been keeping tabs on them, not the easiest of things to do. The reason he was here in person was that his watchful intelligencers had lost them for several hours and Cadbury had become nervous.

'What now?' said Trevor Lugavoy.

'Now? Now you buzz off like the young man said. And I mean out of Spanish Leeds. Go on a pilgrimage to beg forgiveness for your shitload of sins. I hear Lourdes is particularly horrible at this time of year.'

And that was that. The Two Trevors moved to the wall opposite Vague Henri, but before they merged with the dark, Lugavoy nodded towards him. 'See you.'

'Lucky for you, old man,' said Vague Henri, 'that he came when he did.' Then they were gone.

'This way,' said Cadbury. As Vague Henri stepped behind him he let go of the overstrung bow and with an enormous TWANG! the bolt shot into the blackness, bouncing between the narrow walls in a criss-cross series of pings. As Vague Henri and his not-exactly rescuer put on some speed down the road, a mildly offended distant voice called out to them, 'You want to be careful, Cadbury, you could've had someone's eye out.'

It was unfortunate that Cadbury and Vague Henri met under such circumstances. The latter was no fool and was getting less foolish all the time – but if someone saves your life only the most disciplined could fail to be grateful. And he was, after all, still just a boy.

Cadbury's offer to stay with him for the evening was well taken and Vague Henri very much needed the several drinks he was offered on top of the ones he'd had already. No surprise then that he told Cadbury a great deal more than he should have. Cadbury was, when not murdering or carrying out doubtful business on behalf of Kitty the Hare, an amiable and entertaining presence, and as capable and desiring of affection and friendship as anyone else. In short, he quickly developed a fondness for Vague Henri, and not one like that of IdrisPukke's for Cale that was particularly difficult to understand. It even had the mark of true friendship, if by that one means the willingness of friends to put aside their own interests for the other's. Cadbury decided it might be better if Vague Henri were not drawn to Kitty the Hare's attention in any more distinctive way than he already had been (as an unimportant familiar of Thomas Cale). Kitty was skilled at not letting you become aware of what he knew or did not know.

'They are *hoi oligoi* of assassins,' Cadbury replied to Vague Henri's questions. 'The Two Trevors cut down William the Silent in broad daylight, surrounded by a hundred bodyguards; they poisoned the lampreys of Cleopatra even though she had three tasters. When he heard what they'd done to her, the Great Snopes was so afraid that he ate nothing he hadn't picked himself – but one night they smeared all the apples in his orchard using a strange device they made themselves. They leave no survivors. Whoever it is that Cale has upset, they have money and a great deal of it.'

'I'd better disappear.'

'Well, if you can vanish into thin air then by all means do so. But if you can't evaporate you're better off where you are. Not even the Two Trevors will ignore Kitty the Hare's instruction to stay away from Spanish Leeds.'

'I thought they could get to anyone?'

'So they can. But Kitty isn't just anyone. Besides, no one has paid them for such a risk. They'll look for another way. Just stay out of sight for the next week, until I can say for certain that they've gone.'

3

It was mid-morning and Cale was waiting to go mad again. It was a sensation something like the uneasy feeling before a chunder heaves out the poisons of a toxic meal; the sense of a horrible, almost living creature gaining strength in the bowels. It must come but it will take its time, not yours, and the waiting is worse than the spewing up. A juggernaut was on its way, passengered by devils: Legion, Pyro, Martini, Leonard, Nanny Powler and Burnt Jarl, all of them gibbering and shrieking in Cale's poor tum.

Face to the wall, knees to his chest, waiting for it to be over with, he felt a hefty shove in the back. He turned.

'You're in my bed.'

The speaker was a tall young man who looked as if his clothes were filled not by flesh but large ill-shapen potatoes. For all his lumpiness there was real power here.

'What?'

'You're in my bed. Get out.'

'This is my bed. I've had it for weeks.'

'But I want it. So now it's mine. Understand?'

Indeed, Cale did understand. The days of invincibility were over for the foreseeable future. He picked up his few possessions, put them in his sack, went over to a free corner and had his attack of the conniptions as quietly as he could.

In Spanish Leeds, Vague Henri was on his way back to his room in the castle, protected as far as the gate by four of Cadbury's stooges, and with a promise of financial help from his new friend in the matter of the Purgators. Vague Henri detested all one hundred and fifty of these former Redeemers who Cale had saved from Brzca's knife – for the simple reason that they were still Redeemers as far as he was concerned. But they were valuable because they would now follow Cale anywhere, under the entirely mistaken belief that he was their great leader and as devoted to them as they were to him. Cale had used them to fight his way across the Swiss border, intending to desert them as soon as he and Vague Henri were safe. But Cale soon realized that controlling so many trained soldiers willing to die for him would be extremely useful in the violent times ahead, however much he loathed their presence. There was one weakness in Cale's plan: how to pay the ruinous amount of money it cost to keep so many in idleness until the expected war started – which, of course, it might not. With Cale gone, Vague Henri desperately needed money for himself and for the keep of the Purgators. He also needed a friend and he had found both in Cadbury, who thought it useful to have someone indebted to him who could draw on such a resource in these uncertain times. It was clear that Vague Henri was unwilling to discuss Cale's whereabouts and would only say that he was ill but would be back in a few months. Cadbury was too smart to raise Vague Henri's suspicions by pressing him. Instead of asking questions he offered help – a winning strategy in all circumstances.

Now Kitty had an influence over someone who knew and understood the Purgators and who possessed information about the whereabouts of Thomas Cale. This information might become important in due course and now he knew where to get it should this prove necessary. Kitty the Hare was a person of intelligence but also considerable instinct. When it came to Cale, he shared Bosco's belief in his remarkable possibilities, if not their supernatural origin; but news of Cale's illness, however vague, meant that Kitty's plans for him might have to be revised. On the other hand, they might not. It would depend on what kind of sickness was at issue. Desperate and dangerous times were coming and Kitty the Hare needed to prepare for them. The potential usefulness of Thomas Cale was too great to let the question of his current ill-health entirely diminish Kitty's interest in what became of him.

A thumb on every scale and a finger in every pie was Kitty's reputation, but these days most of his concentration was on what was being weighed and cooked in Leeds Castle, the great keep that scraped the skies above the city. Its fame for not having required a defence in over four hundred years was now threatened, and King Zog of Switzerland and Albania had arrived to discuss its defence with his chancellor, Bose Ikard, a man he disliked (his great-grandfather had been in trade) but knew he could not do without. It was said of Zog that he was wise about everything except anything of importance – a worse insult than it appeared, in that his wisdom was confined to skill at setting his favourites against one another, reneging on promises and a talent for taking bribes through his minions. If they were caught, however, he made such a show of punishing them and expressing complete outrage at their crimes that he was generally more renowned for his honesty than otherwise.

All the posh with power, the who whom, the nobs who had gathered in Leeds Castle to discuss the possibility of staying out of the coming war were anxious to become favourites, if they were not already, and to stay that way if they were. Nevertheless, there were many who disliked Zog on a matter of principle. They were particularly agitated at the great gathering because on his way to Leeds he had stuck his royal nose into a village council inquiry (he was a relentless busybody in minor affairs of state) regarding an accusation that a recently arrived refugee from the war was, in fact, a Redeemer spy. Convinced of the man's guilt, Zog had stopped the proceedings and ordered his execution. This upset many of the great and good because it brought home to them the fragile nature of the laws that protected them: if, as one of them said, a man can be hanged before he has been tried, how long before a man can be hanged before he has offended? Besides, even if he were guilty it was obviously foolish to upset the Redeemers by hanging one of them while there was still, they hoped, a chance of peace. His actions were both illegal and thoughtlessly provocative.

Zog was of a fearful disposition and the news from his informers that a notorious pair of assassins had been seen in the city had unnerved him to the extent that he had come into the great meeting hall wearing a jacket reinforced with a leather lining as protection against a knife attack. It was said that his fear of knives came from the fact that his mother's lover had been stabbed in her presence while she was pregnant with Zog, which was also the reason for his bandy legs. This particular weakness also caused him to lean on the shoulders of his chief favourite, at that time the much despised Lord Harwood.

There were perhaps fifty *hoi oligoi* of Swiss society present, most of them beaming with witless subservience as is the way of people in the presence of royalty. The remainder looked at their monarch with much loathing and distrust as he shuffled down the aisle of the great hall, leaning on Harwood, with his left hand fiddling around near his favourite's groin, a habit that increased in intensity whenever he was nervous. Zog's tongue was too large for his mouth, which made him an appallingly messy eater according to IdrisPukke, who had in better times dined with him often. Careless of changing his clothes, you could tell what meals he had golloped in the previous seven days, said IdrisPukke, from looking closely at the front of his shirt.

After much royal faffing about, Bose Ikard began a forty-minute address in which he set out the present situation regarding the intentions of the Redeemers, concluding that while the possibility of war was not to be discounted, there were strong reasons to believe that Swiss neutrality could be maintained. Then, like a magician producing not merely a rabbit but a giraffe out of a hat, he took a piece of paper from his inside pocket and waved it before the meeting. 'Two days ago I met with Pope Bosco himself, just ten miles from our border, and here is a paper which bears his name upon it as well as mine.' There was a gasp and even a single cheer of anticipation. But on the faces of Vipond and IdrisPukke there was only dismay. 'I would like to read it to you. "We, the Pontiff of the true faithful, and Chancellor of all the Swiss by consent of the King of Switzerland, are agreed in recognizing that peace between us is of the first importance."' There was a loud burst of applause, some of it spontaneous. '"And . . ."' more applause, '"and that we are agreed never to go to war with one another again."'

Cheers of high relief rang up to the roof and echoed back. 'Hear, hear!' someone shouted. 'Hear, hear!'

'"We are resolved that discussion and dialogue will be the means we shall use to deal with any outstanding questions that concern our two countries and to resolve all possible sources of difference in order to maintain the peace."'

There were hip hip hoorays for Chancellor Ikard and a chorus of 'For He's a Jolly Good Fellow' all round.

During the commotion, IdrisPukke was able to mutter in Vipond's ear. 'You must say something.'

'Now is not the time,' replied Vipond.

'There won't be another. Stall it.'

Vipond stood up.

'I am prepared to say without any hesitation or doubt that Pope Bosco has another paper,' said Vipond. 'And in this paper he sets out the general scheme for the attack on Switzerland and the destruction of its king.'

There was the distinctive murmur of people who had heard something they didn't care for.

'We are negotiating acceptable peace terms,' said Bose Ikard, 'with an enemy we know to be violent and well prepared. It would be astonishing only if Pope Bosco did not have such a plan.'

The murmur was now one of sophisticated approval: it was reassuring to have a man negotiating for peace who was such a cool realist. Such a man would not have his pocket picked by wishful thinking. Later, as the meeting came to an end and the conference filed out, mulling over what they'd heard, King Zog turned to his chancellor. Ikard was hoping, with good reason, to be complimented for dealing so skilfully with an opponent like Lord Vipond.

'Who,' said Zog, tongue aflutter in his mouth, 'was that striking young man standing behind Vipond?'

'Oh.' A pause. 'That was Conn Materazzi, husband of the Duchess Arbell.'

'Really?' said Zog, breathless. 'And what kind of Materazzi is he?' By this he meant was he one of the clan in general or of the direct line of descent from William Materazzi, known as the Conqueror or the Bastard, depending on whether he had taken your property or given it to you.

'He is a direct descendent, I believe.'

There was a wet sigh of satisfaction from Zog. From Lord Harwood there was a thunderous look of resentment. The royal favourite, who signed his letters to the King as 'Davy, Your Majesty's most humble slave and dog', now had a rival.

An equerry, somewhat hesitant, sidled up to the King. 'Your Majesty, the people are raising a clamour to see you at the great balcony.' This impressive platform, known as El Balcon de los Sicofantes, had been built two hundred years before to show off King Henry 11's much adored Spanish bride. It looked out over a vast mall on which more than two hundred thousand could gather to praise the monarch.

Zog sighed. 'The people will never be satisfied until I take down my trousers and show them my arse.'

He walked off towards the great window and the balcony beyond, calling out to Bose Ikard casually, 'Tell the young Materazzi to come and see me.'

'It would send a wrong signal to many, including Pope Bosco, if you were to see Duchess Arbell personally.'

King Zog of Switzerland and Albania stopped and turned to his chancellor. 'Indeed it would be a mistake. But you are not to teach me to suck eggs, my little dog. Who said anything about seeing Arbell Materazzi?'

Conn had barely returned to his wife's apartments when Zog's most important flunky, Lord Keeper St John Fawsley, arrived to command him to attend the King in two days' time at three o'clock in the afternoon. The Lord Keeper was known to the older princes and princesses as Lord Creepsley On All Fawsley – like royalty everywhere, they demanded servility and also despised it. It was said that on hearing his nickname Lord St John was beside himself with delight at the attention.

'What was that about?' wondered a baffled Conn after

he'd left. 'The King kept looking in my direction and rolling his eyes at me with such distaste I almost got up to leave. Now he wants to have an audience with me on my own. I'll refuse unless he invites Arbell.'

'No, you won't,' said Vipond. 'You'll go and you'll like it. See what he wants.'

'I'd have thought that was obvious. Did you see him fidgeting about in Harwood's groin? I could barely bring myself to look.'

'Don't fash yourself, my Lord,' said IdrisPukke. 'The King was badly frightened in the womb and as a result he is a very singular prince. But if he's mad about you then it's the best news we've had in a long time.'

'What do you mean – mad about me?'

'You know,' taunted IdrisPukke, 'if he looks on you with extreme favour.'

'Don't listen to him,' said Vipond. 'The King is eccentric, or at any rate, given that he is a king, we've all agreed to call it nothing more. Except for a certain over-familiarity with your person you've nothing to worry about. You'll just have to put up with his strangeness for the reasons my brother has referred to.'

'I thought I wasn't supposed to listen to IdrisPukke?'

'Then listen to me. This is a chance for you to do all of us a great deal of good. God knows we need it.'

Arbell, still plump but pale after the birth of her son, reached up from her couch and took Conn's hand. 'See what he wants, my dear, and I know you'll use your good judgement.'

4

Kevin Meatyard might have looked like a sack of potatoes with a large turnip resting on the top but he was tack-sharp and his malice had a subtle ring to it. In other circumstances – if, perhaps, he'd had a loving mother and wise teachers – he might have made something remarkable of himself. But probably not. Murdering a baby in its cradle is, of course, something that should never be done – except in the case of Kevin Meatyard.

We all know we should not judge people by their appearance, just as we also know that this is what we generally do. And this weakness in us all makes this regrettable reality a self-fulfilling prognostication. The beautiful are adored from birth and they become shallow with the lack of effort required in life; the ugly are rejected and become angry. People rejected Kevin Meatyard for the wrong reasons but there were those, not so shallow, who were ready to show him some human sympathy despite his giftless appearance and character. One of these kind people was Headman Nurse Gromek. If he'd never met Meatyard and felt sorry for him then he would have carried on being the blandly good man that he'd been all his life: harmless, competent, pleasant enough, a little blank.

Sensing Gromek's open-mindedness about him, Meatyard began to make himself useful, making cups of tea, cleaning tables, fetching and carrying, listening and watching for any occasion to lighten Gromek's considerable load. Gromek began to realize that mealtimes, always an occasion for the awkward among the patients to kick up a fuss, became much easier when Kevin Meatyard was helping him with the serving-up. How was he to know that Meatyard was issuing threats to his fellow lunatics ('I'll tear off your head and remove your bollocks through the hole') and backing them up at night, most successfully, using a twelve-inch piece of twine and the smallest of stones? Whatever pain you've ever felt was unlikely to compare with that inflicted by Meatyard putting a tiny pebble between your two smallest toes, wrapping string around them and squeezing tight. He liked best of all to do this to Little Brian in the bed next to the one he had instructed Thomas Cale to sleep in.

Something sly and clever in Meatyard drove him to provoke Cale by making him witness cruelty against the weak – and there was no one weaker than Little Brian. Meatyard, along with the grosser pleasure of causing pain, enjoyed the cries of the boy reaching out to Cale as he lay impassively on his back, neither turning away from nor towards the horror happening next to him. Meatyard could sense Cale's weakness: a certain compassion for the frail. It was this weakness that had forced him, however reluctantly, to kill Redeemer Picarbo as he was about to slaughter the beautifully plump Riba.

But he'd been strong then; now he was weak and he had no choice but to endure Little Brian's agony. The trouble was that he could not endure it. What gave Meatyard so much pleasure was that he could feel Cale's soul eroding in front of him. Meatyard's coarser appetite for physical suffering was regularly satisfied, and this place was like a sweetshop to a greedy boy, but he also liked to enjoy the more subtle suffering he got from his awareness of Cale's soul wasting away.

Soon, with Meatyard in charge of the handing out of medicines, even this worst of all occasions for calamity and distress became hushed and orderly.

At night, in Headman Nurse Gromek's little workroom off the ward, Meatyard would talk to him and listen carefully to all his woes. Over days and weeks Meatyard nourished all the nurse's many resentments in life, and one in particular. That Nurse Gromek was an ugly man it would be unkind but not untrue to say. This was partly what drew the two of them together: Gromek felt sorry for Meatyard because he was so unprepossessing in the way he looked. This pity was a way in for Meatyard, and soon he found the weakness in Gromek that lay under his decent qualities and ruled over all the others: he was a man with a loving disposition yet not loved by anyone. He cared for women but they did not care for him. When Meatyard cottoned onto this it showed him at his sharpest best. He could feel the disappointment and resentment in Gromek's apparent resignation to the fact that no one loved him. He could see how angry he really was.

'It's wrong,' said Meatyard, drinking tea and eating toast in the little room, 'that women don't mind you looking at them if they think you're handsome. But if they don't like your face then all of a sudden you're a dirty man – a who-do-you-think-you-are-to-look-at-me skank. They put their tits on display for everyone – except for you or me. We're not worthy to look.' After a few weeks of this, Gromek was puffed up with rage and as easy for Meatyard to play with as a ball. Soon Gromek, a man who'd had enough of being shit upon by girls, was bringing in women from the ward next door. Used to being treated with kindness in the Priory, these women were trusting and were left unsupervised at night because they were among the milder cases of insanity. Meatyard persuaded Gromek to bring them into his little room knowing he could keep shut the mouths of the patients listening outside. Besides, the patients here were often raving mad and full of stories of the terrors of hell that happened solely in their tortured minds. Now Meatyard brought them experience of the real thing. Wherever he went was hell, but in that hell he made a heaven for himself. There was no angry despair involved in being Kevin Meatyard, no torment in his soul acting out revenge against an unkind world. It was bliss: inflicting pain, tormenting of souls, rape. He delighted in being himself.

At night the lunatics listened to the girls whimpering softly – Meatyard liked a bit of crying but it must be quiet. There was the occasional loud cry of pain, and an answering yelp from a madman in the ward thinking it was the call of his own devils coming at last to drag him down. From time to time Meatyard would pop out to have a smoke, playfully swinging the pebble knotted in his piece of string, and chat to Cale as he lay in his bed, staring at rafters and the black beyond.

'You take it easy,' said Meatyard to Cale. 'And if you can't take it easy, take it anyway you can.'

It was during one such break, as Kevin Meatyard, having left Gromek in his little room to take his turn with a girl alone, puffed on a snout and gave Cale the benefit of his opinions, that events took an unexpected turn.

'You have to have the right attitude,' Meatyard was saying to Cale, who was as usual staring up into the void above. 'You've got to make the best of things. There's no point just lying back and feeling sorry for yourself in life. That's your problem. You just have to get on with it, like me. If you can't do that then you're a non-runner. This world is a pig – but you just have to get on with it, like me, see.' He did not expect a reply, nor did he get one.

'What do you want, Gibson?'

This question was addressed to a man in his late forties who had appeared at Meatyard's shoulder. The man didn't reply but stabbed him in the chest with a blade about ten inches long. Meatyard jerked to one side in agony as Gibson tried to wrench the blade free, snapping it off in Meatyard's chest in the process. It was a cheap kitchen knife that one of the men in the ward had found rusting away at the back of an old cupboard in the cookhouse. Horrified and astonished, Meatyard fell and in a moment half a dozen lunatics were on top of him and holding him down. Cale, meanwhile, rolled off his bed and away from the fight, shaky and kitten-weak after a recent visit from Nanny Powler and the rest of his devils. He watched as four other men piled into the annexe and dragged Headman Nurse Gromek out into the main body of the ward, his struggles much restricted by the trousers around his ankles from which he was trying to free himself.

The lunatics had decided to kill Gromek first in order to give Kevin Meatyard a chance to appreciate properly what was to come and to give him a brief taste in this life of what he could expect for all eternity in the next.

Terror can either make men weak or miraculously strong. Freeing one leg from the trousers around his ankles, Gromek managed to get enough purchase, despite the men holding him, to stagger down the ward and get to the locked door, shouting for help as he went. The lunatic with his arm around Gromek's neck immediately shifted it to his mouth, stifling his cries enough to make anyone passing think it was just a patient kicking off. As if they were wading upstream in fast water, the five of them lurched down the ward, then two more grabbed Gromek's legs until his panic-strength gave out and he collapsed onto the floor. Determined to get him away from the door and back to where Meatyard was being held they started to pull Gromek down the central aisle. While this was going on, Kevin Meatyard was loudly but calmly listing what he was going to do to his captors when he got free:

'I'll shove you back up your mother's crack. I'll piss down your throat. I'll fuck you in the ear.'

Once they'd dragged Gromek in front of Meatyard, he was pulled upright with his back against the wall so he could get a good view of Gromek's death.

Without the kitchen knife the lunatics needed to think again. Naturally, anything in the ward that could be used as a weapon had been removed – but even though the bed legs were carefully bolted into place, they had managed to unscrew one. As he was still struggling, grunting and gasping one of the lunatics grabbed Gromek under the chin and yanked his head up to expose his throat so that two of the others could press the bed leg across his neck. A terrible muffled scream erupted from deep in Gromek's chest as he realized what they were going to do. Terror again gave him unnatural strength and this, combined with the sweat pouring off his face, meant the man holding his chin lost his grip. Two more attempts followed as the watching Meatyard kept up his threats of hideous revenge – 'I'll chew off your plums and shove 'em up your winker' – but even he fell silent when Gromek's neck was arched back and the leg of the bed held across his windpipe with a man kneeling on each side. It wasn't quick. The sounds were from out of this world – a wet choking and a crushing of breathing flesh. Cale was transfixed by Gromek's hands, fluttering and quivering in the air, one of his fingers pointing and shaking as if telling off a child. After an age the shivering hands became taut for a moment, then dropped suddenly to the floor. The kneeling lunatics stayed as they were for a full minute and then slowly stood up. They looked at Kevin Meatyard lying pinned down with his back to the wall.

As they moved towards him, Cale called out to them. 'Be careful. Make sure you've got him tight. Don't let him get to his feet.'

But why pay attention to the warnings of a boy who'd done nothing but lie on his bed and retch for a couple of hours a day? They moved on Meatyard. The six lunatics who had a hold on him pulled him to his feet and, knowing this was his one chance, Meatyard took advantage of the momentum of the lift and with all his lumpen strength shook them free. Then he grabbed the astonished Little Brian in his arms and ran up the ward using the boy as a battering ram. He got to the door and turned to face them as the lunatics began edging around him in a semi-circle. He squeezed the boy around the throat and made him cry out in fear and pain. 'Stay where you are or I'll break his bloody neck.' Then he backheeled the door, making it rattle and thud as if a giant was trying to get out. 'Help!' he shouted as he kicked it over and over. 'HELP!'

Now the lunatics were scared – if Meatyard got away they were done for. They'd planned to say the pair of them got into a fight over who'd have the girl first and that they'd killed Meatyard while trying to save Gromek.

With Meatyard free and only the word of murderous lunatics against him they'd be shunted off to the madhouse in Bethlehem, where the lucky ones died in the first year and the unlucky ones didn't.

'Put him down.' Cale pushed through the men surrounding Meatyard.

'I'll break his neck,' said Meatyard.

'I don't care what you do to him, as long as you put him down.'

It's a truism that isn't true that all bullies are cowards – and it was certainly not true of Kevin Meatyard. He was afraid, as he had every reason to be, but he was in control of his fear as much as any brave man might be – although his kind of courage was not bravery. Neither was he a fool and he was at once alert to the peculiarity of Cale's insolence. Cale was one of his victims and he knew how victims behaved, but for the second time that night they weren't behaving as they ought to and, to be fair to Meatyard, as they usually did. Cale was behaving oddly and in an odd way.

'We can all come away from this,' Cale lied.

'How?'

'We say that it was Gromek who took the girl and that all of us, you included, ashamed to let such a thing take place, were forced to drag him off her and he died in the struggle. The girl will back that up.' He looked over his shoulder, still moving forward slowly. 'Won't you?'

'No, I fucking won't!' the girl shouted back. 'I want him hanged.'

'She'll see reason, she's just upset.' All the time Cale was closing in on the suspicious but hopeful Meatyard, his mind fizzing as he tried to think what to do next.

'They nearly squashed his neck off,' said Meatyard. 'No one will believe he got killed by accident. I'll take my chances.'

He backheeled the door again and the first syllable of a scream for help was already out when Cale hit him in the throat with all his strength. Unfortunately for Cale and the lunatics, all his strength didn't amount to much. It was the precision of the blow that hurt Meatyard, that made him jerk to the left and caused the back of Little Brian's head to knock the rusty blade sticking out of his chest. In agony from the knife, he dropped Little Brian. Cale hit the heel of his hand into the middle of Meatyard's chest. When he was ten years old either blow would have dropped Meatyard as if he were standing on a trap door, but he was not ten any more.

Meatyard lashed out and missed, but the follow-on landed a clout on the side of Cale's head. He fell as if he'd been hit by a bear. The blood pounded in his ears and what little strength he had in his arms was draining away to pins and needles. Meatyard took two steps and would have given Cale a kick big enough to land him in the next world, but there was still some brawn left in Cale's legs so he kicked away Meatyard's standing foot and he went down with a wallop on the wooden floor. Luckily for Cale, Meatyard was winded and this gave him time to get to his feet. His head was full of wasps, his arms shaky. He had one punch left in him, but not a good one.

In the struggle the lunatics had backed away, as if Cale emerging to take charge had robbed them of the collective will that had brought them this far. It was the girl who saved them. 'Help him,' she shouted, rushing forward and leaping on top of Meatyard. This decided Meatyard on his most desperate plan, one he'd thought up while his flesh was crawling as he was made to watch poor Gromek choke to death. He grabbed hold of the girl and swung her like a club at the three men barring his way to the large window on the other side of the room. They let him go because it was keeping him away from the door that mattered. Anywhere else he moved was a trap – so they let him back away to the window and shaped up to surround him for the last time. Earlier, desperation and a lack of anything to lose had given them a reckless courage but now none of them wanted to get their neck broken when more caution would see this to its end. So they gave him more time to back away than they might otherwise have done.

'Quickly,' said Cale, on the verge of fainting as the blood swirled in his ears. He felt as if his very brains would burst. Most of them didn't hear him. Meatyard made his way to the window and the lunatics stood and watched. He was, after all, going nowhere. The window was nailed down but it wasn't barred because it was on the fourth floor and some sixty feet from the ground. Meatyard knew this, but he also knew, from his voluntary efforts to get on Gromek's good side by cleaning the ward, that there was a rope anchored to the wall and coiled out of the way behind an old tallboy cupboard. It had been put there many years before as a cheap way of escaping a fire.

The lunatics watched him back off towards the window, then stirred as he reached behind the tallboy and pulled out the long rope. It took them a few seconds to realize what he was going to do and then they moved forward together. Meatyard pulled the tallboy over with an enormous crash and, holding onto the end of the rope, he ran to the window, turning his back at the last moment. The entire frame, much of it rotten, gave way and Meatyard vanished into the night, the rope trailing behind him. It snapped tight for a second then it went loose.

Never tested, the rope was too short. The result was that Meatyard, after falling headlong through the air, had come to a jerking stop twenty feet above the ground, flinging him into a tree which broke the fall that otherwise might have killed him. Good luck, vicious nerve and immense physical strength saw Meatyard limping off painfully to freedom. Cale watched from the shattered window as Meatyard merged into the darkness. He turned away and called the lunatics to him.

'What happened tonight was that the two of them brought the girl here and got into a fight over her. Isn't that right?' Cale said.

The girl nodded.

'Meatyard killed Gromek and when you tried to take hold

of him he smashed through the window – and that's all you know. Now each one of you is going to walk past me and repeat what I just said. And if you get it wrong, now or later, you won't need Kevin Meatyard to chew off your plums and shove them up your winker.'

While the well-intentioned people who ran the asylum were shocked at the terrible violence of the death of Headman Nurse Gromek, brutal attacks by deranged patients were not unknown. What caused more shock was that Gromek was abusing his patients in such a revolting manner. Patients who could pay for their treatment – a small number that should have included Cale – were taken into the asylum in order to provide money to pay for the care for those who could not. It was as kindly a place as such an institution can reasonably hope to be and Gromek had been rightly regarded, at least until the arrival of Kevin Meatyard, as an uninspired but trustworthy overseer. Cale's warning to the lunatics to stick to the story he had outlined taught him subsequently to be more careful when making jokes to people he did not know, particularly those who were not quite right in the head and who were prone to deal with the terrible confusion that existed in their minds by grasping with a grip of iron onto anything they were told with a clear and unambiguous determination. So it was that the unusual repetition of learnt phrases about the incident began to make the superintendents suspicious. Initially the story had been generally accepted – after all, Gromek *had* raped a number of female patients with the help of Kevin Meatyard and he *had* been murdered and the person accused *had* run away and in a desperate manner – but now they were preparing to mine for the truth and would undoubtedly have succeeded in finding out what had really happened had not events turned in Cale's favour. Vague

Henri and IdrisPukke arrived expecting to find him lying in the comfort for which they'd paid and hoping he was on the way to being cured.

'Must you always,' said IdrisPukke to Cale when he was brought down to the private room kept solely for important visitors, 'prove your detractors so unerring in their view that wherever you go calamities follow?'

'And,' said Vague Henri, 'another funeral.'

'And how is,' said Cale to Vague Henri, 'one of God's greatest mistakes?'

'Speak for yourself,' replied Vague Henri.

Cale resentfully explained that not only had he gone to humiliating extremes to avoid trouble, he had been too sick to do anything even if he had wanted to. The details of Meatyard's bullying he kept to himself.

He gave them a detailed account of the truth, the lies he had made everyone tell to cover it up as well as the peculiar bad luck that had put him in the lunatic ward in the first place. IdrisPukke went off to see the newly appointed Director of the asylum and gave her hell about the treatment given to such an important person. What kind of institution was she running? he'd asked, and other rhetorical questions of that sort. In a short time he had gouged a promise from her to end the investigation into the events of that night, and to have Cale brought under the personal daily care of their most skilled mind doctor and at no extra expense. IdrisPukke demanded and received a further promise to cut the fees for Cale's treatment in half.

By no means all of his anger was simulated. He had not expected a cure, given that Cale's collapse had been so great, but he'd hoped for an improvement both because of his great affection for the boy but also because he wanted to work with Cale on a much grander long-term strategy for dealing with the Redeemers. But Cale could not even speak for long without pausing to rest and gather his thoughts: and besides, there was the dreadful look of him. When Cale gave away in passing that today was an unusually good day, IdrisPukke realized that the help they desperately needed from Cale might come too late, if it came at all.

IdrisPukke demanded the Director summon the mind doctor who was to take care of Cale so that he could put his mind at rest as to his quality. The Director, knowing that IdrisPukke had to leave the next day, lied that the doctor was away on retreat and would not return for another three days.

'She's an anomist,' said the Director.

'I'm not familiar with the term.'

'She treats anomie, diseases of the soul, by talking, sometimes for hours a day and for many months. Patients call it the talking cure.' He could be reassured, said the Director, that she was a healer of uncommon skill and she had made headway with even the most intractable cases.

Although he was not sure he believed her about the convenient 'retreat', IdrisPukke could sense the sincerity of the Director's admiration for the supposedly absent woman. He took more hope from this, because he wanted it to be true, than his pessimistic nature would normally allow. That nature would have reasserted itself in full measure when, five minutes after he left to return to Cale, there was a knock on the Director's door which was opened even before she could say 'come in'. The woman who entered, if it was a woman, was of a very curious appearance and holding in her left hand something so strange that not even IdrisPukke, with all his many experiences of the singular and the fantastical, had seen anything like it.

5

Kevin Meatyard was unwell. He had a badly sprained ankle, a dislocated shoulder, a large cut on the left side of his head and assorted welts, cricks and tears. But none of them would kill him. It was the knife in his upper chest that would do that. The Island of Cyprus was not an island at all but a large isthmus that ballooned out into the Wooden Sea. Its system of parochial justice extended fifty miles into the hinterland so that even small villages had a special constable – even if he was only the blacksmith. Meatyard had every reason to believe he would be followed although he also realized it would be too expensive and difficult to keep half a dozen men on the road for long. The problem for him was that he knew he must stay away from any place where he could get the knife removed and the wound cleaned. In the end, he trusted in his constitution to keep him alive long enough to get so far away that no one would have heard of him. So it was that while Kevin Meatyard was trying to leave Cyprus on a road out of the way of nosy strangers, the Two Trevors were trying to enter Cyprus on a road out of the way of nosy strangers. So it was less of a coincidence than it might have been when the two assassins came across Kevin Meatyard lying in a heap beside a small pond. For obvious reasons, while out in the bundu even people very much less experienced in wickedness than the Two Trevors regarded a body lying in the road as something it would be wise to pass by on the other side of. On the other hand, they and their animals were parched. Having satisfied themselves it was not a trap (and who knew more about bushwhacking than they did?) Trevor Lugavoy threw a large rock at the lumpily prone body and, getting only a faint groan in response, decided that whatever danger there was could be avoided by keeping a close eye and not touching him.

A few minutes later, with the horses still slurping the deliciously sweet water, Kevin stirred and awkwardly got to his feet, watched carefully by the two men. He started to walk over to the pond to get a drink but, still unsteady and weak, he collapsed with such a hefty thud it made both Trevors wince.

It might be thought that given their bloody profession the Two Trevors were men without compassion. But while it was certainly the case that they were no nicer than other people, neither, except when they were being paid to kill you, were they very much worse. This was particularly true the older they got and the more superstitious. They were beginning to wonder if a few acts of generosity might be of some help if it turned out that one day there might be an eternal act of reckoning – though they both knew in their heart of hearts that they would have to rescue an epic number of children from a vast number of burning buildings to weigh much in the balance after all the evil deeds they'd been responsible for. Still, it was mean-spirited to leave a clearly wounded man lying within a few feet of a desperately needed drink of water. They frisked him, then woke him up and gave him a drink from one of their own cups.

'Thanks,' said a truly grateful Kevin, after downing five straight cups of what felt like life itself.

'Look, John Smith,' Kevin had, of course, given them a false name. 'You're not going to make it to Drayton – it's fifty miles away, rough going too. That,' he nodded at the broken blade in Meatyard's chest, 'comes out now or we loan you a spade and you can start digging.'

'What's a spade?'

'An implement,' said Trevor Lugavoy, 'that can be used for digging holes several feet deep and six foot long.'

'You can do it?' said a doubtful Kevin. 'Take this out without killing me?'

'Pretty far gone, boy – I'd say seventy/thirty.'

'For?'

'Against.'

This let out of Kevin what little air was left.

'D'you think there'd be a proper surgeon in Drayton?'

'You aren't going to get to Drayton. And even if you did, which you won't, he'll be the local barber. And he'll want paying. And some questions will be asked. Have you got any money? Have you got any answers?'

By now the Two Trevors were beginning to feel their patience wane in the face of Kevin's lack of gratitude.

'My generous friend here is as good as you'll get within two hundred miles. You're lucky to have him. And you don't have much choice. If you want to stay out of heaven, I'd do some grovelling.'

The mention of heaven concentrated Kevin's mind and he made a good fist of apologizing to the now miffed Trevor Lugavoy. After which, Lugavoy got on with it. In fact, he could have earned a fair living as a surgeon. Moved to become skilled for practical reasons, he also took pride in his ability and had paid for tuition from Redeemer surgeons considered by all to be the best, not that this was saying much. He had paid a high price for the medical pliers with which he grasped the little that was left of the blade sticking out of Meatyard's chest. It was out in a moment, accompanied only by a hideous scream of agony.

Worse was to come, as it was clear from the two pieces missing from the blade that there was more to do.

45

'Don't move or I won't answer for the consequences.'

Meatyard was skilled at handing out pain, but he could take it, too.

'Well done,' said Trevor Lugavoy, who was, after five minutes digging about in the wound that must have felt like five days, reassured that there was nothing left behind. 'That's what kills you,' he said to the traumatized Meatyard. He cleaned the wound with several gallons of water and began to pour a mixture of honey and lavender, calendula and powdered myrrh. Kovtun, seeing he was about to use the ointment, pulled Lugavoy to one side and pointed out that it was expensive and they might very well need it themselves. Lugavoy agreed in principle but pointed out that all their efforts would be for nothing if the wound got infected – which it would.

'I take pride in my work. What can I say? Besides, he showed a good deal of courage. I'd have screamed louder. He deserves a bit of generosity.' So that was that. They decided to stay and watch over him in the night; next morning they left him with some rations (not much, at Kovtun's insistence) and were on their way. Though just before they left, a thought occurred to Kovtun.

'You heard of the Priory?' he said to Kevin.

Fortunately for Meatyard his expression of alarm could easily be turned into one of pain. 'No, sorry,' said the ungrateful boy and at that the Two Trevors were gone. Two minutes later Lugavoy was back. He dropped a large block covered in waxed paper, an impulsive addition to the rations they'd already left him.

'Make sure,' he said to Kevin, 'you eat a quarter of this a day. It's good stuff food-wise though it tastes like dog-shit. The Redeemers call it Dead Men's Feet. There's an address inside. If you live, go there and they'll give you work. Tell them Trevor Lugavoy sent you – and nothing else, y'hear?'

If you'd asked Trevor Lugavoy whether virtue was rewarded he would have been both surprised and amused, not because he was a cynic (he regarded himself as having been through all that) but rather that experience had led him not to see the world as a place of balance. On this occasion, however, while returning to ensure that Kevin Meatyard had enough nourishing food to give him the best chance of survival, his kindness was rewarded: he noticed that he was being watched from a hill about three hundred yards away. As he turned back to join Trevor Kovtun he was pretty sure he knew who it was. He caught up with Kovtun rather quicker than he expected to – Kovtun had dismounted and was on all fours with his belt undone, putting two fingers down his throat trying to make himself sick. After a few more unpleasant sounding tries, he succeeded. There was blood in his vomit.

'Any better?'

'A bit.'

'We're being followed.'

'Damn, buggery, bollocks and bullshit,' said Cadbury as he sat down half a mile from the Two Trevors. 'They know we're following them.' Cadbury looked at the girl who had been waiting for him at the bottom of the hill while he was spying on Trevor Lugavoy. Behind her, set apart, were a dozen disagreeable-looking men.

'You let them spot you,' said the girl. She was a stringy-looking thing, but it was the kind of string that you could rely on to take a hard strain, with an odd face – had you seen it in a painting you would have called it underdrawn. It seemed to have something missing, a nose or a pair of lips, except that they were all there.

'You think you can do any better, be my guest.'

'It's your job, not mine.'

'When it comes to tracking people as good as those two you can't get too close and you can't get too far away. It's just bad luck.'

'I don't believe in luck.'

'That's because you're a kiddywink and don't know your arse from your elbow.'

'You'll see what I know. An intelligent heart acquires knowledge, and the ear of the wise seeks it.'

'Will I? How hair-raising.'

But for all his mockery he found the girl's presence decidedly creepy, not least because she was always quoting from some religious tract that had, apparently, an opinion on everything. But she spoke these proverbs and sayings an odd way, so that you couldn't make out what she was driving at exactly. Was she trying to make him uneasy? He had good reason to be jumpy.

Three days earlier, Kitty the Hare had called him in to discuss what was to be done about the Two Trevors and their search for Cale, in the light of the certainty that there was only one thing the Two Trevors did with anyone they were looking for once they found them.

'Do you know who's paying them?' Cadbury had asked.

'The Redeemers, probably,' Kitty cooed. 'Spying things out is not really in their gift. Fanatics find it hard to blend in, as the disgracefully illegal but entirely justified hanging ordered by Zog so clearly established. But it could be the Laconics.' It was a matter of policy as well as amusement to Kitty never to give a completely unambiguous answer. 'They'll struggle to recover from the injury he did to their numbers. Neither could you rule out Solomon Solomon's family. He has a talent for antagonizing people.'

'You could say the same about us.'

'Indeed you could, Cadbury.'

'You don't think he's too much trouble?'

'Oh, indeed I do,' replied Kitty. 'But that's the way it is with the young. It's a question of possibilities. His capacity for ruin needs shaping and I'd very much rather be behind him than in front of him. But there may easily come a time when that will not be the case. You might want to keep that in mind.'

The door opened and Kitty's steward entered with a tray.

'Ah,' said Kitty, 'tea. The cup that cheers but not inebriates.'

The steward laid the table with cups and saucers, plates of ham sandwiches, seedcake, and biccies with custard then left without a word or a bow. The two of them stared at the table but not because of the treats on offer.

'You will have noticed, no doubt, Cadbury, the table's laid for three.'

'I had, yes.'

'There's someone I want you to meet. A young person I'd like you to keep an eye on. Give her the benefit of your experience.' He moved toward the door and called out, 'My dear!' A moment and then a girl of around twenty years appeared and gave Cadbury the most dreadful fright. The sense that you have seen a ghost from the past is disturbing to anyone, but imagine how much worse it is when you were the one responsible for that ghostliness. The last time Cadbury had seen her was while they had both been spying on Cale at Treetops – a chore that had finished with him putting an arrow in her back. In the perpetual gloom required by Kitty the Hare to shield his so-sensitive eyes, it took him a few moments to realize that this was not the late Jennifer Plunkett nor her twin but a younger though disturbingly similar relative. It wasn't just her looks that gave the similarity but the same disfiguring blankness of expression.

'Meet Daniel Cadbury, my lover.' This peculiar endearment was addressed to the girl and was merely an alternative to 'my dear' but deliberately more disconcerting. 'He and your sister were old friends and often worked side by side. Daniel, this is Deidre Plunkett who's come to work with us and share her very considerable skills.'

Even though he realized his mistake quickly enough, there was reason for Cadbury still to be unnerved: the surviving relatives of people you had murdered were generally best avoided.

Kitty had insisted that Cadbury bring Deidre with him in the attempt to track down the Two Trevors: 'Take her under your wing, Cadbury,' he'd said. But the question for Cadbury was what kind of mockery was involved here. Jennifer Plunkett had been a murderous nutcase who, without ever speaking to the boy, had conceived a deep passion for Cale as she spent days watching him swimming naked in the lakes around Treetops. Cale had laughed and shouted for joy for the first time in his life as he swam and fished and ate the wonderful food prepared by IdrisPukke, and sang horribly out-of-tune garbled versions of the songs he'd picked up while he was in Memphis: *Weigh a pie in the sky. The ants are my friends. She's got floppy ears, She's got floppy ears.*

Jennifer had been convinced that Kitty meant Cale harm: this was not the case, in fact, or at least probably not the case. Jennifer had tried to stab Cadbury in a bid to protect her beloved and when she failed had run towards the astonished Cale screaming blue murder. It was at this point that Cadbury had put an arrow in her back. What choice did he have? Afterwards, he had decided it might be better if he told Kitty that Cale was responsible, startled into action by the sudden appearance of a murderous screaming harpy. 'Honesty is the best policy' may not be a virtuous guideline (the man who believes that honesty is the best *policy* is not an honest man) but it was one he should have followed in this instance. Not only was he now left with the problem of what to do about Deidre Plunkett, but also of working out whether her sudden appearance was just a coincidence or Kitty's revenge for having been lied to. If the latter, the question was what sort of lesson his employer had in mind.

At any rate, he took Deidre with him to negotiate with the Two Trevors. If things went fat-fingered, which they easily might, there was a chance the Trevors might solve the problem for him. On the other hand, they might solve all his problems permanently.

'You're coming with me, keep your cake-hole shut and don't make any sudden moves.'

'You've no call to talk to me like that.'

Cadbury didn't bother to reply.

'The rest of you,' he said to the others. 'Keep back but in calling distance.'

They ignored Kevin Meatyard on their way past, it being clear he wasn't going to be any trouble given the state he was in, and in a few minutes they caught up with the Two Trevors.

'Can we talk?' shouted Cadbury from behind a tree.

Lugavoy nodded the two of them forward. 'That's far enough. What do you want?'

'Kitty the Hare thinks there's been a misunderstanding and he'd like to resolve it.'

'Consider it resolved.'

'He'd like to resolve it personally.'

'We'll be sure to drop in next time we're passing.'

'Your friend looks a bit peaky.'

He was, in fact, the colour of half-dry putty.

'He'll live.'

'I'm not sure you're right about that.'

'Who's your skinny friend?' Lugavoy asked.

'This young lady is a most deadly person. I'd show her more respect.'

'You look familiar, sonny.'

'Keep going, mister,' said Deidre, 'and you'll be laughing on the other side of your face.'

'My apologies, but she's very young and doesn't know any better.'

'Don't be apologizing for me,' said Deidre.

Cadbury raised his eyebrows as if to say, 'What can you do?'

'As I see it, Trevor, you're not going to make it to wherever you were planning to go so the question of your intentions coming into conflict with Kitty the Hare's interests doesn't apply for the foreseeable future. If you want your partner to live, I don't really see what the problem is.'

'What's to stop you killing us as we sleep?'

'You shouldn't judge others by your own low standards.'

Trevor laughed. 'Point taken. But still I worry.'

'What can I say? Except that it's not in Kitty the Hare's mind to do so.'

'And what *is* in his mind?'

'Why don't you come back to Spanish Leeds and ask him?'

'So he doesn't trust you enough to tell you?'

'Are you trying to hurt my feelings? I'm touched. The thing is that while Kitty the Hare has considerable respect for you both, it so happens you're on a path that brings your interests into conflict with his. He prefers his own interests.'

'Fair enough.'

'I'm glad that you think so. Are we agreed?'

'Yes.'

'We have kaolin. That should make him feel better.'

'Thanks.'

Cadbury gestured to Deidre Plunkett. She brought out a small flask from her saddlebag and, getting down, walked over to Kovtun.

'Take an eighth,' she said. Cadbury put two fingers in his mouth and let out a whistle so shrill it made Lugavoy flinch. In response the dozen men waiting over the hill emerged in three staggered sets of four and spread out wide.

'Nasty-looking bunch,' said Lugavoy. 'But someone knows what they're doing.'

The skilled approach-work he so admired was being directed by Kleist; the villainous-looking types he was controlling were Klephts, and so rather less dangerous than they appeared. Cadbury had hired them in a hurry because so many of his usual thugs had been struck down with the squits, in fact the same typhoid from which Trevor Kovtun was suffering and from the same source in a water pump in the centre of Spanish Leeds. The rise in the number of people taking refuge there on the rumours of a war with the Redeemers was already exacting a price. It was all very unsatisfactory but the Klephts did look the part and they had clearly fought against the Redeemers and were still alive – no mean recommendation. About Kleist he knew nothing – he was not a Klepht but he seemed always to have the ear of the Klepht gangmaster who, for some reason, was called Dog-End. In fact, Kleist was mostly in charge but it was thought best not to have a boy seen to be their leader.

On their way back they had to pass by Kevin Meatyard.

'Can we take him with us?' said Lugavoy.

'Not enough horses. Besides, I don't like the look of him.' Cadbury signalled to Kleist, who was nearest. 'What's your name, son?'

'Kleist.'

'Give him some food – enough for four days not more.' Kevin had already hidden the rations given him by the Two Trevors.

Kleist approached Kevin slowly: he didn't like the look of him either.

'All right?' he said to Kevin, as he got down and started rifling the ration saddlebag to see what was least palatable and so best for giving away – the staler bread, the harder pieces of cheese.

'Got a smoke?' said Meatyard.

'No.'

Kleist set out what could only be described as an ungenerous interpretation of four days' worth of edibles onto a square of cloth.

'Where you from?' asked Kleist.

'None of your fucking business.'

Kleist's expression did not change. He stood up, looked at Meatyard and then kicked sand all over the food he'd just laid out. Neither of them said anything. Kleist got on his horse and left to catch up with the others.

6

Life is like a pond into which an idle child drops a pebble and from that act the ripples spread outwards. Wrong. Life is a stream and not a stream in spate, just an ordinary piddling sort of stream with its routine eddies, whirls and no-account vortices. But the vortex and the ripple uncover a root, and then another, and then they undermine the bank and the tree by the stream falls down across the stream and diverts the water and villagers come to find out what has happened to their supply and find the coal unearthed by the falling tree and miners come, and whores to serve the miners and men to manage the whores and a town of tents and mud becomes a place of wood and mud, then bricks and mud, then cobbles to pave the street, then the law arrives to walk the cobbles that pave the streets, then the coal gives out but the town lives on or it dies away. And all because of a piddling stream and its piddling whirls and vortices. And so it is with the life of men, driven by the many-fingered hand of the invisible.

The visit that would have brought death to Thomas Cale at the hand of the Two Trevors was stalled by a drink of water from a tainted well, its messengers herded back to where they came from by a long-time friend who couldn't really care less whether he lived or died, back to a city where the wife of the long-time careless friend was wandering the streets with her newborn girl, thinking her husband dead who was now returning towards her and who, in a few days, would pass no more than thirty yards from her in the great crowds that now crushed inside the walls of Spanish Leeds.

Over and again their paths would nearly cross but for the little whirls and vortices pulling them a fraction this way and then a fraction that.

Sometimes we see a cloud that's dragonish, sometimes lionish, sometimes very like a whale, but all the most cheerful philosophers agree that even the blackest cloud has a silver lining. And during the days and nights of wretchedness when Kevin Meatyard ruled, Cale discovered that the old ways he had of dealing with suffering came back to him. In the Sanctuary he had learned to withdraw inside his head, vanish to other places in his mind, places of warmth and food and marvellous things – angels with wings who did whatever you said, talking dogs, adventures without pain, even death without tears and sudden blissful resurrections, peace and quiet and no one anywhere near. Now for a couple of hours a day he could do the same when the retching and the madness gave him some elbow room. Daydreams came to his defence; for minutes at a time he found himself back among the lakes at Treetops, swimming in the cool waters, picking signal crabs out of the streams, thinking about the word he'd found one day for the sound of water on small stones as he pulled the crabs apart and ate them raw with the tops of wild garlic, just the way IdrisPukke had shown him. And then at night, as the long-winged bugs in the wood made their wonderful pulsating racket, they would talk and talk and he'd lap it up, sitting on one of the chairs that were almost like beds as IdrisPukke poured him a light ale and handed out the accumulated wisdom of half a century, insight, as he frequently pointed out, you couldn't buy at any price.

'People treat the present moment as if it is just a stopping point on the way to some great goal that will happen in the future, and then they are surprised that the long day closes; they look back on their life and see that the things they let go by so unregarded, the small pleasures they dismissed so easily were in fact the true significance of their lives – all the time these things were the great and wonderful successes and purpose of their existence.'

Then he would pour Cale another quarter pint, not too much.

'All utopias are the work of cretins and the well-intentioned people who work towards the foundation of a better future are half-wits. Imagine the heaven-on-earth where turkeys fly around ready-roasted and perfect lovers find perfect love with only a little satisfactory delay and live happily ever after. In such a place, men and women would die of boredom or hang themselves in despair, well-tempered men would fight and kill to be relieved of the horrors of contentment. Pretty soon this utopia would contain more suffering than nature inflicts on us as it is.'

'You sound like Bosco.'

'Not so. He wants to wipe cats from the face of the earth because they like to eat fish and catch birds. You might as well wish for a time when the lion will lie down with the lamb. But you're half right, in a way. I agree with Bosco up to a point – it's true that this world is hell. But while I, too, am appalled by humanity as a gross caricature I also feel sorry for it: in this hideous existence so full of suffering, we are at one and the same time the tormented souls in hell and the devils doing the tormenting. We are *fellow* sufferers, so the most necessary qualities to possess are tolerance, patience, forbearance and charity. We all need forgiveness and so we all owe it. Forgive us our trespasses as we forgive those who trespass against us. These are virtues, young man, in which, and I mean this kindly, you are sorely lacking.'

At this last offering, Cale pretended to be asleep, accompanied by exaggerated snores.

But drifting into the past was a place full of traps. He wanted to remember the first time he had seen Arbell naked – bliss it was to be alive that night. But the pleasure and pain, love and anger, lived too much cheek by jowl for this to take him into another world. Better to stick to wonderful meals, to memories of teasing Vague Henri about the enormous size of his head, of listening to IdrisPukke and getting the last word with everyone. But also he would think and argue with himself and try to work out what he really knew: that the world was like a stream full of gyrations, twirls and weedy entanglements, and that wherever you went the water always leaked through your fingers.

The room they had now given him was simple enough: a reasonably comfortable bed, a chair and a table, a window that looked out over a pleasant garden full of slender elm trees. It had two luxuries: he slept on his own and he had a key to lock himself in and everyone else out. They'd been unwilling to provide one at first but he had insisted with a degree of vague menace and, having asked the Director of the Priory, they had warily given him what he wanted.

There was a light tap on the door. He looked through a small hole he had drilled through the thinnest part of the door and, satisfied, he unlocked it with a quick twist and stood well back. After all, you never knew.

Suspicious, the Priory servant stayed where he was.

'There seems,' he said, 'to be a hole in the door.'

'It was like that when I got here.'

'Sister Wray has asked to see you.'

'Who?'

'I believe she has been asked by the Director to investigate your case. She is very highly respected.'

Cale wanted to ask more questions but as is often the case with awkward people he did not like to appear ignorant to someone who clearly disliked him – and for good reason, as this servant was the very person Cale had menaced about having the key. 'People with charm,' IdrisPukke had once said to him, 'can get others to say yes without even asking the question. Having a real talent for charm is most corrupting. But don't worry,' he added, 'that's not something you'll ever have to worry about.'

'I'll take you to her now,' said the servant. 'Then I'll see about the hole in the door.'

'Don't bother. It creates a nice breeze.'

He put on his shoes and they left. The servant was surprised to see, given all the fuss he had made, that the obnoxious young man did not bother to lock the door behind him. But as long as he was not in there Cale couldn't care less who else was.

In silence they walked through the Priory. Some of it was built recently, other parts were older, other parts older still. There were tall and grim-looking buildings with gargoyles grimacing from the walls, then a sudden change to the elegant and well-proportioned, mellow stone structures with large windows of irregular glass that in one piece reflected the sky and in another the grass, so various and changeable that the building seemed to be alive inside. Eventually, through passages in great walls, the silent pair emerged into a courtyard more pleasing in its scale and engaging simplicity than anything Cale had seen even in Memphis. The servant led him through an arch and up two flights of stairs. Each landing had a door in thick black oak to either side of the staircase. He stopped outside one on the top floor and knocked.

PART TWO

Lest we should see where we are,
Lost in a haunted wood,
Children afraid of the night
Who have never been happy or good.

W. H. Auden, 'September 1, 1939'

7

'Come in.' It was a soft and attractive welcome. The servant opened the door and stood back, ushering Cale forward. 'I'll be back in an hour exactly,' he said and pulled the door shut.

There were two large windows to Cale's right, which flooded the room with light, and at the far side, sitting by the fire in a high backed chair that looked comfortable enough to live in, was a tall woman. Even sitting down Cale could see she was more than six foot tall, somewhat taller than Cale himself. Sister Wray was covered from head to foot in what looked like black cotton. Even her eyes were covered with a thin strip of material in which there were numerous small holes to allow her to see. Strange as all this was, there was something much stranger: in her right hand and resting on her lap was some sort of doll. Had one of the children in Memphis been holding it he would not have noticed – the Materazzi girls often had dolls that were spectacularly splendid to behold, with madly expensive costumes for every kind of occasion from a marriage to tea with the Duke. This doll was rather larger, with clothes of grey and white and a simply drawn face without any expression at all.

'Come and sit down.' Again the pleasant voice, warm and good-humoured. 'Can I call you Thomas?'

'No.'

There was a slight nod, but who could know of what kind? The head of the doll, however, moved slowly to look in his direction.

'Please sit.' But the voice was still all warmth and friendliness as it completely discounted his appalling rudeness. He sat down, the doll still watching and – though how, he thought, could it be so? – taking a pretty dim view of what she was looking at.

'I'm Sister Wray. And this,' she said, moving her covered head slightly to look at the puppet on her lap, 'is Poll.'

Cale stared balefully at Poll and Poll stared balefully back. 'What shall we call you?'

'Everybody calls me "sir".'

'That seems a little formal. Can we agree on Cale?'

'Suit yourself.'

'What a horrible little boy.'

It was not especially difficult to surprise Cale, no more than most people, but it was no easy thing to make him show it. It was not the sentiment that widened his eyes – he had, after all, been called a lot worse – but the fact it was the puppet who said it. The mouth didn't move because it wasn't made to, but the voice most definitely came from the puppet and not Sister Wray.

'Be quiet, Poll,' she said, and turned slightly to face Cale. 'You mustn't pay any attention to her. I'm afraid I've indulged her and like many spoilt children she has rather too much to say for herself.'

'What am I here for?'

'You've been very ill. I read the report prepared by the assessor when you arrived.'

'The moron that got me locked up with all the head-bangers?'

'She does seem to have got the wrong end of the stick.'

'Well, I'm sure she's been punished. No? What a surprise.'

'We all make mistakes.'

'Where I come from, when you make a mistake something bad happens – usually involving a lot of screaming.'

64

'I'm sorry.'

'What's there for you to be sorry about? Were you responsible?'

'No.'

'So, what are you going to do to make me all right again?'

'Talk.'

'Is that it?'

'No. We'll talk and then I'll be better able to decide what medicines to prescribe, if that seems called for.'

'Can't we drop the talk and just get to the medicine?'

'I'm afraid not. Talk first, medicine after. How are you today?'

He held up his hand with the missing finger. 'It's acting up.'

'Often?'

'Once a week, perhaps.'

She looked at her notes. 'And your head and shoulder?'

'They do their best to fill in when my hand isn't hurting.'

'You should have had a surgeon look at you. There was a request but it seems to have gone missing. I'll sort out something for the pain.'

For half an hour she asked questions about his past, from time to time interrupted by Poll. When Cale, with some relish, told her he had been bought for sixpence Poll had called out, 'Too much.' But mostly the questions were simple and the answers grim, though Sister Wray didn't dwell on any of them, and soon they were discussing the events of the night Gromek was killed and Kevin Meatyard escaped. When he'd finished she wrote for some time on the several small sheets of paper resting on her left knee as Poll leant over them and tried to read, and was pushed back repeatedly out of the way like a naughty but much loved dog.

'Why,' asked Cale, as Sister Wray took a couple of silent

minutes to finish writing and Poll took to staring at him malevolently, although he also knew this could not be so, 'why don't you treat the nutters in the ward? Not enough money?'

Sister Wray's head moved upright away from her work. 'The people in that ward are there because their madness is of a particular kind. People are sick in the head in as many ways as they're sick in the body. You wouldn't try to talk a broken leg into healing and some breaks in the mind are almost the same. I can't do anything for them.'

'But you can do something for me?'

'I don't know. That's what I'm trying to find out.'

'If you'd let her, you naughty boy.'

'Be quiet, Poll.'

'But it's right.' An unattractive little smirk from Cale. 'I *am* a naughty boy.'

'So I understand.'

'I've done terrible things.'

'Yes.'

There was a silence.

'What happens if the people paying for me stop?'

'Then your treatment will stop as well.'

'That's not very nice.'

'I don't understand.'

'Just stopping – when I'm still sick.'

'Like everyone else I must eat, and have somewhere to live. I'm not part of the order that runs the Priory. They'll keep you in a charity ward but if I stop paying my way they'll turf me out.'

'Yes,' said Poll. 'We haven't had Redeemers to look after us all our lives.'

This time Poll went uncorrected.

'What if I don't like you?' said Cale. He had wanted to

come up with a stinging reply to Poll but couldn't think of one.

'What,' said Sister Wray, 'if I don't like *you*?'

'Can you do that?'

'Not like you? You seem very determined that I shouldn't.'

'I mean decide not to treat me if you don't like me.'

'Does that worry you?'

'I've got a lot of things to worry about in my life – not being liked by you isn't one of them.'

Sister Wray laughed at this – a pleasant, bell-like sound.

'You like answering back,' she said. 'And I'm afraid it's a weakness of mine as well.'

'You have weaknesses?'

'Of course.'

'Then how can you help me?'

'You've met a lot of people without weaknesses?'

'Not so many. But I'm unlucky that way. Vague Henri told me I shouldn't judge people by the fact that I've been unlucky enough to come across so many shit-bags.'

'Perhaps it's not just luck.' Her tone was cooler now.

'What's your drift?'

'Perhaps it's not just a matter of chance, the dreadful people and the dreadful things that have happened to you.'

'You still haven't said what you mean.'

'Because I don't know what I mean.'

'She means you're a horrible little boy who stirs up trouble wherever he goes.' Yet again Poll went uncorrected and she changed the subject.

'Is Vague Henri a friend of yours?'

'You don't have friends in the Sanctuary, just people who share the same fate.' This was not true but for some reason he wanted to appal her.

There was a knock at the door.

67

'Come in,' said Sister Wray. The Priory servant stood at the door silently. Cale, uncertain and angry, got to his feet and walked across the room and onto the landing. Then he turned, about to say something, and saw Sister Wray opening a bedroom door and quickly closing it behind her. All the way back to his own room he considered what he'd seen, or what he thought he'd seen: a plain black-painted coffin.

'Tell me about IdrisPukke.' It was four days later and their sessions began at the same time every day. Poll was on Sister Wray's lap but leaning all the way back on the arm of the chair and drooping over the side to signal her utter boredom and indifference to Cale's presence.

'He helped me in the desert and in Memphis when we were in prison.'

'In what way?'

'He told me how things were. He told me not to trust him or anybody else – not because people are liars, though a lot of them are, but because their interests are not your interests, and that to expect other people not to put what matters to them ahead of what matters to you is stupid.'

'Some people would say that was cynical.'

'I don't know what cynical means.'

'It means believing others are motivated only by self-interest.'

Cale thought about this for a moment. 'Yes,' he said at last.

'Yes, what?'

'Yes, I understand what cynical means.'

'Now you're just trying to provoke me.'

'No, I'm not. IdrisPukke warned me when he didn't have to that I should remember that sometimes what mattered to me and what mattered to him would be different and that even if he might bend a little in my favour other people mostly wouldn't – when push came to shove they'd be forced to choose what was best for them. And only the biggest dunce would believe that other people should put you ahead of themselves.'

'So, no one sacrifices their own interests for others?'

'The Redeemers do. But if that's self-sacrifice you can shove it up your arse.'

Poll slowly raised her head from behind the sofa, looked at him then collapsed backwards with a groan of contempt as if the effort had been utterly worthless.

'And yet you're very angry with Arbell Materazzi. You think she betrayed you.'

'She did betray me.'

'But wasn't she just consulting her own interest? Aren't you being a hypocrite for hating her?'

'What's a hypocrite?'

'Someone who criticizes other people for the same kind of things they do themselves.'

'It's not the same.'

'Yes, it is,' said Poll from behind the arm of the chair.

'Be quiet, Poll.'

'No, it isn't the same,' he said, looking straight at Sister Wray. 'Twice I saved her life, the first time against all reason or odds – and nearly died for it.'

'Did she ask you to?'

'I don't remember her asking to be thrown back – which is what I should've done.'

'But isn't love putting the other person first, no matter what?'

'That's the stupidest thing I ever heard. Why would any-one do that?'

'He's right,' said Poll, still with her head obscured by the arm of the chair.

'I won't tell you again,' said Sister Wray.

'Laugh if you like – I was ready to die for her.'

'I'm not laughing.'

'I am,' said Poll.

'She told me she loved me. I didn't make her do it. She told me and made me think it was true. She didn't have to but she did. Then she sold me to Bosco to save her own skin.'

'And the rest of Memphis – her father, everyone? What do you think she should have done?'

'She should have known I would have found a way. She should have done what she did and then thrown herself into the sea. She should have said that nothing on earth, not the whole world, could make her hand over someone she loved to be burnt alive. Though before they'd set fire to me they'd have cut my balls off and cooked them in front of me. You think I'm making that up?'

'No.'

'Whatever she did it should have been impossible to bear. But she put up with it well enough.'

There was a long silence in which Sister Wray, experienced as she was in the anger of the mad, wondered why the very walls of the room did not catch fire so dazzling was his rage. The silence went on – she was no fool and it was Cale who ended it.

'Why do you have a coffin in your bedroom?'

'May I ask how you know?'

'Me? I've got eyes in the front of my head.'

'Would you be reassured if I told you it has nothing to do with our business together?'

'No. Nobody likes a coffin and me less than most. I'll have to insist.'

'Don't tell that nosy boy anything,' said Poll.

'Go and look for yourself.'

Cale had more or less been expecting her to refuse to tell him anything although he had no idea what he'd have done if she had. He stood up and walked over to the far door and considered what he might be letting himself in for. Was it a trap? Unlikely. Was there something horrible inside? Possibly. What if it wasn't a coffin and he was mistaken and would look foolish? The door was shut tight so he couldn't just push it open. He could kick it open but that would look bad if there weren't a couple of villains waiting on the other side. *Would you rather*, he thought, *be dead or look stupid*? He snatched at the handle, pushed it open, then quickly glanced around the room and dodged back again.

'Cowardy cowardy custard,' sang Poll. 'Your shoes are made of mustard.'

There was no question it was a coffin and the room was empty. Empty except for whatever was inside the coffin. He turned into the bedroom, leant his head back and his arm forward and flipped the lid off then jumped back, windy as you like. He stared at the contents for a few seconds. It was plain wood, no lining. There were even a few wood shavings in the corner. For a moment he felt a surge of pure terror in his chest and thought he was going to throw up. Then he shut it away. He stepped back into the main room, closed the door behind him and went back to his chair.

'Happy now, you big sissy?' said Poll.

'Why do you have an empty coffin in your bedroom?'

'Don't worry,' said Sister Wray. 'It's not for you.'

'I do worry. Who's it for?'

'Me.'

'Worried about cheesed off patients?'

She laughed at the idea – *a lovely sound*, thought Cale. *Is she beautiful*?

'I belong to the order of Hieronymite nuns.'

71

'Never heard of them.'

'Also called the Women of the Grave.'

'Never heard of them either. Don't like the sound of them much.'

'No?' He had the sense that she was smiling. Poll moved her head forward and raised her floppy right arm in a way that managed to indicate loathing and contempt.

'The Hieronymites are an Antagonist order.' She stopped, knowing this would be a disclosure of some significance.

'I never talked to an Antagonist before. Do you wear that thing on your head because you've got green teeth?'

'No. I mean I don't have green teeth and I'm not hiding anything, though I suppose that would be a good enough reason. Did the Redeemers really tell you that Antagonists have green teeth?'

'I don't remember them actually telling us. Not Bosco anyway. It was just sort of generally known.'

'Well, it's not true. The Antagonist Hegemony, a kind of religious committee, declared the Hieronymites to be an extreme error and dissolved the order. They ordered us, death being the alternative, to carry a coffin with us for a hundred miles so that everyone would know not to give us water or food or shelter. We carry the coffin and an ounce of salt.'

'Because?'

'Salt of repentance.'

'And did you? Repent, I mean.'

'No.'

'So we've something in common.'

'We don't,' said Poll, 'have anything in common with you, you godless killing swashbuckler.'

'Don't pay any attention to her,' said Sister Wray.

Cale expected her to continue but Sister Wray could see he was interested and wanted him to be at a disadvantage.

72

'So what did you do wrong?' he asked at last.

'We pointed out that in the Testament of the Hanged Redeemer, although he doesn't actually say that heresy should be forgiven, he does say that we should love those that hate us and forgive their trespasses not once or twice but seventy times seven. St Augustine says that if a person falls into heresy for a second time they must be burnt alive. A Hanged Redeemer who said that if a man strikes you on the cheek you must turn the other and let him strike you a second time is not a God in favour of burning.'

'I heard he said that from the Maid of Blackbird Leys – about turning the other cheek, I mean. But if you turn your cheek when people hit you they'll keep hitting you until your head falls off.'

She laughed. 'I understand what you say.'

'You can understand all you like – I'm right, whatever you think.'

'We'll agree to disagree.'

'They burned her.'

'Who?'

'The Maid of Blackbird Leys.'

'Why?'

'She was saying the kind of stuff you were saying. She'd got hold of a copy of the Testament too. No coffin and no salt though, she went straight to the fire.'

'When you say she got hold of the Testament, you mean a secret copy.'

'Yes.'

'Antagonists don't have secret copies of the Hanged Redeemer's Testament. It's an obligation to read it – it's translated into a dozen languages.'

'P'raps,' he said, 'it's a different Testament.'

'Some things must be the same if they burned her for saying that the Hanged Redeemer is a God of love and not punishment.'

'If it's that obvious why did they punish you for saying the same thing?'

'That's the way mankind is.'

'God's greatest mistake.'

'I don't believe that.'

'Me neither – it's God who's mankind's greatest mistake.'

'Wash your mouth out with soap, you impious sack of shit.'

This time Sister Wray did not rebuke Poll.

'Looks like,' said Cale, triumphant, 'you need to teach your little friend about forgiveness.'

'Perhaps,' replied Sister Wray, 'you've exceeded your limit.'

'Seventy times seven,' Cale laughed. 'I've got loads left. You won't get off that easy.'

'Possibly. It depends on how great the sins you committed are.'

'Does he say that, the Hanged Redeemer?'

'No.'

'There you are then.'

'You're not telling me the truth.'

'I never said I would. Who are you? I don't have to tell you anything I don't want to.'

'About the Maid of Blackbird Leys, I mean.'

'I did what I could to save her.' He wasn't feeling so triumphant now. 'That's all there is.'

'I don't think that can be true. Am I wrong to think there's more to say?'

'No, you're not wrong.'

'Then why not tell me?'

'I'm not afraid to tell you.'

'I didn't say you were.'

'Yes, you did.'

'I agree. Yes, I did.'

He stared at the grid of tiny holes that covered her eyes. Maybe she was blind, he thought, and this was a waste of time. Stupid. Stupid. Stupid.

'I signed the licence for her to be justified.'

'Justified?'

'Burned on a pile of wood. Alive. You ever seen that?'

'No.'

'It's worse than it sounds.'

'I believe you.'

'I oversaw her being burned.'

'Was that necessary – to be so closely involved?'

'Yes, it was necessary.'

'Why?'

'None of your business.'

'But it bothers you?'

'Of course it fucking bothers me. She was a nice little girl. Brave. Very brave but stupid. There was nothing I could do.'

'You're sure?'

'No, I'm not sure – maybe I could have jumped on a magic rope and swashbuckled my way out of a square of five thousand people and twenty-foot-high walls. Yeah, that's what I should have done.'

'Did you have to sign?'

'Yes.'

'Did you have to be there?'

'Yes.'

'Did you have to be there?' she asked again.

'I went because I thought I should suffer . . . for signing . . . even though there was nothing else to do.'

'Then you did all you could. That's my opinion.'

'That's a relief.' Quiet but acid. 'Do you think she would have thought so?'

'I can't say.'

'That's the problem, isn't it? Do you forgive me for what I did to her?'

'God forgives you.'

'I didn't ask about God. Do you forgive me?'

8

Of arms and the man I sing, and of cheese; of the rage of Thomas Cale and of adequate supplies of oats for the horses delivered in the right place at the correct time; I sing of thousands going down to the house of death, carrion for the dogs and birds, and of the provision of tents, of cooks, water for ten thousand in the middle of the barren wilderness; I sing of a sufficiency of axle-grease and cooking oil.

Think of a picnic with family and friends, consider the failure of all to meet up at the proper time and place ('I thought you said twelve o'clock'; 'I thought the meeting place was at the elm tree on the other side of town'). Consider the endless wrongness of things, consider the jam mislaid, the site of the picnic shared with a swarm of bees, the rain, the angry farmer, the row between brothers festering for twenty years. Now imagine the bulls of war let loose to bring about the ending of mankind. To bring about the apocalypse requires cheese, cooking oil, oats, water and axle-grease to be ordered, the order made up and the order delivered. That's why Bosco was not fighting but wasting the time of kings, emperors, supreme rulers, potentates and their armies of ministers and under-secretaries of this and that with an endless blizzard of treaties, pacts, protocols, pledges and covenants all designed to create as much space and time for the essential trivia required in order for the wiping out of the human race to be made possible. The end of the world had been postponed until the following year.

As nothing really happened in a hundred walled towns for

month after month throughout the four quarters, other more imminent threats emerged: disease, fear, the failure to plant a crop, the inflation of money, a longing for home and the hope that everything would somehow sort itself out. The refugees began to return home. As a result, in Spanish Leeds the typhoid abated when an old midden, opened for the influx of alarmed peasants and which had leaked human excrement into the water supply and caused the plague, was shut down because it was no longer needed. Trevor Lugavoy recovered, as did Kevin Meatyard who turned up at the address he'd been given and started work humping sacks of grain around the city.

The Materazzi lived on like a great family fallen on the worst of times. They had no money but they did have capital of sorts: the brains of Vipond and IdrisPukke and the always reliable gold standard of snobbery. Even the surliest barrow-boy-done-good, having made his fortune in bacon or horse-glue, discovered when confronted by the supercilious hauteur of the Materazzi women that something was lacking in their lives: they were as common as muck and only a Materrazi beauty could begin to remove that taint. Imagine the thought of having a wife with a thousand-year-old-name, one that could be passed on to the children. What a triumph! Underneath the stroppy bluster your barrowboy soul would no longer ping an imperfect note. And all you needed to become one of the who whom was the most fair-minded egalitarian of all: buckets of cash.

The Materazzi men may have been shits but they were not snobs in the way their wives and daughters were. They treated the rich common-persons of Spanish Leeds with the affection they gave to their horses and dogs. So well were these horses and dogs beloved that they imagined they were equals. It must be said, though, that the Materazzienne, as the women came to be called in Spanish Leeds, were not always prepared to make the ultimate sacrifice and marry into a family who'd made their money in glue or marmalade. But in time, the reality of what was required when you were special but had no special abilities meant that many were forced to make their way, weeping, down the aisle to a future husband who had made his money in rendered fat or pork scratchings. Vipond had strong-armed a tax on these unions but the flow of money was nothing like as much as he needed, for all his furious urgings to the heads of the Ten Families to 'beat some sense' into their daughters. His old policy of adding his brains to Materazzi money now had to bend to the former. In this, IdrisPukke and Thomas Cale were what he had instead of a treasury. IdrisPukke's return from the Priory with news of what had happened was a disappointment, if for less personal reasons than those of his half-brother. He admired Cale and was fascinated by him but there was no personal affection. Still, he'd hoped that the boy would be nearly better by now.

'Is Cale worth pursuing?' he asked IdrisPukke. 'Be frank with me. There's too much at stake not to be.'

'What are you asking me to be honest with you for?' came the bad-tempered reply. 'You don't have the right to make a demand like that from me. He is what he is.'

'There's no arguing with that.'

'If you want to drop him then you can drop me, too.'

'Don't be so dramatic – you'll burst into an aria next. I misspoke. Let's imagine I never said anything.'

So, strapped for cash though he was, Vipond sent a messenger to Cyprus every two weeks to meet Cale's requests for information: maps, books, rumours, such reports as Vipond and IdrisPukke could borrow or steal. In return, but slowly, came his maps and his guesses and certainties about what

Bosco would do, and how he could be frustrated, and the minimum number of troops and resources it would take. It was slow for one reason: Cale was sick and he was not improving. There were times when it seemed he was on the mend, sleeping for twelve hours a day instead of fourteen, being able to walk for half an hour a day and work for the same. But then the attacks, the retching and terrible weariness came back. For no reason that he or Sister Wray could determine, the illness ebbed and flowed according to laws entirely of its own.

'Perhaps it's the moon,' said Cale.

'It's not,' replied Sister Wray. 'I checked.'

Poll was sure what was wrong. 'You're a very naughty boy and all shagged out by wickedness.'

'P'raps Woodentop is right,' said Cale.

'Perhaps she is, though she has a nerve calling anyone else naughty. You are worn out by the wickedness of others. The Redeemers poured it into you and now your soul is trying to spit it out.'

'There can't be much left.'

'You haven't swallowed a bad pork chop – you've swallowed a mill.'

'One of those things that blow round with the wind?'

'No – like a salt mill. A magic salt mill, like in the fairy tale.'

'Never heard of it.'

'Once upon a time the sea was filled with fresh water. One day a fisherman pulled up an old lamp in his nets. When he started to polish it up a genie came out who'd been imprisoned in the lamp by an evil magician. As a reward, the genie gave him a salt mill that produced salt for ever and ever. Then the genie flew away but the old fisherman was so exhausted that he dropped the mill and it fell to the bottom of the sea where the salt just came pouring out, never stopping. That's why the sea is salty.'

'I don't know what you're talking about.'

'We must stop the mill from grinding. We need to find some medicine.'

'About time.'

Sister Wray did not react. Poll was not so reticent.

'You ungrateful hooligan.'

'Grateful for what?' he said, still looking at Sister Wray who turned to the puppet.

'He has a point. We must do better.'

'Is that dummy part of your religion?'

'No. Poll is just Poll.'

This made it all seem stranger than it had at first sight. It was true that he'd been startled on first meeting them. On the other hand he was used to, expected even, anyone dressed as a priest or nun to proclaim abnormal beliefs and behave in an outlandish manner.

The Redeemers' prayer before breakfast stated their firm belief in the Eight Impossible Things. Almost every minute of every day for his entire life they had told him something about devils flying above him in the air or angels at his shoulder weeping when he sinned. Deranged behaviour and mad beliefs were normal to him. He was not even very impressed by Sister Wray's talent for the different voice that seemed to come from Poll – he had seen voice-throwers outside the Red Opera on bullfight days.

One day he knocked on Sister Wray's door but there was no answer. He was perfectly aware that he should knock once more but he opened the door after the shortest pause possible. He hoped, of course, to find Sister Wray without her obnubilate (she had told him what her veil was called when he asked). Surely she wouldn't wear it when she was on her own? He might even enter to find her naked. Would she be big-breasted and with red nipples the size of the dainty saucers they used at Materazzi tea parties? He had dreamt of her like this. Or would she be ugly and old with the skin hanging from her chest like damp washing on a clothesline? Or something else he hadn't thought of? His distant hopes were to be disappointed. He entered quietly – cats would have begrudged him. She was in her chair but asleep and lightly snoring, as was Poll – though in a completely different tone and rhythm. Sister Wray's snoring was like that of a small child, soft and low. Poll's was like an old man dreaming of grudges.

He sat down and listened to them phewing, susurrating and wheezing for a while, and considered searching her bedroom. He stood up, decided against it, and instead moved to her side and began lifting her veil.

'What are you doing, thou wretched thing of blood?'

'Looking for something I lost,' said Cale.

'Well, you won't find it there,' replied Poll.

Cale dropped the lower edge of the veil as carefully as he had picked it up, then went and sat down as guiltless as a bad cat. Cale sat for a full minute while Poll stared at him.

'Are you going to wake her up?' he said to Poll.

'No.'

'We could talk,' said Cale, affably.

'Why?'

'Get to know each other.'

'I know,' said Poll, 'as much about you as I want to.'

'I'm all right when you get to know me.'

'No, you aren't.'

'You think you understand what I'm really like?'

'You think I don't?'

Sister Wray slept on.

'What have I ever done to you?'

82

It wasn't an aggrieved question, just a matter of curiosity.

'You know very well.'

'No, I don't.'

'She,' said Poll, looking up at Sister Wray, 'is all nobility and grace and generosity.'

'So?'

'Her weakness, though I love her for it, is that these great gifts that she passes on to others smother her proper fear of you.'

Though he tried not to show it, Cale was rattled by this. 'She's got no reason to be afraid of me.'

There was a gasp of impatience from Poll.

'You think that the only thing people should be afraid of is what you can do to them – that you could punch them on the nose or cut their head off? She's afraid of what you *are* – of what your soul can do to hers.'

'What's that strange buzzing noise in my ears?' said Cale. 'It sounds like words but they don't make any sense.'

'You understand what I'm talking about. You think it just as much as I do.'

'No, I don't, because everything you say is camel-shit.'

'You know . . . you infect other people . . . you *know* exactly, you snivelling little chisler.'

'I don't snivel. No one's ever heard me snivel. And it's lucky for you I don't know what a chisler is.'

'Or what?' said a triumphant Poll. 'You'd cut my head off?'

'You don't have a head. You're made of wool.'

'I am not,' said an indignant Poll, quickly. 'But at least I don't suffer from soul murder.'

Then for the first time he heard Poll gasp – a guilty sigh of someone who's let the cat out of the bag.

'What are you talking about?'

'Nothing,' said Poll.

83

'It's not nothing. Why so guilty? What are you afraid of?'

'Not you, anyway.'

'Then tell me, wool-for-brains.'

'You deserve to be told.' Poll looked away at the sleeping Sister Wray, still snoring like a two-year-old. A pause. Making up her mind. Then Poll looked back at Cale with all the kindness, it seemed to the boy, in the eyes of a weasel he had once come across while it was eating a rabbit. It had raised its head and looked at him for a moment, utterly indifferent, and then gone back to its meal.

'I heard her talking to the Director when she thought I was asleep.'

'I thought you two knew everything about each other – little heart-pals.'

'You don't see anything about the two of us. You think you do but you don't.'

'Get on with it. I can feel my left leg going to sleep.'

'You asked for it.'

'Now I can feel my other leg wants forty winks.'

'Soul murder is the worst thing that can happen to you.'

'Worse than death? Worse than five hours dying with your giblets hanging out of your tum? Your liver dribbling out of your bread basket?' Cale was laying it on thick but not thicker than it was.

'Soul murder,' said Poll, 'is living death.'

'Get on with it, I've got fish to fry.'

But the truth was he didn't much like the sound of it, nor, even if Poll did have wool between the ears, the look in her eyes.

'Soul murder is what happens to children who take more than forty blows to the heart.'

'Do blows to the head count? Never had one to the heart.'

'They killed your joy – that's what she said.'

84

'You wouldn't be lying at all? I was wrong about the wool – that nasty tongue of yours sounds like it's made from the arse hairs of a sheep-shagger – most likely I should think that was a considerable possibility.'

'I don't think your joy is dead.'

'I don't care what you think.'

'Your joy is all in laying waste to things – blight and desolation is what makes your soul glad.'

'That's a bloody lie – you were here when I told Wray . . .'

'*Sister* Wray!'

'. . . when I told her about the girl I saved in the Sanctuary. I didn't even know her.'

'And you've regretted it ever since.'

'I was joking.'

'Nobody's laughing – nobody does when you're around, not for long.'

'I got rid of Kevin Meatyard.'

'Says you.'

'I saved Arbell Materazzi.'

'It wasn't your soul doing the thinking, was it? It was your prick.'

'And I saved her brother.'

'That's true,' said Poll. 'I agree that you did good there.'

'So you're wrong – you said it yourself,' said Cale suspiciously.

'I didn't say your heart was dead, lots of soul-dead people have a heart, a good heart. I bet you were a lovely little boy. I bet you would have grown up a real goody-goody. But the Redeemers got you and murdered your soul and that was that. Not everybody can be saved. Some wounds go too deep'

'Drop dead.' He was rattled.

'It's not your fault,' said a delighted Poll. 'You can't help yourself. You weren't born bad but you're bad all the same. Nothing can be done. Poor Cale. Nothing can be done.'

'That's not what *she* believes,' he said, looking at Sister Wray.

'Yes, it is.'

'She never said that.'

'She didn't have to. I know what she thinks even before she thinks it. You're going to make her suffer, aren't you?'

'Sister Wray?'

'Not Sister Wray, you idiot – that treacherous slut you're always whingeing about.'

'I never hurt her.'

'Not yet, you haven't. But you will. And when you cross that river we're all going to suffer – because once she's dead there'll be nothing to stop you. You know the river I'm talking about, don't you?'

'There's that buzzing sound in my ears again.'

'It's the river of no return – THE WATERS OF DEATH – and over that river is the MEADOW OF DESOLATION. That's where you're heading, young man, despair's your destination. You're the salt in our wound, that's what you are. You stink of misery and pretty soon the smell is going to fill the whole world.'

Poll was beginning to shout.

'I'd be sorry for you if we all weren't going to get it in the neck as a result. You're the angel of death all right – you stink of it. Cross over the river of no return into the land of lost content, the valley of the shadow of death . . .'

Poll had raised her voice so much that Sister Wray came to with a loud snort.

'What?' she said.

There was only silence. 'Oh, Thomas, it's you. I fell asleep. Have you been here long?'

86

'No,' said Cale. 'Just got here.'

'I'm sorry, I'm not feeling very well. We could continue tomorrow if you wouldn't mind.'

Cale nodded.

Sister Wray stood up and walked him to the door. As he was about to leave she said, 'Thomas, Poll didn't say anything to you while I was asleep?'

'Don't believe a thing that snivelling little chisler tells you!' squawked an alarmed Poll.

'Be quiet,' said Sister Wray.

Cale looked at her. This was odd stuff to grasp even for a boy who had drunk deeply and at a very early age from the fountain of the strangeness of others.

'No,' he said. 'It didn't say anything and I wouldn't have paid any attention even if it had.'

9

'That's easy for you to say. Have you ever allowed another man to fondle you?'

'Not as far as I can remember.'

Conn was arguing with Lord Vipond, watched by Arbell and a fascinated IdrisPukke.

'*Has* the King ever touched you?' asked Arbell, not altogether patiently.

'No.'

'Then why all this fuss?'

'Every philosopher can stand the toothache,' said Conn to his wife, 'except for the one who has it.'

This was a reference to one of IdrisPukke's most carefully polished sayings.

'Well,' said Vipond, 'if you'd like to swap banalities . . .' this was aimed at his brother . . . 'why don't you consider this one: every problem is an opportunity.'

The difficulty and the golden chance they were discussing involved King Zog of Switzerland and Albania, who'd taken a very particular shine to Conn Materazzi. Many, of course, felt the same about the tall and beautiful blond young man, so strong and graceful with his easy manners and openness to all. The cocky little shit of less than a year before had needed to grow up and had done so in such an appealing way that he surprised even his admirers. Arbell, who had once had a crush upon the spoilt young boy – though she treated him with coolness and even disdain as a result – now found that she was falling in love with him. A little late perhaps, given that they had been married for more than seven months and had a son whose early arrival, yet plump size, had been the subject of some ungenerous rumours. Though certainly more biddable than before, and considerably so, he had his limits, one of them being his aversion to everything about his royal admirer: his stained clothes ('I can tell you everything he has eaten in the last month'), his tongue ('It flaps about in his mouth like a wet sheet on a washing line'), his hands ('Always fidgeting with himself and his favourite's trousers'). His eyes ('watery'). His feet ('enormous'). Even the way he stood ('Repulsive!').

'The King,' said Vipond, 'holds all of us in his hands – and more besides. Every country nervous about the Redeemers looks to him for a sign of what they might do. Without him, the Materazzi will descend into a kind of nothing – that's to say your wife, your child and you.'

'So you want me to lick his arse?'

'Conn!' A sharp rebuke from his wife.

There was an unpleasant pause.

'I'm sorry,' said Conn at last.

'I've heard worse,' replied Vipond.

'Can I say something?' asked IdrisPukke.

'Must you?' said Vipond.

IdrisPukke smiled and looked at Conn.

'My dear boy,' he began, winking at Conn so the others couldn't see – a sign that he was on his side in conspiring against the other two.

'If he touches me, I'll cut his bloody head off,' Conn said, interrupting IdrisPukke's attempt to handle him.

IdrisPukke smiled again as the others sighed and grimaced in exasperation.

'You're not going to cut his head off because you're not going to let him touch you.'

'And what if he does?'

'You stand up,' said IdrisPukke, 'look at him as if you'd seen more lovely things coming out of the back end of a dog and leave the room in silence. You *say* nothing.'

'If that's the best you can do, don't let us keep you,' said Vipond.

'The King is a snob,' replied IdrisPukke, 'and, like all snobs, at heart he's a worshipper. All his life he's been looking for someone who looks down on him to adore. Conn looks like a young god – a young god with a bloodline that goes back as far as the great freeze. He's wonderstruck.'

'I can think of another word,' said Conn.

'Maybe that, too. But he wants you to treat him with contempt. He won't dare touch you. Every time you look at him – and don't look at him except once or twice a meeting – you pour every quintilla of your loathing and disgust into it.'

'That won't be hard.'

'There you are, then.'

With this unexpected resolution, IdrisPukke chatted away about a dinner he'd been at the previous night and then Arbell eased Conn out of the door and the two brothers were left on their own.

'I thought that went very well.' It was not IdrisPukke talking in honeyed tones of self-congratulation but Vipond, whose scowl had vanished completely, to be replaced by a look of considerable satisfaction.

'Do you think she caught on?'

'Probably,' replied Vipond. 'But she's a smart little miss. She won't say anything.'

'You're wrong, by the way' said IdrisPukke.

'What do you mean?'

'You said, "Every problem is an opportunity."' IdrisPukke walked over to the window to catch the last rays of the setting sun. 'What I actually always say is, "Every opportunity is a problem."'

Vague Henri was disturbed, but in an unusual a-fish-has-just-fallen-out-of-the-sky-in-front-of-you way. Two days earlier he had reached into his pocket to pay for a pack of cigarillos at Mr Sobranie's Health Tobacco shop and discovered that his loose change was gone and had been replaced by a carrot. More precisely, a carrot that had been not very skilfully carved into the shape of an erect penis with the word 'YOU' cut into the testicles. Eventually he decided that he'd been the victim of some smart alec street lurcher. The question why a skilled thief would steal the loose change in his left pocket but not the wallet in his right, which had nearly thirty dollars in it, he put to the back of his mind. But now the oddly peculiar thing that he had put to the back of his mind couldn't stay there any longer because it had happened again. This time he had discovered a hard-boiled egg, with the two staring eyes of a village idiot and a mouth with the tongue flapping to one side drawn on the shell. On the reverse of the egg was a statement:

VAGUE HENRI
TRUE

All through the night Vague Henri turned over in his brain what the significance of the two gibes might be and whether they were a threat or not. Then there was a knock at the door; he answered it, taking the precaution of hiding a long knife behind his back. But his visitor had the sense to stand well back.

'So, it was you?'

'Who else would it be?' said Kleist. 'Nobody else knows what a prick you are the way I do.'

Vague Henri was so pleased to see his old friend that the bollocking that followed for running off on his own when they were in the Scablands lasted barely five minutes before they were sitting down and smoking two cigarillos of Mr Sobranie's Health Tobacco and drinking what remained of a bottle of hideous Swiss wine. Both of them, of course, had extraordinary events to speak of. 'You first as you've sinned the most,' said Vague Henri and was astonished as Kleist, without warning, began to weep uncontrollably. It was half an hour before Kleist had recovered enough to tell him what had happened. As he listened Vague Henri grew pale and then red with anger and disgust.

'There, there,' he said to the weeping boy, patting him on the shoulder because he didn't know what else to do. 'There, there.'

It's not all the world that is a stage but each human soul: the cast list in each of our souls is long and varied and most of the characters queue in the wings and down the dark passages and into the basement, never to be auditioned for a part. Even for the ones who do make it onto the stage it's only to carry a spear or announce the arrival of the King. In this expectant but likely to be disappointed line of inner selves waiting for the chance to strut out in the world we usually find our inner fool, our private liar, our unrevealed oaf and, next to him, our wisest, best self; our hero and then our coward, our cheat and saint and next to him our child, then next our brat, our thief, our slut, our man of principle, our glutton, our lunatic, our man of honour and our thug.

Called unexpectedly to the front of Vague Henri's soul queue that night was a most dangerous character (for Vague Henri at any rate): the part in him that believed in justice and fair play.

Cale dealt with his past through being in a state of almost

constant rage, Kleist by disdain for everything that might touch his heart, Vague Henri by being cheerful in the face of adversity. The strategies of the first two had failed (Cale had gone mad and Kleist had fallen in love) and now it was Vague Henri's turn. The idea that one of them could have married and made another human being, an actual baby, pink, small and helpless, touched him with rage at the Redeemers so deep that the deaths of Kleist's wife and son at their hands burnt like the sun. So he called on the maddest of all his cast of characters: the one who wanted life to be fair, who wanted those who had done harm to be punished and justice for all.

While an exhausted Kleist snored in miserable oblivion on the bed, Vague Henri smoked his way through the last snout of his Health Tobacco and worked on his spidery and ill-advised conspiracy. Demoted to the back of the line in Vague Henri's inner cast list, his wiser self was calling to him: delay, fudge, avoid, put off as long as possible the moment when you must commit yourself and others to the business of death. But it was the voice of rage that had his ear.

If IdrisPukke had known what Vague Henri was planning he would have had a stroke – instead he was enjoying the absolute success of his plan to manipulate Conn in the matter of the King. With every disdainful look and every sigh of contempt Zog was only the more enthralled by Conn. He'd finally reached snob heaven: he'd met someone who was worthy to look down on him.

Swift though his rise had been, and along with it that of the Materazzi in general, even Conn's most star-struck admirers were astonished at the announcement that the King was to make him commander of all the armies of Switzerland and Albania. This extraordinary and apparently foolish step, given the threat to their existence that faced the

Swiss, was less opposed than it might have been because everyone had been expecting the job to go to Viscount Harwood, King Zog's now former favourite, a man of no military experience or indeed talent of any kind. It was reliably said that, on learning of Conn's preferment, Harwood retired to his bed and cried for a week. The more scurrilous rumours, probably untrue, whispered that his penis had shrunk to the size of an acorn. In light of this, Conn's appointment was less absurd than it first appeared. He had changed a good deal since the ruinous shambles at Silbury Hill. He had come very close to a hideous death there and been forced to endure rescue by someone he'd once bullied and despised. Even IdrisPukke, who had burst into laughter on hearing the news of his appointment to such a ludicrously powerful position, began to realize after a few days of meetings with Conn and Vipond that defeat, death and humiliation at Silbury had been the making of the young man. Here was someone who had been brought up to fight and who had learnt his bitter lessons early. In addition Conn, as Vipond had advised him to do, listened carefully to IdrisPukke and was clearly and genuinely impressed by the work he had done on the coming war with the Redeemers. Conn was not to know that much of the intelligence had been supplied by Thomas Cale.

'But what if Cale comes back? How is Conn going to take to that?' said IdrisPukke.

'Does he know?' asked Vipond.

'Does he know what?'

'The thing it would be better if he didn't know.'

'Probably not. If we're thinking of the same thing.'

'We are.'

'Is he likely to come back – Cale, I mean?' asked his brother.

94

'Apparently not.'

It was an unhappy reply and it would have been even more unhappy if he could have seen the boy who he continued, to his surprise, to miss so much. The circles around Cale's eyes were, if anything, darker – the skin ever whiter with exhaustion at the retching that afflicted him sometimes for a few seconds, sometimes for hours. Some days were better – there were even weeks when he thought perhaps it was lifting from him. But the attacks always returned eventually, greater or lesser according to their own devices and desires.

During one of these better weeks, Sister Wray said that she wanted to climb to the top of a nearby hill, both in search of the truth of the rumours that blue sage and orange neem grew at the top and because the view of the sea and mountains was said to be the best in Cyprus.

'It may be a hill,' said a breathless Cale, a few hundred feet into their climb, 'but it feels like a mountain.'

It was as well they started early as Cale had to rest every few hundred yards. At their sixth stop he fell asleep for nearly an hour. Sister Wray went for a wander up and down through the dry scrub and crumbly earth. Even though there had been little rain in the last few months, everywhere, hidden amongst the scraggy burberry bushes and thistle trees, were the tiny pleasures of purple knapweed, rock roses, the tiny eggy flowers of thorowax.

When she got back Cale was awake, and looking pale and even more black around the eyes.

'We'll go back.'

'I won't make the top but we can go on a bit longer.'

'Big cry-baby pansy,' said Poll.

'One day,' replied Cale, his voice a whisper, 'I'm going to unravel you and knit someone a new arsehole.'

*

Some fifteen hundred feet above them, and two hundred feet below the top of the hill, was a V-shaped rift cut into the hill by the winter rains. It was the easiest way up, and waiting for Cale and Sister Wray to pass through it were the Two Trevors and Kevin Meatyard. Kevin was all puppyish excitement but the Two Trevors were uneasy. They were too well aware that the iron law of unintended consequences seemed to apply even more sharply to the planned act of murder than to other enterprises. They always designed their assassinations as a story where the chain of events could be upset at any point by a trivial detail. They had failed to kill the Archduke Ferdinand in Sarajevo because the carriage driver, a late replacement for the usual driver who'd cut his arm that morning while replacing a wheel as a precaution, had panicked over the hastily given instructions over where to go and taken a wrong turn, not once (the Two Trevors had taken this into account) but twice. Had they succeeded in killing the old buffer who knows what the consequences might have been – but they didn't, so something else happened instead.

The return of the Two Trevors to Spanish Leeds had been something of a welcome anti-climax. Kitty seemed to believe their reassurances that while they could not reveal their client's business they were not in any way a threat to Kitty's interests (not true, as it happened, but neither realized that the other had a stake in Thomas Cale). Kitty guessed that the Redeemers were probably involved but while the political situation was so confused he didn't want to antagonize them without good reason. He'd considered, of course, disappearing the Two Trevors into the rubbish tips at Oxyrinchus just to be on the safe side. But he now decided that being on the safe side meant letting them go – much to Cadbury's irritation, given the trouble he'd been put to in order to bring them back. In addition to their lives, the Two Trevors had a

96

lesser stroke of luck: they'd discovered where Cale had taken refuge when Lugavoy had his ear bent by Kevin Meatyard's boastfulness. A delighted Kevin had discovered Thomas Cale's reputation as some sort of flinty desperado and was determined to let everyone know that he'd given this celebrity hardcase any number of bloody good hidings. No one really believed him but Kevin's appearance, as well as his violent boasting, made people nervous. If the human body was the best picture of the human soul, Kevin was clearly someone best avoided. Hence the complaints to Trevor Lugavoy from Kevin's employer and hence their jammy discovery of Cale's precise whereabouts. 'I don't like ridiculous good luck,' said Trevor Kovtun, 'it reminds me of preposterous bad luck.'

The three of them had arrived at Yoxhall, the town outside the Priory, just the day before Cale and Sister Wray's trip up Biggin Hill. For a hundred years Yoxhall had been a spa town where the reasonably well-off came to take the waters and visit their relatives in the Priory, which had grown up there in the belief that the local hot spring was beneficial in the treatment of those suffering from 'nerves'. It was out of season and easy to get lodgings with a view of the main gate of the Priory. It wasn't possible to arrive at an exact plan until they'd thoroughly examined the site and laid out a strategy or two for escaping. While they were eating breakfast early that morning, an excited Kevin had rushed down from overlooking the gates to report that Cale, and some sort of strange nun he'd seen about the place a couple of times when he was incarcerated, were headed towards Biggin Hill. They followed, realizing that more suspicious good luck was offering them a golden opportunity even though the Two Trevors didn't believe in golden opportunities. It was clear Cale and the nun were heading for the top but they kept stopping to rest so the three of them were able to get well ahead, even though they had to take a much steeper route to scrutinize the cut in the hillside that Kevin assured them would be an excellent place for an ambush. He turned out to be right – he was ugly and offensive but not stupid. In fact, when he wasn't boasting or making people uneasy he was astute in a distastefully coarse way.

In addition to their dislike of unexpected good fortune, there was also the problem of the nun or whatever she was. It was more than just a professional reluctance to kill someone they hadn't been paid to, but a moral uneasiness. The Trevors weren't deluded enough to believe that everyone they killed had got what was coming to them, though it was usually true. Indeed it was probably always true. Why would anyone spend the huge amounts needed to hire the Two Trevors on some-one who was innocent? But however ideal a place this was to slaughter Thomas Cale – who unquestionably deserved what was coming to him – there was no way they could leave either a witness or someone to raise the alarm. Therefore it was with peculiar mixed feelings that they watched as Cale and the nun turned back. There were no mixed feelings from Kevin Meat-yard: he punched the ground with frustration and swore so loudly that Trevor Lugavoy told him to shut up or he'd be sorry. They waited an hour and then made their silent and bad-tempered way back down the hill.

The Trevors were not the only observers that day. Watching from a beautifully kept *maison de maître* at the bottom of Big-gin Hill were Daniel Cadbury and Deidre Plunkett.

Their late arrival that morning in pursuit of the Two Tre-vors meant that it was only when Cale and Sister Wray returned, followed an hour later by the two men and their lumpy companion, that Cadbury realized he'd come close to failing to protect Cale. Either something had gone wrong or for some reason the Two Trevors were following Cale but were not intending to kill him. But what could they be up to if it wasn't a killing?

Even though it was off-season for Yoxhall there was enough business from the families of the wealthy mad to keep things ticking over. Cadbury didn't want to risk going into the town and stumbling into the Two Trevors so he decided to send Deidre instead. They had, of course, seen her briefly when he brought them back to Spanish Leeds but she'd been dressed in her usual sexless serge outfit. Something could be done about that.

Cadbury ordered the bumpkin who looked after the house to fetch a dressmaker.

'You *do* have dressmakers?'

'Oh yes, sir.'

'Tell him to bring a selection of wigs. And keep your mouth shut, and tell the dressmaker to do the same.' He gave the bumpkin two dollars, and five for the dressmaker.

'Do you think five dollars was enough?' he said to Deidre when the old man had left. He wasn't interested in her opinion concerning the hush money, he was just trying to get her to talk. He needed to find out if she was aware that he had murdered her sister. The more time he spent with this woman, who was even more peculiar than the late Jennifer, the more it preyed on his mind. Deidre rarely said anything much. But whenever he asked her a direct question she would reply with some gnomic saying – or what seemed like one. Whatever she said was delivered with a faint smile and in a tone so laconic that it was hard not to think that she was mocking him. At times she seemed as silently knowing as a smug Buddha. But what was she wise and silently knowing *about*? Was she just biding her time?

'Enough is as good as a feast to a wise man,' she said, in reply to his question about the money. Was there a glint of scorn flickering in the depths of those flat and unresponsive eyes? And if so, what did it mean? Did she know and was waiting? That was the question. Did she know?

As there was nothing else to be done until the bumpkin reappeared, he tried to read. He brought out his new copy of *The Melancholy Prince*, the old one having fallen apart during a visit to Oxyrinchus to arrange for the removal of a corrupt official responsible for the city's rubbish tips. He was corrupt in the sense that he was holding back on Kitty the Hare's share of the profits, owed to him by virtue of the fact that it was Kitty the Hare who had paid the bribe to put him in charge. When he sadly decided to throw away his crumbling copy of *The Melancholy Prince* – so many memories – he was intrigued to see that his soon-to-be victim had rather cleverly divided the local bins into different ones for food, miscellaneous trash and paper. According to his contract with the city he was supposed to take the paper to Memphis, where he claimed it could be sold to offset the cost of disposal and hence explain why his bid for the contract was lower than that of his rivals. This was a lie. In fact he took the paper out into the nearby desert and buried it.

Now Cadbury opened his new copy and began reading, but though it was pleasurable to read again the familiar words ('Nymph, in thy orisons be all my sins remember'd'), Deidre's silent presence put him off.

'Are you much for books at all?' he asked.

'Of making many books, there is no end,' she replied. 'And much study is a weariness of the flesh.'

Was there a smile there? he thought. *There was definitely a smile.*

'You don't think that knowledge is a good thing, then?' Cadbury's tetchy sarcasm was not at all in doubt.

'He that increases knowledge,' she said, 'increases sorrow.'

This actually did annoy him. Cadbury was an educated man and took his own learning, and the learning of others, seriously.

'So you don't take the view that the unexamined life isn't worth living?' More sarcasm.

She did not say anything for a moment, as if allowing his outburst to land in the dry air of the room, dusty with motes in the shafts of sunlight coming through the small windows.

'For him that is joined to the living there is hope; for a living dog is better than a dead lion.'

To Cadbury this seemed like a threat, the more threatening because delivered even more flatly than usual.

Was her sister the dead lion? Was he the living dog?

'Perhaps,' he said, 'some new clothes will cheer you up.'

She smiled, a rare event.

'There's nothing new under the sun.'

Twenty minutes later the bumpkin returned with the dressmaker, weighed down with holdalls. Cadbury had explained that he wanted Deidre to put on a dress and a wig – her hair was cut almost to the skull – and go to look for the Two Trevors. He couldn't imagine they would recognize her; once the dressmaker was finished, neither did Cadbury. The dress and the false hair did not transform her into a beauty. If anything she looked even stranger than before – like a doll, an automaton that he'd seen demonstrated at Old King Cole's Palace in Boston. Once the powder and lip rouge had been painted on, Deidre looked very strange indeed, as if someone had described a woman to a sculptor blind from birth, who'd then had a stab at making one that had turned out impressive in its way, given his limitations, but still not entirely convincing. Still, it would certainly do the trick. No one was going to recognize her.

By now it was dark. He paid off the dressmaker and the bumpkin, gestured Deidre over to the largest window and raised up the lantern so she could see herself reflected in the glass. He thought her expression softened for a moment as she swayed back and forth and then he saw an expression of pure delight.

'Who is this?' she said. 'Who comes out of the desert like a pillar of smoke scented with myrrh and frankincense?' And then she laughed.

'I've never heard you laugh before,' said Cadbury, mystified.

'There is a time to laugh,' said Deidre, as she swayed back and forth admiring herself in the window, 'and a time to weep.'

Having taken Cadbury's instructions as to what she should and should not do ('Don't be seen by the Two Trevors and don't kill anyone'), she was gone for nearly two hours, during which Cadbury had plenty of time to consider what his grandmother had meant when she repeatedly told him that worrying is the Devil's favourite pastime.

If he'd known the truth about Deidre he would have been less worried for his own sake but even more concerned for the successful accomplishment of their business. Deidre Plunkett, if not an imbecile, was certainly at the high end of simple-minded. Her mother, a devout member of the Plain People, who feared her daughter's oddness more than her lack of understanding, read out loud to Deidre daily from the Holy Book in the hope that its wisdom would drive away her strangeness. In this she failed, not least because of the influence of her equally odd but much more quick-witted sister, the late Jennifer. Devoted to Deidre, Jennifer showed her greater powers of intellect by devising games for her sister, the least appalling of which involved torturing small animals to obtain a confession, putting them on trial on trumped up charges and then inventing hideously complicated executions. Though Deidre's powers of understanding were weak she was naturally cunning when it came to killing in the way a wolf is cunning. No wolf can speak or count but a mathematician who speaks a dozen languages would be unlikely to last an hour with a single wolf in a dark wood on a cold mountain. And she was not so simple that, by keeping her mouth shut and adopting the enigmatic nearly-smile her sister had taught her, she hadn't gained a reputation for shrewdness and acumen, one which seemed ably supported by her talent for murder.

Anyone who tried to strike up a conversation with Deidre soon felt awkward under an empty gaze that, paradoxically, seemed to suggest profound and dismissive guile. Her terse replies, terse because she rarely understood what was being said to her, seemed to imply she regarded anyone speaking to her as a wordy fool. The enigmatic, often vaguely menacing, quotations from the bible of the Plain People were triggered by the words of whoever was talking to her. In this way her replies always seemed relevant if mockingly at odds. In other circumstances a savvy operator like Daniel Cadbury would have seen through her, but fear (not guilt, mind, because Jennifer had tried to murder him first and had unquestionably got what was coming to her) and worry that she knew everything and was biding her time blinded him to the truth, one of these truths being that Deidre had taken a liking to him. The fact that she fancied him was what made her, in fact, more talkative than usual – the only way she had of flirting with him was by waiting until a word triggered off something she recognized from the Holy Book. Unfortunately much of the Holy Book consisted of rather brilliant threats of one kind or another against unbelievers, hence Cadbury's feeling that there was something menacing about her way of talking to him.

Deidre had been gone nearly an hour and a half when he could endure no more. He decided to risk the clear chance of walking into the Trevors and find out what was going on.

She may have been disguised but she was easy to spot, so odd was her appearance and manner. It was just as well Cadbury found her when he did because she'd come to the attention of a trio of what passed for dandies in that part of the world: top hats, red braces and pointed slippers. The four of them, Deidre with her blonde wig, mad eyes and painted cheeks, looked like the bad dream of an unhappy child.

'Any more like you at home, gorgeous?' mocked the gurrier, who clearly regarded himself as the Mr Big. Deidre stared at him then let out a kind of strangulated whine, her best attempt at playing the reluctant coquette.

'How about a blow dry in the entry?' said one of the others. Deidre did not know what either a blow dry or an entry was but she knew violence when she heard it. The third top-hatted gurrier grabbed her by the arm. 'Kissy-kissy!' he said, laughing.

Cadbury was about to step in when a man in his fifties called out nervously to the gurriers, 'Leave her alone.' All three turned to Deidre's saviour.

'Why don't you come and make us, fatso?'

Already pale, the man turned paler and didn't move. Cadbury decided to pretend to be a relieved lover finding his lost sweetheart ('There you are, my dear. I've been looking for you for half an hour!'). But he was too late. The gurrier's grip on Deidre's arm tightened as he turned away from her. Her left hand was already in her pocket and pulling out a short knife with a wide blade. With all her skinny strength she punched it into his back between the sixth and seventh ribs, tearing her right arm free as he fell, crying out. The leader jerked away and turned so that the blow aimed at his back struck him in the stomach, followed by a strike to the heart. The third gurrier tried to speak, holding his hands out to protect his chest and stomach. 'I . . .' But he never finished what he had to say. Deidre's knife took him through the eye. She looked around the crowd to check if anyone else was coming for her. But the crowd was still and soundless, unable to make sense of the painted doll of a woman, the savage emptiness of her eyes and the blood on the ground.

Cadbury walked towards her in the silence, broken as he approached her by the eyeless third man calling for his mum. 'My dear,' said Cadbury, 'my dear,' careful to bring her back from whatever ecstasy had taken hold of her. She blinked, recognizing him. Slowly he placed his open palm on her hand, careful not to hold or grip as he urged her away.

Unsurprisingly no one followed, and turning and twisting in the pretty but narrow streets they were secure enough for the moment, the peaceful town's watchmen not being used to more than an occasional late night drunken fight. The result of everything turning to vinegar in such a fashion was at least clarity: get out, keep going. But waiting in Spanish Leeds for Cadbury was an expectant Kitty the Hare, and explaining to him how this fiasco had taken place along with the probability of Cale being lost to the Two Trevors didn't bear much thinking about. Cadbury needed to show that he'd made a serious attempt to do something to recover the situation. There could be no greater contrast than between Bosco and Kitty the Hare, except that they both thought that Thomas Cale was a talisman for the future. ('The spirit of the age, my dear Cadbury, possesses some people and the thing to do when you find one is to ride on their tails until they burn themselves out.')

Reaching a small trough set into the wall of a church Cadbury told Deidre to wash off the make-up while he tried to work out what to do. The problem was one of time: it was like deciding when to leave the flats of an estuary as the tide turned – keeping just a few seconds ahead made the difference between strolling up on the foreshore in good time or being drowned.

He looked at Deidre. All the water had done was smear the rouge and black kohl and powder all over her face. She was a vision of something out of the eighth circle of hell.

'Did you see anything of them – the Two Trevors?'

'No.'

'And that lout of theirs?'

'No.'

He was trying to work out how to get to Cale at this time of night – presumably they wouldn't just let you walk into a madhouse unannounced – but he was also considering where to hide Deidre. If the Two Trevors hadn't murdered Cale when they had such an easy chance that morning they were hardly likely to try to get up to anything tonight. So he didn't need Deidre with him, but finding somewhere to hide her where they could cut loose as soon as he'd finished warning Cale – he didn't have time for that. And then the answer became clear: who looked more like a madwoman than Deidre?

Quick now, the tide is coming. Pulling Deidre behind him he made for the Priory, its tall clock tower dominating the edge of the town. In less than five minutes he was knocking on the heavy front door.

10

A small door within the Priory's main gate opened up.

'We're closed. Come back tomorrow.'

'Yes, I'm sorry I'm late,' Cadbury said. 'But it was . . . the wheel on the carriage broke . . . it was all arranged. She's very ill.'

The gatekeeper opened a flap on the lamp he was holding and pointed it at Deidre who had her head bowed low. A shake on her sleeve from Cadbury made her look up. Familiar with the harrowing of the face that lunacy caused, still the man gasped at her staring eyes, black smears and mouth that looked as if it had melted too close to the fire.

'Please,' said Cadbury, and pressed a five-dollar piece into the man's hand. 'For pity's sake.'

Compassion and greed melted the keeper's heart. There was, after all, not so much to be wary of. This was a place people tried to break out of, not to break into. And the girl certainly looked like she needed to be locked up.

He let them in through the small door.

'Have you got your letter?'

'I'm afraid I left it in my travel bag. That's why we don't have any cases. The driver will bring them in the morning.' It sounded horribly unconvincing.

But the gatekeeper seemed to have given up on questions. Except for one: 'Who was the letter from?'

'Ah . . . my memory . , . oh . . . Doctor . . . ah . . . Mr . . .'

'Mr Butler? Because he's still in his office over there. Lights still on.'

'Yes,' said a grateful Cadbury. 'It was Mr Butler.'

'Is she safe?' the gatekeeper said quietly.

'Safe?'

'Do you need a guardian?'

'Oh no. She's very tender-hearted. Just . . . not right.'

'Busy night tonight.'

'Really?' said Cadbury, not interested in anyone's night but his own.

'You're the second unexpected arrival in the last ten minutes.' Cadbury felt his ears begin to burn. 'Two gentlemen from Spanish Leeds with a royal warrant.' He looked up, having found the key to unlock the second gate allowing them into the Priory itself. 'Sent them to Mr Butler, too – there's nothing in the logbook, of course. The paperwork in this place couldn't be any more bloody useless if the patients were in charge.'

The gatekeeper let them through and pointed over to the other side of the quadrangle and the one window still lit.

'That's Mr Butler's office.'

Once they were through and the second gate locked behind them Cadbury stopped to think what to do next.

'What's the matter?' said Deidre. It was rare for Deidre to begin a conversation but she had an animal talent for dangerous action and felt instinctively at ease now where normally she was on the edge of understanding what people were saying to her.

'The Two Trevors are here looking to kill Thomas Cale.'

'Where is he?'

'Don't know,' he said, looking over at Butler's window. 'The man in that room could tell us but he's dead.'

'Then call out to Thomas Cale.'

'What?' He was still so surprised by her manner that he had trouble picking up on her line of thought.

'Go up that,' she said, pointing at the bell tower. 'Ring it. Call out a warning.'

He had begun to suspect there was something witless about Deidre. But, predator-sharp, she'd seen the situation instantly and she was right. Wandering around a place with perhaps three hundred rooms, armed warders and unlit quadrangles was a sure way to get killed, especially with the Two Trevors waiting in the dark like a pair of ill-disposed spiders.

'You hide down here,' he said. She didn't reply and, assuming her consent, he moved quickly through the shadowed side of the quad and into the unlocked bell tower. She waited to be sure he was out of sight and then, keeping to the shadows, made her way to the centre of the Priory.

Cadbury climbed the stairs, feeling his chest begin to rasp and worrying that in order to warn Cale he had to give away his own position, a position with only one exit. He was going to have to leave very quickly down two hundred steps in the dark. Once he was at the top he took two full minutes to recover for his escape. He pulled the bell rope four times. The deafening ring would get the attention of everyone within a mile. He let the ringing die away, took a deep breath and bellowed. 'Thomas Cale! Thomas Cale! Two men are here to murder you!' He rang the bell once more. 'Thomas Cale! Two men are here to murder you!'

With that he went back down the stairs, hoping that the Two Trevors had more to worry about than him. If Cale really was the virtuoso roughneck he was cracked up to be then they were now in trouble. If that didn't satisfy Kitty the Hare that he'd done his best, then Kitty could get stuffed. He'd collect Loopy-lou Plunkett and worry about what to do with her later.

Coming to the last few steps of the tower he stopped, took

out a long knife and a short one, his preferred combination when fighting two people, and burst into the quad as if he'd been blasted by Hooke's gunpowder. He was across the quad and into the safety of the shadows in a few seconds, desperately trying to control the wheezing he was suffering from his exertions as it treacherously called, or so it sounded to his ears, a deafening appeal to the two vengeful Trevors to find him and cut his throat. But they did not come and soon he was breathing almost silently. Slowly he began to feel his way to the point where he'd left Deidre. But Deidre was gone.

By now the quad was filling up with the curious mad, the wealthier and non-violent mad, at any rate, those who had access to the bulk of the Priory, all wanting to break their routine by coming out of their rooms to find out what all the fuss was about. Added to their number were alarmed doctors and nurses trying to usher them back to safety. Some of the more highly strung got the wrong end of the stick: 'Help!' they cried. 'They're coming to get me. Murderers! Assassins! I'm sorry! I didn't mean it! Help the poor struggler! Help the poor struggler!'

The fuss certainly helped Cadbury to move more safely within the crowd in the hope of finding Deidre and getting out without, he hoped, having to deal with either of the Two Trevors.

Before all of this, Cale had been sitting in the Priory cloisters with Sister Wray, discussing the existence of God – it was on Cale's insistence, a challenge to her born out of his bad mood at failing to make it to the top of the hill.

'Don't,' she said, 'be taking your ill-temper out on me – but in case something else inside you is listening I'll tell you about God. When I was upon the hill today, looking out over the sea and sky and the mountains, I could feel him everywhere. Don't ask me why, I just could. And don't worry, I know just as well as you do that much of life is hard and cruel.' She turned her head and he had the strongest sense she was smiling. 'Well, not perhaps quite as well as you. But hard and cruel as it is I still feel his presence. I still find the world beautiful.' She laughed, such a pleasant sound.

'What?' he said.

'Tell me what you saw when you were up there. With the mountains and the sea and the sky. Tell me honestly.'

'All right,' he said. 'I saw a river delta easy for a landing from the sea but impossible to defend. Up from that I saw a river plain – you could bring an army up easy . . . but then it narrows and a land slip cuts it in two, about eight feet deep. You could defend for days against four times the men. But there's a small bypass to the left cut into the hill. If they took that it would be over. But there's also a path to the back of the valley. If you timed it right you could pull your men back in packs of a hundred or so and get them out even though it's constricted. They could cover the remainder from the hills when they needed to abandon the line. But any attempt to follow with numbers and you'd be jammed tight like a cork in a bottle.' He laughed. 'Sorry, not what you want to hear.'

'I'm not trying to reform you.'

'Don't mind if you do. I'm sick of myself. Sick of being like this.' He smiled again. 'Redeem me all you want.' A pause. 'Can you make me better?'

'I can try.'

'Does that mean no?'

'It means I can try.'

Another silence, or as much as the pulsing thrum of the tree cicadas would permit.

'What about you?' he said, after a minute or two.

'When you saw the sun over the mountain today did you see a round disc of fire somewhat like a gold dollar?' Sister Wray asked.

'Yes.'

'I saw an innumerable company of the heavenly host crying "Holy, Holy, Holy is the Lord God Almighty."'

Yet another silence.

'Quite a bit different then,' Cale said eventually.

'Yes,' said Sister Wray.

'There is no God,' said Cale. He did not intend this as an insult. He did not intend to say it at all. It burst out of him. He felt Poll moving up his arm and whispering very quietly in his ear, so that Sister Wray would not overhear, 'Blasphemous cunt!'

At that moment something extraordinary happened, a coincidence so outrageous that it could only be encountered in either an improbable fiction or life itself: four resounding clangs sounded from the bell tower and a powerful voice from above shouted: 'Thomas Cale! Thomas Cale! Two men are here to murder you.' But Cale misunderstood – although Cadbury's shout was intended as a warning he interpreted it as a threat from the heavens, to punish him for his sacrilegious outburst.

At once he looked around into the dark and realized that the cloister was a natural trap – a box with only one entrance, four times longer than it was wide with a covered walkway creating deep shadows on all four sides. The bell rang out again, followed by the shout, 'Thomas Cale! Thomas Cale! Two men are here to murder you.'

Sister Wray began to rise. He grasped her arm and at the same time pushed against the ground, so that the wooden high-backed bench on which they were sitting toppled backwards.

As they moved through the shadows of the cloisters, getting into position, the bells and the warning astonished the Trevors. Having separated to move either side of the covered walkway, both decided to let fly with their small overstrungs – but by toppling backwards on the bench Cale was a fraction faster and the bolts moithered overhead with a venomous zip. On his feet, Cale grabbed Sister Wray with his other hand and dragged her backwards into the darkness of the covered walkway. He dumped her forcefully next to a statue of St Frideswide and whispered, 'Stay here – don't move.'

There was only one course possible for his killers. One of them would stay near the only exit to his left, while the other would already be moving up the other walkway to close in on him from the right. Cale was in a pinch. If he tried to make the diagonal run across the open centre of the cloisters they'd have plenty of time to put a bolt in him front and back. He couldn't stay where he was.

'Give me your habit and your veil. Quick.'

She did not waste time being shocked, but she was afraid and fumbled at the line of buttons. 'Quickly!' He reached for the front of her habit and ripped it apart. She gasped but did not flap and helped him haul it down to her feet. Then, without asking, he lifted off her veil. Too much afraid to stop and stare at what he saw, Cale stepped into the habit and dragged on the veil, ripping away the small, perforated patch that covered her eyes. 'Don't you move,' he said again and, black habit pulled up to his knees, launched himself into the middle part of the cloister. But he didn't try for the long diagonal run to the exit but sprinted straight across by the shortest way towards the opposite side. Lighter than the deeply shadowed walkway, it was still only dimly lit by the clouded moon and the poor light and black habit made his movements indistinct and odd. Thrown by the strange appearance of the nun, and wary of a decoy being used to force them to give their position away, the Two Trevors hesitated and let the figure go as it flapped into the unseeable shadows of the walkway.

Cale had given the Two Trevors a problem: what was simple had become complicated. They were, of course, not long in working out what had probably happened. But only probably. It was *probably* Cale wrapped in the nun's habit. But only probably. Perhaps she was young and fit. Perhaps Cale had threatened to cut off her head if she didn't make the dash. Perhaps the nun had decided to sacrifice herself for Cale and got away with it. Lugavoy had the exit covered and it was clear that he must stay there; it was Kovtun at the top of the cloister who had to decide whether Cale was still to his left or now to his right dressed head to toe in black. And he had to be quick. The warning from the tower meant that they were being looked for. The problem about being quick was that it meant they might easily make a mistake. But to act more slowly meant dealing with the guards of the more dangerous lunatics farther inside the Priory. He was now in a trap himself – to one side a presumably harmless nun, to the other a homicidal maniac. He was unnerved even more by a strange convulsive sound like an animal bellowing in the dark.

He was not to know, of course, that his position was considerably less serious than he thought. He wasn't to know that the sound was nothing more than Cale chucking up his guts at the terrible demands he had made of his miserably collapsing constitution. But Kovtun had to move and his skill and instinct made him choose correctly. He went back the way he'd come, closing in on the distressed and exhausted boy. Cale was unarmed, not that it would have made much difference if he'd been holding the Danzig Shank itself, and he knew that he must make his move to the exit or die where he was. He was soaked in sweat, his lips full of pins and needles. He moved towards the exit slowly – any faster and he would have fallen down. Fortunately for him, the still spooked Kovtun was following pretty gingerly himself. Neither Cale nor the Two Trevors had time on their side but all three knew that too little patience could get them killed. Cale was on all fours, feeling his way towards the right-hand corner of the cloister, heading for the exit and whoever was waiting there and trying not to breathe too hard or give himself away by throwing up again. Behind him, Kovtun was slowly beating up the walkway. Cale realized the greatest obstacle to his having any chance of getting out was the moonlight coming through the large entry into the cloisters. Anyone trying to make it through would be lit up like St Catherine on a wheel. He shuffled forwards to the edge of the light and braced himself to run, hoping to catch whoever was guarding the exit by surprise. Behind him he heard the sound of Kovtun scuffing his foot lightly on an uneven slab. He ran for it – one second, one and a half, two seconds – and then felt a huge crack to the side of his head as Trevor Lugavoy, who'd been waiting just the other side of the line of moonlight, stepped in and struck him with the heavy end of his overstrung. It would have taken a lot less to knock Cale down in his dreadful state and he fell like a sack of hammers, collapsing with his back to a statue of St Hemma of Gurk.

11

Drawing his long knife, Lugavoy reached down and pulled the veil from Cale's head to make sure he was going to kill the right person.

'Thomas Cale?' he asked.

'Never heard of him,' whispered Cale. Lugavoy, who was left-handed, drew back the long knife and stabbed at Cale who cried out, but then there was a loud THWACK! like an old woman beating a carpet of its dust. Trevor Lugavoy saw but did not understand that the lower half of his forearm, with the hand that had been holding the long knife, was now lying on the cloister floor. He raised his amputated arm and stared at the stump, utterly bemused.

Then the shock hit him and he sat down heavily on his backside. A blurred figure moved in front of him and struck Trevor Kovtun, who had moved directly behind Cale, in the chest. It is no easy thing to kill a man instantly with a sword but Kovtun was close to death within seconds of slumping to the ground. Lugavoy had moved onto his knees and had taken hold of his severed forearm, as if in the preliminary stages of putting it back on. Then he looked up and saw a creature whose very eyes and nose and mouth seemed to have been smeared across its face in colours of blue and red. Whether he saw anything more terrible after that cannot be known – no one returns from that place, scheduled or unscheduled.

Having finished off Trevor Lugavoy, something that, to Deidre's vexation, took three strokes rather than one, she turned back to the astonished boy sitting knackered before her and said, 'Are you Thomas Cale?'

Dog-weary as he was, Cale was too suspicious by nature to answer quickly. What if she was just a rival assassin and wanted to kill him herself? He panted more heavily to signal he could not speak and held out his right hand, palm forward, in a gesture of compliance. It didn't work.

'Are you Thomas Cale?' she demanded.

'It's all right, Deidre. It's him.' It was Cadbury, with four alarmingly large men from the dangerous lunatic section of the Priory. 'Marvellous work, Deidre. Marvellous, marvellous, marvellous. Now be a good girl and put away the sword.'

Meek as a little girl made from sugar and spice, Deidre did as she was told.

'If I may say so,' said Cadbury, to Cale, 'you don't look at all well.'

'I'd say,' a pause to stop being sick, 'that things,' another pause, 'could be a lot worse,' replied Cale, putting out his hand.

Cadbury pulled him up and looked him over, smiling. 'I appreciate your desire to make up for all your wickedness but are you really sure you're cut out for Holy Orders?'

Cale took off Sister Wray's habit and picked up the veil Lugavoy had dropped on the pavement.

'Stay here,' he said to Cadbury and walked off wearily into the shadows of the covered walkway.

'It's all right, it's me,' he called out into the dark. 'You're safe, I've got your . . .' he wasn't sure what to call them, '. . . clothes.' He placed the habit and the veil on a small section of pavement illuminated by the moon and then stood back. 'The face thing's a bit torn. Sorry.' Nothing happened for a moment and then a shockingly white arm moved into the light and pulled the habit and veil slowly into the dark. There was a short period of rustling.

'Are you all right? Not hurt?' said Sister Wray from the shadows.

'Not hurt.' A pause. 'Are you all right?' Cale asked her.

'Yes.'

'Somebody rescued me. Do you think it was God?'

'After you told him to his face he didn't exist?'

'Perhaps he wants to save me – for better things.'

'You must think pretty well of yourself.'

'As it happens I don't think it was God – the woman who saved me, she doesn't look like she's had much to do with angels. Perhaps the devil was behind me all the time.'

'So,' said Poll, from the dark. 'So you're still the chosen one and not just a nasty little boy with a gift for bloodshed.'

'I was hoping,' replied Cale, 'that you might have taken one in the gob. You'd better come and meet our redeemers.'

But halfway down the cloisters he changed his mind. 'Perhaps you shouldn't. There are people, I don't know . . . it's better not to come to their attention.'

He vanished into the dark but Sister Wray decided she'd had enough of doing as she was told by Cale. She eased forward until she was able to hide at the left-hand corner of the cloister. Cale was talking to a tall man, elegantly dressed in black, and next to them a woman with her back to Sister Wray who had clearly lost interest in what was going on around her and was looking away into the darkness at the back of the cloister. When Deidre Plunkett turned around, Sister Wray drew back into the shadows and began to take the view that Cale had been right. It was a face best avoided.

'We can't stay,' said Cadbury. 'There was some unpleasantness earlier in the town and it's time we weren't here. She needs a scrub and to get out of these clothes.'

'What about the bodies?'

'Considering they were about to kill you before we stepped in I don't think it's unreasonable to ask you to sort them out. Don't think you have to thank her, by the way.'

'Oh, yes. Thanks,' said Cale, calling out to Deidre, who merely stared at him for a moment and then looked away again. He would have offered to take his rescuers to his room but it was clear from the presence of the watchmen that they were going nowhere. Then the furious Director of the Priory arrived and was about to demand an explanation when she saw the two dead men and the dismembered arm followed by Deidre Plunkett's face. The blood drained from her lips, as well it might, but she was made of heavy-duty cloth. 'Come here,' she said to them both, and backed away from the cloisters' entrance.

For several futile minutes Cale and Cadbury tried to explain what had happened until they were interrupted by Sister Wray. 'I was a witness and participant. Those two men came to kill us both. Why I can't say, but it was completely unprovoked and had the . . .' she paused, '. . . young woman and this man not intervened it would be our bodies lying in the cloister.'

'And what,' said the Director, 'am I supposed to do with the bodies that *are* here?'

'I'll deal with them,' said Cale.

'I'm sure you will,' said the Director. 'I'm sure that's the kind of talent you have in abundance.'

'Call the magistrate,' said Sister Wray.

'He's in Heraklion,' replied the Director. 'He couldn't get here until late afternoon tomorrow at best.' She looked at Cadbury and Deidre. 'We'll have to keep you in custody until then.'

'I don't think that I, nor my young colleague,' Cadbury

nodded at Deidre, 'would be at all happy about that.' The news of the three deaths in the market had obviously not yet reached the Priory. Once it did they were cooked: there would be no explaining away those deaths as well as the Trevors. He started to consider their chances of cutting their way out of the Priory.

'They can stay with me in my room,' said Cale. 'The windows are barred and you can put as many guards outside as you like. I think that's fair.'

The Director had the sense to be unnerved by the prospect of actually arresting Cadbury and the weird young woman – if that was what it was. 'I give you my word,' said Cale, something that meant absolutely nothing but which, he noted, seemed to satisfy many people. But wanting the easiest outcome persuaded the Director. She turned to the most senior of the guards.

'Show them to Mr Cale's room. You and all of your men remain outside until I have you relieved.' She turned to Sister Wray. 'I'd like to talk to you in private.'

Five minutes later the three of them had been delivered to Cale's room and the door locked. Before the key had turned Cadbury was checking the impressive looking bars on the window. He turned to Cale.

'And we're better off here because?'

'Because I don't care to have bars on the window if I can do anything about it.' Cale took a shiv from the drawer in the single desk and started stabbing at the wall. It crumbled surprisingly easily, because it was made of gravel and dust stuck together with soap, to reveal a metal stud, the anchor to bars that looped through the wall under the window itself. 'I've been loosening them off for a while. You can be out in ten minutes.'

'How far down is it?'

'About three feet. They haven't kept dangerous head-bangers in here for years. The bars look impressive but inside the wall it's mostly rust.'

'Not bad,' said Cadbury. 'Forgive me for doubting you but one of my greatest faults is lack of trust.' He looked over at Deidre. 'Got any soap?'

It took Cadbury nearly half an hour of sullenly endured scrubbing to rid Deidre's face of the greasepaint while Cale dug away at the already weakened wall. What gradually emerged from the soap and water was a more familiar Deidre – pale, thin-lipped but still mad-eyed. They put her in one of Cale's suits; it was baggy, with the trousers held up by a belt that they had to cut out an extra notch a good six inches further on.

During the ten minutes more it took to remove the bars, Cale mined Cadbury for information about the Two Trevors. 'I can't be sure it was the Redeemers who sent them but for years they operated out of Redeemer territory for a price: if you want a peaceful retirement under our protection do what we ask when we ask it.'

'There are other people who don't care for me,' said Cale.

'Not who could get to the Two Trevors or afford them if they could. It was the Redeemers.'

'You can't be certain.'

'Certain. No.'

'If they were so wonderful, how come a little girl killed them?'

'She's not a little girl and the Trevors got unlucky. One job too far.'

'The thing about your friend . . .'

'She's not my friend.'

'. . . is she looks sort of familiar.'

Cadbury changed the subject.

'You might want to think about coming with us.'

'Me? I haven't done anything wrong.'

'I don't think the old dear who runs this place will think that.'

'I'm not worried about her.'

'You can't stay here. They won't stop.'

'I know the Redeemers a lot better than you do. I'll have to have a think.'

'Got a message for Kitty?'

Cale laughed. 'Tell him I'm grateful. And to you, and your mad friend.'

'I told you, she's not my friend, and I'm not sure Kitty is looking for gratitude exactly. You might be safer in Leeds than anywhere else.'

'P'raps I'll look you both up next time I'm there.'

And that was that.

Next morning the Director arrived with Sister Wray and flew into an almighty rage. 'They overpowered me,' said Cale, and that was all. There was much shouting and a good deal of personal abuse, and even more when it became clear that the two fugitives had been responsible for three further deaths, all of which had to be explained to the magistrate from Heraklion. They locked Cale up for three days, but as he had patently had nothing to do with the murders in the town and, as Sister Wray pointed out with considerable force, he'd been the intended victim in the cloisters, they were forced to let him go. The Director gave Cale one week's notice to leave on the entirely justifiable grounds that he posed a serious risk to everyone at the Priory.

'To be honest,' he said to Sister Wray, 'I was a bit surprised she gave me as long as that. I should thank you, no?'

'I thought it was only fair,' she said. 'Where will you go? Don't tell me.'

He laughed at the change of direction. 'Not sure. I could go north but I hear it's grim up there. Besides, Bosco won't leave me alone wherever I go. Probably Cadbury was right, I'm safer in Spanish Leeds than wandering about in the bundu.'

'I don't know what a bundu is but you're not well enough to be on your own – or anything like it.'

'Then it's settled. Leeds it is.'

'Can I ask you to promise me one thing?'

'You can ask.'

'Stay away from that Kitty the Hare person.'

'Easier said than done. I need money and power and Kitty has both.'

'IdrisPukke cares for you – stick with him.'

'He doesn't have money or power. And he has his own problems.'

There was a moment's silence. Sister Wray went over to a cupboard in which there were many small drawers and opened two of them before placing two packets on the table, one sizeable, the other small.

'This is Tipton's Weed.' She opened the packet and poured a tiny amount into the palm of her hand. 'Use this much in a cup of boiling water, let it cool and drink it every day at the same time. You'll be able to get it from any herbalist in Spanish Leeds but they will call it Singen's Wort or Chase-Devil.'

'What's it for?'

'It helps to chase away the devil. It will help you feel better – even things out. If you start to feel dizzy or sensitive to the light cut down the dose till it stops. It's good for wounds as well.'

She tapped the other packet twice. 'This is Phedra and Morphine. I've thought more than twice about giving you this.' She opened the packet and tipped a tiny amount of green and white speckled powder onto the table then, picking up a small knife, separated enough to cover a fingernail. 'Take this when you're desperate. As desperate as you were the other night, not otherwise. It will give you strength for a few hours. But it builds up in the body so if you take it for more than a few weeks what you've suffered over the last few months will feel like a minor inconvenience. Do you understand?'

'I'm not stupid.'

'No. But the time is coming, I guess, when it may seem the lesser of two evils. Take it for more than three weeks in all – I mean twenty doses – and you'll find out it probably isn't.'

'Take it all now,' said Poll. 'Put yourself and the rest of the world out of its misery.'

Telling Poll to keep quiet, Sister Wray took Cale through the boiling up of the Tipton's and made him count out the Phedra and Morphine into twenty lots so he could see how little he could take. There was a knock at the door. 'Come in.' One of the Priory servants entered.

'Please, Sister,' said the girl, clearly excited. 'A beautiful woman in a carriage is asking for Thomas Cale. She has soldiers and servants dressed a la mode and with white horses. The Director says he's to come at once.'

'Who do you . . . ?' But Sister Wray was already talking to Cale's back.

I 2

It's one of the greatest mistakes of the cultivated person to take it as given that because they have sophisticated minds they also have sophisticated emotions. But what kind of soul feels sophisticated hatred or sophisticated grief for, say, a murdered child? Is the broken heart of the educated and refined person different from that of the savage? Why not say that the enlightened and knowledgeable feel the pain of childbirth, or the kidney stone, in a different way to unpolished commoner or chav? Intelligence has many shades, but rage is the same colour everywhere. Humiliation tastes the same to everyone.

As for Cale's heart, it was as much a sophisticated as a savage thing. No grand master in the game of chess possessed the subtle skills that Cale had at his command when reading a landscape – how to defend or to attack it, or to adjust that reading in a second because of a change in the wind or rain, how to finesse the known and unknown rules of a battle that can be altered by the gods at any time without consent or consultation. Life itself, in all its horror and incomprehensibility, plays out in even the simplest skirmish. Who was cooler or more intelligent than Cale in this most terrible of human trials? But this prodigy of the complexity of things rushed down the stairs, heart bursting with hope: *She's come back to throw herself on my forgiveness. Everything will be explained. I'll turn her down and threaten her. I'll treat her as if I can't remember her. I'll wring her neck. She deserves it. I'll make her weep.*

Then sanity of a kind returned: *What if it's not her? What if it's someone else? Who else could it possibly be? She wants something. She won't get it.* And on it went, the madness breaking inside him as both his wild and intelligent hearts contended with each other for command. He stopped and found himself breathing hard. 'Get some grasp,' he said aloud. 'Control yourself, take it easy. Simmer down and keep your head.'

He was sweating. *Maybe,* he thought, *it was that tea she gave me. Don't go in like this.* Then the insanity returned. *Perhaps she'll leave if I come late. Perhaps she happened to be passing and she came in on a whim and she's already regretting it. She might just leave, worrying about what I'll do.* And then the greater madman visited. *She's come to laugh at me, knowing she is safe now that I'm sick and weak.*

But pride of a kind won out over even madness, fear and love. He went back to his room, washed quickly in the basin – he needed to – and changed his shirt. Slowly, because of the fear that he might again sweat too much, he made his way to the Director's office. Another moment outside the door to gather himself. Then the firm knock. Then the entrance before the words 'Come in' were halfway out of the Director's mouth. And there she was – Riba not Arbell. Break, fracture, split, fragment and smash. What did his poor heart not endure? It was all he could do to stop a cry of dreadful loss. He stood quite still, staring at her.

'Would you mind terribly if I spoke to Thomas alone?' she said to the Director. In other circumstances Cale would have been astonished, even if pleasantly, at the gracious tone of Riba's request and the clear understanding by both women that it could not be confused for the kind of question to which the answer might be 'No'. The tone of her voice was one of charming and implacable authority. The Director simpered in obedience to Riba, looked malignantly at Cale and left, closing the doors behind her. A silence followed, weighty with strange emotions, all of them horrible.

'I can see you were expecting someone else,' she said at last. 'I'm sorry.' It's true that she was sorry to see him so disappointed and so ill, the circles around his eyes so dark – but it was also true that she was put out at being the cause of such terrible disappointment. It was not flattering, particularly when she had expected to surprise him with delight at her wonderful story of love and transformation. But in this legend of pain, misery, slaughter and madness it is as well to be reminded that everything is not for the worst in the worst of all possible worlds, a story where today is bad, tomorrow dreadful until at last the most appalling thing of all happens. There *are* happy endings, virtue is something rewarded, the kind and generous get what they deserve. This is how it was with Riba. She came into the story of poor, tormented, miserable Cale in the most revolting of ways: bound hand and foot and waiting to be eviscerated in order to satisfy the curiosity of Redeemer Picarbo concerning the bodily source of the monstrous impurity that possessed all women. Riba knew perfectly well, because Cale had constantly reminded her, that he was history's most reluctant saviour and that if he'd had it to do again he would have left Picarbo to his repellent investigations. She didn't really believe he'd have left her to die, at least she probably didn't believe it. You never quite knew what he was capable of. After this narrowest of squeaks, her climb to prominence was remarkably easy. She was a beautiful girl, if unusually plump, but in Memphis beauty was commonplace. Helen of Troy had been born in Memphis and was generally considered to be rather plain compared to others. What brought Riba to the attention of a great many men in the city was that she was kind, good-natured and intelligent, but also that her body, sonsy to the point of fubsy, expressed

127

in flesh the generosity and comfort of her heart. Servant to the hated Arbell (though not hated by Riba), she had been caught as much as her mistress in the fall of Memphis and the dreadful flight from the Redeemers, in which so many of the Materazzi who survived Silbury Hill died from hunger and disease. Though she was still Arbell's servant when those that remained of the Materazzi stumbled into Spanish Leeds, it was inevitable that her easy charm and wit would bring her the attention of men of every kind and class. And, unlike the Materazziennes, she had the overwhelming advantage of liking men rather than despising them. Such choice she had! She was adored by coal-carriers, butchers, lawyers and doctors, as well as the aristocrats of Memphis and Spanish Leeds. Fortunately for her peace of mind, from among this array of possible futures (bigwig or nonentity?) she fell in love with Arthur Wittenberg, Ambassador to the Court of King Zog and only son of the President of the Hanse, the syndicate of all the wealthy countries of the Baltic Axis. His father opposed their marriage, understandably, until he met her and was so charmed he almost forgot himself and was on the verge of attempting to betray his son in the manner of a Greek tragedy before he pulled himself together and determined to behave. How would storytellers and makers of operas live if everyone was so restrained? At any rate, in a matter of a few months she rose from starving nobody to becoming a woman of vast wealth and enormous political influence.

Still, despite Cale's shock she was sympathetic to his disappointment – if a little piqued concerning her hurt vanity – and slowly allowed him time to pull himself together by chatting away amusingly, and self-deprecatingly, about her rise to fortune. After an hour or so, Cale was himself again and able to hide his disappointment and his considerable shame over the depth of that disappointment. He was, in the end, pleased to see her, amused by her current good luck while also considering how it might be made use of. She chatted away about the past and had a fund of amusing stories to tell about the absurdity of life amongst the nobility.

'Was Arbell at your wedding?'

'She was, and very happy to be so.'

'I'm sure she probably fitted you in before popping over to the pigman to help feed his porkers. I hear they're very hard up, the Materazzi.'

'Not quite so much any more. Conn has become a great darling of the King and he listens to no one else. There's money about and a position discussed.'

'What?'

'The skinder is that he'll be made second-in-command to General Musgrove to run the army of the entire Axis – if he can get them to agree to fight the Redeemers.'

'Will they?'

'Arthur says they'll talk but do nothing until the Redeemers make a move, by which time it'll be too late.'

'Is Vipond employed?'

'Yes, but not with any of the power he wants or needs. The Swiss have put him out to pasture, Arthur says, and IdrisPukke eats the grass with him.'

Cale looked at her, sizing up any change her good luck might have made in her sympathies towards him.

'Do you trust your husband – his ability, I mean?'

'Yes.'

'Then do him a good turn and introduce him properly to Vipond and IdrisPukke. He'll see that they've been about their business and he needs them. They need his influence and money.'

'He's my husband. I can't tell him what to do.'

Cale nodded and remained silent, allowing her to realize she had disappointed him, and deeply. As they walked through the gardens, avoiding the cloister, he chatted about the birds and the flowers and what it was like at night to look up at the milk-white road of stars that wheeled across the sky. There was a pause. He laughed. That was good, she thought, he'd let go of the business about Vipond and IdrisPukke.

'It's a funny old world,' he said, casually.

'Because?'

'Well, I was thinking how very singular and spooky-like life is – that now you're a beautiful lady with a great big nabob to look after you, when hardly any time ago you were lying on a wooden table bound and beaten and about to have your giblets spilt all over the shop. What if I'd kept on walking? I was a bad boy in those days – I might have. But I didn't. I turned around and I . . .'

'Very well. Enough. You've made your point.'

Cale shrugged. 'I wasn't making a point. I was just talking about old times.'

'I'm well aware of how much I owe you, Cale.'

'So am I.'

And with that they walked the remainder of the gardens in silence.

The next day he asked Riba to let him return with her to Spanish Leeds.

'Is it safe?' she asked.

'For you?'

'For you to go back. Are you well enough?'

'No – I'm not well enough. But it's not safe here or any-where. I thought if I got far enough away he'd leave me alone but Bosco's going to come for me whatever I do.'

Cale was wrong about this but his wrong conclusion was the only reasonable one.

'You're going to destroy the Redeemers?'

'You make me sound mad when you put it like that. Give me another choice and I'll take it.'

'You must have travelling clothes and a nice hat.'

'I'd like a nice hat.' He thought for a minute. 'Will I be allowed inside the carriage with you?'

'You must be more agreeable if you're going to do great things. Arthur has a lot to teach you. He knows you saved my life and is desperate to repay you. Don't throw his goodwill away.'

He laughed. 'Teach me how to behave on the journey. I'll listen, I promise.'

'You'd better – your fists can't protect you now.'

He looked at her. Baleful would be the word.

'Sorry,' she said, and laughed. 'My good luck has made me puffed up and snooty. That's what Arthur says.'

'When can we leave?'

'Tomorrow morning. Early.'

'How about tomorrow morning, late?'

But even late morning was bad for Cale. He made it glass-eyed into the coach but laid himself down on the padded seat and fell asleep for more than six hours.

Watching him from a distance was Kevin Meatyard, who had realized that the rumours of the deaths at the Priory must be true and that he was now unemployed as well as unprotected in a town where he was wanted, admittedly for a murder he had not committed. No one in Cyprus was to hear of him for many years, but when they did it was in the hope that he had forgotten all about them. But that's another story.

The carriage carrying Cale and Riba stopped after four hours' travel but he refused to be disturbed and Riba and her entourage ate well without him. He woke up slowly an hour after they restarted the journey but it was more like regaining consciousness than emerging from restful sleep. He did not, could not, open his eyes for a good twenty minutes. But there was something pleasurable to be heard: Riba singing and humming softly to herself a song that was the very latest thing in Spanish Leeds.

> *Please tell me the truth about love,*
> *Is it really true what they sing?*
> *Is it really true what they sing?*
> *That love has no ending?*
>
> *Come into the shade of my parasol,*
> *Come under the cover of my umbrella,*
> *I will always be true to you,*
> *And you will love me, my love, for ever.*
>
> *Oh tell me the truth about love,*
> *Is it true or is it lies,*
> *That first love never dies?*
>
> *But please don't tell me if it isn't so,*
> *Please don't tell me if it isn't so,*
> *For I don't want to know,*
> *For I don't want to know.*

He sat up slowly and she stopped singing.

'Are you sick?'

'Yes.'

'Are you very sick?'

'Yes.'

'I was afraid to ask you, do you have any news of the girls?'

'Girls?'

'The girls I was with in the Sanctuary. Do you think Bosco has killed them already?'

'Probably not.'

She was surprised at this and hopeful.

'Why?'

'He has no reason to kill them.'

'He has no reason to keep them alive.'

'No.'

'I thought,' she said, after a silence, 'he might be keeping them to use against you.'

'Not any more, obviously.'

'Can I do anything to help them?'

'No.'

'Are you sure?'

'You know you can't help them so why keep asking if you can? Feeling guilty?'

'For being alive and happy? Sometimes.'

'But not all the time.'

She let out a sigh.

'Not all the time. Not even most of the time.'

'Just enough guilt to make you feel better about yourself and make it all right to enjoy your happiness. Go ahead. They can't be happy, so be happy *for* them.'

'It's not up to you to tell me what to do. I'm a very important person and you have to do as I say.'

He laughed. 'Yes. I've decided to do as I'm told from now on. A beautiful rich woman who owes me her life – I could take orders from someone like that.'

'Well, you can't kill everyone you don't like any more. I meant it when I said you'll have to learn to be agreeable.'

'Agreeable?' He said the word as if it were one he'd heard before but never expected to need in any practical way. It was good to see Riba again and it was a pleasure to see her so well accounted for. He didn't know whether to say it but he said it anyway. 'I found out what Picarbo wanted you for, what he was doing.' He told her plainly and quickly.

'Horrible,' she said softly, 'and mad.'

'Bosco thought pretty much the same – that he was mad, I mean – that's why he might keep the rest of them alive. Bosco disapproved.'

'You don't seem,' she said, 'to think of Bosco as badly as you used to.'

'I wouldn't say that. I understand him better and I'd like to understand him even more before I cut his head off.'

13

Far away from the Four Quarters, in the great, green, greasy jungles of Brazil, a storm of measureless power is approaching its height. Winds blow, rain lashes, there is lightning and thunder enough to crack open the world – and then it moves into decline by a fraction of a fraction of an infinitesimal not even a puff of air strong enough to blow a single speck of dust off a slippery slope. The great storm is beginning to disperse.

Redeemer General Gil, now with the honorary title of Defender of the Holy Glee, came into Pope Bosco's war room and bowed slightly less humbly than was owed.

'Anything?'

There was no doubt, despite the fact that they were supposed to be going about the business of bringing the world to an end, that this enquiry referred to Thomas Cale.

'As I told Your Holiness yesterday, the last news was that he was in Leeds and probably suffering the effects of dysentery – ill at any rate. He's left now but I'm not able as yet to say where.'

'Have you put more people on it?'

'As I said I would –' he paused, 'yesterday.'

'Good people?'

'The best.' This was true enough as far as it went, which was not very far, given that the good people he had out looking for Cale were the Two Trevors. Gil had decided that the end of the world, a project in which he deeply believed, would take place a good deal sooner if it were preceded by Cale announcing it to

God personally. Bosco's obsessive belief that the death of the world could not come unless Cale administered it was a delusion in Gil's estimation – a blasphemy he was careful to conceal. Cale was never the incarnation of God's anger, he was just a delinquent boy. Once he was confirmed as dead Bosco would just have to get on with it.

'I want to know immediately you hear anything.'

'Of course, Your Holiness.'

It was a dismissal but Gil did not move. Throughout the conversation Bosco had not taken his eyes from the great map of the Axis powers laid out on one of the four massive tables in the room.

'You aren't worried he'll give away your plan to attack the Axis through Arnhemland?'

'Away from here, Cale is merely a thorn in his own side. He could shout it out in the middle of Kirkgate on market day and no one would listen – least of all Ikard or that buffoon Zog. Was there something else?'

'Yes, Your Holiness. The end of the world. There are problems.'

Bosco laughed, delighted at this.

'Did you expect to bring about the apocalypse without them?'

'There are *unanticipated* problems.' Gil was finding it harder these days not to be irritated by his pontiff.

'Yes?'

'Moving the populations out of the territories we've annexed is diverting more supplies and materials than we can easily provide. There are too many people to move to the west and not enough food or transport to do the job without robbing the exact same stocks from our militants. We must slow down one or the other.'

'I'll think about it. What else?'

'Brzca came to see me.' Brzca was a man with a talent, a

genius if you will, in the matter of killing in numbers. He was in charge of the practical problem of transporting captured people into the west and beginning the process of bringing an end to God's greatest mistake. 'He's having problems with his executioners.'

'He has complete freedom of access to any suitable person in the militant. I made it clear he has priority.'

'I've done everything you asked,' said an increasingly irritated Gil.

'Then what's the problem?'

'Too many executioners are becoming sick – in the head, I mean.'

'He knows the importance of this, why didn't he say something before now?'

'Mostly they only began their duties three months ago. It turns out that killing two thousand people a week begins to take a toll after a few months. Nearly half of his people are unable to continue. It's not so hard to understand. I know it's necessary but I wouldn't want to do it. But there it is.'

Bosco said nothing for a while and then walked to the window. Finally, after some time, he turned back to Gil.

'You know I am proud of them, my poor labourers. When I think of what we are obliged to do it makes me sick with dread. To endure what they must endure and remain a decent person – well, it's clear what spiritual strength it requires. Is he still here?'

'Yes.'

'Send him to me. Together we will discover a way to help our people find the spiritual courage to continue.'

'Your Holiness.' Gil started to withdraw. Bosco called out after him.

'I know Brzca of old: tell him not to kill those who've failed. We must make an allowance for human weakness.'

137

14

'Name?'

Vague Henri looked at his interrogator with an expression of helpful bewilderment.

'I'm sorry, they didn't tell me your name.'

'Not my name. *Your* name.'

A pause – for just as long as he thought he could get away with.

'Yes.'

'What?'

'Yes, I see.'

'So, what is it?'

Despite the difficulty of his situation, Vague Henri was enjoying appearing to be dim while really being a cheeky little sod, a dangerous line he had perfected over many years of tormenting Redeemers and the reason for the name Cale had given him five years ago. Now no one knew him as anything else.

'Dominic Savio.'

'Well, Mr Savio. You've committed a serious offence.'

'What does *offence* mean?'

'It means a crime.'

'What does *committed* mean?'

'It means "done". It means you've done a crime.'

'I'm a good boy.'

You're also an idiot, thought the interrogator. He sat back. 'I'm sure you are. But it's a crime to cross the border without papers and it's another crime to enter the country at any point unless that point is an official border crossing.'

'I don't have any papers.'

'I know you don't have any papers, that's why you're here.'

'Where can I get the papers?'

'Not the point. It's a crime to *try* to come into the country without papers.'

'I didn't know about the papers.'

'Ignorance of the law is no excuse.'

'Why not?'

'Because then everyone would say they didn't know about the law. They could say they didn't know murder was against the law. Would you let someone go who'd committed murder if he said he didn't know killing people was against the law?'

'Soldiers kill people, that's not against the law.'

'That's not murder.'

'You said "killing people".'

'I meant murder.'

'I understand.'

The interrogator was not sure how he had let the questioning of the boy slip in such a way. Once again he attempted to get control of the situation.

'Why did you try to enter the country at an illegal place?'

'I didn't know it was illegal.'

'All right. Why were you trying to get into the country?'

'The Redeemers were trying to murder us. Sorry, to kill us.'

'What do you mean?'

Vague Henri looked at him wide-eyed with alarm at the question.

'I mean make us not live.'

'I know what *kill* means. Why did you say murder and then change it to kill?'

'You told me soldiers can't do murder.'

139

'I don't think I did.'

Vague Henri looked at him. Blank.

'Why were they trying to kill you?'

'I don't know.'

'They must have had a reason.'

'No.'

'Even Redeemers have to have a reason to kill someone.'

Vague Henri was tempted to say something sarcastic but had the sense to stop himself.

'Perhaps they thought we were Antagonists.'

'Are you?'

'Is that a crime?'

'No.'

'I'm not an Antagonist.'

'Then who are you?'

'I'm from Memphis.'

'At last.'

'Sorry?'

'Never mind.'

'What did you do in Memphis?'

'I worked in the kitchens at the Palazzo.'

'Good job?'

'No. I cleaned dishes.'

'Parents?'

'Don't know. Dead, I think. Maybe they're just going about like me.'

'Going about?'

'Going about from place to place looking for work. Staying away from Redeemers.'

'But you didn't – stay away from them, I mean.'

'Will I go to prison?'

'Not worried about your friends?'

'They're not my friends.' This was true enough. 'I was

just travelling with them. Did some cooking. It seemed safer.'

'Do you know who they are?'

'Just people going about trying to find work and stay away from the Redeemers. You would if you were them – if you were me.'

The interrogator was silent for a moment.

'No – in answer to your question. You won't go to prison. We have a camp for crossovers, people like you, about thirty miles away in Koniz. You'll have to live in a tent. But you'll be fed. There are guards to keep you safe. There might be more questions.'

'Will I be able to leave?'

'No.'

'So it *is* a prison?'

'No, it's a sort of holding place while we find out more about you. There are thousands doing what you're doing. We can't have them just wandering all over the country. We'd have Redeemer fifth columnists everywhere.'

Vague Henri appeared to consider this. 'What's a fifth columnist?'

'A sort of spy. You understand now?'

'Yes,' said Vague Henri.

'Fair enough, then. You go to the camp and you'll be safe there. Then we'll see. Things will probably settle down. Then you can go on your way.'

'Is that what you think? That it will all settle down?'

The interrogator smiled. He wanted to reassure the boy. 'Yes. That's what I think.' And on the balance of probabilities this was truly what he did believe. What was the point, after all, of the Redeemers fighting a war on so many fronts? There had been serious concessions to the annexation of Nassau and Rockall and plausible reassurance from the Pope

as a result of them. It was difficult for a cautious and pessimistic person, which is what he considered himself to be, to
see what the Redeemers could gain from a total war. There
was nothing left to concede, everything had already been
given away. Anything more would merely be unconditional
surrender and not even the most recalcitrant and feeble
would tolerate that. From now on the Redeemers would
either be happy with the significant concessions offered
them, and which had cost them nothing, or risk everything
they had in a universal war, which might cost them everything. A war did not, on balance, seem plausible. He pushed
a piece of paper across the table.

'Sign this,' he said softly.

'What is it?'

'Read it if you like.'

'I can't read,' said Vague Henri.

'It asks you whether or not you brought any meat or flow-
ering vegetables into the country. And to give details, where
applicable, of any misfeasance committed here or in another
country. Misfeasance means bad things.'

'Oh,' said Vague Henri. 'No bad things. Here or anywhere.
I'm a good boy.'

The next day he was in a walking convoy on his way to the
tent city the interrogator had told him about. He thought it
was unlikely they'd actually get him there as there were
around three hundred refugees, some of them women and
children, and only fifteen guards. As it turned out, the camp
at Koniz was on the way to Spanish Leeds so it made sense
to let the border guards feed him and keep him safe as the
interrogator had said they would. He'd probably skip out
before they got there, or after if it seemed more sensible.

A prison with tents wasn't going to be able to hold someone

who'd got out of the Sanctuary – boastful thoughts he had to revise over the following days. The Swiss guards knew their job and so maybe the guards at Koniz would too. Still, things could be worse. He could be dead like most of the dozen Redeemers he and Kleist had taken over the border to kill Redeemer Santos Hall for murdering Kleist's wife and baby in the wilderness on the way to Silesia.

Of the four kinds of military failure Vague Henri's small expedition to kill Hall was the worst: disaster from the word go. Nothing went right: the rain started as they left and did not stop, the horses became sick and so did the men. They stumbled into three Redeemer patrols when a minute later or earlier they would have passed unobserved. Even before they arrived at Santos Hall's camp in Moza they'd lost two men. When they arrived they just walked into the camp, well able to blend in with men they'd lived with most of their lives; unluckily one of the Purgators was immediately recognized by an oblate who was being sent back to Chartres with hideous foot rot. Again, a fraction earlier or later and everything might have been reclaimed from the previous week of disasters.

Having only passed through the first wall of defence they were able to fight their way out, but not without losing another four Purgators. In the dark of their escape he lost Kleist and had no idea whether he was alive or dead. And yet although it had failed miserably, and was a foolish idea in the first place, their attempt to kill Santos Hall had been well planned by two people who knew what they were doing. No one could have foreseen their dreadful bad luck nor its frequency. They had thrown a coin twelve times and twelve times it had come up tails. Vague Henri had plenty of time to consider what he'd done wrong in planning and executing the attack and was very willing to learn from his mistakes.

But as far as he could see he hadn't really made any, other than doing it in the first place.

In a few days his run of misfortune deserted him and a storm helped him slip away just before the column made it to Koniz. In a week he was back in Spanish Leeds having learnt an important lesson – although he wasn't quite sure what it was. Never *do* anything, perhaps.

Within two days he was delighted and relieved by the arrival of Kleist, only for both of them to learn from Cadbury that Cale was back and being looked after in some luxury by Riba, now wife of the Hanseatic Ambassador to the Court of the King. Vague Henri was delighted by the return of Cale but put out by the news of Riba, having nursed something of a crush on her since he had shamefully spied on her washing naked in a pool in the Scablands after their escape from the Sanctuary. But both he and Kleist had more pressing problems. Cadbury had not turned up to tell them the local gossip but to summon them before Kitty the Hare, who knew very well what they'd been up to and was aggrieved at their stupidity.

'If you have prayers, prepare to say them now,' said Cadbury, ushering them to the door.

Cadbury's light-hearted attempt at alarming the two boys seemed less amusing when he delivered them to Kitty's house by the canal. Cadbury saw two men entering Kitty's rooms. He didn't recognize them, but he had spent too much time among the wicked not to recognize this quality when he saw it in someone. The way they held themselves, the way they moved and gazed at others betrayed their grudge against life. There were other explanations, of course: few people of an elevated moral stature came to do business with Kitty the Hare. Still, his nose for bad business was twitching. He sent one of Kitty's servants to fetch Deidre. He turned to the two boys and gestured them over to the table by the wall.

'Gentlemen, your material.'

He grimaced to signal that any claim not to know what he was talking about would be an insult to all three of them. They started to empty their various hidden pockets onto the table: a knife, a shiv, an awl, a hammer, another knife, a razor, a small pick, a wimble, a gouge and finally a pair of pliers.

There was a pause.

'And the rest,' said Cadbury.

Yet another knife, a bolt, a punch (large), an axe (small), a mace (surprisingly not small) and finally a needle of the kind use to repair thick sails.

'What's the matter – nobody like you?'

'No,' said Kleist.

'But we don't care,' added Vague Henri.

Cadbury knew that there must be more, even though he was surprised how much there already was. But he had covered himself and he could not bring himself to send the two boys naked into the chamber. It was not often that Cadbury felt dread, except on his own behalf, but he was feeling it now. His bad conscience called out to him, angry and mocking. *You've no right to be having a conscience now, you hypocrite, after all the evil you've had a finger in.* Kitty's door opened and his steward emerged.

'They must come in now,' he said. Cadbury nodded to the two boys who were alarmed now, Vague Henri more than Kleist. They were gestured through by the steward, who closed the door after them. Usually, thought Cadbury, he would have entered with them but not this time. The steward looked at Cadbury, obviously uneasy. What did that mean? 'My master says you can leave now.'

The steward turned and walked away, his disquiet

contained within the set of his shoulders and even the way he walked. To work for Kitty meant you had a considerable capacity for looking the other way when it came to evil-doing; but almost everyone has their standards, the line beyond which they will not go. Even in prison the murderer looks down on the common thief, the thief looks down on the rapist and all of them are disgusted by the nonce. It was all very well the steward hinting that something nasty was about to take place. But what could he do about it? Cadbury had been told to leave and so that's what he did.

Walking out into daylight felt like emerging into the sun after a year in the dark. But the dread at what was going to happen came with him too, and could be seen so plainly that on meeting Deidre Plunkett hurrying towards him, even she could see that he was in a state of intense anxiety.

'What's the matter?' she asked.

'I'm not well. We need to go home.'

'I've just come from home.'

'Then we'll go back,' he shouted, and pulled her to the other side of the street and away from Kitty the Hare's house.

Once the door closed behind them it would have made no difference if Kleist and Vague Henri had been carrying all of the weapons Cadbury had removed and twice as many like them besides. It took a few seconds to become accustomed to the gloom after the door was shut but anyway there was nothing to be done about the pair of small overstrungs pointed at them by one of the men Cadbury had been so disturbed by. The other man was holding two broom-handle-sized sticks with loops on the end of the kind used to catch wild dogs.

'Turn around.'

They did as they were told and with great deftness the

loops were dropped over their necks and shoulders and pulled tight around their midriffs, binding their arms. It was not the first time that Kitty had admired the finesse of such large men. Neither of the boys said anything or tried to escape, something that also impressed Kitty.

'We're going to sit you down on these two stools,' said one of the men. They pushed lightly on the wooden shafts holding the loops and eased the boys forward and onto the stools. Then they set the wooden shafts into two small slots in the floor. There was a loud CLICK! and the ends of the shafts were secured.

'Tug away, if you like,' mocked one of the men.

'Mr Mach,' cooed Kitty the Hare. 'You'll not behave rudely. These two boys are going to die here. Show them the respect due to that fact or be quiet.'

Vague Henri and Kleist had been used to threats all their lives and they had seen them being carried out with great, even if pious, cruelty. They knew this wasn't a threat. This thing was going to happen. Behind them the two men got on with their preparations, Mach with his nose somewhat out of joint at being corrected. It took them little effort. From their inside pockets both took out a length of strong wire, wrapped at either end around wooden handles about four inches long.

'Why?' cried out Vague Henri. The two men, more out of a sense of ritual than need, tested the robustness of the wood and the wire by pulling them apart twice. Satisfied, they moved to loop the twine around the boys' necks.

'Wait,' Kitty murmured. 'Since you've asked, you must want to make this last longer than it needs. I'll tell you. Your stupid actions against the Redeemers have upset the balance of my peace. I have gone to trouble and expense to ensure that nothing *happens* – that this war is as drawn out and delayed as it suits me and my business for it to be drawn out and delayed. You've tried to begin a war that I do not want begun. Once a war starts all sorts of unpleasant things happen which means I don't get paid. But a war that might or might not happen is utter bliss — 50,000 dollars a week in supplies. That's why the great door opens for you. I cannot say it will be painless but it will be quick if you give in to it.'

The two men stepped forward and circled the wire around their necks. 'For God's sake,' whispered Kleist.

'I know when they'll come — the Redeemers!' shouted Vague Henri. 'I know to the day.'

'Wait a little,' said Kitty.

'All right, I admit,' Vague Henri was still able to lie well under dreadful circumstances, all his years of practice at deceiving the Redeemers coming to his aid, 'not to the day, but to the week.'

A pause. Kitty seemed convinced by the admission; after all, who wouldn't exaggerate under such conditions?

'Go on.'

'Before we tried to get into the camp I watched the place for nearly twenty hours. In that time, fifty carts arrived. Each cart carries half a ton, give or take. Thirty of the carts were just food. A commissariat tent takes five tons. There were over two hundred of them. That's a thousand tons. The camp only has around two thousand men all told. That's half a ton of food for every man.'

'So the camp is a distribution point.'

'No. Nothing beyond a couple of carts went out and none of them took food. Commissariat carts are different.'

'Storage for the winter, then?'

'You don't build up stores before the summer. Most of it would rot in a tent. You don't need a mass of stores to keep a camp in the summer. At this time of year you can live off the countryside – buying and commandeering.'

'And so?'

'They must be fuelling an attack. If they were staying where they were, they wouldn't need a twentieth of such stores.'

'Two thousand men aren't going to advance on Switzerland.'

'It would only take two weeks to bring in another forty thousand – but then they have to attack. No choice. Forty-odd thousand men eat at a rate of around thirty to fifty tons a day. They can't stay in one place together in such numbers. Santos can't bring them up in less than ten to fourteen days. And he can't keep them there just eating up the stores. He'll have to move in a week, two at the most.'

'I've heard, you know, a great many plausible lies.'

'They're not lies.'

'How do you know so much about bacon and flour?'

'I'm not like Cale or Kleist. They were trained for the militant; I'm commissariat. Nobody fights without supplies – wood and water and meat and flour.'

Kitty considered, a hideous pondering for the boys.

'I'll send for someone who has competence in all this. If he finds out this is all buncombe – which I suspect . . . I suspect it is – you'll wish you'd kept your mouth shut because by now you'd be dead and your suffering would be over.'

Ten minutes later, both of them shaking with terror, Vague Henri and Kleist were locked in a surprisingly comfortable room in the basement of the house.

'Good lies,' said Kleist, after a while. '*Damned* good lies.'

PART THREE

The superpowers often behave like two heavily armed blind men feeling their way around a room, each believing himself in mortal peril from the other, whom he assumes to have perfect vision. Each side should know that frequently uncertainty, compromise, and incoherence are the essence of policymaking. Yet each tends to ascribe to the other a consistency, foresight, and coherence that its own experience belies. Of course, over time, even two armed blind men can do enormous damage to each other, not to speak of the room.

Henry Kissinger, *The White House Years* (1979)

15

'So,' said IdrisPukke, 'you're back.'

'I am.'

'And what did you learn while you were away?'

'That I must avoid pain and get as much happiness as I can.'

IdrisPukke gasped with derision. 'Ridiculous.'

'So you say.'

'I do indeed. Consider a healthy young person, every muscle and sinew strong and supple. Except for one thing – he has a toothache. Does he rejoice in his strength and take pleasure in the overwhelming multiform wonderfulness of his young body, even if only a tiny fraction of it is hurting? No, he does not. He thinks only of the dreadful pain in his tooth.'

'All he needs to do is get his tooth pulled and then he'll think he's in heaven.'

'You have fallen, rather too easily if I may say so, into my trap. Exactly. He feels absolutely the intense pleasure of the absence of suffering not the pleasure that all the other bits and pieces of his body give him.'

'I'm sick to the back teeth of being miserable. I've had more than my portion. Look at me. You can't say otherwise.'

'Yes, I can. In this paradise that you've decided to believe in as your ultimate goal everything comes to you without much trouble and the turkeys fly around ready-roasted – but what would become of people even much less troublesome than you in such a happy place? Even the most pleasant-natured person would die of boredom or hang themselves or get into a fight and kill or be killed by someone who is even more driven to madness by the lack of struggle. Struggle has made us what we are and has suited us to the nature of things so that no other existence is possible. You might as well take a fish out of the sea and encourage it to fly.'

'As usual you try to make out I'm saying something stupid so you can win the argument. I don't expect a rose garden. God knows, just better than this – a bit less pain and a bit more beer and skittles.'

'I understand you've had some hard rain in your life. All I can say is that you're mistaken in thinking that more pleasure is the answer. The truth is, no matter what people think, pleasure has little hold over us. And if you disagree, consider the pleasure and pain of two animals, one being eaten by the other. The one doing the eating feels pleasure but that pleasure is soon forgotten as hunger, as it always does, returns. Consider in contrast the feelings of suffering of the animal being eaten – they are experiencing something of quite another order. Pain is not the opposite of pleasure – it is something altogether different.'

'Have you been saving that up for my return?'

'If you mean to ask me whether I just *happened* to have such thoughts as you just *happened* to say something more than usually stupid, of course not. I have thought very carefully about everything I have to say. Only inferior minds speak or write in order to discover what they think.'

Their pleasant argument was interrupted by the noisy arrival of Cadbury, quarrelling with the guard outside and demanding to see Cale. Once inside he was to the point.

'Do you think they're still alive?'

'Possibly. Probably not.'

'Why's he doing this?' said IdrisPukke.

'Kitty doesn't take to people acting against his interests,

especially if he's been paying them. He has a lot to lose if this war starts now. "Don't touch me" is his motto and he'll do what's needed to make it stick.'

'It's not two weeks since he went to so much trouble to save my life – now this.'

'Your value has fallen,' replied Cadbury. 'He was not impressed by the account given of your fight with the late Trevors.'

'Your account, you mean,' said IdrisPukke.

'Kitty the Hare pays my wages. I don't owe Thomas Cale anything.'

'So why are you here?' asked Cale.

'A question I've yet to answer to my own satisfaction. It can't be redemption. Who could make amends in the eyes of God by saving you?'

But Cale wasn't listening.

'If I need something to raise my price,' he said at last, 'what does Kitty want?'

'Not money. He's got money. Power – give him the power to protect what he already has.'

'Meaning?' said IdrisPukke.

'What do you know that *he* doesn't? Sorry – time I wasn't here. Kitty's going to want my head on a stick when he finds out what I've done.'

He was at the door and almost gone.

'How do I get in?' asked Cale.

Cadbury looked at him.

'You don't. You so much as knock on his front door too loudly and they'll tab you in two shakes of a lamb's tail.'

'How many guards?'

'Fifteen, give or take. But all the doors are iron plate – the wood on either side is just veneer. Every door would take a dozen men an hour to get through. But you won't have an hour. He's taken against those boys and he won't give them up without a bung – and a bloody big one too.'

'Thanks,' said Cale. 'I owe you.'

'You already owe me and look where that's got me.'

When Cadbury had gone, Cale sat down and looked at IdrisPukke for some time.

'It wouldn't matter,' said IdrisPukke at last, 'even if I did know something big enough, I couldn't tell you if my life depended on it.'

'I thought you cared for Henri.'

'I care for Kleist as well, even if you don't. I know what affection is. There are, I admit it, things I know. But I can't put them in the hands of someone like Kitty, not if they were my own sons.'

'That's easy enough to say.'

'I suppose it is. I can't help you. I'm sorry.'

Within fifteen minutes Cale was in his new lodgings in the Embassy of the Hanse and putting the crush on Riba's husband.

'I don't have time to be ladylike about this: I saved your wife at the pretty certain cost of my own life. Now it's time to settle up.'

'Have you discussed this with Riba?'

'No, but I will, if you like.'

'I'm not just Riba's husband. The lives of many thousands – more – depend on me.'

'I don't care.'

'I'll come with you and we'll try to get your friends out together. My life is not the issue here.'

Cale almost said something deeply offensive. 'It wouldn't matter if I had two hundred like you. I know force. Force isn't going to do it. He wants what you know.'

'I can't.' It was as agonized a refusal as Cale had ever heard. This was good.

'You don't have to.'

'I'm sorry?'

'You don't have to tell him what you really know, you just have to tell him what you might know.'

'I'm being obtuse, I realize. Could you plod a little more?' Cale closed his eyes, his irritation plain.

'You must have thought about all the different stuff you could do in the face of the threat from the Redeemers, right?'

'Explored alternative responses?'

'Yes. That. I don't want to know what you've decided. Don't tell me. I don't care. I just want one of the choices you didn't make, whatever it is, and all the detail written down.'

A long pause.

'I can't write anything down. If it got out the Hanse could be ruined.'

It was not easy for Cale to avoid picking up the handsome ornament on the table next to him and throwing it at the wall. His head hurt and he thought he was probably going to die in the next few hours.

'Listen to me,' he said, 'Kitty the Hare could eat you up and spit you out and a dozen more like you. He's not going to accept my word for anything. He knows I'm a lying little shit, all right?'

'Putting a lie in writing is as bad as telling the truth. It *will* get out – and if it's written down people will believe it. I can't.'

Now Cale's head was throbbing as if it were expanding and contracting by a couple of inches with each breath.

'What if I promise I'll see it's destroyed?'

'How can you be certain?'

'I'm giving you the word of someone who prevented your

wife from being paunched while she was still alive – you ungrateful fuck.' He looked at Wittenberg and decided he had nothing to lose. 'And I'd have to tell Riba that you refused to help the three people who saved her life – even when one of them promised to keep you out of it.'

'A particularly ugly threat, if I may say so – but I suppose you're desperate.'

'I'm an ugly sort of person.'

'At any rate you are a very violent one.'

'Luckily for your wife.'

'But you're very sick. Your skill in moving armies isn't of much use if you've left those armies behind. Ugly or violent, you're now ordinary. I can't help you in this, no matter what my personal obligations are. Leave my house by midday tomorrow, if you wouldn't mind.'

'Actually I do mind.'

'Leave it anyway.'

Cale went to his room, took out one of the small packets of Phedra and Morphine, tapped the tiny amount of white powder onto the back of his hand, put one finger to his left nostril, bent down and took a huge snort. He called out in pain; it was as if a packet of pins and needles had exploded in his head. The sensation took a minute to fade and once he had wiped the tears from his eyes he began to feel better. Then very much better. Then better than he had ever felt: sharp, clear and strong. On his way out he passed Riba. 'You've been talking to Arthur,' she said.

'Yes.'

'And?'

'He's not as dumb as he looks.'

As he walked to Kitty's house it was through a city and a world filled with confusion. It was either the eve of destruction or the crisis had passed. Some people were leaving, some people had decided to stay. Prices had been rising on fears of a war, but now they were falling on rumours of peace. Men of experience were selling off gold, men of experience were buying it back. Things might go this way or things might go that. The first casualty, the day after the declaration of war, is the memory of the confusion that preceded it. Nothing fades from the powers of recall like the recollection of uncertainty.

On his way from the Embassy of the Hanse, Cale stopped briefly at a depot used by the outdraggers – tinkers who hired out their handcarts for deliveries of just about anything, though mostly the meat and vegetables from the market across the square. He gave one of them, angry-looking but beefy, five dollars and the promise of another five if he'd head for the street where Kitty lived and watch for two or three people coming out who might need to be carried away. He'd need to be quick, no hanging about.

'Sounds like there could be trouble,' said the man. 'Ten dollars and then another ten.'

'What's your name?'

The tinker was careful about the business of giving names, but there was serious money involved. 'Michael Nevin.'

'Do the job and there'll be more.'

'More money or more jobs?'

'Both.'

Knocking softly on Kitty's door, Cale was admitted, searched, relieved of his collection of devices and then taken in to see Kitty. He was seated behind a large desk, his face indistinct in the semi-darkness. Sitting against the shutters at the back of the room were the two men who had come so close to killing Kleist and Vague Henri a couple of hours earlier.

'You've disimproved since we last met, Mr Cale. Sit down.'

Cale's fear at having two such obvious evil-doers behind him was not in any way eased by the oddness of the fit of the chair. It was slightly too low, the arms slightly too high, the seat awkwardly sloped. And it was fastened to the floor.

'I have to talk to you alone,' said Cale.

'No, you don't.'

'Are they still alive?'

'I wouldn't worry about them, sick little boy.'

'I have to know if they're dead or alive.'

'They are in a waiting room. The question is whether or not you are going to wait with them.'

'Me? How have I offended?'

'You, sir, have not delivered on your undertakings for which you have been paid and cared for.'

'I've been a bad servant, I admit. I've come to put that right.'

'Well?'

'I've two things to tell you. The first is to repay what I owe you. The second is a swap for my friends.'

'And why shouldn't I make you give me this second thing without the cost of looking weak?'

'Because I have to prove it as well as tell you. And the proof isn't here.'

'We'll see. Go on.'

'They leave.'

'We'll see after you pay me what you owe.'

Cale tried to give the impression that he was considering this.

'All right. You've a map of the four quarters?'

'Yes.'

'I need to show you.'

It took a few minutes for the two men to unroll the map and hang it from hooks high up on one of the walls. It was obvious to Cale that Kitty would have commissioned a survey of some kind but he was surprised at its size and detail, better than anything even the Redeemers had made and they were skilled cartographers.

'You're impressed,' said Kitty.

'Yes.'

One of the men handed him a pointer with little more substance to it than a stalk of wheat – no chance of using it as a weapon. Cale looked at Kitty, hooded and in the shadows, still as a stump. If there had been anyone to tell him fairy stories as a boy, Kitty would have been a sight to bring back the true fear of the child's nightmare. Cale had no choice, so he got on with it.

'This is what I think, based on what I know,' Cale said. 'Some of it's guesswork. But it's there or thereabouts.'

There was a high-pitched wheezing sound from Kitty, laughter perhaps, and the smell of something hot and damp momentarily carried in the still air.

'Your scruples are noted.'

'The Swiss mountains make an attack almost impossible from anywhere except the north. As far as the Swiss are concerned, the other countries in the Swiss Alliance exist to act as a series of three buffers against any attack from there. Farthest north is Gaul, protected by the Maginot Line and the Arnhemland desert. The Axis think the strength of the defences in the Maginot Line will protect them and that Arnhemland is too wide and waterless for an army of any real size to cross. They're wrong. Bosco has been delaying so he can dig a network of wells and water stores across the desert.'

'And you know this because . . . ?'

'Because I thought of it. The Gauls think that even if an army does come through the desert and hit their weaker defences, an army that's spent six days in Arnhemland isn't going to be in much of a shape to fight – even weak defences should be more than enough to stop them until they can bring in reinforcements.'

'And they're wrong because . . . ?'

'The Redeemers won't take six days, they'll take one day and two nights.'

'Are they going to run all the way?'

'They'll come on horseback.'

'I seem to remember you saying in one of your less than informative reports that the Redeemers had no cavalry to speak of and would take years to develop one.'

'They're not cavalry – just mounted infantry. It takes six weeks to learn to ride a horse, if that's all you're going to do.'

'And if the Gaul cavalry catches them?'

'Then they'll get off and deal with them the way they dealt with the Materazzi at Silbury Hill. And they'll be in a great deal better shape than the Redeemers were there. Half of them were fighting with paper shoved up their squeakers to stop them from crapping on their feet.'

'Spare me the details.'

'More battles are lost because of the squits than because of bad generals.'

'What then?'

'Speed – at first. They'll take Gaul in six weeks.'

'Optimistic, wouldn't you say?'

'No, I wouldn't. If I say it can be done, then it can be done. The defence against the Redeemers is based on how quickly they moved in the past – how quickly all armies moved in the past. Everyone fights the war they're used to.'

'So the Redeemers will roll over Gaul, then Palestine, then Albion and Yugoslavia and all the rest until they're at the gates of Zurich.'

'It won't be that easy.'

'You surprise me.'

'Always.'

Again the high-pitched, wheezing laugh. 'What a conceited young man you are.'

'I'm not conceited. I'm just honest about being so much better than other people.'

Kitty was silent for a moment. Another waft of the hot damp smell.

'Well then,' said Kitty. 'Allowance must be made for your boastfulness, being a person so much above others. Go on.'

Cale turned back to the map and pointed to the river that cut Gaul in half on its way to the sea.

'All the Redeemers need to do is make it quickly to the Mississippi. Then they'll have a defensive line they can hold or retreat to if things go wrong, and for as long as they like.'

'And from the Mississippi onwards . . . ?'

'War the usual way, probably – slow and nasty. But the Redeemers are good at that.'

'And where are the Laconics in all of this?'

'Paid to stay out of it if Bosco does what I said.'

'And what if he doesn't do what you said? Or the Laconics think once the Redeemers have taken the Swiss they'll come for them next?'

'Once they've taken the Swiss that's exactly what Bosco will do.'

'So why should they go along just because it's convenient for your plan that they do so?'

'Because that's what they want to believe. This way they get money and a guarantee.'

'Worthless.'

'But they don't know that. It doesn't make sense to attack them after all. There's no great strategic use for Laconia and there's bugger all there. The cost of taking it doesn't bear thinking about – even for the Redeemers.'

'But Bosco will try.'

'Yes.'

'Why?'

'I don't know. He just asked me to make it possible. Something to do with God, I imagine.'

'So you don't know everything.'

'I know everything I know about.'

Cale needed to be honest with Kitty for the reason that his life and Vague Henri's and Kleist's depended on him being convincing. Nothing convinces like the truth. But Bosco's plan to create a final solution to the problem of evil would have seemed impossible even to someone as vile as Kitty the Hare. Such a thing was outside the kingdom of even his appalling imagination because it had no purpose – there was no money or power to be had from such a vision.

'What about the purpose of the Redeemer camp at Moza your friends so foolishly chose to attack?'

This was tricky. They must have told Kitty something useful or they'd be dead. But then maybe he hadn't intended to kill but just to scare them. If Cale told Kitty something that conflicted with what they'd told him he'd know they'd been lying. And then there were other possibilities to the left, and the right, and to the left again, always intelligent guesses to be made and got completely wrong. Gambling that Vague Henri would have decided to tell something close to the truth, Cale committed himself.

'The Redeemers will attack from the north through Arnhemland but they'll want to squeeze from opposite ends and the only way to attack the Swiss from the south is up through the Mittelland, then through the Schallenberg Pass to Spanish Leeds.'

'How many?'

'Forty thousand, give or take. I'm not saying he won't just stay where he is and seal the Swiss in and wait for the attack from the north to work its way down. But if he can draw the Swiss into an attack in the Mittelland it might be worth it. And if they don't come out to fight he can seal off the Schallenberg then wait them out there.'

'Why?'

'Five thousand men in front of the Schallenberg could hold the Swiss in for ever. That's nearly thirty-five thousand less than staying where he is.'

'Why not go through and take the city?'

'Because five thousand men can hold it from the other end just as well. But then it's just a question of how long it takes the Redeemers to make it down from the north. See – everything depends on them getting across Arnhemland in a day and two nights. After that it's just a matter of time.'

'And have you told anyone else about this?'

'Who I tell and what I tell them is my business.'

'You're very insolent for someone who's come looking for charity.'

'No, I haven't told anyone.'

'Why?'

'What I know is all I've got. Besides, my reputation isn't what it used to be. Who's going to believe a sickly boy who used to be good at throwing his weight around?'

'What about your Materazzi patrons?'

'Everybody and his mother want them to drop dead, if at all possible.'

'And yet Conn Materazzi is much slobbered over by the King.'

'Conn won't stomach me at any price.'

'So I've heard. Is it true?'

'Sorry, I don't understand.'

'That you're the father of the little boy?'

'She sold me to the Redeemers.'

'Not really an answer. But it doesn't matter.'

'What about my friends?'

'You'll have to do better.'

'I can.'

'Then do.'

'Not with them here.'

'Your reputation may have declined but I know you to be a person of violent talents who is not always wise in your use of them.'

'I'm not the person I used to be.'

'So you say.'

'Cadbury told you what happened at the Priory – I couldn't lift even a finger to save myself. Look at me.'

For some time Cale sat as Kitty considered his white skin and the black circles and the stoop of his shoulders and the weight loss.

'I could get these gentlemen to chastise it out of you.'

'You're going to need more than what I tell you. You're going to need proof. And I haven't brought that with me. Let them go.'

'I don't think so.'

'You'll still have me. Nobody knows who the two boys are. Killing them won't send much of a message. But my death would send a signal. Not right?'

'You're offering to sacrifice yourself for your friends? I'd thought better of you.'

'I intend to walk out of here. I'm just pointing out that you can afford to let them go if you've got me.'

Kitty considered but not for long.

'Go and get them – both of you.'

They did as they were told, closing the heavy door quietly behind them.

'You know where I'm living now.'

It was a statement. In reply, a long cooing hoot – Kitty was laughing.

'Why would I care where you lay your hat?'

Cale stayed silent.

'Yes, I know where you live.'

'I've found out what the Hanse are going to do. Interested?'

'Oh, yes,' said Kitty, casual. 'You've proof?'

'Yes.'

'Show it me.' The unpleasant laugh again. There was a knock at the door.

'Come in.'

It opened. The two men who had left, and several others, entered holding Vague Henri and Kleist, their hands tied. But the restraint was more for form than otherwise. They were in a terrible state, Kleist in particular unrecognizable, his face bloody, both eyes bagged with pockets of blood, though one had split like a small gaping mouth and was pouring a delta of red down his right cheek. Vague Henri looked as if someone had wiped his face with some toxic plant – bloated and inflamed. His tongue slipped out of his mouth as if he were an old man gone in the head. Their left hands had been crushed and both of the boys shook uncontrollably.

Cale did not react at all. 'Put them outside. Someone will collect them and when they're safe they'll bring proof of what I'm saying to you.'

'Play the fraud with me and you'll find that death has ten thousand doors and I'm there to show you through every one.'

'Can we get on? I have a dinner to go to.'

A slight nod of the head and the two boys were pushed, stumbling, to the door.

'Make them tell me what they see in the street.'

Two minutes later and one of Kitty's guards returned. 'Some outdragger with a handcart has come to collect them.'

'While we wait for the letter I'll tell you what's to come. Once they shut the door.' A moment, then Cale continued. 'The Hanseatic League are going to declare their support for the Axis and promise to send ships and troops and money. The money will come but not the ships or the troops. They'll make a show of assembling ships in Danzig and Lubeck but even if they put to sea they'll be driven back by storms or plague or woodworm or an attack of barnacles for all I know. But they won't come – at least not until they're reasonably sure who's going to win.'

'And Wittenberg told you this over tea and cucumber sandwiches? I'd heard that he was a man of intelligence and discretion. Why would he say these things to someone like you?'

'I used to like cucumber sandwiches – when I could get them.'

'Answer me.'

'I saved Wittenberg's wife from some Redeemer nasty business. I own his happiness, if you like. But he didn't tell me directly and I wouldn't have believed him if he had.'

'So she told you? That's what you're saying?'

'No. I tried and I even twisted her arm, so to speak. But she's a clever girl, Riba, and wasn't having any of it. I stole his key and took the letter from his room.'

'Sounds unlikely.'

'It does, yes, but it's true all the same. Wittenberg's a clever man, subtle, like you say, in talks and discussions and that,

168

but he's above stealing in a personal way. I mean someone like him could let thousands die but couldn't kill a man standing in front of them. It never crossed his mind I'd betray his wife's generosity or his. I suppose he hasn't had my disadvantages.'

'What else do you know?'

'What I told you. It's a letter not a confession. You have to read a bit between the lines but not much. See for yourself when it comes.'

Even though Cale was lying he had more or less accurately set out the position of the Hanse, not so very surprising in that there were only a limited number of options available to them, given that they were a trading federation who used military power to protect their financial interests only when it was unavoidable. But it was about more than just money because they had already provided a great deal to the Axis and would provide more. Partly it was the open-ended financial risk of war: there was a limit to giving money, even if it was a great deal of money, but there was no limit to the treasure that a war could swallow up. And they were also mindful of the view that war was the father of everything – it produced changes even for the victorious that could have untold consequences. Far better to stay on the sidelines, making vague promises you had no intention of honouring, handing over cash and staying out of it as long as possible.

Sadly for Cale, this happy guesswork was of no practical value beyond being plausible – Kitty expected proof and there wasn't any. And he expected it in the next few minutes.

16

Since he had come into Kitty's room, hammers had been working in Cale's brain to come up with an escape plan and decide what to do about Kitty the Hare. He had never seen Kitty do anything more than stand or sit. What was he? He had seen the peculiar paw-like right hand and since he had taken to wearing the peaked cap and the dirty looking brown linen veil there was only the cooingly precise voice to go by. What if he had teeth to tear you with, claws as sharp as razors to cut, arms so brutal they could rip your bone casings apart like Grendel, or worse, like Grendel's mum? He was unknown until the moment he was attacked. Then there was the door and the men outside who could open it whenever they wanted to. Then there was getting away. Too many unknowns for someone who, even at sixteen (if that was Cale's age), was no longer the man he used to be. His position was so evil that, even as he was pouring camel manure into Kitty's ear and looking around the room for a means of blocking the door and finding something that might help in the infliction of the violence that was certainly coming, he was also cursing himself for failing to observe one of IdrisPukke's mostly highly polished aphorisms: always resist your first impulses, they are often generous. After all, those two cretins had gone off on their demented frolic entirely of their own free will. Why should he die for their stupidity? But it was too late for that now.

It began. Cale ran to the large bookcase that stretched from floor to ceiling, packed with Kitty's accounts. He jumped as high as he could and started heaving on it like a deranged monkey. Luckily it was freestanding and toppled easily and so quickly that he almost fell under it as it crashed to the floor in front of the door and blocked it from opening.

Kitty's bodyguards started pushing against it with all their strength. Kitty stood up from behind his enormous desk and moved a few steps backward. Was he waiting in terror for his guards to break in or was he calmly preparing himself to tear Thomas Cale into small, meaty pieces? Cale had been beaten by Bosco into believing one thing above all others – once you decide to attack, commit without let or hindrance. Cale took four steps towards Kitty and jabbed the heel of his hand into his face. The scream Kitty let out as he fell shook even Cale. It wasn't the scream of a man mutilated on the battlefield or a cornered animal, but more like a furious and frightened baby – high-pitched and harrowing. A spot of blood appeared on the linen mask as Kitty wailed and thrashed to get a grip on the polished floor, all the while the red stain spreading. Behind him, the bodyguards were charging the door so heavily that the great frame shook with each blow. Cale turned to the desk and heaved. It was so heavy it might have been screwed to the floor. But fear pumped him up enough to shift the desk an inch, then two, then again with greater and greater speed as his frantic roar of effort mixed with the heaving crashes of the door, until he hit the now shifting bookcase with the desk just as the bodyguards had stepped back for a final push. The collision of desk and bookcase slammed the door shut, taking the fingertips of two men's hands with it.

His brain was buzzing with the screams inside the room, the cries of agony outside, and his lips throbbed with pins and needles as the power of the Phedra and Morphine began to lag. He stared at Kitty, still shrieking in the corner of the room. Outside the guards had gone silent, planning something.

It is a business full of difficulty, killing a living thing. Even with the means – the blunt object, the useful blade, the stillness induced by dread. Anything more awkward than the wringing of a chicken's neck takes nerve and practice and familiarity. Cale considered the task ahead. Already his legs and his hands were shaking. Nothing in the room would help, it was more or less empty but for the bound red ledgers on the floor. And what was he dealing with? Kitty the Hare was frightened, to be sure, but that didn't mean he wasn't dangerous. Cale felt his artificial powder strength begin to drain away. Could he beat Kitty to death with his fists? And what was behind the veil?

The shoving on the other side of the door began again. He stepped forward and, bending down, grabbed Kitty and shifted him over. He fumbled for his neck and tried to hold it in the crook of his elbow. Kitty realized what he was going to do and began howling and screaming again, so high-pitched it hurt the ears, his feet scrabbling on the polished floor. Terror made him strong and he wrenched free and backed away, still screaming, to the far wall. Again the room-shaking battering from the guards crashing against the door. It was impossible to go on without seeing his face – Cale needed to see who or what was so vulnerable to being hurt. He tore off the peaked cap and bloody linen veil.

Disgust made him pull back, shocked at the ugliness of what he saw. The face and skull seemed to belong to two different creatures, one more deformed than the other. The right side of his head was distended along its entire length, as if the skin had been filled with stones. His right cheek was a mat of warty growths, his lips on one side swollen by three or four inches. But halfway along his mouth the lips narrowed and became quite normal, and with a recognizably human expression. On the left side of his head, above his ear, Kitty had grown the strands of hair more than twelve inches long and combed them over in an effort to hide a huge tumour. His left hand, too, was perfectly ordinary and rather delicate, his right was paw-like but huge, as if it had been cut and healed into three parts, each with the large and pointed nails from which Kitty got his name.

'Pease! Pease!' said Kitty. 'Pease! Pease!'

But it was his eyes that got to Cale, deep brown and delicate as a girl's, shining with fear and dread. Imagine what it is to beat a living thing to death with weakening hands and aching shoulders. The time it took, the crying out, the blood in Kitty's throat choking him, the feet scrabbling on the floor. But the blows with his fist and elbow had to carry on no matter what. It must be done.

When it was over, Cale sat back on the floor. He did not feel horror and he did not feel pity. Kitty the Hare didn't deserve to live; Kitty the Hare deserved to die. But then he, Thomas Cale, probably deserved to die as well for all the horrible things he'd done. But he wasn't dead and Kitty was. For the moment at any rate.

During the killing of Kitty, the guards had been battering against the door. Now they'd stopped. Cale was soaked in sweat, now cooling, and not just from the effort of putting an end to Kitty. His lips were firing pins and needles ever faster, his head throbbing. 'It's midnight, Goldilocks,' he said aloud, misremembering the story he'd heard Arbell telling her little nieces in Memphis.

He stood up and began opening the drawers in the great ebony desk. Nothing but papers, except for a brass paperweight and a bag of boiled sweets – humbugs. He ate a couple, splintering them in order to get the sugar into his body, then stepped next to the door and banged it three times with the paperweight. He thought he heard whispering.

'Kitty the Hare. He's dead,' said Cale.

A silence, then, 'Then you're going to sing him to his rest, shit-bag.'

'Why?'

'Why the fuck do you think?'

'Did you love Kitty? Was Kitty a father to you?'

'Never you mind about what Kitty was. Prepare to not be.'

'You want to kill the only friend you have in the world? Kitty's dead and that means all his enemies, many and unkind, are going to disjoint his goods and services among them. Not including you – your share of the profits is going to be a six-foot by two-foot space in one of Kitty's illegal rubbish tips in Oxyrinchus.'

Cale was sure he could hear muttering and arguing. This ought to be the easiest part. What he was telling them was true and it was obvious. The trouble was that riffraff had their loyalties and affections like everyone else. And they also were puffed up with the drama and action of the last fifteen minutes. There was going to be violent change one way or the other and Thomas Cale had caused it. If people could be trusted to act in their own best interests it would be a different world. He needed to let tempers cool.

'Go and get Cadbury. Bring him here and then we'll talk.'

Silence for a few moments.

'Cadbury's buggered off to Zurich.'

'Anyway,' shouted the man who'd taken the lead, 'fuck Cadbury. You talk to us. Let us in.'

The request for Cadbury had backfired. What could he do, after all? He'd expected they'd have taken time to go and find him only to discover he was gone. Now all he'd done was annoyed whoever had taken control. He considered bluster. Dangerous. He chose bluster.

'I'm Thomas Cale, I've just beaten Kitty the Hare to death with my bare hands. I killed Solomon Solomon in the Red Opera in two seconds and there are ten thousand Laconics rotting in the shadow of the Golan Heights, and I was the one who left them there.' Though he felt dreadful and his situation was dire, declaring his glorious achievements aloud was exhilarating. *It all was true, wasn't it?* he thought.

There was no reply.

'Look. I've got nothing against any of you. You were doing what you were paid for. Kitty got his portion and that's the way it is. You can either work for me, with all the money and whatever privileges Kitty gave you, and a bonus of two hundred dollars and no questions asked, or you can take your chances with General Butt-Naked and Lord Peanut Butter – I'm told that General Butt-Naked keeps his troops lively by stringing the intestines of those who disappoint him across the streets of the slums he controls.'

These lurid stories of Kitty's rivals were, in fact, true. Even in Switzerland, a civilized place of trade with admirably clean streets where all was ordered, its people prosperous and law-abiding, there were parts of it that were the very bowels of darkness. A stone's throw from generous streets and the generous souls who lived in them a savagery and a cruelty of a kind that was impossible to imagine except for the fact that it happened took place at all hours and within a short walk. Isn't it the same with all cities everywhere, and in all times? The civilized and the inhumanly cruel are separated only by a short stroll.

After a few minutes' more talking, Cale filibustering to draw out the time and let them calm down and see things as they were, he pushed back the desk just enough to give them purchase – no easy matter, his strength was fading in jabs and bursts. He went and sat down, casual, in Kitty's chair and waited for his bodyguards to push back the heavy bookcase.

So they filed in, obviously wary but also subdued by the body in the middle of the floor. It was not death or blood that worried them – that was their calling, after all – but the sight of unstoppable power suddenly stopped. Kitty was myth – his reach ran everywhere. Now even in the gloom it wasn't just that death had robbed him of power but that he was revealed as deformed, eaten and swollen by growths, distended and spoilt. What they had feared now revolted them and all the more intensely because of the intensity of that fear. Now their terror demeaned them.

'I saw a sea-cow,' said one, 'dead in the water for a week who looked like that.' He prodded him with his feet.

'Leave him alone,' said Cale.

'You killed him,' protested the man.

'Leave him alone.'

'Who are you to give us orders?'

That, thought Cale, *is a good question.*

'Because I'm the one who knows what to do next.'

Some of the men in the room were stupid, others intelligent and ambitious, but Cale's assertion threw them badly. It was not that Cale had the answer, because really he had no idea what to do next. His advantage over them lay in realizing that what to do next was the only thing that mattered.

'How many of you can write?'

Three of the fifteen men slowly put up their hands.

'Have any of you worked for General Butt-Naked?'

Two hands went up.

'Peanut Butter?'

Three hands.

'I want the three of you that can write to set down everything you know on paper. If the rest of you have anything to add then say so.' He stood up. 'I'll be back in three hours. Lock the door behind me and don't let anyone in or out. If the news of Kitty's death gets around, you know what that means.' Then he walked out, full of purpose and clarity. At any moment he expected to be stopped, to be asked the obvious two questions that he couldn't answer. But no one said anything. He was out of the door and down the stairs to the most welcoming sound he had ever heard: the lock turning behind him.

Feeling sicker with every step, Cale had gone to IdrisPukke on his way to find Vague Henri and Kleist. The relief on IdrisPukke's face was evident even to Cale, wretched and angry with him as he was; it was the look of a man who'd come to feel he'd done something dreadful but which had turned out all right in the end. Cale told him what had happened and asked him to come with him to see the boys and send someone for a doctor.

It was not easy to astonish IdrisPukke and for the first few minutes of the walk he was silent, then just as they were about to enter the digs, IdrisPukke took Cale's arm and stopped him.

'What was it like?'

'It was a bad do. I can't say it wasn't. I don't feel sorry for Kitty – he got what he deserved – but when I was walking to you after I got out I understood something about why he wanted to make the world afraid of him. What were his choices? Make his living in a freak show with the geek who eats frogs or the boneless wonder? Depend on the kindness of others? Don't get me wrong, though – I wasn't thinking that when I bashed his brains out.'

'I feel I've let you down,' said IdrisPukke. Cale said nothing at first, thinking about what he said. This had all been Vague Henri's and Kleist's fault. IdrisPukke had been pretty good to them all, ever since he'd met them, for no very good reason. Cale had asked him to cheat on his brother. But something had been pecking in his soul – even though he couldn't see why, he agreed that IdrisPukke had in some way been disloyal to him.

'No. No, you didn't,' he said. And they moved on.

Just from the brief glimpse he'd had of them in the house he knew the boys were in bad nick. Now he was able to look them over properly they looked even worse. Kleist was unable to speak his mouth was so swollen. The little fingers on both their left hands had been broken along with the thumbs. Cale told them Kitty was dead.

'Was it slow?' said Vague Henri.

'As slow as you like.'

When the doctor arrived he cleaned them up carefully; it was painful stuff. Except for their faces and hands most of the damage was bruising. Kleist kept spitting blood and the doctor quietly worried to them that there might be a haemorrhage inside. 'If he starts shitting blood, call me at once.' Still not altogether down from the Phedra and Morphine, Cale could not help but admire that the stitching of Vague Henri's face from the wound of the year before had held up nicely. But Kleist didn't seem all there and kept drifting in and out.

'Kitty,' he mumbled.

'Kitty's dead.'

'Kitty,' he mumbled again, and kept on till he passed out completely.

The doctor put Vague Henri to sleep with a mixture of Valerian and Poppy Oil and Cale and IdrisPukke watched over them.

'What will you do with them, Kitty's people, now?'

Cale seemed surprised.

'Nothing. Let them rot.'

'There's too much money and power at stake just to let it go.'

'You have it then.'

'I was hoping you'd say that.'

'You don't need my say-so.'

IdrisPukke detected the sourness. He did not blame him – he was ashamed of his refusal to help in the rescue of Vague Henri and Kleist but this was too important an opportunity to pass up. An empire of sorts was going begging.

'I thought I'd send for Cadbury,' IdrisPukke said. 'He'll know the SP on everything Kitty was up to.'

'I think you'll make a lovely couple,' said Cale. And with that he went to sleep.

It did indeed turn out to be a great match, if not one made in heaven. Criminal scum are often sentimental about their mothers but, in general, this is the furthest extent of their loyalty. Outsiders almost by definition, they aren't usually moved by the idea of innate rank, social order or hierarchy, except when it's imposed by the continuous threat of violence. Where there are beggars there can never be a king resting easy with his crown.

IdrisPukke surrounded Kitty's house to prevent the occupants from leaving. He didn't want a fuss and told them he was waiting for Cadbury to arrive to sort everything out. He also promised to raise their bonus to five hundred dollars. The following morning Cadbury arrived, having been halted during his flight to Oxyrinchus, still amazed by the news of Kitty's death. Though there was no general affection for Cadbury among those inside the house, he was at least familiar to them and had a reputation for being smart. By now they needed a saviour and the changeover from Kitty the Hare to IdrisPukke and Cadbury was so quick that in barely a week Kitty was already passing into the myth in which he most naturally belonged. From now on, stories would be told about him by mothers sweetly threatening their children to be good or Kitty the Hare would come for them. Then these same children in their later years would scare their younger siblings with blood-curdling accounts of the deformed Kitty wielding a chain and a saw over hapless maids doomed to being dismembered and eaten; and then, as the years passed, his reputation reached the Celts in the east, where they transformed him into a friendly old hare selling pegs and telling ghost stories for a penny a go.

17

As the swellings went down and the bruises came out in purples and browns, Vague Henri became almost ecstatically cheerful. Kleist not so – he seemed to have been struck hard by the events in Kitty's house. He slept a lot and wouldn't talk much when he was awake. They thought it best to leave him alone, that he'd come out of it in his own time. Once Vague Henri was up to walking he and Cale went for a stroll along the Promenade des Bastions and watched the girls in their spring dresses forgetting the dreadful rumours of war that were in the air, and the two boys forgot along with them. They bought chocolate cake bursting with cream and Cale tormented Vague Henri by breaking off pieces and almost feeding him but then putting the cake in his own mouth.

On the bandstand a dozen musicians played 'I've Got a Luverly Bunch of Coconuts', that spring's most popular song. A group of girls of about the same age as the boys scolded Cale and took the cake away and began feeding the boy with the bandaged hands as if he was a baby. And he loved it.

'What happened to your poor hands?' said one of them, a wayward-looking redhead.

'He fell off his horse,' said Cale. 'Drunk.'

'Don't listen to him,' said Vague Henri. 'I did it saving a small puppy from drowning.'

More giggles at this – a lovely sound, like running water.

For ten minutes he flirted with the girls, nibbling their fingers as they fed him so they told him off for biting, though not the girl with red hair who let him suck the thick white cream off her middle finger for much too long while her friends chattered like starlings and gasped delightedly at her shocking behaviour. Cale sat in the sun at the other end of the bench, looked at by two of the girls who wouldn't have minded feeding him something more than cake if they'd only had the encouragement. Cale lapped it all up: the warm sun, the pretty girls and his friend's pleasure. But it was as if it were a scene only to be observed, not in itself to do with him. He didn't even notice the girls looking at him.

Eventually a responsible adult came and rounded the girls up and took them away.

'We're often here,' they said. 'Goodbye! Goodbye!'

'Odd,' said Vague Henri, 'a couple of days ago it was the deep six and now it's girls and cake.'

'What'll you remember best?'

'Sorry?'

'Pain and suffering or girls and cake? What'll you remember best a year from now?'

'What are you on about?'

'IdrisPukke said pain was much more than pleasure – that you remembered it more. If you were a python eating a pig, it'd be a bit pleasurable for the python but mighty nasty for the pig. And that's life, he said. So you should know, having had both in a week. Pain and suffering or girls and cake?'

'Why just me?' said Vague Henri. 'Weren't you shitting yourself before you killed Kitty?'

'Me? Not me. I'm your swashbuckling hero-type person. I'm not afraid of anything.'

They both started giggling at this, not unlike the girls who'd been there a few minutes before and who knew nothing about pain and suffering – although, of course, you could never tell just by looking at someone.

'Me? I'm for girls and cake,' said Vague Henri. 'You?'

'Pain and suffering.'

They both started laughing again.

'Sounds barn owl to me,' said Vague Henri.

For the next few days they tried cheering up Kleist but he refused to be made any happier. Eventually Cale gave him tea from his daily supply of Chase-Devil given him by Sister Wray and hoped that would bring him round. It didn't seem to do much other than make him feel sick.

A few days later Cale and Vague Henri went off to find the outdragger who'd picked up the pair from Kitty's and taken them home.

'My friend here wanted to thank you personally,' said Cale when they tracked him down.

'Thank you,' said Vague Henri.

The man looked at him, not hostile but certainly not grateful.

Cale gave him the rest of the money he'd promised and another five dollars on top.

'You're welcome,' said the outdragger to Vague Henri, clearly indifferent to what he thought one way or the other.

'You probably saved our lives,' said Vague Henri, awkward and irritated by the outdragger's refusal to be grateful for his gratitude.

'Fifteen dollars?' said the outdragger. 'Your lives aren't worth much, are they?'

Vague Henri stared at him then gave him another ten dollars, all he had on him. He waited for some sign of appreciation but the outdragger made no acknowledgement beyond putting the money in a purse he took from his pocket. It was pulled tight by a cord from which hung a small iron gibbet dangling a tiny Hanged Redeemer. Antagonists of whatever kind did not approve of these holy gibbets. Everybody was suspicious of the Tinkers whose own version of the faith went back to before the great split.

'Let me give you some advice,' said Vague Henri, not at all awkward any more, 'worth more than ten dollars. Put away the holy gibbet there and don't bring it out until the conversion of the Masons.' The Redeemers believed the Masons to be the most blasphemous of all religions and that their conversion would take place at the end of time.

Cale's interest was elsewhere. 'Tell me about your cart,' he said, looking at the handcart Kleist and Vague Henri had been hauled away in.

For the first time since they'd arrived, Cale's question seemed to inspire enthusiasm. The tinker was clearly proud of his barrow. The design, he said, was as old as the outdraggers themselves but he'd made many improvements over the years; and always, he pointed out resentfully, to the disapproval of other outdraggers.

'They drop dead while they're still young pushing the porky hulks of the Gorges that killed their fathers and their grandfathers before them. I made this cart from a pile of bamboo scaffolding I found in the dump. Got the idea for the springs from a bouncy horse I saw at a carnival. Cost me two dollars to get it made up.' Cale and the outdragger talked about the cart and everything its lightness and mobility allowed him to do in the way of delivering heavier loads up steeper streets. *Why?* thought Vague Henri.

'What a stink,' said Vague Henri, as they walked away into the city.

'You've got very swanky for someone whose idea of heaven used to be a nice juicy rat.'

'What was that all about then, the cart?'

'I'm interested in how things work. An ignorant man from

ignorant people that outdragger – but clever. Interesting bloke.'

When they got back to their lodgings, an irritated IdrisPukke was waiting for them along with Cadbury and Deidre Plunkett who, with her scarlet lips and rouged cheeks, looked like nothing on God's earth.

'Punctuality is the politeness of kings,' said IdrisPukke to Cale. 'Let alone someone who was sold for sixpence.'

'We were held up. Hello, Deidre. Are you well?'

'Nothing shall be well with the wicked.'

There was a short silence.

'Speaking of the wicked, Deidre,' said Cadbury, 'would you mind keeping an eye out for anyone behaving oddly?' She left silently.

'She's lovely,' said Vague Henri.

'Hold your tongue, you little twerp,' replied Cadbury. 'We've come from Kitty the Hare's office.'

Cale nodded.

'IdrisPukke tells me you're always complaining about your bad luck – but I have to say if you'd asked me what your chances were of getting out alive from your interview with Kitty I'd have said about as thin as a homeopathic soup made from the shadow of a pigeon that'd died of starvation.'

'I don't know what homeopathic means.'

'In this instance, it means not worth the steam off a bucket of piss.'

'I'll try to remember – good word, homeopathic.'

'I don't have time for this,' said IdrisPukke. 'Whatever people thought of Kitty they underestimated him. His loan books are a maze with an exit in every treasury this side of the Great Wall of China. They didn't know Kitty was behind them – I've counted more than twenty front men as it is. Most of them should have known better than to deal with someone like Kitty. My guess is that he was blackmailing them. But you never know with splendid financiers what they'll do for even more money.'

'I don't complain about my bad luck,' said Cale.

'Yes, you do,' replied IdrisPukke. 'At any rate, a lot of people owe Kitty a lot of money. Now, thanks to you, we've inherited their obligations to pay up.'

'What if they don't want to? Kitty's dead, after all.'

'But, as Cadbury has pointed out, exacting payment from Kitty's debtors is very much his line of work.'

'What's my share?'

'We thought a tenth,' said Cadbury.

'He kills Kitty and you get nine-tenths? Seems the wrong way round to me,' said Vague Henri.

'You know a lot do you, you ungrateful young pup, about running a criminal enterprise? You're both, I'm sure, deeply knowledgeable about trading in options and futures in the collateralization of debt and what to do when an entire country threatens to default.'

'No,' said Vague Henri.

'Then shut up.' IdrisPukke turned to Cale. 'Do you think I'd steal from you or do you a bad turn?'

'No.'

'So we're agreed. Ten per cent. You'll be very rich if Cadbury is telling the truth, or half the truth.'

'Now you've hurt my feelings,' said Cadbury.

'You know those boys Kitty had in Memphis? Did he bring them here?'

'Nothing to do with me, that stuff.'

'It is now. I want you to find them and let them go. Give them fifty dollars each.'

'Fifty dollars for a rent boy?'

Cadbury could see immediately that Cale was not in the

mood to be disagreed with. 'All right, I'll see to it but it'll come out of your share.' But he couldn't leave it. 'You can't do anything for them. Not now. This is what they're used to. They'll spend the money and end up with Peanut Butter or Butt-Naked. They'll be worse off than they were with Kitty. Either leave them as they are or take care of them.'

'Do I look like somebody's mother? The four of us did all right. Riba's practically the Queen of the Russians. And now the three of us are rich. Give them the money and let them go. Then it's up to them.'

On his way home, Cadbury thought about what Cale wanted. What he said about Riba was true enough. Cadbury had seen her looking gorgeous at some social thrash Kitty had sent him to, to have a word with some Fauntleroy or other who was late with his payments and who had important information Kitty wanted, much more important than the piffling three thousand that was owed. He'd seen Riba at high table. She was something to look at in her red gown, hair piled up like a loaf. But as to Cale and the others being all right, you just had to look at the state of them.

18

Vague Henri and Cale had made one further condition, of a kind: Cadbury had to kill the two men who had beaten the boys so badly. Cadbury was going to do this anyway because he'd been told they were looking for a chance to take over Kitty's operation themselves, but it wouldn't do any harm to let Cale think he'd conceded something.

'It'll have to be quick,' he told the three boys. 'I only torture people when I really need to know something: if you want them to suffer you must do it yourself.'

Quick would be all right, they said.

That night the two men were tied up and when they demanded to know what would happen to them Cadbury said, 'You must die and not live.' The next day, along with Kitty the Hare, their bodies were taken to be buried in the rubbish tips at Oxyrinchus.

Meanwhile, in the civilized places a few hundred yards away, Vipond was in the ascendant. Now that he was in possession of Kitty's red books, and the money secrets inside them, the doors that were once closed to him were now opening.

Conn Materazzi, whose cold disdain for the King made him ever more agreeable in his admirer's adoring eyes, was now in command of ten thousand household Switzers, soldiers of considerable skill and reputation. He was opposed in his rise by the Swiss chancellor, Bose Ikard, but not because of his youth and inexperience. In fact, such things were last of all on his mind: the alternative to Conn could only be drawn from the Swiss aristocracy, who may have been older but were generally not very bright and had considerably less military training than the young man. What alarmed Ikard was the influence this gave to Vipond and his no less dangerous half-brother. He feared any power moving into their hands because all that concerned them was what was good for the self-serving war-mongering Materazzi and not what was good for anyone else. Vipond would have understood his fears but would have pointed out that for the foreseeable future their mutual interests lay in opposing the Redeemers. But Ikard feared war more than anything while Vipond thought it was inevitable.

In fact Bose Ikard and Vipond, and even IdrisPukke, were not so different, in that they were experienced enough to be suspicious of decisive action in war or anything else. Life had taught them to spin everything out until the last minute, then appear to agree to some major concession and then, when all seemed to be decided, find some way to spin things out again.

'The trouble with decisive agreement, just as with decisive battles,' lectured Vipond to Cale, 'is that they decide things and logic dictates that there must be an extremely good chance of them being decided against you. When anyone talks to me about a decisive battle I'm inclined to have him locked up. They're an easy solution and easy solutions are usually wrong. Assassinations, for example, never change history – not really.'

'The Two Trevors tried to assassinate me at the Priory. It would have changed things if they had,' said Cale.

'You must take a more nuanced view. What would it have *changed*?'

'Well, Kitty the Hare would still be alive and you wouldn't have his money and his secrets.'

'I don't consider Kitty's death to have been an assassination – by which I mean the pursuit of impersonal political ends by an act of personal violence. Kitty's death was just common murder. If you want to make something of yourself you must stop slaughtering people, or at least stop slaughtering them for purely private reasons.'

Cale was always reluctant not to have the last word with anyone, even Vipond – but his head ached and he was tired.

'Leave the boy alone, he's not well,' said IdrisPukke.

'What do you mean? The boy knows I'm only giving him the benefit of my experience.' He smiled at Cale. 'Pearls beyond price.' Cale smiled back despite himself.

'I wanted to talk to you about a difficult matter: Conn Materazzi won't have you on his staff.'

A puzzled silence from Cale. 'Never crossed my mind he would.'

'His dislike of you is quite understandable,' said Vipond. 'Nearly everyone takes exception to you.'

'He dislikes me even more since he was in my debt,' said Cale, referring to his long regretted rescue of Conn from the crushed and gasping piles of the dead at Silbury Hill.

'He's grown up a good deal since then. Transformed, I'd say. But he won't be doing with you at any price. We need you to be advising him and very badly. But he's adamant against even my considerable temper when I don't get my own way on something so important. Why?'

'No idea. Ask him.'

'I have.'

Cale sat in silence.

'Moving on,' continued Vipond, after a moment. 'On balance, we've decided not to tell anyone about the likelihood of the Redeemers beginning their attack through the Arnhemland desert.'

'You don't believe me?'

'I believe you. But the problem is that if we warn the Axis

and they do something about it by reinforcing the border next to the Maginot Line the Redeemers will have to re-think everything. If I understand you correctly,' he did, this was merely flattery, 'the Redeemers' entire strategy for the war depends on a swift breakthrough there.'

'So?'

'If that entry is blocked, they'll have to think again.'

'Yes'

'Would you say a long delay?'

'Probably.'

'Perhaps another year if they must miss the summer and autumn. They won't attack in the winter.'

'They probably won't.'

'If you say so. But you agree that blocking Arnhemland now will probably delay the war for a year?'

'Probably.'

'Well, we can't afford that. By *we* I mean the Materazzi and you.'

'Because?'

'Bose Ikard is pouring plausible but false hope into the ear of the King. He's saying that the Axis in general and the Swiss in particular are sealed up tight against Bosco, that either the mountains or the Maginot Line will keep him out. He's telling him the lands the Redeemers have already taken may be considerable but that things are not as alarming as they appear. The territories they have conquered have nothing much in the way of resources worth having and so the trouble of occupying them with Redeemer forces will consume more Redeemer blood and treasure than they can possibly gain from occupying them.'

'He has a point,' said Cale.

'Indeed he does – but our point is different. If we are to believe you, then Bosco will come because he must, now or later. But if it's later then we will lose all credibility. It will appear that Ikard is correct – the Redeemers have taken land that's more trouble than it's worth and are barred by axis defences from taking any more. Bosco can't go forward, he can only go back. If we warn them about the attack through Arnhemland it will stop Bosco and it will look as if Ikard is right and we are wrong. We'll decline into a kind of nothing.'

'So you're going to let the Redeemers in.'

'Exactly. You disagree?'

'It sounds a bit clever dick to me. But you might be right. I'll have to think about it.'

'If you have a better idea let me know.'

'I will.'

But half an hour after he'd left, Cale was pretty sure Vipond was right. The question was what if the Redeemers weren't held at the Mississippi? What if they crossed over and kept on coming? The mountains that protected them from anyone getting in would be the mountains that stopped anyone from getting out. The only exit was through the Schallenberg Pass and Bosco was ready to shut that tight as a cork in a bottle.

That evening Vipond and IdrisPukke were trying to browbeat Arbell Materazzi in the same course.

'You must persuade him,' said Vipond.

'He won't be told and that's that. If I tried to persuade him I'd make him a good deal angrier at me than he is at you – and he's pissed off with you, I can tell you.'

'Don't be so vulgar.'

'Then don't tell me to make an enemy out of my own husband.'

'She has a point,' said IdrisPukke. 'We don't want to send him where we can't get him back.'

'He's not at your beck and call anyway,' she said, angry

now herself. 'He's not a pipe for you to play on.'

'I stand corrected,' said IdrisPukke, touchy himself.

'Besides, you think Thomas Cale is your saviour and ours. Are you so sure?'

'You did pretty well out of him, you ungrateful madam.'

'If he hadn't come to Memphis I'd never have needed rescuing. I'm not ungrateful.'

'I've never understood the "not" in front of "ungrateful",' said IdrisPukke. 'It doesn't mean grateful, does it?'

'All right,' she said, 'I'm a thankless bitch. But wherever he goes, everyone says it, a funeral follows. He was the cause of us losing everything. You think you're clever enough to make use of him to destroy the people you hate – and he'll do it. And he'll take you with him. And my husband and my son.' She stopped for a moment. The two men said nothing because there was no point. 'You should have more trust in Conn. He can be a great man if you can make friends with him again.'

'It doesn't look like we have much choice,' said Vipond the next day when they met up with Cale and Vague Henri to discuss what should be done next. 'We must let the pig pass through the python.'

The two of them started sniggering at this like two naughty schoolboys at the back of the class. 'Grow up!' he said to them, but it only made them worse. When they eventually stopped, Cale told them what he thought.

'I know everyone thinks I'm not good for anything but murder – but this is a wicked thing we're doing here.'

'So I'm told,' said Vipond.

'What if we're wrong? What if someone finds out?'

'You think you're the only one with reservations? I have the reputation for being a wise man, despite the fact that I lost an entire empire while I was supposed to be its steward.

But my experience is still worth something, I think. Great powers, and the men who rule them, are like blind men feeling their way around a room, each believing himself in deadly peril from the other whom he assumes to have perfect vision. They ought to know that all the policies of great powers are made of uncertainty and confusion. Yet each power fears that the other has greater wisdom, clarity and foresight – although they never do. You and I and Bosco are three blind men and before we're finished we're probably going to do a great deal of damage to each other and to the room.'

Twelve days later the Redeemers raced across Arnhemland in less than thirty-six hours and destroyed the first army of the Axis in five days, the eighth army of the Axis in six days and the fourth army of the Axis in two days. The problem was that all the armies guarding Arnhemland and those backing it were increasingly poorly equipped in terms of experience and weaponry, all the best soldiers and equipment having been reserved for the expected line of attack on the impressively well-guarded Maginot Line. These were soldiers who would have had a good chance of either checking or at least slowing the advance of the lightly armed first attack by the Redeemers but having been cut off from all means of re-supply were obliged to surrender without much more than a cross word. This all happened with such speed that Vipond had every reason to fear that he had indeed been too clever by half and that his decision to say nothing was not only wicked but foolish. Temporary rescue of a sort came from an unexpected source.

Artemisia Halicarnassus is already a name long forgotten – but of all great men of military genius never given the credit they deserved she was, perhaps, the greatest. Artemisia was no Amazon or Valkyrie – she was barely five foot tall and was so concerned with her appearance, with her banded painted toenails and elaborately curled hair, that one surly diplomat had described her as more pansy than feminine. In addition she spoke with a slight lisp, which many thought to be an affectation but was not. Along with her tendency to seem easily distracted (due to boredom at the dullness or stupidity of what she was listening to), and her habit of interjecting ideas that seemed merely to have drifted across her mind in the way soft clouds move with a light breeze, there was no one who could look past her appearance and manner to recognize her original and penetrating intelligence. As it happened, the collapse of the armies of the Flag, and the almost as quick defeat of the Regime of the 14th of August that lay in reserve behind, created an extraordinary and definitely once in a lifetime chance for Artemisia to show what she was made of.

Halicarnassus, which had its northern boundary formed by the Mississippi, was unusual in its geography in that, unlike the other countries that bordered that great river, Halicarnassus was a place of limestone gorges and awkward hills. Seeing the terrible collapse in front of her and realizing the vast numbers of retreating soldiers would be slaughtered as they were pinned up against the northern bank of such a difficult to cross river, she emerged from Halicarnassus with the small army left to her by her husband and, spreading her troops like a funnel, managed to guide large numbers of fleeing soldiers into the temporary safety of Halicarnassus. There she re-organized the terrified troops and arranged for as many as a hundred and fifty thousand to be evacuated across the Mississippi – a mile wide at that point. In the ten days that the rescue took she fought in Halicarnassus itself to slow down the advancing Redeemers. For three weeks

Halicarnassus bulged alone into the Redeemer army as it reached the banks of the Mississippi and murdered the thousands of soldiers she had not been able to protect who were trapped by the river around Halicarnassus. Eventually Artemisia was forced to withdraw and cross the river herself. It is not recorded if she expected to be greeted by cheering crowds, the ringing of church bells and the holding of many banquets in her honour. If so, she was to be disappointed.

On her arrival in Spanish Leeds, having been more than anyone else responsible for stopping the Redeemers at the Mississippi, and therefore preventing them from swarming into Switzerland to begin the first stage of the end of the world, she was greeted with polite, if brief, applause and a place at the bottom of the table, like a wedding guest who'd been invited for form's sake but no one wanted to talk to. She was being ignored not just because she was a woman, although it was partly that; even if Artemisia had been a man it would have been hard to place her in the scheme of things. No one whose judgement they especially trusted had actually seen her in action. Perhaps her successes were just good luck or exaggerated. History was full of striking successes by people who either never repeated that success or who spectacularly failed when they attempted to do so. There's a reason why we feel that trust has to be earned – by and large it's the product of repeated success. But Artemisia had emerged from nowhere and her manner would not necessarily have inspired confidence even in an open-minded person. She deserved that confidence but it was not impossible to understand why she didn't have it. She had asked to be put in charge of the defence of the South Bank of the Mississippi but this had not been so much refused as simply referred to various war committees where her request would evaporate like a shallow puddle in Arnhemland. She could have returned to command her own small private army, but only on the banks opposite Halicarnassus where no one, certainly not Artemisia, thought the Redeemers would cross because there were so many better places to do so. So she decided to stay in Spanish Leeds and see what she could do to find a position where she could properly influence events.

Five days after arriving she was already in despair. Whenever she spoke at the interminable meetings to discuss the war her observations were followed by a short, slightly puzzled, silence and then the arguments continued as if she had never spoken. It was at a garden party on the sixth day that she first met Thomas Cale. She had been trying to insert herself in the discussion around various military advisors without success – once she offered an opinion it acted like soap on oil – the group quickly dispersed, leaving her holding a glass of wine and an *amuse bouche* of toasted bread and anchovies and feeling like an idiot. Eventually, in high frustration, she went up to a young man, not much more than a boy, who was leaning against a wall and eating a vol-au-vent with his right hand, while holding two others in his left.

'Hello,' she said. 'I'm Artemisia Halicarnassus.'

The boy looked her over while continuing to chew slowly like, she thought, an unusually intelligent goat.

'Big name for such a little girl.'

'Well,' she replied, 'after you tell me your name perhaps you can give me a list of *your* achievements.'

In most other circumstances this would have been successful at putting such an obvious nobody in his place. 'I'm Thomas Cale,' he said, and set out all his great deeds in a boastfully matter-of-fact way.

'I've heard of you,' she said.

'Everyone's heard of me.'

'I've heard that you're a well-poisoning yob who lets children and women starve and brings carnage and massacre wherever he goes.'

'I've done my fair share of well-poisoning and murder. But I'm not all bad.'

He was used to hearing abuse like this, if not directly. What was strange about it this time was not just that it was said to his face, but that it was done in a slightly distracted manner, her blue eyes fluttering, and in a tone that if she were not accusing him of dreadful infamies would have been almost sickly sweet. She was looking at her fingernails as if they were an object of total fascination.

'I've heard of you, too.'

She looked up at him, eyes fluttering, for all the world like some fabulous social butterfly about to receive yet another compliment about her refulgent beauty. She knew, of course, an insult was coming. Cale spun the moment out. 'Not bad,' he said at last. 'If what I heard was true.'

'It *is* true.'

She had not meant to show she cared for other people's good opinion so much. And indeed she didn't. At least not *so* much. But she did care for it. And she had been so cross about not being given her due that this surprising compliment caught her out.

'Then tell me about it,' said Cale.

Perhaps not even girls or cake can equal the pleasures offered by someone of the highest reputation informing you of your unique brilliance. Cale may have been a well-poisoning murderer but Artemisia found these unhappy qualities receding into the background as it became clear both that he knew what he was talking about and that he admired her enormously. It was not just his flattery that warmed her. His questions, scepticism and doubts, all of which she was able to answer, gave as much delight as having the sore muscles of her delicate neck and shoulders massaged by expert hands. She was, by this time, nearly thirty years old and while she had liked her late husband, who had adored her and indulged her in her peculiar interest, she had not loved him or any man. Men desired her not because she was beautiful in any conventional way, but because of the very quality of other-worldly distraction and a lack of interest in them that also perplexed them. In short, they found her excitingly enigmatic but what they failed to realize as they praised her mysterious-ness was that she did not want to be mysterious. She wanted to be admired for her abilities, appreciated for her good judgement, cunning and brains. Cale, without showing any apparent interest in her as a woman, understood her bril-liance and set it out to her in adorable detail, and for several hours.

By the end of the evening she was (how could she not be?) already half in love. Both were equally astonished that the other was not in some position of great importance, given how wonderful they were. Neither of them, perhaps for similar reasons, had any idea how galling and irritating it was to be around them. They could not easily grasp that no one, especially if they were untalented, wanted to have their lack of ability made plain. He arranged to meet her the next day at the wine garden in Roundhay Park, which delighted her, and said that he would bring a friend of his if he was well enough, which did not delight her quite so much. Then he was gone. His sudden departure made him seem mysteri-ous to her and it also left her off-balance; he had seemed so fascinated by her but had then left suddenly and in an almost off-hand way. She was somewhat put out that this only made him seem more attractive. The truth was he'd left so sud-denly because he felt as if he was going to throw up. Anxious to avoid the bad impression this might make he left abruptly

and only made it to the street outside before he started retching.

'Artemisia Whasername?' said IdrisPukke, the next morning.
'I wouldn't have thought she was your type at all.'

'Meaning?'

'A bit winsome.'

'Windsom?'

'Affected.'

'Affected?'

'Making a show of being endearing and mysterious – all
those fluttering eyelashes and staring into the distance.'

'She wasn't making a show – she was just bored. She's a
brilliant woman.'

'You don't think all that stuff about her is exaggerated?'

'If I say it wasn't exaggerated, then it wasn't. I went
through everything, tried to dismantle her head to foot, but
she stood it up. As it happens, she's a marvel.'

'Well if the Great Bighead thinks so well of her we must
take a look.'

'Why?'

'Someone with such a great ability but less full of herself
than you could be very useful.'

'IdrisPukke wants to meet you, and Vipond.'

Artemisia was excited by this and was not someone able to
hide her enthusiasm – her eyes widened, her eyelashes, long
as a spaniel's, fluttered away as if signalling desperately to a
distant shore. There was something about her; perhaps most
importantly, she was not Thomas Cale. He was very sick of
himself indeed. Being in the company of a sick person all
the time was a strain even if you were the sick person: always
feeling horrible, never wanting to go anywhere, always asleep

or, when awake, wanting to go back to sleep. She liked him a great deal, which was a considerable help, as girls seemed mostly to be afraid of him or sometimes, more worryingly, they imagined that this enticingly bad reputation was a mask that could be removed by a sensitive woman to reveal the soulmate beneath. They didn't appreciate that there are some souls, not necessarily the cruel or the bad, with which it might be better not to join.

Another thing that fascinated Cale about Artemisia was that for the first time he had met someone whose story was odder than his own. Artemisia had always been a puzzle because she was no tomboy. In fact, she had been considered the girliest of little girls – not at all like her older sister, who was notorious for her rough and noisy habits. Artemisia liked pink and feminine colours that made your eyes ache to look at them, wore so many frills and flounces that it could be hard to find the little girl hidden inside them and had a collection of red-lipped dress-me-up dolls that numbered in the hundreds. Courtiers began to notice that in the morning she would dress and undress the dolls, babbling away like the lunatic so many small children resemble, scolding her dolls for getting dirty or squabbling with each other or wearing the wrong gloves for a Tuesday – but in the afternoon she would arrange them in great effeminate phalanxes of pink and cerulean and work out the best way of slaughtering them. Soldiers in mulberry petticoats fought to the death with irregulars in lavender pastel bonnets and cavalry riding on cotton reels in bloomers coloured baby blue.

It was assumed that in time her taste for these mincingly effeminate soldiering games would fade but her interest in everything military seemed only to grow more intense the older she got. She had no interest in any form of personal violence at all. She did not want to practise with swords or knives or, God forbid, wrestle with boys like her older sister. She did not have to be ordered not to box (like her sister), any more than she had to be ordered not to fly. She was an excellent horsewoman but no one tried to prevent this because Halicarnassus was famous for its horses and riding was considered perfectly acceptable for girls.

'You don't know how to fight?' Cale asked.

'No. My arms are so weak I get out of breath lifting up a powder puff.'

'I could teach you,' he offered.

'Only if you let me teach you how to wear a corset.'

'Why would I want to do that?'

'Exactly.'

'Not exactly at all. I don't want to be a girl.'

'And I don't want to be a soldier. I want to be a general. And that's what I am. You can carry on cutting people's heads off and spilling their insides on the ground in great piles of giblets the size of Mount Geneva. But you don't have to – there are plenty of people who are good at that.'

He wondered if he should tell his new friend that, without a snort of a drug powerful enough to kill, his days as a scourge of the battlefield were long gone. But he thought better of it for now. How did he know she could be trusted? However, it had to be said that something in him longed to tell her the truth.

She finished her story. She had been married off at fourteen, protesting noisily at the age of the man, his obscurity, and that where the country was flat it was *too* flat and where it was mountainous it was hideously so. In addition it was too hot in the summer and too cold in the winter. It took nearly four years of petulance and general disagreeableness before she began to appreciate her good fortune. Daniel, fortieth Margrave of Halicarnassus, was an intelligent, wise and unconventional man, though it was an unconventionality he had carefully hidden lest it frighten his family and neighbours. In addition, he adored and was amused by Artemisia rather than irritated, which he had every right to be given how awkward and rude she was to him at first. While he didn't always indulge her, he did encourage her in her peculiar interests, in part out of affection and to win her heart and in part out of curiosity to see where it would lead. He wasn't interested in war but he recognized his small militia was almost completely useless and so there was no harm in letting her loose on them.

Artemisia won the support of the militia, and rid herself of the officers who out of natural self-interest opposed her, by dividing the soldiers in two and offering to fight three war games. Then she bet the officers three thousand dollars she would win all three. If they lost they were to resign. She had three thousand left in her dowry (Daniel had given it back to her on their wedding day) and she used a thousand of it to bribe the militia now under her command and who, until she paid them so much money, were not very happy about it either. She had two and a half thousand men, mostly farmers and their hired workers and an assortment of brewers, bakers and metal workers. She had three months.

At first the men worked hard because they were paid to – but only on results. Each week the men were paid more but only if they ran the length of this field faster, or carried a heavy weight for longer. But she also divided them up into groups with different fierce-sounding names and dressed them in waistcoats of different colours – though wisely not the baby blue or cerulean of her childhood dolls. Anyone who failed to improve was stripped of their waistcoat publicly and thrown out. But if they subsequently passed the test they'd failed, and bettered it, they'd be reinstated. She made mistakes – but money and an apology seemed to cure everything. When the three months were up, the games began. They were rough enough, though with padded sticks instead of swords and spears, and there were many injuries. She won all three easily because of her talent but also because her opponents were made up of intelligent officers who were complacent and complacent officers who were stupid. She retained some of the former and began a further series of rough games to correct her mistakes – which she knew were many. She ordered books by great authorities on the art of war from everywhere possible – and found most of them maddeningly vague when it came to what she wanted to know: the details of how something was actually done. One bombastic authority after another would tell of, say, the night march by General A that had daringly outflanked and surprised General B – but the details of how you moved a thousand men over rocky, lousy paths without lights and without the men breaking their legs or falling over the edge of a cliff – the things you actually needed to know – were nearly always absent. What was left were just stories for children and daydreamers.

'I still don't understand,' Cale said, laughing, 'how you got to be so good. I've been taught to do nothing else my whole life.'

'Perhaps I'm more talented and clever than you.'

'I doubt it,' he said. 'I've never met anyone more talented than me.'

She burst out laughing.

'I don't know what's so funny,' he said, smiling.

'You are. I'm not surprised nobody likes you.'

'Some people like me. But not many, it's true,' he admitted. 'So how did you do it?'

'I played.'

'All children do that. Even *we* used to play.'

'I played a different way from everyone else.'

'Now who's boasting?'

'I'm not boasting. It's true.'

'Go on then.'

'I watched other children playing even when I was very small – all they ever did was make things come out the way they wanted them to. But things never do – I knew that even when I was five. So I took an old pack of my mother's cards and I used to write things on them – your best general falls off his horse and breaks his neck, a spy steals your plan of attack, thunder makes your enemies' horses stampede, you suddenly go blind.'

Cale laughed again. 'I take it back. You are cleverer than me.'

'It's not a question of being clever. Nothing's lost on me, that's all. Just like everyone, I see what I want to see – only I know that's what I'm like, so sometimes I can make myself see things as they are. Only sometimes, though. That would be really clever – seeing things as they are all the time.'

But she was wrong about that, as time would tell.

And so what happened was everything you would expect. He told her about the Sanctuary and his life there (not everything, of course, some things are better left unsaid) and she was close to tears hearing him talk about the things he experienced there, which was, of course, very satisfactory to Cale. They talked and walked and kissed – something that to her surprise he was puzzling good at. To the great scandal of her servants, she brought him to the small house she had rented not far from Boundary Park and – a little guiltily, though not too much – spent several hours making a shameless beast of herself with her young lover's body. She was aware at some level that he was very much more familiar with how to touch her than his age and history would have suggested. Her suspicions were moved to the place where all uncomfortable suspicions go – to the back of her mind. There they joined all her other anxieties and shames, including the one which she was most guilty about, that she was deeply excited by Cale's certainty that there would be no agreement that kept the Redeemers on the other side of the Mississippi in exchange for money and more concessions of territory. They were coming and nothing would stop them except force. The realization that she wanted a war appalled her because she knew perfectly well that it would bring terrible pain and suffering everywhere, especially to the people she had built her private army to protect. Although they turned out to be a tough collection, the farmers and carpenters who had made up her militia were interested in cows and barley not war. The thing which she was most talented at, most excited by, most passionate about was an exercise in blood and suffering, though it wasn't this that drew her to fighting but the delight she felt in trying to control the uncontrollable. There are some men and at least one woman for whom life is meaningless unless the greatest prize of all, life itself, is at stake. What was the point of chess, she used to complain to her husband when he was alive? He used to spend hours playing and claimed that it was a game so full of traps and subtleties it mirrored the deepest and most complex levels of the human mind.

'Bollocks!' she had said to him. She had heard this expression just that Sunday on the training ground and was not completely aware of the strength of its vulgarity. Bollocks was not a word that a Margravine ought to use to a Margrave and certainly not about chess. Eye-widening, startled at her outburst, he pretended only polite uncertainty.

'Your exquisite reasons, my dear?'

'I don't have any exquisite reasons. It's just that chess has rules and life doesn't have rules. You can't burn your opponent's bishop, you can't stab him either, or pour a bucket of water over the board or play when you haven't eaten for three days. However clever you have to be to play it, it's just a stupid game. To fight a battle,' she said, 'needs a mind a hundred times better than any stupid game.' She was so rude because she felt guilty about wanting to go to war.

Her husband had thought about this for a moment. 'Let us hope, my dear, that at some time in the future you get your chance to butcher as many of our friends and neighbours as will satisfy your ambition.'

She didn't talk to him for three days – but unusually he was not the one to give in.

It was a secret relief that, when the time came to play with real death and destruction, she had absolutely no choice but to do the one thing that in all the world she most wanted to. The extreme nature of the Redeemers cleared her conscience.

At the war conference in Spanish Leeds (Cale was as dismissive of it as he was desperate to be there), there emerged a sudden demand for decisive action from the King himself. It was intolerable, he said, that so much had been lost to the Redeemers and he would not endure it and neither would his people, and he sincerely believed his allies would take the same view.

He did not sincerely believe anything of the kind. It is a truth, declared Vipond later, that the sincerity of anything said aloud should be divided by the number of people listening to it. Like nearly all kings, in another world Zog would have been an inadequate cattle farmer, a better than average grower of turnips or a mediocre butcher. The same would be true for many of the great and the good who surrounded him. This is why the best picture of the world is as a lunatic asylum. 'If you only knew,' IdrisPukke was fond of saying to Cale, 'with how much stupidity the world is run.'

*

The last we heard of the great storm above the forests of Brazil it had passed the height of its unimaginable power by merely a fraction. Now, months later, it has dispersed that power across five thousand miles in all directions to the north and south and east and west. Descending from the warm skies above the Aleatoire Bridge over the River Imprevu, a great tributary of the Mississippi, it approached a large buddleia, as purple as the hat of an Antagonist bishop, covered in butterflies feeding on its nectar. As it touched the bush the last breath of wind of the great Brazilian storm finally died – but not before it ever so slightly lifted the wings of one of the butterflies, causing it to take to the air. The movement of the long-tailed blue just caught the eye of a passing swallow who dipped and, in a fraction of a second, took it in its beak, startling the mass of other butterflies who took to the air in hundreds like a bursting cloud and frightened a passing horse pulling a wagon badly loaded with rocks for the repair of a wall. The horse reared, turning the cart on its side and pitching the rocks into the River Imprevu below.

Some agricultural language followed this accident, and a kick for the unfortunate horse, but only some rocks were lost and not worth the effort of getting them out. So the wheel was put back on the wagon, the horse given another kick, and that was that.

In the river below, the not especially large pile of stones caused the current to flow more quickly round its sides and pointed the faster stream directly at the roots of one of the oldest and largest oak trees on the banks of the great tributary.

At the same moment, Zog was proposing that an army of the best Swiss troops and those of its allies should be sent through the Schallenberg Pass to engage the Redeemer army on the plains of the Mittelland. 'We can do nothing less. In putting this plan forward I rededicate myself to the service of this great country and this great alliance.' The speaker thanked the King and tearfully stated, 'You have become for us all, your Majesty, a kaleidoscope king of our kaleidoscope alliance.' There was loud applause.

The speaker then threw the King's plan open for discussion to the Axis members gathered – which is to say that he threw the King's plan open to them for their agreement, a consent that had already been guaranteed by persuasion and threats from Bose Ikard, despite the fact that he was profoundly opposed to doing anything of the kind. Given that he had not persuaded the King against a fight he realized that he must make up for disagreeing with him by now being deeply enthusiastic in its favour. He had neglected, however, to talk to Artemisia, because he didn't consider her important enough. She listened for twenty minutes to various speeches in response, all supporting the King and all pretty much the same. She tried catching the eye of the speaker of the meeting but he refused to recognize her. In the end she simply stood up, as one of the prearranged speeches of support ended, and started talking.

'With all respect to His Majesty, while I understand his impatience to engage the Redeemers, what you suggest is too hazardous. The only force that stopped the Redeemers from walking into this room has not been any army but the existence of the Mississippi. But for a mile of water we would not be talking together now.'

This simple and straightforward truth was the cause of huge and vocal resentment: 'Army'; 'Noble traditions'; 'Heroism'; 'Brave lads'; 'Our heroes'; 'Courage'; 'Second to none'.

'I'm not questioning the courage of anyone,' she shouted above the racket of objections. 'But the Redeemers are stuck where they are in the north until early next year. They must build an uncountable number of boats and train enough shoremen to get them across the river. I can tell you because I know that it's the work of years to know how to navigate the currents of the Mississippi. Now's the time to reconstruct what's left of the armies that made it across.' A reminder here, a little too subtle, that so many were still alive because of her. 'We must send the best of the troops we have north to retrain the troops that were rescued and use the greatest ally we have – the size and currents of the Mississippi.'

Enormous howls of protest went up at this and the speaker had to work himself up into a fury to bring the meeting to order.

'We thank the Margravine of Halicarnassus for her forthright views but she understandably may not know that it is not done in this place to speak slightingly of the brave heroes who have made the ultimate sacrifice for the safety of others.'

'Hear! Hear! Hear! Hear! Hear!' And that was that.

'If you will forgive me for being blunt, Margravine,' said Ikard, half an hour later in his office, 'but you have behaved like a complete twerp.'

'I'm afraid I'm not familiar with the term. Not a compliment, I s'pose.'

'No, it's not. Whatever the merits of your views – and I know there are others of reputation who agree with you – you made any chance of influencing matters impossible with your ridiculous defiance.'

She made a brief sound with her tongue against her front teeth.

'Do I take it that signals disagreement?' said Ikard.

'You didn't bother asking my opinion before, what possible reason could I have to believe you'd have listened if I'd kept my mouth shut?'

'The King,' lied the Chancellor, 'has until now spoken of you with respect and admiration. Now you hang in his favour like an icicle on a Dutchman's beard.'

'So,' she said, 'I must be like Cassandra, doomed always to tell the truth but never to be believed.'

'You flatter yourself, Margravine. I have always understood the story about Cassandra to demonstrate not that she was so wise but that she was so foolish: there's no point in telling people the truth when there's no chance of them hearing. You must wait until they're ready. That's the moral of the story. Take it from someone who knows. The course you suggested, whatever its merits militarily, is in every way socially and politically impossible. The army will not stand for such abuse, the aristocracy will not endure it, and the people whose sons and husbands died in their thousands will neither stand for it nor endure it. You may know something about war but you know nothing about politics. Something must be *done*.'

Then she was dismissed. It was ten minutes before she thought of a strong reply – although the young man she told about her dressing-down didn't have to know that.

'So what did you say?' asked Cale.

'I said, "Unfortunately for you, Chancellor, the facts don't give a damn about politics."'

He laughed. 'A good shout, that.' She was a little ashamed but not too much.

For Cale and Artemisia, waiting for the pig to pass through the python was in some ways a frustrating experience and in other ways delightful. Great events that they wanted to influence were taking place without them but they had endless hours for each other, and though there was more talking than the giving of pleasure, there was not very much more. If the Axis failed (and what was to stop them?) he could soon be on top of a bonfire big enough to be seen all the way to the moon. On the other hand, neither Vague Henri nor Kleist were well enough to make it out over the mountains. Besides, he was used to waiting for the unspeakably grim, used to it all his life; but the pleasure of being with the woman asleep next to him was a rare thing and he knew it. Now was the time for girls and cake.

There was one way in which he was involved in the new plan to attack the Redeemers. He was sworn to secrecy by Vipond, who risked a great deal by showing him a copy of the plans drawn up by Conn Materazzi for the advance through the Schallenberg and the attack on the Redeemers. It was a trust Cale immediately betrayed by discussing what he'd been shown in great detail with Artemisia.

Cale's feelings on going through the plan were oddly mixed. It was not at all bad. In Conn's position he would not have done much different. It turned out he wasn't just an over-privileged, chinless wonder after all. Apparently he had expressed sympathy with Artemisia's dismissal of the King's idea (irritatingly showing even more good sense) but Cale realized Conn had no choice but to attack if he wanted to stay as Commander in Chief, and he'd made a pretty good fist of coming up with a decent plan. But it was still too risky.

'The trouble with decisive battles,' said IdrisPukke, not for the first time, 'is that they decide things.'

'If you get the chance,' said Cale, 'you might want to suggest he cuts out a couple of thousand extra men to stay in the Schallenberg, just in case it all goes a bit porcupine. If he loses that's all there'll be between the Redeemers and us and a lot of running about and screaming.'

Later, on his way back to Artemisia, he stopped to see

Arbell's brother, Simon. It was a visit he'd been avoiding, not for lack of affection – he'd rescued the boy from the isolation and contempt of being unable to hear or speak – but because he both feared and – horribly, hatefully – desperately desired to see his sister.

He spent several hours talking to Simon through his reluctant and disagreeable aide, Koolhaus. Koolhaus had been a low-ranking civil servant in rank-obsessed Memphis, not because he lacked ability, but because his father was a *merdapis*, an untouchable who carried away the excrement and urine from the palaces of the Materazzi. Koolhaus was two parts of resentment to three parts of intelligence. It was Koolhaus who, in a matter of days, had devised an expressive language out of the short list of signs given to him by Cale, which was based on the simple signing system the Redeemers used to direct an attack when silence was required. Cale and Vague Henri had developed it a little in order to make offensive remarks about the monks around them during the brain-destroyingly boring three hour high masses at the Sanctuary

'I'd like to borrow Koolhaus for an hour or so a day.'

The attempt to bend Koolhaus out of shape by suggesting he was some sort of useful household item was deliberate. Annoying Koolhaus was something that had always delighted the three boys ('If you were an egg, Koolhaus, would you rather be fried or boiled?'). They could have been friends and allies – and should have been – but they were not. That's boys for you.

Simon could see that his interpreter was annoyed – it didn't take much. Their master and servant relationship was awkward, the balance of power shifting between Simon's dependency on him to make contact with the world – which he often resented – and Koolhaus's entirely justified feeling that he was meant for greater things than being a talking puppet. An offer to pay Koolhaus more money usually mollified him, but only temporarily.

'Tomorrow at six, then,' said Cale, and made his way through the low-ceilinged corridors where he had so disgraced himself during his last uninvited visit. What hideously mixed feelings twisted in his soul; dread and hope, hope and dread. Then – and he might have made the same visit fifty times and they would have never met – she was in front of him, having decided to take her son to see Simon, who delighted in the baby because he could neither fear Simon nor pity him. Cale's heart lurched in his chest as if it would tear itself from his body. For a moment they stared at each other – the boiling sea off Cape Wrath was nothing to it. Not love or hate but some braying mule of an emotion, ugly and raucously alive. The baby waved his hand about happily then suddenly slapped his mouth against his mother's cheek and began making loud slurping noises.

'Is that good for him?' Cale said. 'You might be catching.'

'Have you come to threaten us again?' She was also shocked at the change in him, gaunt where he was once muscular, with the dark circles around his eyes that no good night's sleep would ever wipe away.

'You remember every sin of mine that was just words and forget everything I did to keep you safe at any cost. You're still alive because of me – now the dogs bark at me in the street because of you.'

Ah, self-pity and blame, a combination to win the heart of any woman. But he couldn't help himself.

'Abl blab abl baddle de dah,' said the baby, nearly poking his mother in the eye.

'Shshshsh.' She settled him on her hip and started to swing from side to side.

'If there was any good in you, you'd leave us alone now.'

'He seems happy enough.'

'That's because he's a baby and would play with a snake if I let him.'

'Is that supposed to be me – that's what I am to you?'

'You're frightening me – let me go.'

But he couldn't. He could feel the pointlessness of talking to her but there was no way to stop. Part of him wanted to say he was sorry and part of him was furious with himself for feeling so. There was nothing to be sorry for – his soul demanded that she throw herself to the floor and, weeping, beg his completely undeserved forgiveness. But not even that would have been enough, she would have needed to spend the rest of her life on her knees to stop his heart from scalding him about what she'd done. But not even that.

'The man you sold me to told me he'd already bought me once before – for sixpence.'

'Then your price has risen, hasn't it?'

Angry and guilty, and therefore angrier, it was unwise to say something like that to him. But like Cale she had a taste for the last word. As much as her presence was poison to him he couldn't bear to see her go. But he couldn't think of anything to say. She pushed past, the baby on the far side, away from him. Into his chest something seeped: oil of vitriol. Acid was kind next to it.

'Yaaar! Blah baa! Pluh!' shouted the baby.

19

History teaches us that there are approximately twice as many triumphant military exits from great cities as there are triumphant returns. The exodus from Spanish Leeds was greater than most in terms of trumpets, rows of well-drilled troops, cheering crowds and emotional young women shouting goodbyes to their heart-burstingly proud men. And then there were the horses – the power and glory, the head-brasses and the colours of blue and yellow and red – and the gorgeous men riding them. There were children present who would remember the splendour and the noise of steel on stone and the cheers until the day they died.

Twenty minutes outside the city, off came the armour and most of the horses were sent back to their stables. Not only did they consume fodder the way a bear eats buns, but Conn Materazzi would not be allowing the Redeemer archers to destroy a cavalry charge from three hundred yards away as they'd done at Silbury Hill. The cavalry were mostly useful for gathering information before a battle and running away afterwards if it all went wrong.

Even though Conn's vanity and pride had largely given way to an impressively mature good judgement he still had a blind spot, understandably enough, when it came to Thomas Cale. Although Cale had no intention of fighting in a battle where he wasn't in control, he was furious when he was told that he wouldn't be allowed to bring the Purgators anywhere near the army. Even Artemisia, guilty by association, was refused a part on the grounds that her troops were irregular and not suited to a pitched battle. She would be allowed, however, to lead the sixty or so reconnaissance riders who had helped her slow the Redeemer movement through Halicarnassus. Artemisia had let Cale sulk for several days then suggested he come with her, pointing out that he wouldn't be able to fight but he might be able to watch.

'I'm not sure if I can,' he said. 'I don't know if I have the strength even for watching.' He had not told her anything like the whole story of his illness but it was too obvious that something was seriously wrong with him not to give some explanation. He claimed he was suffering from bad-air disease caught in the Scablands. The symptoms were well known to be vague and recurring. Why shouldn't she believe him?

'Try it for a few days. You can always come back.'

Six days into the march to the border the news reached Conn that a Redeemer army of around thirty-five thousand was heading to the Mittelland in two parts of twenty-five and ten thousand respectively, the latter coming through the Vaud, probably in an attempt to take Conn's army from behind. Unfortunately, but not unusually, some of this information was wrong.

The Redeemer army under Santos Hall had, on balance, decided to move forward only to take the high ground outside the village of Bex and again on balance to divide the army so that they could move more quickly to do so. Shifting thirty-five thousand men with all their carts and baggage could easily lead to a queue two miles wide and twenty miles back. The speed needed to reach the best ground outside Bex was the priority here. But by the time the Redeemers arrived a delighted Conn was solidly placed in front of Bex, protected on his left by the River Gar and to the right by a dense wood, full of lacerating briars thick as fingers and wince-sharp thorns known as dog's teeth. This gave Conn a space about a mile wide into which to fit thirty-two thousand men. Just before nightfall, the Redeemers started to set up in a position they glumly realized was very much second best. Between the two armies was a slope, much shallower down the Redeemer front and much steeper up to the Swiss army. Conn had won the first battle: he had control of the steeper slope and he had archers almost as good as the Redeemers, and more of them. The battle tomorrow would start with a forty-minute exchange between the two. In that time more tens of thousands of arrows would be exchanged, arriving at one hundred and fifty miles an hour, fired into packed ranks. One of the sides would not be able to endure such a killing squall and would be forced to attack. The side that did so would probably lose the battle, defence being far easier than attack. Odds against the Redeemers were much worse because they had to advance up a steep slope under fire and with fewer men when they got to the top because of the numbers of the dying and dead. More alarming than this was that the ten thousand troops Santos Hall had moved separately from his main army in order to outflank the Axis had got lost and were now blundering around the Swiss countryside.

During the night something changed that might make the situation better for the Redeemers or very much worse, although it was nothing either side could do anything about. It was a feature of the local climate that because of the effect of the nearby mountains the weather could change dramatically. The unusually hot sun that day emerged out of a clear sky, which at nightfall allowed the heat to escape upwards in minutes. In turn, cold air off the mountains began flowing into the valley so that the temperature dropped quickly to freezing in a few hours and a deep frost covered everything.

By two o'clock in the morning the ground was like iron. But then the wind picked up. It blew over the battlefield first one way then the other, and then back again. Conn and Little Fauconberg, not much more than five foot two, stood in the freezing cold at the top of the hill outside Bex and looked over their own ineffective fires at the equally ineffective fires of the Redeemers, who didn't even have the shelter of the wood to protect them from the cold wind.

'Odd if the wind settles it,' said Conn.

'There's nowt you could do about it. But it might drop altogether now or blow in their face and we'd be even better off.'

A horse intelligencer arrived and ran up to the two men, slipping on the icy ground and landing heavily on his poor arse. Embarrassed and in pain, he got to his feet. 'We sighted the rest of the Redeemers at the far end of the Vaud, heading the wrong way. They've turned for us now but they won't be here before mid-afternoon.'

'Should we divide and go to meet them?' said Fauconberg. 'We don't need to stop them, just slow them down. Three thousand could keep them away long past them being of any use here.'

Conn thought about it.

'Is that Cale oik in camp?' Fauconberg went on. 'We could send him off to squeeze them at Bagpuize – they've got to come that way. His glorious death would be jolly useful all round.'

'He's not here. It's a damn good idea, Fauconberg, but I'm going to stick. Triple the intelligencers – I want to know every mile they make towards us. We can send Vennegor or Waller if things go all right here.'

'If the wind settles going down from us towards them, we'll win.'

'And what if it doesn't?' said Conn.

Conn was right to ask. By five in the morning the wind was driving constantly into their faces like a blast from a furnace for forging ice. All the advantages won by Conn's speed and grasp were blown away in a cold wind from the worst cold snap in thirty years.

'They won't wait,' said Little Fauconberg. 'If the wind can change once it can change twice. They'll take the advantage while they can. Bloody bollocks and damn our luck!'

There was nothing he could say to improve on Fauconberg's assessment so Conn just ordered the massed ranks up into line. With the wind so bitter he ordered the men at the front to swap with the men behind, seven deep, every ten minutes. What may sound a tricky manoeuvre was easy enough: for all the romantic heroics of tall tales of warfare in the penny-dreadfuls of Geneva and Johannesburg and Spanish Leeds, the man never lived who could fight for ten or five or even two hours at a stretch. Men were in ranks so that they could replace the men in front not just if they died or were wounded, but mostly to give them a breather and to be given one in their turn. Depending on circumstances a man in pitched battle might fight for no more than ten minutes in every hour. Now, like the emperor penguins of the northern pole, they shuffled side to side into the numbing sleet.

Little Fauconberg was right. Santos Hall ordered his archers forward. So hard was the ground they could not grab even a pinch of earth to eat to make it clear to God that they were ready to be buried for his sake. This put many Redeemers into a state of hysteria, so terrified were they of dying in a state of sin yet hardly terrified at all of death itself. An exasperated Santos Hall had to send non-militant priests up and down the ranks issuing pardons, something that took ten minutes. A more practical matter of concern was that the earth was so hard they couldn't stick their arrows into the ground for ease of use.

Once forgiveness for sins of omission had calmed them down, the Redeemer archers moved forward into position to shoot. As they did so they began to call out to their enemies.

'Baaaa! Baaaa! Baaaa! Baaaa! The sleet wind blew the sound across the four hundred yards that separated them.

'Isn't that sheep?' asked Little Fauconberg. 'Why are they making the sound of sheep?'

'Baaaa! Baaaa! Baaaa!' The call came louder and softer with the rhythm of the wind.

'They're saying we're lambs to the slaughter,' said Conn.

'Are they?' said Fauconberg. 'Hand out sprigs of mint to the men and when we come together we'll shove it up their arse.'

'Shouldn't that be arses, Fauconberg?' said one of the knights-in-arms standing just behind.

'Shut your gob, Rutland, or I'll use you to show the men how it's done.'

Much laughter at this.

'If you must shove something up my bottom,' said Rutland, 'I'd prefer a nice hot pepper. It might have a warming effect in this fucking wind.'

Then it began and in a few seconds the first stage of the battle was lost. The wind against them blew with so much power that the Swiss arrows lost fifty yards in range and those of their enemy gained the fifty they'd lost. They might just as well have used harsh words. It hardly mattered that the thick sleet blinded them and they kept losing sight of their opponents, now dim, now completely obscured by the driving mixture of snow and freezing rain, because everything they shot fell short. But the first volley from the

Redeemers no longer fell from the sky but was driven by the wind with malice into knee and chest, mouth and nose at such speed not even the highest quality of steel could defend against a full strike. Rutland, pierced through the ear, no longer worried about the cold.

There were ten thousand Redeemer archers shooting, at a less than usual rate of about seven arrows in every minute because of the hard ground. The thirty-two thousand Swiss on the steeper hill were hit by nearly seventy thousand arrows every sixty seconds, each weighing a quarter of a pound and, with the wind behind each one, travelling nearly a hundred yards every second. There was nothing coming back at the Redeemers to frighten or harm them. After twenty minutes more than a million arrows landed on a space half a mile wide and ten yards deep. In all, one hundred and fifty-eight tons of malignant rain pissing it down on men, none of them with shields and more than half of them with no more armour than a heavy jacket with metal discs sown into it. To retreat out of range would have meant rout – an army cannot turn its back and live – and to stay was impossible, but to advance made for a probable defeat.

'We've to attack!' shouted Fauconberg over the hideous rattle of iron on steel. PINGAPINGAPINGAPINGAPING-APINGAPINGAPING! The racket merging with screams of pain and the roaring shouts of the sergeants trying to stop their men from running away. Few die well or quickly on a battlefield.

Shocked and more *astonished* by the collapse of his clever and wonderfully executed plans, Conn looked at Fauconberg. 'Yes, I agree.' Despite himself, Fauconberg, fifty-five years old and bad-tempered, as dismissive as any thirty-year mercenary, was impressed by Conn: *Not bad, sonny, in a shitstorm like this.*

How many of us have a finest hour? The moment when everything you were made for, everything you have become, arrives; the great event that opens you up and calls out, 'This is for you.' With his carefully laid plans in wind-driven ruin, Conn Materazzi gathered himself up and caught fire. He bellowed the order to advance and its tone of power and conviction was picked up by each of the sergeants in their turn as it echoed down the line. The great army afflicted by the squall of sharps moved forward to come to grips. Four hundred yards will take an army moving with care to keep its shape more than three minutes – an age under the arrows pelting into feet and knees and mouths and throats. But now the murder of arrows had to end because the Swiss were closing. The Redeemer archers had to leave off and retreat behind the infantry standing still behind them and who would now have to bar the way of the advancing Swiss hand-to-hand. The arrows stopped falling like a sudden squall suddenly over. But the real wind grew more blustery as they advanced, the sleet more blinding. As both sides moved in the storm, the slack visibility and the confusion of movement of so many men so quickly meant that the left side of Conn's attacking line and the right side of the Redeemers overlapped as they finally met. Seeing the problem, the centenars and sergeants on either side threw in reserves to seal up the edges and to prevent their opponents coming around the sides to take them from behind. But these uneven counter pushes began to skew the line of battle so that it slowly began to rotate against the clock.

At nearly six foot four, in armour that cost the price of the better kind of manor house, Conn was the man observed by all observers, Axis and Redeemer alike. He was the latter's target, too. Redeemer marksmen, a couple hiding in the trees that defined one side of the battlefield, fired at him repeatedly – but even when they hit their man the fortune lavished on his suit of lights showed that in armour you get what you pay for. The arrows pinged harmlessly away as he moved across the back of the line, shouting and moving to the front. Like some towering elegant insect, silver and gold, he stabbed, crushed and punched his opponents, whose armour he seemed to open up as if it was made of tin. There were few swords here – Conn preferred the hideous poleaxe for fighting in this press, men trying to get at each other with hardly a couple of feet to either side.

The poleaxe was a thug's weapon used by gentlemen. Not more than four foot long it was hammer, hatchet, club and spike. Of all the weapons of killing it was the most honest because anyone could tell what it was for just by looking at it. Poets might blather on about magic swords or holy spears but none of them had ever used a poleaxe to symbolize anything: it was made to crush and split and didn't pretend otherwise.

For ten minutes at a time Conn punched the life out of everyone who came at him: brutality was never so graceful, splintering of bones never so deft, the bursting and crushing of flesh never so debonair; his reach the greater, his heart the stronger, muscle and sinew bound together in his ugly skill and beautiful violence.

A few hundred yards away, keeping shtum in the trees, Cale watched Conn fighting like an angel and envied him his strength. But he admired him too. He was quite something out there in the blood and chaos.

'We have to go,' whispered Artemisia, as loud as a whisper can go. She was standing at the foot of the tree with two of her hefty-looking soldiers. She had declined to climb up with Cale.

'What's the matter?' he said. 'Worried about your nails?'

'The Swiss Pickers are coming to root out the archers. They won't know who we are – it's too dangerous. We've to go.'

He was down almost before she'd finished, breathing heavily and sweating not at all healthily. They moved off but not quickly; too much in the way of razor briars. Careful of the dog's teeth thorns they pushed through into a clearing. Ten yards away, so did others. Four Redeemers, the marksmen the Pickers were looking for. No one did anything. No one moved. For years Bosco had set Cale tests in which he was faced with the completely unexpected with only a few seconds to solve the problem before the blow to the back of his head that followed if he failed. To make things worse, the punishment was not always immediate; sometimes the blow fell a few hours or a day or a week later. This was to teach him to assess things before he acted, no matter how immediate the danger. Four Redeemers against four of them. Artemisia would be no use – the two guards with her would be handy but not a match. And neither was he. Turn their backs and run? Not through the briars. Take the Redeemers on? Not a chance. *Never expect rescue*, Bosco used to say, *because rescue never comes*. But it came to Cale then, and by means of the greatest curse of his life. The four Redeemers knelt down; one of them – the leader apparently – burst into tears.

'We were told,' he said, beating his breast three times in terrible remorse, 'that the Left Hand of God would be watching over us. But I did not believe. Forgive me.'

Fortunately Artemisia and her bodyguards did not need to be told to stay still. The four Redeemers looked at Cale fearfully and lovingly. He raised his hand and drew a circle in the air. It was the sign of the noose, a gesture only permitted to the Pope. And now, it seemed, also to the incarnation of the

Wrath of God. It was as if he had opened a door into the next world and through it passed eternal grace into the hearts of the four men. Cale said nothing but waved them away with a kindly smile. Open-mouthed, struck by the love of God, the four Redeemers left.

When they'd gone he turned to Artemisia. 'Perhaps, in future,' he said, 'you won't answer back so often.'

'They think you're a God?' said an astonished Artemisia.

'That'd be blasphemy. They think I'm one of God's feelings made flesh.'

'Really?'

'Disappointment. And anger, in case you were wondering.'

'That's two feelings.'

'I thought you weren't going to answer back.'

'*I* don't think you're anything made flesh. I think you're just a horrible little boy.'

'A horrible little boy who just saved your life.'

'What's he angry about, your God?'

'He's not my God. He's angry and disappointed because he sent mankind his only son and they hanged him.'

'You can see his point, I suppose.'

On the battlefield the next crisis was approaching, but this time for the Redeemers. Between Conn's blistering violence driving the Swiss and their allies forward as he moved up and down the line and Fauconberg, some fifty yards behind, disposing and allocating, assigning and putting things right, the Redeemer line began to buckle and also to twist ever more quickly against the clock so that now the front moved slantwise across the field. But though they came close they did not break. Not yet, at any rate, but without the ten thousand Redeemers who had failed to turn up, it was only a question of time. What had become of the missing Redeemers? They were still lost. Not by much, a couple of miles, but the battle-field was only the size of four of the larger fields the locals used for wheat. And the hideous wind that had worked so wonderfully to favour the Redeemers earlier now worked against them. The screams of orders and agony, of anger and effort, made for a hefty din. Only a couple of miles away, the arriving Redeemers would normally have followed the sound and that was what they did. But the wind had thrown the noise to the east and following the sound took them away from and not towards the fight. Now the line of battle had been turned so that the Redeemers were being pushed back towards the woods, where the thickly planted trees and the razor briars formed a barrier through which only the first few hundred men would be able to escape. For the rest it might as well have been a wall of brick.

But battles breathe out as well as in. In its sixth hour some-thing in the Swiss began to fade, something in the Redeemers to emerge. In the continuous circulation of fighting men, no one should fight for more than half an hour. But change destroys the rhythm of the side that's fighting well, brings, perhaps, new impetus to the soldiers doing badly. Conn had fought too long; at Fauconberg's insistence he needed a longer rest, a drink and something to eat. Conn removed his helmet and, so that he could drink, the metal gorge that pro-tected his throat. Three of his friends around him, Cosmo Materazzi, Otis Manfredi and Valentine Sforza, did the same. The legend afterwards was that the Redeemer marksmen in the trees had waited for this chance for hours. But legends are often wrong, or only partly right. There was nothing aimed at Conn by cunning assassins, it was just bad luck, a gust of a few haphazard arrows, not even ten. But three of them took Cosmo in the face, one hit Otis in the neck and another struck Valentine in the back of the head. Friends of a lifetime were gone inside a minute.

Where Conn had shone before, he now burned. Rage stoked his talent and focused it to break, blow, smash and maim so that everywhere he went the Redeemer line fell back and sent the message of strain like weakening magic along the line, which now lost its rhythm for a second time and began to fail again, shifting back towards the woods and murderous defeat.

Then, desperate and panic-stricken, the ten thousand missing Redeemers, under the command of Holy Gaffer Jude Stylites, stumbled upon the fight that was almost lost and found themselves as if by means of the most cunning intelligence not just on the battlefield but at exactly the right place at exactly the right time to save the day. What Stylites had been sensibly trying to do was to approach the Redeemers who'd been fighting all day long from the rear, at a point where his men could be used as replacements for the exhausted men in the front line. Instead, their run of accidents and the anti-clockwise turn of the battle line brought them into the side of the Swiss line, forcing it to bend into an L-shape to prevent being taken from behind. Now the pressure was on the Swiss and slowly the Redeemers began to push back from the line of trees and the certainty of defeat.

Then, late in the afternoon, after whatever it is that controls a battlefield moved first with one side and then the other, the Swiss line broke – a man slipped, perhaps, and took down his neighbour as he fell and he in turn hampered another. Perhaps a Redeemer, with one late surge of strength, pushed into this gap and others, seeing the space opening, followed – and so from one slip a battle was lost, a war, a country, the lives of millions. Or perhaps it was that the confused arrival of the Redeemers' reserve was just too much for the tired Swiss and that from the moment they stumbled into the exact weak point of the Axis the matter was decided.

Whatever the cause, in minutes the Axis line crumbled and the few who ran became the many – and seeing them run, the many became the mass. Like a great building whose foundations had slowly been demolished underground, the collapse was great and sudden. Face to face, armour to armour, side by side, it's not easy to kill an enemy. Perhaps only three or four thousand died in the seven hours of battle that preceded the collapse. Now was when the slaughter began.

20

The Swiss and their allies had only two lines of escape: up the slope to the side from where they'd attacked or back and down a muddy slope into a meadow contained in the meander of a river not much more than ten foot wide, but moving fast for being swollen by mountain rain. This glorified stream might just as well have been the Mississippi. Men in armour jumped into its waters and were dragged under by the weight. The exhausted ordinary soldiers in padded jackets struggled across the stream getting in each other's way. Slipping and falling, they found the water soaked into the hand-painted mix of cotton and metal discs, which then pulled them under too. Meanwhile, the Redeemers were following at their heels, slicing and cutting and killing. Men they'd fought all day and could not harm were now easier to kill than herds in a knacker's yard. From the top of the forty-foot slope the Redeemer archers formed a line and now, invulnerable, loosed ten a minute into the thousands packed in a space no bigger than a paddock, trapped not just against the almost impossible-to-cross stream but against each other as more and more panicked and terrified running men added to the crushing press.

Those who'd seen what was happening and looked for escape elsewhere did no better. Most ran further along the river, heading for the bridge at Glane, but were easily caught by the mounted infantry of the Redeemers. Seeing they weren't going to make the crossing, many tried to swim for it. But here the swollen stream was even deeper and they drowned again in their thousands. Realizing there was no escape across the river, those who turned back were slaughtered on the banks. Perhaps a thousand made it to the bridge and safely across. They would have died once the Redeemers made it over the bridge but they were stopped. Someone with foresight set the bridge alight as soon as they saw the Redeemers coming. It was a cold decision because a thousand men were still trying to cross when it began to burn. Fire in front and Redeemers behind, the terrified men had no choice but to try, and fail, to swim across this deepest part of the river. It was claimed that some survived because the numbers of the drowned packed into the river were so great they were able to walk across the bodies to escape.

Thousands more had run away along the uplands to the rear of the position where they had begun the day, discarding armour as they went. The mounted Redeemers followed them – they were as vulnerable as little boys. Now the sky had cleared and the brightest of moons began to rise and take away what help the dark could bring. When the sun came up at six the dead lay everywhere, for ten miles from the battle and for six miles wide. More than a hundred of the great and the good were captured but not for ransom or as useful hostages. Santos Hall established first who they were and what degree of power they held and then executed them. For the second time in little more than a year the Redeemers had destroyed a ruling class inside a single day – and also finished most of what they'd started in the destruction of the Materazzi at Silbury Hill. But Conn lived, even if Fauconberg had needed to practically drag him onto a horse to make his getaway. 'There's nothing you can do except survive,' the old man had shouted at him. 'Living is the best revenge.'

Mostly heroes die, mostly heroes fail. The darkest hour is

not before dawn and nor does every cloud have a silver lining. Life is not a lottery: in a lottery, finally, there is a winner. But it is also the case that no news is ever as good or as bad as it first seems. In this instance, the hideous defeat at Bex did have a silver lining and more than that. What kind of disaster it was – and for those involved it was certainly that – depended very much on who you were. For Artemisia Halicarnassus and Thomas Cale it worked out very well. Within sixteen hours it became clear there were only some two thousand survivors from the Swiss and their allies, half of whom had made it over the Glane bridge before it was set alight. But the survivors were very far from safe – mostly unarmed and unarmoured, they were still a long way from the protection of the Schallenberg Pass some eighty miles away. The burnt bridge had slowed their pursuers but not stopped them. In a matter of hours the Redeemers were over the stream and intent on finishing what they'd started.

But it was precisely on this kind of rearguard action that Artemisia had cut her teeth. Adding to her own guerrilla militia of three hundred with a small number of escapees still able to fight – less than two hundred – she divided her forces with Cale, who made it clear he expected not to take orders but to do as he saw fit; she made it equally clear that he would not.

'Do as I say or you can bugger off back to Leeds. I know what I'm doing and these are my men.'

Cale thought about this.

'There's no need,' he said at last, 'to use such bad language.'

The ground between Bex and the Schallenberg Pass was always rising and the roads passed through any number of woods and over small hills. From these positions, always retreating slowly and avoiding a direct fight, Artemisia plagued the Redeemers as they began to catch the exhausted and often wounded Swiss with volleys of arrows and individual snipers in an endless hit and run. While sacrifice and martyrdom were enthusiastically pursued by the Redeemers in general, even they had a limited taste for being struck by someone they couldn't even see in pursuit of the scraggy remnants of a defeated army. They backed off and contented themselves with murdering the occasional straggler. In short order they lost their enthusiasm even for this when Artemisia started setting traps for them using carefully placed men pretending to be wounded in places where the Redeemers could be easily ambushed. Over the following two days, nearly fifteen hundred men made it back to the Schallenberg Pass and safety. Among them were Conn Materazzi and Little Fauconberg.

21

The aftermath of any disaster usually demands two things: first, the person responsible for the disaster must be named, shamed and punished in the most elaborate manner possible; second, though less important, it was highly desirable to find someone who demonstrated, through their personal courage, intelligence and skill, that the dreadful disaster could and should have been averted. In the case of the disaster at Bex, that there wasn't anyone to blame or anyone particularly to praise was neither here nor there. Already, by virtue of his great experience of triumph and disaster, Little Fauconberg was alert to the likelihood of retribution and some three days after the miserable remnants of the Swiss army returned to Spanish Leeds, Fauconberg realized the way things were going and sent a message to Conn Materazzi that he might do well to make himself scarce. He took his own advice and by nightfall was well on his way towards a little-known pass over the mountains that he had marked out for this purpose as soon as he was appointed second-in-command.

But by then Conn had already been arrested and charged with misfeasance in the face of the enemy and failure to strive. In short, he was accused of not winning a battle, a crime of which he was unquestionably guilty. The rage of the King and the people did not permit any great amount of time to pass and Conn's trial was ordered to take place in the Commons on the following Wednesday. Just as Conn was being unjustifiably blamed, Cale found himself being unjustifiably praised, much to the fury of Artemisia Halicarnassus.

All the credit for heroically saving the remnants of the army and seeing them safely to the Schallenberg Pass had been given to Cale: the idea that the only soldier who'd shown the necessary bravery and skill was a woman was not just unacceptable in a crude sense but impossible to grasp.

'There's no point blaming me,' said Cale.

'Why not?'

This was hard to answer. He entirely understood her anger but, as he unwisely pointed out, that was just the way things were. 'There's no point whining about it.'

'Take that back!'

'All right. Whining will make an enormous difference.'

'I'm not whining. I deserve the credit.'

'I agree. You deserve the credit for saving fifteen hundred men. Absolutely.'

'What do you mean?'

'I don't *mean* anything.'

'Yes, you do. What are you driving at?'

'All right. You deserve the credit for saving fifteen hundred men. They're giving it to me and I don't deserve it – but what they're really saying is that whoever's responsible for that – which is you – would have beaten the Redeemers.'

'And you're saying that I couldn't.'

'Yes.'

'How do you know?'

'Conn did everything right. I couldn't have done it better.'

'So of course that's proof enough. No one could do better than you.'

'I didn't say that.'

'You didn't have to.'

'I admire you.'

'Not as much as you admire yourself.'

'That would be asking a lot,' he said, smiling.

'I can see right through you, don't worry. You're not joking, I know.'

'You could run that battle a hundred times and Conn would have won fifty of them. What the people are screaming is that whoever saved the fifteen hundred – you – would have won the battle. That's credit you don't deserve, even if it's been given to someone who deserves it less.'

'You, you mean?'

'Yes.'

'Say it.'

'I don't deserve the credit. You do.'

She said nothing for a moment.

In the meantime another charge had been added to the accusations levelled against Conn: that he had, in a manner cowardly and craven, set fire to the bridge at Glane and, in order to save his own treacherous skin, condemned thousands to die at the hands of the Redeemers. Of all the counts against him this was the most damaging. It was also the most unfair. Conn hadn't been within five miles of the bridge and couldn't, therefore, have set fire to it. But even if he had, it had been a necessary act. The stranded men killed on the left bank would have made it over and survived only to be chased down and killed once the Redeemers crossed to the right behind them. Those already on the right bank survived only because someone took the hard decision to burn the bridge. The person who had set fire to the bridge, disguised by means of an abandoned helmet, was Thomas Cale.

Perhaps no historical subject has been written about so thoroughly as the rise of the Fifth Reich under Alois Huttler. The failure to explain how a man of little education, less intelligence and no obvious talent except for windy inspirational speeches about his country's manifest destiny to rule the world could come as close as any man in history to achieving this end is obvious. No one knows how he managed the rise from imprisonment for aggressive begging to ruling the lives of millions across vast territories and bringing a level of destruction to the world never seen before in human history. No historian will conclude at the end of a book that there is no explanation for the things he describes. In the case of Alois there is none. That it happened is all the reason that will ever be uncovered. It is a good deal easier to explain satisfactorily how, by the end of the week following the disaster at Bex, Thomas Cale, boy lunatic, had become the second most important military commander in the Swiss Alliance.

Because of his new-found heroic status he had been invited to attend the conference to discuss what to do now that the Redeemers had sealed up Switzerland from the rear and had only to cross the Mississippi to crush Spanish Leeds in a vice. There was no army left to stop them and no one left alive to lead it even if there had been. There were a fair number of speeches given indignantly making it clear that the speakers had never been in favour of attacking the Redeemers in such a disastrous fashion, although solid evidence of their stand was somehow lacking. The only person who'd clearly stood out against the action, Artemisia, went unmentioned, although she had without any fuss been allowed back in to attend the conference.

Before she attended Vipond had tried to mark her card as well as Cale's.

'Whatever you say at the conference you won't say "I told you so", will you?'

'Why shouldn't I?' said Artemisia.

'She won't say it,' said Cale.

'I will.'

Cale looked at her. 'She won't say it.'

It was not an order, or even a demand. Indeed it was hard

to say what it was – a laying out of an inevitable fact, perhaps. With a sigh, she less than gracefully accepted the advice.

At the conference itself Cale made a point of saying nothing at first in order to let the accusations and hand-wringing go on for long enough for them to demoralize everyone in the room. Then the lamentations began.

'How long before they come?' asked the King. It was a morose Supreme Leader of the Allied Forces who replied.

'They'll take all summer to build the boats needed to come across the Mississippi. The autumn floods will make the river treacherous and the winter ice more treacherous still. It will be late spring next year.'

'Can we rebuild an army in seven months and hold them at the river?' asked the King.

It was the question, or something like it, that Cale had been waiting for.

'No, you can't, Your Majesty,' he said, and stood up. Thin and pale in his elegant black cassock (he was comfortable in them after all the years he'd worn them, although his tailor designed the cut more elegantly and made it out of the softest Sertsey wool), Cale looked like something out of a fairy story to frighten intelligent children. The King, affronted, turned his hand aside and an explanation was given in whispers as to who this was and his (largely undeserved) heroic status.

'You were a Redeemer, I understand.'

'I was brought up as one,' said Cale. 'But I was never one of them.' There was more whispering in the King's ear.

'Is this true that you commanded a Redeemer army?'

'Yes.'

'It seems unlikely – you're very young.'

'I'm a very remarkable person, Your Majesty.'

'Are you?'

'Yes. I destroyed the Folk and after I destroyed the Folk I

238

came back to Chartres and destroyed the Laconic army at the Golan. You had no one to rival me even before Bex. Now I'm all there is.'

'You're very boastful.'

'I'm not boasting, Your Majesty, I'm simply telling you the truth.'

'Are you telling us you can hold the Redeemers at the Mississippi?'

'No. It can't be done. You couldn't have stopped them there even with an army and now you don't even have an army.'

There was an outcry at this: that the Swiss and their allies would raise thousands to their cause, that you could take their land but you could never take their freedom, that the people would fight them in the woods and on the plains and in the streets, that they would never give in, and so on. Zog, a very much more sober person than he'd been only a week before, signalled them to stop.

'Are you saying that we must lose?'

'I'm saying that you can win.'

'With no army?'

'I'll give you a new army.'

'That's very good of you.'

'Goodness has nothing to do with it.'

'How can you do this?'

'If you will see me tomorrow in private I'll show Your Majesty.'

It's been said that a confidence trickster gets his name not by gaining the confidence of those he tricks, but by giving them some of his own. The truth was very simple: they were utterly lost and now one person was claiming he could find them again. In such circumstances his implausibility was a sign in his favour: only something unbelievably strange could save them.

*

239

At Bex, the Redeemers now had the appalling job of burying the thirty thousand they'd killed there. It was a week after the battle itself and the two days of intense cold directly following the fight had given way, as it often did in that part of the world, to a warm spell. The bodies that stank the worst were those who had died from internal injuries caused by the heft of the poleaxes. The blood stayed inside and rotted and when the Redeemers moved the bodies the blood poured out of the noses and mouths. Then it got hotter still and the bodies began to bloat, so big that on the cheaper armour the rivets burst open with an enormous SNAP! Then the bodies went blue and then black and the skin peeled and those who had to burn them thought they'd never get the smell out of the backs of their throats.

Most news is never as bad or as good as it first seems. This was certainly true of the great Redeemer victory at Bex. Redeemer General Gil was impressed by the skill with which the Office of the Propagation of the Faith had managed to pull off the contradiction involved in praising the courage, strength and sacrifice of the Redeemer army while also suggesting that God had ensured victory was inevitable. As Gil knew from his many protégés who had been in the fight at Bex, it had been a damned close-run thing. The bad news was that Cale had been seen by a handful of Redeemers but he hadn't heard of it early enough to quarantine them and stop the news from spreading.

'Tell me exactly what you saw – don't add anything. You understand?'

'Yes, Redeemer General.'

He'd decided to see the snipers who'd stumbled into Cale in the woods one by one, starting with the sergeant.

'Go on.'

'He was seven foot tall and a great light shone from his

face. Around his head was a halo of red fire and the mother of the Hanged Redeemer was next to him all in blue and with seven stars at her forehead and she was weeping tears of sorrow for our glorious dead. And there were two angels holding arrows of fire.'

'And did they have halos as well?'

'I don't think so, Redeemer General.'

For half an hour he tried to get some sense out of the sergeant but someone who believed Cale was seven-foot tall and that his face shone with anything but suspicion and loathing was clearly not going to be of much help. After interrogating two more of the group, whose accounts were even more ridiculous, he gave up.

He was now faced with two questions. Was this just an excess of holy glee, or had they really seen Cale? If so, what did it mean? Why was he skulking in the woods and not leading troops in the battle? It didn't even solve the problem of what had happened to Cale after the Two Trevors had been killed. Gil had hoped he'd died of his injuries – surely the Trevors must have got in at least one blow before he killed them? They were supposed to be the best murderers in the Four Quarters and Cale was supposed to be sick. Maybe Cale was dead, in which case the stories about him appearing at the battle were even more worrying. Or were they? Was it better to have him alive and without power or dead and turning up seven-foot tall and with a halo, creating God-knows-what havoc among the unwary faithful? If this seems unusually sceptical for a man of deep spiritual beliefs in the One True Faith, the fact of the matter was that Gil was changing in his old age. As long as miracles and visions concerned people or things he hadn't experienced directly he'd been ready to accept them without question. But the reality of his personal experience of Cale and the progressively more nonsensical stories about him increasingly stuck in his throat. He had known Cale since he was a smelly little boy, had trained him day after day under Bosco's instructions, had seen him wet himself with fear after a fight before the blow on the head gave him that odd talent no one could match. It was the work of God, said Bosco. But it was just too hard for Gil to think of Cale as someone chosen by the Lord to bring about the end of everything. In his heart, Gil thought of him as a boy he didn't like. What Gil did not realize, or want to realize, was that such realism was poisoning his faith. Not to believe in Cale was not to believe in Bosco: not to believe in Bosco was not to believe in the need for the end of the world. To acknowledge this was to question his central place in bringing it about. Better not to go there. But it was easier not done than not thought about.

The more immediate problem was what, if anything, to tell Bosco. Tell him about this miraculous drivel and he'd be certain to be inspired. Not tell him and if he found out there would be trouble. He decided not to take the risk and several hours later he was with Pope Bosco and coming to the conclusion of his report on the unusual sighting of Thomas Cale.

'Do you believe them?' said Bosco when Gil had finished. Answering this was tricky. Hedge his reply with thoughtful doubt and perhaps he might be able to shape Bosco's response. But he decided it was a test and he was right. But even telling Bosco what he wanted to hear presented problems. Too much enthusiasm would make him suspicious and Gil feared what might happen if Bosco cooled any more towards him.

'I remain reasonably sure, Your Holiness, that Cale has not grown by more than a foot and nor does his face shine with a holy light, but I believe they saw him. The question is: what was he doing there?'

Bosco looked at him but he, too, wanted the old trust between them to return. It was lonely and strange to stand on your own to bring about the promised end.

'Whatever he thinks his purpose is, he is about God's business whether he knows it or not. But while God may not have increased his height or blessed his face to illuminate the faithful he's given us a signal. We must attack Arnhemland now and not wait for another year as you advised. And we must increase the speed at which we send people to the west.'

The private meeting with the King that Cale attended the next day was not really private in the way he'd either expected or hoped. In fact, the King was no more used to privacy than Cale had been growing up in his dormitory of hundreds. Being on your own was a sin to the Redeemers and it might just as well have been the same for the King to all intents and purposes. Unlike Cale, he didn't seem either to mind or even to notice, unsurprising, perhaps, in a monarch who had a special appointee of considerable power, the Keeper of the King's Stool, to examine his excrement on a daily basis.

'You expect us to hand over our army to a boy?' said Bose Ikard.

'No,' said Cale. 'Keep your army. Do what you want with it. I'll create a New Model Army.'

'From where? There are no men.'

'Yes, there are.'

'Where?'

'The Campasinos.'

All were startled; not everyone laughed.

'Our peasants are the salt of the earth, of course. But they are not soldiers.'

'How do you know, Your Majesty?'

'Mind your manners,' said Bose Ikard. 'But as it happens

you're not the first to come up with this idea. Twenty years ago Count Bechstein created a company made up of bogtrotters and bumpkins and took them off to the wars against the Falange. I believe one or two who had the sense to desert in the first week might have survived.'

'I don't care.'

'But we do. It will not work.'

'Yes, it will. I'll show you how.'

With that he went to work with his designs and plans.

An hour later he finished: 'The simple fact is this: there's no other way. If I fail you can have the satisfaction of watching the Redeemers roast me in the town square. That is, Chancellor, if they don't start with you.' He turned to the King. 'All I need is money.'

They might have barely any soldiers but money was something they had in great quantities. After the slaughter at Bex, no one believed, not even Bose Ikard, that surrender was an alternative. It was clear that the Redeemers didn't recognize the notion of allowing their enemies to give in. Cale was right. There was no other way.

'You can do this in seven months? You seem very sure.'

'I told you, Your Majesty. I'm a remarkable person.'

If Cale was not as confident as he claimed, neither was he as desperate as he seemed to Ikard. He had been working on his New Model Army since he was ten years old (or nine – he was not sure about his date of birth). Since then, whenever he'd had a few minutes, sometimes only once a week or once a month, he'd draw a diagram or make a note about something of the working habits and the different kinds of tools the peasants around him were used to handling, the hammers and flails, the sharpened small shovel used by the Folk in the fight at Duffer's Drift. Even in the worst days at the Priory, when Kevin Meatyard was tormenting him, he'd watch the threshers and pickers at work in the fields with their scythes and hoes and wonder what might be made of them and their way of life. He'd worry about what to do if it worked or not when things became clear. But here was a chance to work on a plan of retreat as well – one which would likely involve heading over a mountain pass with as much cash as possible.

Zog was curious about Cale in the way he might have been curious about a monkey that could write better than a human being or a uniquely elegant dancing dog. He recognized that the boy was someone exceptional but it would never have occurred to him that he was anything but a wondrous freak of nature.

'Tell me more, dear boy, about your defeat of an entire army of Laconics. Tell me all about it . . . Tell me all about it . . . everything . . . the entire history.'

What Cale thought was that you might as well ask him to tell the history of a storm. He was, of course, about to start when Bose Ikard interrupted.

'I'm afraid that Your Majesty has an important meeting with the Ambassador for the Hanse.'

'Oh. Another time, perhaps,' he said to Cale. 'Most interesting.' Then he was on his way out. Cale himself had an appointment too. The next day he was required to give evidence at Conn Materazzi's trial, to which the Swiss had devoted almost an entire afternoon. The appointment was to make it clear to Cale what his evidence would be.

'You are the most notorious traitor that ever lived!'

The House of Malls would comfortably seat four hundred, ranged in banks on three sides. Today there were eight hundred, with thousands waiting outside for news. On the fourth side was a judge's bench occupied that day by Justice Popham, a man who could be relied upon to engineer the correct verdict. Next to it, slightly to one side, was a prisoner's dock, in which stood an unimpressed Conn Materazzi who looked disdainfully at the prosecuting attorney, Sir Edward Coke, the man who had just shouted at him.

'You can say it, Sir Edward,' replied Conn, 'but you cannot prove it.'

'By God, I will!' said Coke, who looked like a bull without a neck, all foul temper and belligerence.

'How do you plead?' asked Judge Popham.

'Not guilty.'

'Ha!' shouted Coke. 'You are the absolutist traitor there ever was.'

Conn turned his hand slightly, as if he had to swat away a horsefly.

'It does not become a gentleman to insult me in this way. Though I take comfort from your bad manners – it is all you *can* do.'

'So I see I've angered you.'

'Not at all,' said Conn. 'Why would I be angry? I haven't yet heard one word against me that can be proved.'

'Didn't Fauconberg run away over the mountains because he had betrayed us at Bex? And didn't that tergiversating sneak also plan to kill the King and his children?' He sniffed loudly as if it were all too much. 'Those poor babies who never gave offence to anyone.'

'If Lord Fauconberg is a traitor what's that got to do with me?'

'Everything he did, you viper, was at your instigation!'

At this there was a huge boiling over in the crowd. TRAITOR! MURDERER! HEAR! HEAR! HEAR! CONFESS! THE BABIES! THE POOR BABIES! Popham let them fulminate. He wanted Conn to get the point that his refusal to play the role of abject penitent, as he'd been told to, was doing him no good. 'Silence in the court,' he said. The trouble with trying to bribe Conn to go along with his part was that Popham knew perfectly well that sacrificing a goat required that the goat understood that he was *it* no matter what he said or did not say.

Coke, now red in the face with fury, waved a piece of paper in the air. 'This is a letter found hidden in a secret drawer in the house of that renegade Fauconberg. On it he states clearly that the vile Pope Bosco intended to pay six hundred thousand dollars to Conn Materazzi and that he would give Fauconberg two hundred thousand to assist him in losing the battle.' He waved the paper once more and then brought it close to read with an expression on his face as if someone had used it to wipe their arse. 'It says here, "Conn Materazzi would never let me alone".' He turned to the clerk. 'Read that line again.' Startled, the recording clerk blushed bright red. 'Get a bloody move on, man!' shouted Coke.

'"Conn Materazzi would never let me alone."'

Coke looked around the room, nodding his head in grim triumph. SHAME! called out the crowd. SHAME! TRAITOR!

'Is this,' shouted Conn, above the noise, 'is this ... is this all the evidence you can bring against me? A more suspicious person than I might suggest that Sir Edward can recite this nonsense so well, because it was he that wrote it.'

'You are an odious fellow. I lack the words to express your viperous treason.'

'Indeed you do lack works, Sir Edward – you've said the same thing half a dozen times.'

Coke stared, eyes bulging with a spasm of fury.

'You are the most hated man in Switzerland!'

'As to that honour, Sir Edward, there isn't a gnat's wing between you and me.' From one side of the court, those who knew Coke well and therefore loathed him, there was laughter.

'If Fauconberg was a traitor,' said Conn (although he knew he was not), 'I knew nothing about it. I trusted him in the same way that the King and his counsellors trusted him when they, not me, appointed him as my second-in-command.'

'You are the most vile traitor that ever lived.'

'So you keep saying, Sir Edward, but where's your proof? The law states there must be two witnesses to treason. You don't even have one.'

An enormous bilious smile from Coke, that made him look like a smirking toad.

'You have read the law, Conn Materazzi, but you don't understand it.'

Popham cleared his throat. 'The law you speak of that used to require two witnesses in cases of treason has been deemed to be inconvenient. On Monday another law was passed to repeal it.'

Perhaps in the thrill of answering his accusers Conn had forgotten that the verdict was always certain. If so, he now remembered. But he was rattled all the same.

'I don't know how you conceive the law,' he said quietly.

'We don't *conceive* the law, Conn Materazzi,' boasted a triumphant Coke, 'we *know* the law.'

During the next two hours there was more evidence produced as assorted liars, falsifiers, inventors, actors and bullshitters were brought in to testify to the traitorous remarks before the fight and traitorous tactics during it that proved beyond question that Conn had deliberately lost the battle. 'I never saw the like case,' declaimed Coke, 'and I hope I shall never see the like again.' In the last hour they moved on to the second charge: that Conn had set fire to the bridge at Glane to preserve his own life at the cost of thousands of his men. Six witnesses were called who swore they had seen him, without his helmet, light the fire himself. The seventh witness was Thomas Cale. It had been made clear to him that the golden opinions he had won had made his evidence particularly valuable and that telling the court what he had seen of Conn's actions during the battle, and his subsequent setting fire to the bridge over the river was essential if those who still wavered over the granting of money towards his New Model Army were to be persuaded as to the true depth of his devotion to the interests of the state.

'Your name.'

'Thomas Cale.'

'Put your right hand on the Good Book and repeat after me: "I swear that what I am about to say is the truth, the whole truth and nothing but the truth."'

'It is.'

'You have to say it.'

'What?'

'You have to repeat the words.'

A pause.

'I swear that what I am about to say is the truth, the whole truth and nothing but the truth.'

'So help me God.'

'So help me God.'

By now he was barely audible.

Just as they had rehearsed it the day before, Coke fed Cale the questions and Cale fed back the answers as if they were a conjuror and his amazing dancing bear passing a ball to each other. The questions and answers were designed to demonstrate one thing: that, youthful as he was, Thomas Cale was an experienced soldier, utterly versed in the battle tactics of the Redeemers. He was also asked in detail to set out his heroic and skilful actions in saving the lives of fifteen hundred Swiss soldiers and their noble allies so miserably betrayed by Conn Materazzi.

'At one point, Mr Cale, you were able to observe the battle from a tree in the nearby woods?'

'Yes.'

'Did this give you a complete view of the battle?'

'I don't know about complete – but as good as you were likely to get.'

Coke stared at Cale. This was not the straightforward line they'd agreed.

'Why was someone of your experience not involved directly?'

'It was prevented.'

'By the defendant?'

'I don't know.'

Coke stared at him. Yet again the bear was not returning the ball as he'd been taught.

'Is it not the case,' said Coke, offering him an opportunity to do better, 'that Sir Harry Beauchamp, at Conn Materazzi's instruction, told you not to involve yourself in the battle directly, on pain of death?'

'He told me to stay out of it or suffer the consequence – yes. But he didn't mention anyone by name.'

'But it was what you understood?'

This was too much, even for Popham. The forms might be bent but they could not be broken quite so grossly.

'Sir Edward, I realize that you speak out of zeal for your duty and horror at the defendant's crimes – but you must not lead the witness to repeat hearsay, particularly when there was none to repeat.'

That Coke lacked a neck seemed to be confirmed by his habit of turning his whole body to look at whoever spoke to him, giving him the look of a statue of hideous aspect. The observant would have noticed a small muscle twitching on his right temple. *If he was a bomb*, thought Hooke, watching from the back of the court, *he'd be ready to explode*.

'My apologies to the court.' He turned back to Cale, the small muscle still twitching.

'Is it true that at the Battle of Silbury Hill you saved the life of the defendant?'

'Yes.'

'Clear proof, ladies and gentlemen of the jury, that the witness bears him no ill will. Is that so?'

'I don't understand.'

'Really?'

'No.'

'Do you,' said Coke, the muscle now twitching on his left temple, 'bear the defendant any ill will?'

'No.'

'Did you put your own life at risk when saving him?'

'Yes.'

'Has he ever thanked you for this most courageous act?'

'I can't remember, to be honest.'

'Does this make you angry?'

'No.'

'Why not, Mr Cale? I think most of us would be angry at such wretched ingratitude.'

'The ingratitude of princes is a proverb, isn't it?'

'I have never found princes of any kind in this country to be ungrateful, but I believe it of Conn Materazzi.'

'Well, that was why I wasn't angry. I didn't expect it.'

For the first time since he'd come into court, Cale looked directly at Conn. What passed passed between them was odd stuff.

'Would you tell us,' said Coke, 'what was your estimation of the conduct of the battle from your unique viewpoint?'

'Do you mean from the tree or based on my experience?'

'Both, Mr Cale, both.'

'It was a good three hours into the battle, I'd say, maybe more. It looked like it could go either way.'

'Did you see the defendant on the field?'

'For a while. It was at a distance, though.'

'You formed an opinion, based,' he turned back to the jury, 'based on your *considerable experience*, as to his conduct of that tragic engagement?'

There was a pause as if Cale was thinking something over. 'Yes.'

The muscles in Coke's forehead stopped twitching.

'And what was that considered opinion?'

If he was going to be true to his oath, something he had no intention of doing, Cale should have said that Conn had demonstrated outstanding personal and tactical courage. He could not have done better himself – or even as well. Mind you, he might have added he would never have fought the battle in the first place. But no one wanted to hear that. The simple truth – the facts-as-they-stood kind of truth, as opposed to the whole-and-nothing-but truth – was that Conn was a dead man. Defending him because it was the honest thing to do was idle and futile.

Cale genuinely believed he was the only person who could stop Bosco and that without his New Model Army everyone in the city, possibly including Cale, would be dead inside twelve months. It was not just idle and futile to defend Conn, it was wrong. So it was hard for him to explain why he could not bring himself to lie directly in order to ensure a good thing was done as opposed to beating about the bush and risking that good thing. He realized the stupidity of what he was doing and, given a few minutes to think about it, he would have demonstrated to himself that risking the lives of millions to save the life of a shit-bag like Conn Materazzi, however admirably he had behaved at Bex, was wicked, evil, wrong and, worse than all of this, bad for Thomas Cale.

'He had done all the things that any commander in such a battle might have considered, given the circumstances. Although he might have considered other actions.'

'Actions that would have been more effective – that's what you're saying?'

'More effective?'

'Yes – you're saying he could probably have chosen to behave otherwise and so win the battle.'

A pause.

'Um. Yes.'

'Mr Cale,' interrupted Justice Popham. 'We come to the heart of the matter here. Are you saying that if the accused had acted differently then defeat would have been averted and victory achieved?'

'I can definitely say that,' said Cale, relieved. 'Yes. Had he acted differently the battle might have been won.'

'I want . . .' What Coke wanted was to get a plain assertion, as had been agreed, that Cale would state unequivocally that Conn had deliberately lost the battle. Popham realized that, for whatever reason, the creature in the witness box had changed his mind, and that by trying to wring an assertion of Conn's guilt out of Cale, Coke was making things look bad. There were plenty of others to state Conn had lost deliberately and that he had personally set fire to the bridge. This was a horse that wouldn't run.

'I think we've troubled the witness long enough.'

'One more question,' demanded Coke, temple muscles twitching again, and asked it before permission was refused. 'Did you witness Conn Materazzi setting fire to the bridge over the River Gar?'

'No. I wasn't anywhere near it.'

22

Along the banks of the River Imprevu one of its greatest
oaks had fallen into the river, its roots undermined by the
current created by the rocks that had fallen a few months
earlier from the bridge above. A hazard to shipping, the local
mayor had ordered the branches to be stripped as far as possible so that it could be hauled to lie flush with the bank.
They were lucky in that once the branches had been cut from
the tree above the water a flash surge of water from rain in
the mountains pushed it over so that the other side could
also have its branches removed. Unfortunately, when they
were almost finished, a second surge jerked it free of its temporary moorings and flushed the great trunk down the river
towards the Mississippi where it would now become someone else's problem.

That night, after the trial, IdrisPukke cooked dinner, a morose
affair. The guests consisted of Cale, Artemisia, Vague Henri,
Kleist and Cadbury.

'Is Vipond angry with me?' asked Cale.

'Would you blame him?' said Cadbury. 'Isn't Conn his
great nephew or something?' He looked at IdrisPukke, taunt-
ing. 'He's even related to you, isn't he? How's that work?'

IdrisPukke ignored him. 'Vipond isn't a hypocrite. He
understands why you felt obliged to give evidence. But he *is*
puzzled.'

'Include the rest of us,' said Vague Henri. 'I never saw
anything so stupid in my entire life.'

Kleist said nothing. He hardly seemed to be in the room at all.

'God,' said Artemisia, clearly shocked by her lover's behaviour, 'has a particular punishment for perjurers.' It was a sign of her failing affection for Cale that this was a harsher way of construing the events of the day than was strictly fair. Why were her affections failing and so suddenly? Why do they ever? Perhaps she had been impressed by Conn's lonely courage and compared him, as they stood opposite one another, to Cale, so unblond, so strange and so lacking in nobility or grace.

'He sends them to bed without any pudding?' offered Cale.

'No.'

'I didn't think so. God always has something nasty lying in wait for naughty boys.'

'He's got a devil put aside to torment you through all eternity by shoving a red hot poker up your bottom.' This was from Vague Henri.

'Sorry,' said Cale. 'He'll have to go to the back of the queue. Besides, the devil they've put aside for me for poisoning wells is supposed to shove a pipe down my throat to fill my stomach full of shit-water. They'll just cancel each other out.'

'Going under oath isn't a joke. He's going to die because of you.'

'The only reason he's alive to be sentenced to death is because of me – so we're even.'

'I think we should all calm down,' said IdrisPukke. 'Wine, anyone?'

No one seemed interested in wine so he started handing out what looked like small crackers wrapped into a small thumb-sized parcel. There was one each and they all stared unenthusiastically at the hard and unappetizing pastries.

'You're not supposed to eat them, just break them open. I've decided to publish a short collection of my ideas carefully reduced to their essence in one sentence. It's to be called *The Maxims of IdrisPukke*. I thought these would amuse you.' He gestured them to break them open. 'Now read them out: Cadbury.'

Cadbury, who was becoming longsighted, had to hold the small roll of paper at some distance.

'It says nothing against the ripeness of a man's soul if it has a few worms.'

Cadbury suspected, wrongly as it happened, that this particular maxim was supposed to be about him.

IdrisPukke realized his attempt to lighten the mood of the evening had started badly. He gestured to Artemisia. She cracked open the pastry.

'I would believe only in a god who knows how to dance.'

She smiled weakly but as she grasped what he was driving at her smile broadened a little.

IdrisPukke's heart sank – but ploughed on as if his plan wasn't deflating like a child's balloon. It was Vague Henri's turn.

'To act in the world is the only way to understand it. In this life it is given only to God and his angels and poets to be lookers-on.'

Like Cadbury, Vague Henri wondered if IdrisPukke had chosen this especially for him. Was he accusing him of something?

Next it was Kleist, who crumbled the pastry with unnecessary force in the palm of one hand.

'To live is to suffer, to survive is to find some meaning in the suffering.'

Then it was Cale's turn. What he read out seemed only to confirm that IdrisPukke was smugly having a laugh at their expense.

'Whoever battles with monsters had better see that it does not turn him into a monster. If you gaze long enough into the abyss, the abyss will start to gaze back into you.'

A silence followed. 'How about you?' said Cale. Idris Pukke's heart sank just a little – having heard the others he knew the only saying that was left. He crumbled the pastry and read it out.

'If there exist men whose ridiculous side has never been seen it is because it has never been properly looked for.'

'Spot on,' said Cadbury but he still wanted his own back for what he took to be the criticism of the word-pastry.

'So, Idris Pukke, isn't the unfortunate Conn Materazzi a relative of yours, then?' From that day on Cadbury always mockingly referred to him as 'the unfortunate Conn Materazzi.'

'Of some kind – half a grand-nephew, I suppose. Couldn't abide him myself. Though, to be fair, he was coming along pretty well.'

'So explain why Vipond isn't sweating for revenge,' said Cadbury. 'I thought the Materazzi were mad for their relations.'

'My brother merely understands the impossible position Cale found himself in. Obviously he likes Conn and worked hard to support him – not with much gratitude, it has to be said, though there were other reasons for that. But he is neither a fool nor a hypocrite nor lacking in affection. He's obliged for obvious reasons not to be seen to have anything to do with Cale, but he knows perfectly well that Conn has been a dead man since the line broke at Bex. What puzzles him is that Thomas,' and here he looked pointedly at Cale, 'should go to so much trouble to give evidence that neither condemned him nor helped to save him, so that he annoyed all sides for no obvious benefit.'

Everyone looked at Cale.

'It was a mistake. All right? I knew I couldn't do Conn any good by telling the truth and that if I went along with the trial they'd give me what I need . . . what everyone needs. It was just that, when it came to it, I just lost it . . . for a bit. I had a worthless attack of the truth – I admit it.'

'Why was it worthless?' asked Artemisia.

'Because telling the truth just isn't going to do any good. There's one thing standing between all of us and a lot of blood and screaming – the New Model Army. There's nothing complicated about it.'

'So why didn't you give evidence *against* him?'

'Because as it turned out it was easier said than done, all right?'

'Let justice rule – even though the heavens fall.' IdrisPukke was lightly mocking Artemisia's idealism but Cale was now in a touchy mood and took it as some sort of criticism.

'Stick it back in your cracker, granddad.'

The dinner crumbled like one of IdrisPukke's aphorisms and everyone went home in a bad mood. Outside the evening air was heavy and not so much lukewarm as tepid, vaguely unpleasant as if it was atomized with the dead souls of the sons and husbands of Spanish Leeds gathered to attend the execution of Conn Materazzi in two days. Cale and Vague Henri and Kleist, whose growing misery made the other two feel worse, got back to their elegant townhouse. They were still slightly intimidated by living there, as if expecting someone important to come and chase them out for living above their station. They were used to other people's servants by now but not their own. It wasn't that they minded someone cooking and cleaning for them, it was more that the power of servants to creep up on them at unexpected moments reminded them of the unprivacy of the Sanctuary, with its horror of doors and its punishments for being caught on your own. Servants seemed to think they could just appear like Redeemers. They took it badly when Cale insisted they knocked before entering, something they regarded as evidence that he was common. He also made a point of thanking them when they did something for him, a habit that also revealed him as common. The proper thing for any employer to do was to treat them as if they did not exist.

Before they had rung the bell the door, unusually, was opened by Bechete, the over-valet.

'You have company, sir,' he said, as he gestured towards the *chambre des visiteurs*.

'Who?'

'They declined to give their names, sir and I would have refused them entry under normal circumstances. But I recognized them and I thought . . .' He allowed his sentence to trail off meaningfully.

'So who is it?'

'The Duchess of Memphis, sir, and I believe the wife of the Hanse Ambassador.'

'I'm going to bed,' said Kleist as if he'd heard nothing.

'Guess why she brought Riba?' said Vague Henri. 'Do you want me to come with you?'

'Yes. Arbell thinks I'll come on my own. You go first and be cold with them. I'll come in a bit. Leave the door open.'

Vague Henri almost knocked – but stopped himself and opened the door a little too energetically to compensate. Both Arbell and Riba stood up, a little startled, and he noticed the disappointment on Arbell's face. One up to Cale.

'This is late to be calling, ladies. What do you want?'

'Good manners, perhaps,' said Riba. But Vague Henri was no pushover.

'So it's a social visit? I'm surprised because there's been plenty of time to call on us before now. Obviously I was wrong to think you wanted something. I apologize.'

'Don't be like this, Henri. It's not worthy of you.'

'Yes, it is.'

'No. You're the kindest of people.' This time it was Arbell who spoke, but gently, not at all the proud Materazzienne.

'Not so much any more. I had time to think while I was waiting to be beaten to death — about kindness, I mean. You're a kind person, Riba, but you'd have let me die in Kitty the Hare's basement. Cale, now, he's not a kind person but he wouldn't do that, let me die, I mean. So I've gone off kindness. What do you want?'

Vague Henri sensed there was something strange about his own indignation, something that he couldn't put his finger on until much later. He was enjoying it.

Cale, carefully waiting the right time for a dramatic entrance, thought this was good enough.

'Why don't you tell him? I'd be interested to hear, too.'

Seeing her shook him. She was beautiful, certainly, with that touching bloom that had made such an impression on him when they'd met in the corridor. But there are fish-in-the-sea numbers of beautiful women in the world, many of them with that same flush of youth and power — but something about her touched him, always had and always would, like a malign twin of the lost chord, whose discovery the late Montagnards believed would generate a great and infinite calm. He wanted to be loved by her and to wring her neck in equal measure.

'We were all friends once,' said Riba, then turned to Vague Henri. 'Can we talk somewhere?' she said to him, so sadly and sweetly that, soft and sentimental as he was, he felt ashamed by his outburst. Cale nodded at him and he showed her out, but not before Riba had taken Cale's hand. 'Please be kind,' she said, and was gone.

*

The two of them stared at each other for some time.

'I suppose you . . .'

'Help him,' interrupted Arbell. 'Please.'

Agitated and trying to hide it, he went over to the elegant and uncomfortable chair and sat down.

'How?' he said. 'And why?'

'They think – the Swiss – that you're their saviour.'

'They wouldn't be the first to get that wrong.'

'They'll listen to you.'

'Not about this, they won't. It was a disaster and someone has to pay.'

'Would you have done any better?'

'I wouldn't have been there in the first place.'

'He doesn't deserve to die.'

'I can't tell you how little that's got to do with it.'

'Are you so full of hatred for me you'll let a good man die to get your own back?'

'I saved his life once already, probably the stupidest thing I've ever done, and if I wanted to pay you back, you treacherous bitch, you'd be dead already.'

'He doesn't deserve to die.'

'No.'

'So help him.'

'No.'

'Please.'

'No.'

It was a rare and intense pleasure to watch her suffer. He felt as if he could never have enough of it. And yet he also felt the dread of the loss of her, a horror that increased the greater his delight at watching her in pain. It was like scratching an itch that only made the pain worse even as it ecstatically soothed the very same.

She was shaking now and pale with fear.

'I know it was you who set fire to the bridge.'

This was a bit of a shock.

'Did I?'

'Yes.'

'And the proof?'

'I know you.'

'They'll need more than that.'

'And I know two witnesses who know you too.'

This was entirely possible; there were a lot of people at the bridge and maybe some of Artemisia's men had snitched.

'You've changed your tune,' said Cale. 'First it's tears, now it's threats.'

'It *was* you.'

'Nobody cares. Whoever set fire to the bridge was a god-damned hero. It just wasn't me. Even if someone confessed it wouldn't matter. Someone has to be to blame. Conn's the one. That's all. Now take your sniffles and menaces and shove off.'

He stood up and walked out, half of him pleased, the other half devastated. Outside in the hall, Riba and Vague Henri broke off the earnest conversation they were having. She moved towards him and started to speak.

'Shut up!' he said, and like a spoilt and angry child stormed off up the stairs to bed.

23

'What did Arbell Materazzi want?' asked Bose Ikard.

The meeting with Cale had started badly with another ill-tempered question. 'What the bloody hell did you think you were playing at?' This was in regard to Cale's peculiar performance at Conn Materazzi's trial. 'It was made perfectly clear to you what you were supposed to say.'

This was true enough.

'That was before I realized you had your witnesses queuing up to give the same story. I don't know why you didn't go the whole hog and pay them on their way down from the witness stand. I made the whole thing look plausible at least.'

This was entirely true. Cale's half-baked prevarication had indeed had the effect of drawing the sting, if only in part, of the Materazzi claim that the trial was a mere show. Conn's impressive performance at the trial had won him some sympathy and when at Riba's urging her husband had raised objections on behalf of the Hanse as to its fairness, Ikard had been able to point to Cale's testimony as proof that the evidence had not been fixed in advance. It had also benefit-ted Cale by giving the impression he was honest and had refused to do a bad turn to a fellow soldier even when it was in his interests to do so. Besides, a kind of mania had lifted Cale out of the realm of ordinary men. In a matter of days he had become famous. It was hardly surprising given the hideous circumstances in which the Axis found itself. If ever a saviour was required it was now.

'Are you spying on me?' asked Cale, very well aware of the answer.

'You are the observed of all observers, Mr Cale. You can't piss in a pot without its significance being discussed at every dinner table in the city. What did she want?'

'What do you think?'

'And?'

'And nothing.'

'You aren't going to intercede on his behalf?'

'Would it help if I did?'

'You could put in a plea for leniency, if you wished. In writing. I'd make sure the King received it personally.'

That was it then.

'No, it's nothing to do with me.'

A pity, thought Bose. He would certainly not have passed it to the King had Cale been foolish enough to write such a plea. The King had forgotten his obsession with Conn – or rather he now regarded himself as having been overly influenced by Bose Ikard's enthusiasm for the young man (as if his Chancellor had had any choice but to go along with his master's hysterical favouritism). For now, Cale was everyone's favourite, including the King's, so it wouldn't do to be seen to work against him. But Bose was sceptical about the boy's ability to keep people happy for long. Whatever his skills, politics wasn't one of them. And in the end ability and talent were nothing in the face of politics. It might have been useful to have a letter in his back pocket.

'Are you sure?'

'Yeah,' said Cale, touching himself just under the chin with the flat of his right hand. 'I'm up to here with sureness.'

'Is that supposed to be some sort of pleasantry at my expense?'

'No.'

'And are you also sure that you have the men to create your New Model Army?'

'Yes.'

'Because I have experienced and knowledgeable advisors who say it's not possible to create an army out of peasants, not in general and certainly not one capable of beating the Redeemers. Let's not even consider the lack of time involved.'

'They're right.'

'I see. But it's possible for you?'

'Yes.'

'Why?'

'At the Golan the Laconics inflicted the greatest defeat on the Redeemers in their history. Ten days later the Redeemers inflicted on the Laconics the greatest defeat of theirs. The difference was me.' Cale had been slumped insolently in his chair but now stretched upright. 'Is that sneak behind the screen going to join in or am I going to have to go over there and drag him out?'

Bose sighed. 'Come out.' A young man, smiling amiably and in his early twenties, emerged. It was Robert Fanshawe, Laconic scout. Cale had last seen him when they'd cut a deal over prisoners after the battle he'd just been boasting about.

'You don't look well, Cale, if you don't mind me saying.'

'I *do* mind.'

'You don't look well all the same.'

'Well,' said Bose Ikard. 'At least it proves you know him.'

'Know him?' said Fanshawe. 'We're special pals.'

'No, we're not!' said Cale, his alarm at how this might be taken delighting Fanshawe who laughed, revelling in his discomfort.

'Do Mr Cale's claims about his importance to the Redeemer victory have merit?'

'I'm not *claiming* anything,' said Cale. Fanshawe looked at him, cool, not laughing any more.

'Yes, this young man was the difference.'

'So why are you so sure his New Model Army will fail?'

'There have been peasant rebellions as long as there have been peasants,' said Fanshawe. 'Tell me one that succeeded?' He looked at them both, head mockingly turned, waiting for a reply. 'The Laconics have fought six wars against our Helots in the last hundred years – if you can call the slaughter of untrained hillbillies a war. It ends one way. Always.'

'Not this time,' said Cale.

'Why?'

'I'd rather show than tell.'

'Excellent. I look forward to your presentation of the details.'

'No.'

'What do you mean?' said Bose Ikard.

'I'm not giving a performance so your dunces get to offer me the benefit of their experience. There's going to be a fight and whoever's left standing at the end wins the argument. One hundred each side.'

'The rules?'

'There are no *rules*.'

'A real fight?'

'Is there any other kind? Bring who you like, how you like.'

'And you'll just have your peasants?'

'I'll bring whoever I damn well please.' But it was too hard to resist. 'There'll be eighty plebs and twenty of my veterans.'

'And you?'

'I'll be watching Fanshawe getting the shit kicked out of him.'

'Me? I'm just a Laconic advisor. I couldn't possibly take part.'

Bose Ikard was suspicious, always, but considered that perhaps it was for the best: he wanted to know what Cale was up to and it was hard to think of a better way than something like this. There were Swiss soldiers who felt they deserved recognition before some miserable-looking boy. Now they'd have the chance to prove it.

'I'll get back to you,' he said. 'Close the door on your way out, Mr Cale. A word, Mr Fanshawe.'

24

The sun came up on the morning of Conn's execution with as much warmth and honeyed light as if it had been the Jubilee celebrations of a much-loved monarch. At ten in the morning he was taken from his cell in the Swarthmore, then down to the West Gate and through the Parc Beaulieu to the place of execution on the Quai des Moulins. Five of his men, but not Vipond, or his wife, walked with him, bareheaded and unarmed. There he ate a piece of bread and drank a glass of wine in the Vetch Gallery. From before dawn a huge crowd had been gathering in order to get the best places from which to see the action.

Along with the usual excitement of a crowd who delighted in the hideous suffering of a fellow human being was added the hatred of citizens who held Conn Materazzi responsible not only for the defeat at Bex but for their justified fear that in the spring of next year the Redeemers would be doing very much the same to them as they were now about to do to him.

A brass band of sorts, sponsored by the city's biggest pie-maker, belted out rough versions of popular songs and blaring versions of boastful martial anthems about Switzer-landers never being slaves. The crowd was a peculiar mixture of unequals: do-bads, thieves, tarts and lollygaggers, carpenters and shopkeepers, merchants and their wives and daughters and, of course, a specially erected terrace for those who really mattered. In all, it was such a crush of spiteful humanity that those not used to it suffered terribly, namely the wives and daughters of the gentility who fainted in the heat and had to be carried out with their plunging necklines all disordered, which got the drunk apprentices going ('GET YOUR TITS OUT FOR THE LADS!'). As always, it was a bad day for cats: at least a dozen were thrown into the air to bellowing shouts around the great space in front of the place of execution.

In general, throughout the Four Quarters, judicial death came about through hanging, beheading with an axe or burning – sometimes all three, if you were particularly unfortunate. But in Spanish Leeds, commoner and aristocrat were both beheaded after a peculiar manner and by a most unusual executioner. Formally it was called the Leeds Gibbet but the *polloi* called it Topping Bob. It consisted of a frame of wood about sixteen foot high and four foot wide bolted into a large block. It was something like a French guillotine, although much bigger and much cruder. But unlike the guillotine there is no single executioner for the Leeds Gibbet: there are many. Once the block and axe is pulled to the top of the frame and held with a pin, the rope holding the pin in place is handed out to any of the people below who can get a grasp of it. Those who can't stretch out their hands to show that they assent and agree to the execution. This, then, was the sight that waited for Conn as he stepped out onto the platform and his death.

His shirt of black silk had been cut around the collar without much skill to leave his neck visible. Black silk shirts, then the height of fashion, were unpopular for many years afterwards. The gibbet, of course, dominated the scene and if beauty is the shape that most conveys the purpose of an object then its ugliness was beautiful. It looked like what it was. It was a pity that none of Conn's friends had been allowed out onto the platform with him: he deserved someone to witness his bravery in the face of that awful device. Perhaps there were some in the crowd, not many, who sensed the young man's courage. It was true that he'd shown great courage in battle but that was courage shown where all around were to share a part in the same fate; where there was fear but also fellow feeling and the prospect of honour and purpose. Here it was all isolation among the taunts and the cruelty; giving people the pleasure of watching hideous suffering inflicted without risk to themselves. But there was at least one person there who admired him, who knew the injustice and unfairness, the *wrongness* of his death. Cale was in the bell tower of St Anne's cathedral, which looked down on the square – a distance from the gibbet of about fifty yards and a hundred and thirty feet high. He was alone and smoking one of the fine Swiss cigars, a Diplomat No. 4, to which he had become addicted now that he could afford them every day. He couldn't have told you how he felt – not sick to his stomach, as he'd been at the death of the Maid of Blackbird Leys, but a kind of dead tranquillity in which he seemed, paradoxically, alive to everything: the mocking obscenities, the whistles, the man smiling at Conn and holding two fingers to his forehead, delighting in the horror to come. But he also felt removed, as if the tower had taken him above the fog of malice and pleasure below. A small tribe of dogs chased each other, barking happily, in and out of the legs of the soldiers who faced the crowd from the platform, not armed but carrying drums.

Conn waited to be instructed what to do. A curate approached him. 'It has been agreed that you may speak but I'm warning you not to say anything against the Crown or the people.'

Conn moved forward. The noise of the crowd diminished a little – a good speech could be dined out on.

Thirty yards away the bookies at their trestles were taking bets on how many spurts of blood there'd be.

'I haven't come here to talk,' said Conn, startled by the firmness of his voice as his stomach surged. 'I've come here to die.'

'Speak up,' shouted someone in the crowd.

'I'd be heard little if I shouted myself to death. I'll be brief – I'd prefer to say nothing if it weren't that going to my death silently would make some men think I submitted to the guilt as well as to the punishment. I die innocent . . .'

Up in the tower Cale heard the word 'innocent' but nothing more as the curate signalled the drummers to drown out Conn's accusation of injustice. Whether he cut it short because of the drums or he didn't have much to say, Conn finished and walked towards, if not the executioner exactly, at least the man responsible for the workings of the gibbet.

'I hope you sharpened the blade as duty obliges you. And I'll have my head cut off at the neck and not topped like an egg as I hear you did with my Lord the Cavalier of Zurich. Botch it and there'll be no tip. See it done properly and you'll be glad you killed Conn Materazzi.'

'Thank you, zir,' said the almost-executioner, who depended on such tips for payment, 'we have a new doings to prevent such han unfortunate thing happenin' agayne.'

Conn walked to the gibbet, took a deep breath as if to swallow back his terror, and knelt down, his neck fitting into a clearly brand new semi-circle made in the wood. The new cross plank above was swiftly put in place with the matching half of the circle and locked into position. Above him, the flat blade in its heavy wooden block was held in place by two pins, each one attached to a separate rope. One of the pins was held in place by a clip and it was the rope leading from this one that the gibbet-master threw into the crowd. He waited until the scrabble for a handhold on the rope was finished then went up a ladder placed against the gibbet and put his right hand to the clip holding the pin in place, so that no one in the crowd could prematurely pull it out. He addressed the people.

'I will count to three – any man's hand now on the rope that stays on the rope after the count of three will be whipped.' Satisfied that those holding the rope were in command of themselves he called out: 'One!'

'TWO!' shouted back the crowd. 'THREE!'

He whipped the clip free with a great flourish.

The rope and pin whipped loose, the block and blade rattled in the rail and struck with a dreadful bang. Conn's head shot from the gibbet as if it'd been launched from a sling and flew over the platform and into the crowd, vanishing among the Sunday best of the men and women of fashion.

Cale stared down for a moment. *Why this?* he thought. *Why like this?* then he turned away, dropped what was left of the cigar on the stone floor and left.

But just as he could see what had happened, Cale could also be seen. Afterwards it was put about that he had not only smoked during Conn's death but that he had laughed at the horrible conclusion. In time this did great damage to his reputation.

Arbell was standing at the far end of the room, staring out of the window and holding her baby tightly, slowly rocking backward and forward.

To Riba and her husband it seemed like a very long walk indeed. They stopped a few feet away; both said after they had left it was as if the very air between them and Arbell trembled with terror and held them back.

'Is it finished?'

'Yes.'

'Did he suffer?'

'It was very quick and he was calm and showed great courage.'

'But he didn't suffer?'

'No, he didn't suffer.'

She turned to Riba.

'You weren't there?' It was an accusation.

'No, I wasn't there,' Riba said.

'I wouldn't let her.' Arthur Wittenberg thought he was helping. He was not.

'Of course I couldn't go, I couldn't,' said Riba, reassuring.

'I should have gone,' said Arbell. 'I should have been with him.'

'He would have hated that,' said Riba. 'Hated it.'

'He made it very clear to me,' said Wittenberg, 'last night when I spoke to him that he wouldn't countenance your being there – under any circumstance.'

A lie was seldom told so clumsily. But Arbell was not in any state of mind to judge very much of anything. The baby, who had been very calm because he liked being held tightly, started to wriggle. 'Yaaaaaaaaach!' shouted the baby. 'Bleeuch!' Finally he managed to free his right arm and started pulling on a lock of Arbell's hair. Yank. Yank. Pull. Pull. She didn't seem to notice.

'Shall I take him?'

Arbell turned away from Riba as if it were an offer to remove the child permanently. Gently she unfastened the baby's hands from her hair.

At the door a servant called out, 'Lady Satchell to . . .'

But the end of his sentence was drowned in the dramatic bustle and noisiness of the woman herself.

'My darling girl,' she wept from the other side of the room.

273

'My darling girl . . . what a *cauchemor*, what a *nagmerrie*, a *kosmorro*!' No single language was enough for Lady Satchell to perform herself in. She was known, even among the Materazzienne, as the Great Blurter. There was no situation that, by her instant appearance, she could not puff up with hysteria. Not even this one.

'I am *so* sorry, my dear,' she said, grasping Arbell to her chest. No trembling shield of grief would put Lady Satchell off. She no more saw Arbell's pain than the bull sees the spider's web. 'It was dreadful, *strasny*! *Terribile*! The poor boy – to see that handsome head go *weerkats* down the Quai des Moulins.'

Fortunately the sheer power of Satchell's hysterical capacity for stirring caused her to shift into Afrikaans so that Arbell barely understood what she was talking about.

'And that *mostruoso* Thomas Cale – I heard from one who was with him he laughed at the Misero Conn as he died and smoked a cigar and blew rings at his *disgraziafo* corpse.'

Arbell stared at her. It was hard to imagine that someone would go so white and still live. Riba took her by the elbow, pulled her physically away, whispering, 'Shut your mouth, you heartless bitch!' and signalled to the two servants at the door.

'What are you doing? I'm her dear cousin. Who do you think you are, you toilet scrubbing slut to . . .'

'Get her away from here,' said Riba, to the servants. 'And if I see her here again I'll make you both wish you'd never been born.'

Lady Satchell was so startled at being manhandled by the servants now gleefully licensed to mistreat one of their betters that she was outside before she could start flapping her mouth again.

Riba walked back to her former mistress, working out her story.

'Is it true?' Her voice so quiet Riba could barely hear her.
'I don't believe it.'

'But you heard it, too?'

'Yes. But I don't believe it, not a word. It's not like him.'

'It's exactly like him.'

'He saved my life. He saved Conn's life too, for your sake.'

'And he perjured himself against Conn because he thinks
I betrayed him. There was nothing else I could do. But you
don't know him when he's against you – what he's capable of
doing.'

Torn between the two of them as she was, Riba's first
thoughts were not generous to her former mistress. *If you
hadn't betrayed him, Conn would still be alive. Everything would have
been different.* Of course, part of her knew that this was unfair,
but it didn't stop it from being true.

'I told you. I don't believe a word of it.' But this was not
entirely the case. Which of us, on hearing that our closest
friend had been arrested for a dreadful crime, would not
think, buried in the deepest recess of our soul, hidden in the
shadows concealed in our heart's most crepuscular oubliette,
that it might possibly be true? How much easier then for
Arbell to believe that Cale had laughed at her darling husband
as he died. She should not be blamed for this lack of faith in
Cale – it's only human to hate the person you have hurt.

'Is it true?'

'Sounds bad – so probably it is,' said Cale. There was no
mistaking Artemisia's suspicious and angry tone.

'Answer me. Did you laugh at Conn Materazzi when he
died?'

He'd many years of practice at not giving away his feelings
– control of spontaneous emotions was a matter of survival
at the Sanctuary – but a less angry person than Artemisia

might have noticed his eyes widen at the accusation. Not for long and not by much.

'What do you think?' he said, casual.

'I don't know what to think, that's why I'm asking you.'

'The thing is – I was in the tower on my own. I could have sacrificed a goat in there and no one would have known.'

'You still haven't answered the question.'

'No.'

'No what?'

'No, I didn't laugh at Conn Materazzi when he died.'

And with that he stood up and left.

'I'm impressed,' said IdrisPukke.

'Because?'

'It's not long ago that you would have told her you did laugh at Conn, just to punish her for asking.'

'I thought about it.'

'Of course you did.'

'Why would she believe something like that?'

'You are widely referred to as the Exterminating Angel. It's not so surprising that people fail to give you the benefit of the doubt. Besides, the times need a man with a reputation for unmitigated cruelty – people want to feel that with such a creature on their side they might have a chance of living through the next year.'

'But *they* don't know me.'

'To be fair, it's not an easy thing to do – know you, I mean.'

'She should by now.'

'Really? She knows you lied under oath with as much ease as if you were telling an old woman that you liked her hat.'

'Not *that* again. What was I supposed to do? If I'd confessed we'd both have had our heads bouncing across the square.'

'I agree. But for all her eccentric skills, Artemisia doesn't understand things as they really are. She's one of *them*. The more money you have, the nicer the world is; if you have money *and* power the world's niceness is almost heavenly. To such people the world's cruelty is an aberration not the normal state of things. You've had the good fortune never to believe that anything was fair. You must allow her time to learn that she's living in another world now. She hasn't had your disadvantages. The spirit of the times used to move through her and Conn and the King – now it moves through you. This is your time, for however long it lasts.'

'Meaning?'

'There'll come a time when it isn't.'

'When?'

'Hard to say. The thing is that whenever it comes to an end the person whose time it used to be is usually the last to realize.'

25

There's not much to be said for being sick, except that if you're sick for long enough it gives you endless opportunities to think. For the permanently unwell there are not enough distractions to fill the endless days and, besides, illness can drain you easily of the energy you need to read or play a game. Then you must think, even if it's the drifting sort of thinking that floats you aimlessly from past to present, from meals eaten, lovers kissed, to nights of humiliation, bitter regrets. Cale had a talent for this kind of thing. In the madhouse ruled by Kevin Meatyard he had been able to use the skills honed in the Sanctuary for all those years to go into hiding somewhere inside his head. But in those days he'd been as ignorant of the world as a stone: there was his hideous real life and his imaginary world where everything was wonderful. Now the drifting daydreams were all mixed up with the numerous things that had happened to him since then. Daydreaming was not so much a pleasure any more. So he tried to think of useful things – the mulling of ideas, the beating out of plans and working up of notions that had he been well he would have brushed to the back of his mind and left to the dust.

The religion of the upper classes of the Swiss and their allies was an odd affair. It had come as a considerable surprise to Cale that they also worshipped the Hanged Redeemer – but as the true Redeemers had created a religion full of sin and punishment and hell, of things that filled every waking moment, the religion of the Swiss aristocrats and merchants had developed in more or less precisely the other direction: beyond church on Sundays, weddings and funerals, there seemed to be no specific demands made nor any reference to the dire consequences that would result from failing to meet these loosely-hinted-at suggestions. But this was not the case with the working people and the peasants. The latter in particular were extremely religious, so much so that they had a large number of creeds to service them but at the bottom of them all was the Hanged Redeemer. Though each sect considered itself to be the sole true heir of his beliefs, they recognized to varying degrees that they belonged to a family. But one thing that united them was their universal loathing for the Redeemers themselves, whom they regarded as corrupt, idol-worshipping, usurping, murderous heretics. Whatever the differences between the Plain People and the Millerites, the Two by Twos and the Gnostic Jennifers, Cale had talked to enough of them to know that their commitment to destroying the Redeemers was of a kind where death would be a privilege rather than a price. Whatever his own feelings about martyrs he was used to making them work for him. It was a currency that he understood. It was now nearly three weeks after the death of Conn Materazzi, and he had used the time to persuade the various heads of the important religious factions (Moderators, Pastors, Archimandrites, Apostles) that he was as deeply committed to destroying the Redeemers and their hideous perversion of the true teachings of the Hanged Redeemer as only someone who had suffered personally under their yoke could be. Fortunately this did not require Hanseatic diplomatic skills: they were only too ready to believe in him. And hence why all of them were present on the Silver Field at ten in the morning to witness the very far from mock battle between Cale's fledgling New Model Army and the Swiss. Also present were Vague Henri, IdrisPukke, Kleist and a still frosty

Artemisia Halicarnassus. Standing to one side, looking suspicious, was Bose Ikard and an assortment of newly appointed Swiss generals, elevated to their new positions courtesy of the cull of their former senior officers now rotting gently in the grave pits at Bex.

The day after the meeting with Bose Ikard and Fanshawe, Cale had written to demand that, as the fate of several nations hung on his successful attempt to create this New Model Army, the fight of his one hundred against that of the Swiss Knights should be fought with sharp weapons and without rules, except that surrender would be permissible. As intended this alarmed the Swiss who, rightly suspicious, demanded that only blunt practice arms be used. Cale refused. Eventually a compromise was reached: unsharpened weapons, no spikes or points, and crossbow bolts and arrows to have dull tips and bars to prevent deep entry.

The day began with a strange incident involving Cale, which in the telling and re-telling gave rise to a peculiar legend. The person involved was only a very minor member of the country aristocracy who had arrived in Spanish Leeds the night before and had managed to hang onto the coat-tails of some prince or other and was enjoying the attention of the various flunkeys seeing to the needs of the assembled gentry. Not realizing that the white-faced boy standing next to him in his plain black cassock was the incarnation of the Wrath of God and all-round exterminating angel, he had mistaken him for a servant and politely, it must be said, asked for a glass of water with a slice of lemon. The servant ignored him.

'Look here,' he said to Cale more forcefully. 'Get me a glass of water and a slice of lemon and do it now. I won't ask you again.' The servant looked at him, eyes blazing with an incredulity and disdain that he took for the worst kind of dumb insolence.

'What?' said Cale.

The newly arrived country toff was anxious not to be regarded as a bumpkin of the kind who would allow himself to be intimidated by a dogsbody and took the stunned silence from those around to signal that they were waiting to see whether he was up to dealing with insolence from a servant. He fetched Cale an enormous blow to the side of his face. There followed a paralysed stillness that made the previous silence seem raucous. It was the prince who'd invited him who broke it.

'My God, man, this is Thomas Cale.'

There is no adjective in any language fit to describe the whiteness of the country gentleman's face as the blood drained into his boots. His mouth opened. The others waited for something horrible to happen.

Cale looked at him. There was a long pause, a dreadful silence, suddenly broken when Cale let out a single loud bark of amusement. Then he walked away.

Each side had been allowed forty horses and when the Swiss entered the field they certainly looked impressive, the horses pulling at their bits, anxious to get on, and beside them seventy knights on foot, armour carapaces sparkling in the morning sun. Beautiful. Formidable. They took up a line and waited. Not for long. From the other side of the park what looked like a peasant wagon came into view, and another one after it and another – fifteen in all. Each one was led by two heavy shirehorses, bigger than the hunters ridden by the knights by half as much again. As they approached it became clear that these were not the usual wagons for carrying hay or pigs – they were smaller, the sides slanted and they had roofs. By contrast, the fifteen wagons were flanked by ten of Artemisia's horse scouts, slight men on fast and famously agile

Manipur ponies. They were carrying crossbows, not a weapon used much in Halicarnassus. They'd been designed by Vague Henri for use on horseback – light, nothing like as powerful as his own overstrung but very much easier to draw and load. The wagons came to their marked place and then curved round into a circle. The drivers leapt off and unhitched the horses, pulling them into the centre. The gap between the wagons was not very great as the horses had been carefully trained to offset them before they were unharnessed. Each driver quickly removed a detachable wooden shield hung from the back of the wagons, which they slotted between them so that now the wagons and shields formed a continuous circle without gaps.

The Swiss looked on, some amused, the more intelligent suspicious. The only way through the wagons was through the spaces underneath – but this was soon closed as four more planks of wood were lowered through slots in the floor. For a moment nothing happened. Then there was a shout from inside the circle and the outriders started firing their crossbows at the Swiss ranks. Vague Henri's design might have been less powerful but from a hundred yards the bolts, blunt as they were, hit the massed ranks of armoured men with a ferocious clang. The Swiss had only brought ten archers and they were trained for shooting at massed ranks, not ten men on agile horses. In a five-minute exchange only two New Model Army riders were hit, painfully enough and drawing blood, but they themselves hit more than twenty of the Swiss. Their armour and the bluntness of the bolts prevented any deep wounds but it was clear that a real bolt would have killed or badly wounded nearly all of them. After five minutes there was a trumpet burst from the wagons and the outriders moved back to the circle. A wooden shield was removed to let them in and they were gone.

Then three other walls were taken out and about twenty men with mallets and stakes rushed out and began hammering them into the ground. This was more to the Swiss archers' taste, but before they could start shooting, volley after volley of arrows emerged from the centre of the wagons, causing huge confusion and yet more considerable injury to the lightly armoured Swiss archers.

Under this fearsome protective cover, the peasants knocking in the posts finished the job and ran back to the safety of the wagons, leaving behind the wooden stakes connected by thin ropes with sharp metal barbs woven into them every six inches. The odd thing about this was that the stakes and barbed ropes only covered about an eighth of the circle, leaving the attackers free to go round this unpleasant obstacle. It was hard to see the point.

With the arrows still raining on them, the Swiss had no choice but to advance and take the wagons in hand-to-hand combat. The blunted arrows were nothing more than nuisance value to men in such high-quality armour and fighting close was their life's work. Skirting the barbed ropes – several of the knights slashed at them as they went past but wire had been threaded through the rope to prevent such an easy cure – they approached the wagons, determined to break their way in and give the occupants a bloody good thrashing. Although the wagons were neither particularly big nor tall, once they were close there seemed no obvious or easy way in. As they approached they noticed small square holes in the sides of the wagons – six in each. Out of them, crossbow bolts shattered into them, devastating at such short range despite their bluntness. And fast too – one fired every three or four seconds. They were forced to come right up to the wagon sides to grasp the wheels and heave them over. But the wheels had been hammered into the ground with hoops of steel. Then the roofs of the wagons were heaved up and crashed over the side on a hinge with blunted spikes on the leading edge, designed not to pierce the armour of anyone they hit but to deal a crushing blow. Dozens of arms and heads were broken in this move. Then the reason for the low height of the wagons became clearer. In each there were six peasants, armed with the wooden flails they'd been used to using all their lives as much as the Swiss professional soldiers had used swords and poleaxes. Even without the addition of the nails that would have been used in a real fight, the head of the flail moved with such ferocious speed that it crushed hands and chests and heads alike, armoured or not. And still the bolts kept coming. They may not have been able to kill but they caused terrible pain and deep bruising. The Swiss were hardly able to land a blow in return. The killing range of a few feet they were used to, dictated by the length of a sword or poleaxe, had been extended by Cale by no more than a few feet – but it was everything. Men they could have dismembered in a few seconds in the open were made untouchable by strong wood and a few extra feet in height. And now they were vulnerable to an insulting collection of modified agricultural tools wielded with confidence and familiarity by mere peasants. After fifteen minutes of pain and damage they withdrew – angry and frustrated, poison-ously impotent. Their retreat was conducted to a mocking but still painful volley of blunt arrows from a dozen of Cale's Purgators until he signalled them to stop. He watched with great pleasure as the Swiss generals went to inspect the dam-age to their baffled elite. He was gracious enough not to go with them; even from forty yards away, the effect of the metal flails, clubs, hammers, blunt woodaxes and rocks was clear.

After ten minutes of inspection it was Fanshawe who walked back to Cale, apparently as easy-going and frivolous as usual; but the truth was that he was shaken by the implications of what he'd seen.

'I was wrong,' he said to Bose Ikard. 'It could work. I've got questions though.'

'And I have answers,' said Cale. They adjourned to a meeting later that day. On the way off the field Bose Ikard caught up with Fanshawe and spoke quietly.

'Can this really work?'

'You saw for yourself.'

'And we can win?'

'Possibly. But what if you do? What then?'

'I don't follow you.'

'You've shown your hillbillies that they're as good as their masters. Are they going to fight and die in their thousands – and they will die – and then just hand it all back? Would *you*?'

At their meeting that afternoon there were a great many surly questions, all of them dealt with easily enough by Cale. If he'd been them he would have made things much more awkward – he knew there were weaknesses even if they couldn't see them. The questions from Fanshawe failed to materialize: he could see the flaws too, but also that they could be managed. Cale answered calmly and pleasantly until the very last comment – the suggestion that once it was a matter of life and death the peasants would break in the face of blood and mutilation.

'Then bring your men back tomorrow and we'll fight with sharp weapons, and no mercy,' said Cale, still calm. 'You won't be back for a third time.'

Bose Ikard, however, though mulling over the long-term consequences pointed out by Fanshawe, saw that he had no choice but to support Cale: there was no point in long-term thinking if there wasn't going to be a long-term. He sent away his new High Command and got down to the details of money and the requisition powers Cale demanded.

This did not come easily to the Chancellor: giving away money and power was physically painful to him. But he'd worry about getting them back, as well as the dangers of an armed and trained peasantry, when this was all over. By the end of the meeting, Thomas Cale was the most powerful little boy in the history of the Four Quarters. It felt to Cale, as the letter was signed, as if deep in his peculiar soul a small sweet spring of cool water had started to flow.

Outside, Fanshawe signalled him to one side.

'You were very quiet,' said Cale.

'Professional courtesy,' said Fanshawe. 'Didn't want to piss on your pageant.'

'And you think you could have?'

'How are you going to supply them?'

'Oh no! You've seen the big weakness – there's no fooling you.'

Fanshawe smiled.

'Then you won't have a problem answering, will you?'

Ten minutes later they were in an old workshop deep in the slums of Spanish Leeds and Michael Nevin, outdragger and inventor, was proudly showing off one of his new supply wagons. Now he had money to back his ingenuity, the result, while still distantly related to his outdragger cart, was a thing of elegance and style.

'Move it,' said Cale.

Fanshawe picked up a two-wheeled cart by the shafts at the front. It was much bigger than the original it was based on, and he was astonished at how light it was. Nevin was a peacock puffed with pride. 'It'll shift four times as quick as the supply wagons them junkie Redeemers use, turn right enough and heft near half as much. Don't over-pack it and you only need one horse 'stead of six bullocks. Push comes to shove you don't even need a beast – y'could budge it with four men and half a cargo and still resupply near as quick as the Redeemers. I'm salivatin' right enough. Haven't I made it to be all things to all men.' It was a statement not a question.

Cale was almost as delighted with Nevin as Nevin was delighted with himself.

'Mr Nevin worked with me on the war wagon as well. It was his idea to cut down the size so they can move maybe twice as fast as the Redeemer supply carts. The only way they can move with enough speed to follow and attack us is by sending mounted infantry after us but without supply wagons. Even if they catch up, Artemisia's outriders will tell us hours before they arrive. We circle up, dig a six-foot trench around the outside, and what will they do? If they attack we'll cut them to pieces, worse than we did today. If they wait, the outriders will have ridden for more troops to relieve us. Remember, there'll be two hundred of these forts on the move every day of every week. Even if they can isolate one and destroy it we'll take ten times as many of them with us.'

'As easy as that?'

'No,' replied Cale. 'But they'll lose two men for every one of ours.'

'Even if you're right, and I concede you might be, the Redeemers are ready to die in numbers – are your hillbillies?'

Cale smiled again.

'We'll find out, I suppose.'

'Do you really think you can win a battle with your wagons?'

'Don't know that either, but I don't intend to try. It's like IdrisPukke says: the trouble with decisive battles is that they decide things. I'm not going to crush the Redeemers, I'm going to bleed them.'

26

According to the great Ludwig, the human body is the best picture of the human soul and so, like the body, the human spirit has its cancers and growths and infected organs. Just as the purpose of the liver is to act as a sump for the poisons of the body, the soul has its organs for containing and isolating the toxic discharge of human suffering.

It is an axiom of the hopeful that whatever doesn't kill you makes you strong: but the truth is that such deadly suffering can be held in isolation in this poison reservoir only for a time: like the liver it can deal with only so much poison before it begins to rot.

Survivors of the Sanctuary had already taken more than their due share of grief. Add to this the loss of his wife and child, and the horror of the events in Kitty's basement, and Kleist was on the brink of drowning in his past. The day after the mock battle on Silver Field he was delivering a pair of boots he had been working on for the campaign ahead (leather work had been one of Kleist's designated skills at the Sanctuary) and was heading for the bootmakers in New York Road. Bosco had drummed into Cale that decent boots were third only to food and weapons for an army. Kleist was heading through the market, crowded because the weekly horse fair was on, when he brushed past Daisy carrying their son.

He walked on for a few yards and then stopped. He had barely taken in the face of the young woman – he'd not been looking at her directly and they'd passed in a fraction of a second – but something shivered in him, even though she was older and thinner than his dead wife, much more drawn. He knew it could not be her – her dust was blowing about on a prairie three hundred miles away – and he did not want to look again and drag his misery out of the depths, but he could not stop himself. He turned to stare at her as she moved away through the crowd, baby on hip. But she was quickly hidden in the crush of buyers and sellers. He stood still as a stump and told himself to go after her, but then he told himself there was no point. A shiver of desolation passed through him, his grief now uncontainable, spreading slowly, a slow and malignant leak. He stood for a moment longer but he had things to do and he turned for the boot-maker's. But from that moment in the marketplace Kleist was on borrowed time.

'So what do you think?'

For the last ten minutes Cale had been watching Robert Hooke examining a four-foot-long tube of pig iron.

'Have you tried to use it?' asked Hooke.

'Me? No. I saw one like it at Bex. The first time it fired it went through three Redeemers at one go – the second time it blew up and killed half a dozen Swiss. But if you could make it work it'd be a hell of a thing.'

Hooke eyed the ugly-looking contraption. 'I'm astonished it worked at all.'

'Of course you are.'

'I'd need a lot of money.'

'Of course you will. But I'm not stupid. I know you were working on a tube for your collider. I'm not paying for you to research into the nature of things.'

'You think all knowledge must be practical.'

'I don't think anything about knowledge one way or the other – what I think about is not being on top of a bonfire,

289

one you'll be joining me on if we don't find a way to stop Bosco. Understand?'

'Oh, indeed I do, Mr Cale.'

'So, is it possible?'

'It's not *im*possible.'

'Then give me a bill and get on with it.' Cale walked off towards the door.

'By the way,' called out Hooke.

'Yes?'

'Is it true you cut off a man's head because he told you to bring him a glass of water?'

Even for someone as sound as a roach Cale's workload would have been murderous and he was very far from sound. Necessity forced him to delegate. There were candidates enough: IdrisPukke and a reluctant Cadbury ('I have criminal enterprises to run') could be trusted, Kleist even, silent and grim as he was, seemed to want work to occupy his mind. Vague Henri was everywhere doing everything. But it was still not enough. He went with IdrisPukke to ask Vipond for his help.

'I'm sorry about Conn.'

'I am,' replied Vipond, 'quite clear that you have nothing to be sorry for. There was no choice.'

'I didn't laugh at him.'

'I know. But I'm afraid it doesn't matter. You must bring in Bose Ikard.'

'How?'

'Yes . . . not easy. He's an able man in his way but he has the besetting fault of power: it's become an end in itself. And he's addicted to conspiracy. Leave him alone for five minutes and he'd start plotting against himself.'

'I need control of the regular army,' said Cale. 'I thought I could build my own separate force. But it won't work on its own. I need troops who can fight outside the forts.'

'I understand you promised him otherwise.'

'Well, I was wrong. The hillbillies are fine as long as they're protected behind the walls and out of reach. But away from the wagons they're as dangerous as a bald porcupine.'

Vipond said nothing for a moment.

'Desperate situations require desperate remedies,' he said at last. 'Try telling the truth.'

'Meaning?'

'What it suggests. Be frank with him. He knows how desperate things are or you wouldn't be where you are now. Point out to him that you'll succeed together or you'll die together. Or you could try blackmail if that person Cadbury has anything on him.'

'Not enough,' said IdrisPukke.

'Then honesty it is.'

'And if honesty doesn't work?'

'Assassination.'

'I thought you said it never worked.'

'Did I say that?'

'Yes.'

'Extraordinary.'

To Cale's surprise his subsequent meeting with Bose Ikard was not just successful but pleasurable. Lies had to be elaborate and there was always something you hadn't thought of to catch you out. It was a strain, lying. Telling the truth, on the other hand, was easy. It was so *true*. He liked telling the truth so much he decided that one day he'd like to tell it again. And so it turned out as Vipond had hoped: a lack of choice would drive Bose Ikard towards simplicity.

'I can tell you that the High Command won't be convinced. They don't want anything to do with you.'

'Then they'll have to be replaced.'

'They've only just been appointed.'

'Is this true of all of them or just some of them?' asked IdrisPukke.

'If you could remove the triad that might be enough. If.'

'Are you averse to special means?'

'Special?'

'You know: desperate times require desperate remedies.'

Within ten days, two resignations and a suicide had accounted for the triad by way of Kitty the Hare's red books. As a matter of courtesy and a show of good faith, one of the books was handed over to Bose Ikard, one that contained some unorthodox financial dealings involving Bose Ikard himself. IdrisPukke had, of course, made a copy.

For different reason the Laconics and the Redeemers were societies built on the notion that war was an inevitable constant of human existence. The Axis armies were just armies. Cale was helped in his reforms, however, by the increasing awareness that it was not defeat that was at stake in the war but annihilation. This awareness was made all the greater by reprints of sermons given in the Great Cathedral of Chartres by Pope Bosco himself. In them, Bosco, quoting in precise detail from the Good Book, called on his followers to carry out God's explicit command that 'you shall not leave alive anything that breathes. In Makkedah utterly destroy it and all the souls therein. In Libnah destroy it and all the souls therein; and in Luchish and Eglon and Hebron and Debir, they utterly destroyed all them that breathed and they did not spare any, putting to death men, women and children and infants, cattle and sheep and camels and donkeys.'

There were suggestions, entirely true as it happened, that these blood-curdling sermons were fakes. But though it was true that they had been made up by Cale and Vague Henri and printed in secret, most people became reluctantly persuaded they were real and for two reasons. From the few refugees who had recently made it across the Mississippi from the territory now occupied by the Redeemers, there were numerous reports of the mass evacuation of entire cities, moving to the north and then the west. But there was also the disturbing truth that all the religions of the Four Quarters shared a belief in the same Good Book, and though most chose to ignore the many occasions on which God had demanded the divine massacring of entire countries, down to the last dog, it was no longer possible to do so in quite the same way. The inconvenient truth was that the promise of an apocalypse, whether local (Man Hattan, Sodom) or universal (the end time of Geddon), was woven into the very fabric of their oddly shared beliefs.

For the next six weeks it was duck soup all round as Cale's new government department, the Office Against the Redeemers (the OAR) found itself pushing at open doors everywhere. Partly this was due to fear of the Redeemers and partly fear of Thomas Cale: the story about him cutting off a man's head for ordering him to bring a drink of water was now accepted truth. 'You have a talent for being legendary,' said IdrisPukke. 'I wonder if that can be entirely a good thing.' His access to Kitty the Hare's red books also encouraged co-operation. After the replacement of the triad, everyone, for the moment, now relied for their position on Thomas, with the result that a new enthusiasm about his plans for everything began to permeate the halls of power. Much was done and much quicker than the OAR could have expected. But all this good news couldn't last, nor did it. But the blow, when it came, was unexpected in its expectedness.

Two months into their preparations they had planned the first delivery of supplies of food, uniforms, weapons and the wagons so central to their campaign. The boots, mostly designed by Cale and Kleist, had been contracted in detail according to a strict model – the Redeemer way. The same with the food. The same with the weapons – from the high quality but simple flails to the newly created crossbows designed for speed of loading and close fighting rather than power. Standing in the food depot, where the first lot of rations had been delivered, Cale watched as box after box was broken open to reveal tack biscuits infected with maggots and weevils. Those that weren't were either tainted by rancid fat or adulterated with God-knew-what to make them not just inedible (soldiers could endure the merely inedible if they had to) but worthless in providing energy to fighting men. In the previous four hours he had been through the same routine with all the other supplies: the boots were already falling apart, the crossbows couldn't fire a bolt powerful enough to break the skin of a child suffering from rickets. The wagons seemed to be built to their specifications but a thirty-minute ride with half a dozen of them showed they'd barely last a week of serious use.

'I want those responsible,' said Cale, as cold as anyone had ever seen him.

But this turned out to be a good deal trickier than it seemed. Corruption in the matter of military supplies was rooted not just in the suppliers but in the people the suppliers corrupted in order to get the contracts. It was so grown into the business of procurement that those involved did not think of it as fraud. Worse than the fact that it was an ingrained habit was that control of procurement was exclusively in the gift of members of the Royal Family. It should not be thought that they actually did anything for the money except endure the strain of opening up their pockets, but the amount they expected for doing nothing was so great that there simply wasn't enough money left to provide decent weapons and food and make any kind of profit.

Warfare seemed almost easy next to this. If the OAR could not resupply quickly enough, and with the right quality of equipment for the likelihood of an early spring crossing by the Redeemers, they were finished. Yet the people responsible for creating this disaster were beyond Cale's reach.

'There's nothing I can do,' said Bose Ikard who, to be fair, saw the problem clearly enough.

'It has to stop. It has to be taken out of their hands. It's mad. Don't they realize the Redeemers will destroy them as well?'

'They're royal. Their lives are themselves a form of insanity. They are princes of the blood – a real power – an anointed power created by God flows through their veins. They're not the same as you or me.'

'And I thought the Redeemers were mad.'

'Welcome to the rest of the world,' said Ikard. 'If I intervened I'd be in a cell within an hour. What good would that do you? There must be a solution.'

'Meaning?'

'It's up to you. You're in charge now.'

'Do I have your support?'

'No. But whatever you do, make it dazzle.'

Gil had known for some time that Cale had managed to cover himself with, mostly, stolen glory from the great Redeemer victory at Bex, but everything he could learn was vague and generalized, not much better than the gossip people knew on the streets. He also had a third-hand account of Conn's trial and a first-hand account of his execution, along with the widely believed rumour that Cale had laughed and smoked as Conn's head bounced along the Quai des Moulins. If only, he thought, the claims made in Spanish Leeds about Redeemer spies were true – the only people he had in his pay were criminals, the only fellow travellers were outsiders and inadequates. But Gil was beginning to realize that it was no longer a case of separating fact from fiction when it came to Cale – it became important not to dismiss, however ludicrous, the stories of him being seven foot tall or blinding an assassin by holding his hand up in the air (though the story about him cutting off someone's head because they'd told him to get them a glass of water struck him as all too plausible). Something about Cale caused people to clothe him in their hopes and fears – the fact that they were afraid of him and yet had ridiculous expectations of his ability to save them were bound up together. And it wasn't just the stupid and desperate – look at Bosco. He was the cleverest man he knew and yet nothing could shake his belief in Cale. But that didn't stop Gil from trying.

'He's becoming powerful, Your Holiness.'

'Then,' said Bosco, 'it shows that Ikard and Zog are more intelligent than I gave them credit for.'

'He either knows or can guess what we intend to do. This is a great threat to us.'

'Not so, I think. His knowledge of our plan to attack through Arnhemland could have been serious – but at that time he was not able to persuade anyone to listen. Now we're at the Mississippi in the north and have sealed off the Brunner Pass to Leeds in the south it's perfectly obvious what we're going to do. What he knows or can guess doesn't matter.'

'Only we're not going to be facing some chinless wonder of Zog's. He knows what he's doing.'

'Of course. What else would you expect from the Left Hand of God?' He was smiling but Gil was not sure what kind of smile it was.

'What does the fact that he directly opposes us say about your plan to bring about the promised end?'

'I thought it was *our* plan – and God's plan.' Still the same smile.

'I deserve better, Your Holiness, than to be mocked for a slip of the tongue.'

'Of course, Gil. I stand corrected. The Pope begs your forgiveness. You have always been the best of servants to the harshest of all causes.'

The smile had gone but the tone of his apology was still wrong.

'What does it mean, Your Holiness, that Cale is against us?'

'It means that the Lord is sending us a message.'

'Which is?'

'I don't know. It's my fault that I can't see what he's telling me – but after all I am one of his mistakes.'

'Why doesn't he just tell you?' This was dangerous stuff and once he'd said it Gil wished he'd kept his mouth shut.

'Because my God is a subtle God. He made us because he did not want to be alone – if he has to tell us what to do and intervene on our behalf then we're no more than pets, like the lap dogs of the rich sluts in Spanish Leeds. God hints because he loves us.'

'Then why destroy us?'

Why not, thought Gil to himself as soon as he said it, *follow up a blasphemous question with an even more blasphemous one?* But he'd not taken into account how intelligent his odd master was.

'I have often thought that myself. Why, Lord, ask me to do this terrible thing?'

'And?'

'God moves in a mysterious way. I think perhaps he is

more merciful and loving than I had thought. I was arrogant,' he added bitterly, 'because I was so angry at what mankind had done to his only son. I now believe that once all our dead souls are gathered together he is going to remake us – but this time in his own image. I think so. I think that's why we must do this revolting thing.'

'But you aren't sure?'

Bosco smiled, but this time it was easy to read – it was a smile of simple humility.

'I refer you to my previous answer.'

It was clear the audience was over and it would be best to get out before he said something even more stupid. Gil bowed.

'Your Holiness.'

He had his hand on the door when Bosco called out to him.

'I will have some plans sent to you this afternoon.'

'Yes, Your Holiness.'

'It will take some effort but I'm sure it's necessary – better safe than sorry and all that. I want you to move the shipyards on the Mississippi back a hundred miles or so.'

'May I ask why, Your Holiness?' His voice clearly showed he thought the idea was absurd – but Bosco seemed not to notice. Or had decided not to.

'If I were Cale, I'd try and destroy them. It's wise to be cautious, I think.'

Outside, as he walked down the corridor, one thought was repeating itself in Gil's mind: *I must find some way to leave him.*

27

'What *will* you do?' said IdrisPukke.

'You don't want to know.'

'You haven't thought of anything, have you?'

'No, but I will.'

'Be careful.'

'I meant to ask,' said Cale, 'if you've finished the plans about going over the mountains?'

'As near as.'

'We might need them sooner than you think.' He was obviously thinking about something else. 'Does this plan include the Purgators?'

'No.'

'It should.'

'You've got very sentimental.'

'Sentiment has nothing to do with it – except my loathing for them has clouded my judgement. It's time to count my blessings. Two hundred men who'll do whatever you want, no questions asked, are worth having, wouldn't you say?'

'You're not going to like this,' said Cale to Vague Henri.

'Don't tell me there aren't any cucumber sandwiches.' Vague Henri was only partly joking. He was unusually partial to cucumber sandwiches, which had been invented only ten years before by the Materazzi dandy Lord 'Cucumber' Harris when the vegetables had first been imported to Memphis and no one knew what to do with them. Every day that he was not out and about taking care of business for the OAR Vague

Henri took high tea at four o'clock (cucumber sandwiches, cream cakes, scones) and pretended it was done to mock his former betters. In fact, he looked forward to high tea as the greatest pleasure in his life next to his very frequent visits to the Empire Of Soap in the Rue De Confort Sensuelle.

'The princes of the blood – they're going to get away with it.'

The three of them had discussed the retribution against the princes (Cale and Vague Henri always included Kleist even though he seemed indifferent to anything but his own particular tasks), as well as the manufacturers who bribed them, in terms of what should happen and how extreme and how public the acts of violence committed towards them would need to be.

'Why?' Vague Henri was no longer in a good mood. His fury at the shoddy material that had been delivered was as intense as Cale's.

'Because getting away with things that other people don't get away with is what they're good at.'

'So you're not going to cut their heads off and stick them on a spike?' This had been Vague Henri's preferred solution.

'Worse than that.'

'Go on.'

'We're going to have to reward them,' said Cale.

'You want to give them a bung?'

'Yes.'

'Why?'

'We're not strong enough to move against them. I talked to IdrisPukke and Vipond and they put me right. There isn't time to start a revolution. Bosco took twenty years to take down his enemies in Chartres and even then he had to move more quickly than he wanted to. We can't kill a dozen members of the Royal Family – we can't even afford to upset them too much. We have to bribe them to get out of the way. We need to make them anxious and then offer them a way out.

Not too anxious, and a generous exit. Tricky but possible.'

'And the factory owners?'

'We can do whatever we like to them.'

There was a short silence.

'Bollocks!' shouted Vague Henri, truly frustrated and angry. 'Promise that if we're still alive when this is over we'll come back and fuck them up. Tell me we'll do that.'

'Put them on the list,' said Cale, laughing. 'Along with all the others.'

Let us consider the acts of Thomas Cale and how they came about: the saving of Riba from a dreadful death, though only after he had run away; the somewhat reluctant return to save his not quite friends; the vandalous breaking of the beautiful Danzig Shiv; the killing of men in their sleep; the rescuing of Arbell Materazzi; the killing, sans merci, of Solomon Solomon at the Red Opera; the restoration of the Palace idiot, Simon Materazzi; Arbell saved again; the much regretted deliverance of Conn at Silbury Hill; the signing of the warrant of execution for the Maid of Blackbird Leys; the poisoning of the waters at the Golan Heights; the destruction and invention of the camps, in which five thousand women and children died of starvation and disease; the strangling of Kitty the Hare; the burning of the bridge after Bex; and perjuring himself at Conn Materazzi's trial. To these he now added the kidnap and murder of the twenty merchants he held responsible for the trash delivered to his depots the week before. Naked as worms, the men were strung up in front of the palacios of the royal princes of the blood who had accepted bribes from them. Their bodies were horribly mutilated, noses and ears cut off, lips and fingers stitched together holding a coin in their tongueless mouths and clenched hands. Their left eyes were gouged, their gallbladders – held to be the seat of greed – removed.

Around their necks a sheet of paper, later distributed in hundreds throughout the city, revealed the terrible nature of their crimes against every man, woman and child whose lives they were prepared to sell in pursuit of money. The pamphlet was signed 'The Knights of the Left Hand'.

To be strictly fair to Cale and Vague Henri, the men had been murdered as quickly and painlessly as time and circumstances allowed. The terrible torture inflicted on them as a lesson to the rest was done after they had been killed. History cannot judge: history is written by historians. Only the reader in possession of the facts can decide whether he could have acted otherwise in the circumstances or reasonably seen the consequences of his acts.

On the walls of the palacios from which the bodies were hung a sentence was written in old Spanish, it being an affectation of the aristocracy that they should speak a language among themselves of a kind not spoken in Spain for several hundred years.

Pesado has sido en balanza, y fuiste hallado falto.

Broadly speaking this could be translated as 'You have been weighed in the balance and found wanting' – an observation that would be found meaningless to *hoi polloi* but menacing enough to the twelve princes of the blood involved in taking money from the dead men hanging upside down outside their mansions. Cale let them fret for twenty-four hours and then IdrisPukke, on behalf of the OAR, delivered a large paper bag of money to compensate them for the loss of revenue from their entirely legitimate contract with the late factory owners that the OAR had now been obliged, in the face of grave national emergency, to take over in the greater interest of all. The twelve princes of the blood acquiesced because they were not sure what else to do: they had been threatened although they did not know precisely how, and rewarded although they did not know precisely why.

Not only was there very little fuss concerning the kidnapping, torture and murder of men who had faced no trial, let alone their accusers, rather there was a clamour to root out anyone else involved, and much support from the slums upwards for the Knights of the Left Hand and their methods.

A week after Spanish Leeds had been set alight by the murders, Robert Hooke received a visit from Cale to hear his initial report on the possibility of manufacturing guns.

'There's nothing wrong with the *idea* of guns,' said Hooke, as they looked over the expensively bought shooting iron. 'It's the practice that's the problem. The villainous saltpetre that's packed in at this end – it's too much for the iron. That's why it explodes. Simple as that really.'

'Then get better iron.'

'It doesn't exist. Not yet.'

'How long?'

'No idea – months, years. Not enough time anyway.'

'So that's it?'

'Mmm . . . no . . . maybe not. I was talking to Vague Henri. He told me he'd made his crossbows much easier to load – but it means they're much less powerful.'

'We don't need them to be powerful – they're for close range fighting – a few feet.'

'You never said that.'

'So?'

'So? It's everything. What's the maximum range you'll be fighting at?'

'A few yards mostly – our men will be behind wooden walls – as little man to man fighting as possible.'

'Will the Redeemers have armour?'

'Some, but not much. But I suppose they'll start using more.'

Hooke looked down at the shooting iron. 'Then you don't need this.' He held up a large lead shot the size of a chicken's egg. 'You don't need this either.' He gestured Cale over to a table covered by a cloth and drew it off like a conjuror at a children's party revealing a magic cake.

'It's just a wooden mock-up – but you can see the principle.'

It was similar to the shooting iron – a tube sealed at one end and open at the other – but cut longways in two so you could see the inner workings.

'The thing is,' said Hooke, 'is not to overload it. You need the right amount of villainous saltpetre – as little as possible – and something light to be exploded out the other end.'

'How light?'

Hooke opened up a small canvas bag and spread its contents on the table. It was just a collection of nails, small shards and nuggets of metal – even a few stones. It was hard to be impressed. 'The main thing is to get the size of the charge right. Every time. No offence but your men'll overdo it. And then I thought – why not put a uniform charge in a little canvas bag, easy to load, always the same charge? Then I thought, why not do the same with the metal and stone shot? *Then,*' he said, warming to his brilliance, 'I thought – why not put them both into another bag? Easy to load, and damn quick. Brilliant.'

'Will it work?'

'Come and see.'

Hooke ushered Cale outside where two of his assistants stood next to an iron pipe, much like the shooting iron, held in a wooden vice. About ten yards away was a dead dog strapped to a plank. Hooke, Cale and the assistants took cover behind a pouisse. One of the assistants lit a taper on the end of a long stick and carefully eased it out to the shooting iron. As he was trying to expose as little of himself as possible it took several tries to light the pan. Able to watch through a set of drilled holes, Cale saw the villainous saltpetre in the pan flash, followed a few seconds later by a BANG! – loud, but not as loud as he'd expected. They waited a few seconds and Hooke walked out through the dense smoke, followed by Cale, and over to the dead dog. He'd expected to see something terrible but at first he thought the shot must have missed. It hadn't – at least, not entirely. Once Hooke pointed out the wounds there were clearly half a dozen bits of nail and stone embedded quite deep in the animal's flesh.

'It might not kill. But you get hit by this and you won't be taking part in anything more than groaning in agony for some time. And the thing is – if you only use it at mass ranks close in, each shot will wound two or three or more every time.'

'How many times a minute to load and fire?'

'We can do three. But we're not in battle conditions. I'd say – conservative – two.'

They spent another hour discussing the men and materials he needed and where the new shooting irons could be cast and how reliable the supply would be.

'There shouldn't be a problem. The stress on these will be much lower so it shouldn't be too hard to come up with the quality we need. Besides, I suppose it's pretty clear what'll happen if they deliver anything second-rate.'

He looked at Cale thoughtfully.

'Everyone knows it was you.'

Cale looked back at him.

'Everyone knows it was me who laughed at Conn when he died. Everyone knows it was me who cut off a man's head for ordering me to bring him a drink of water.'

Hooke smiled.

'Everyone knows it was you.'

'Everyone,' said Bose Ikard, 'knows it was him.'

'There was an old lady,' said Fanshawe in reply, 'who swallowed a bird.'

'I don't follow you.'

'You see, she swallowed the bird to catch the spider that she swallowed in order to catch the fly that she swallowed.'

'You mean something but I'm too irritable for your cockiness.'

'I was merely suggesting that even if the cure for the disease is not as bad as the disease, Thomas Cale might be very bad indeed for you.'

'But not you?'

'Indeed he might. The Laconics are outnumbered four to one by serfs.'

'Our peasants are the salt of the earth, not slaves. We don't kill them without compunction. So we're not afraid to go to sleep in case they cut our throats. We are one nation.'

'I truly doubt that. But of course you're in the middle of a wonderful experiment to test your confidence. It will be so interesting if Cale pulls it off to see whether your people are happy to go back to a life of sheep-shagging and forelock-tugging.'

'What's your point, if you have one?'

'That you have to know when to stop swallowing. Do you want to know how the song ends?'

'Not particularly,' said Bose Ikard.

'But it's enchanting. "There was an old lady who swallowed a horse. She's dead of course."'

28

'Fanshawe has offered to supply a hundred Laconics to train the New Model Army.'

The three boys, Kleist ever more silent, were eating oysters in lemon juice with IdrisPukke, accompanied by a dry, flinty Sancerre to cut out the saltiness.

'Obviously you can't trust him,' said IdrisPukke, enjoying the puzzle concerning what Fanshawe was up to as much as the oysters and the wine. 'But in what *way* can't you trust him?'

'He doesn't expect me to believe he's doing it out of the goodness of his heart. He doesn't think I'm that stupid.'

'So how stupid does he think you are?'

There was a delightful snigger from Vague Henri at this. Nothing from Kleist. He seemed not to be listening.

'I think Fanshawe's realized we might stop Bosco and they want to be on the . . . not losing side.'

At this point they were joined by Artemisia.

'Oysters, my dear?' said IdrisPukke.

'No, thank you,' she said sweetly. 'Where I come from we feed them to the pigs.' He was highly amused by this, rather to her surprise, because she'd intended to take him down a peg: for some reason she wrongly suspected him of condescending to her. He turned back to Cale.

'How is he intending to explain the presence of so many Laconics to the Redeemers?'

'It's only a hundred. He's going to claim they're renegades.'

'All right. You don't believe him. But again, *how* don't you believe him?'

'I don't know. Not yet. But I need his instructors whatever his reasons. Losses are going to be high. We need to churn out replacements at five thousand a month. And that's cutting it fine. It's going to be a damn close-run thing.'

'It's an idea,' said Kleist, 'worth discussing, I think.' When he spoke these days, which was rarely, it was about details. He seemed to find some peace in the minute particulars of the heel of a boot or the way the leather was stitched to keep out the wet. 'We've been assuming they aren't going to try to come across the Mississippi in the winter.'

Artemisia groaned in irritation.

'I've told you – the Mississippi doesn't freeze over like other rivers, not completely. It becomes a mass of ice blocks breaking and crashing into each other. Treacherous doesn't begin to describe it. They're not coming over in numbers until well into the spring.'

'I believe you,' said Kleist, quietly. 'But you said they couldn't come over in numbers.'

'So?'

'But it would be possible to cross . . .'

'Not with an army or anything like it.'

Kleist didn't react to the irritated interruption, he just kept on in his dull monotone. 'But it would be possible to cross a small force.'

'What good would that do?'

'I don't mean for the Redeemers to cross in small numbers, I mean for us to cross in small numbers over to them.'

There was a short silence.

'To do what?' said Cale.

'You said it would be close.'

'It will.'

'What if you had more time . . . months, maybe a whole year?'

'Go on.'

'The Redeemers are building boats over the winter for an invasion in the spring. Do you know where they're building them?'

'I don't see . . .' said Artemisia.

'Do you know where they're building them?' Now it was Kleist doing the interrupting.

'Yes,' she said. 'The section on the North Bank between Athens and Austerlitz is packed with boatyards but the Redeemers have moved the factories back, along with the builders, to Lucknow so they can control construction of the fleet.'

'So all their boats are in one place?'

'Mostly, as far as I know.'

'So if you could get a force of, say, a thousand across the river in maybe early spring, could you attack Lucknow and burn their fleet?'

'I couldn't get a thousand across,' said Artemisia. 'Or anything like it.'

'How many then?' said Cale, clearly excited.

'I don't know. I'd have to talk to the river pilots. I don't know.'

'Two hundred?'

'I don't know. Maybe.'

'It would be worth the risk,' said Cale.

'It would be my people taking it,' said Artemisia.

'I'm sorry,' said Cale. 'That's true. But if it could be done.'

'I'd have to lead it,' she said.

Cale wasn't happy with this.

'I need you here and alive. Your outriders are the eyes and ears of the fortress wagons.' This was true enough, but it was not the only, or even the main, reason. 'Besides,' he lied, 'it's an unbroken rule that the man . . . the person who comes up with the plan has the right to put it into operation.'

Artemisia stared at Kleist. 'You have an extensive knowledge of riverwork and know the North Bank of the Mississippi in Halicarnassus?'

'No.'

'I *do* have an extensive knowledge of riverwork and, as it happens, I *own* the North Bank of the Mississippi in Halicarnassus.'

This even made Kleist smile.

'I withdraw,' he said. Cale looked at him, not pleasantly.

'There's another problem,' said IdrisPukke.

'Are you an expert on riverwork and Halicarnassus as well as all your other achievements?'

'No, my dear, I know nothing about either. This is more politics.'

'What's that got to do with it?'

'Everything comes down to politics one way or another. Is this a risky venture, would you say?'

'Of course.'

'You might easily fail then?'

'Cale's right,' said Artemisia. 'If there's even a limited chance of causing such damage we should take it. It's my life and those of my people.'

'I wasn't so much, I'm afraid, worrying about the lives of two hundred people – there'll be many sets of two hundred dead before this is over. I was worrying more about what the implications for everything else would be if you fail.'

'I admit I don't follow, but then that's the point, isn't it? You want me to seem like a stupid girl.'

'Not at all,' replied IdrisPukke. 'But think about it. If you attack in late spring this will be the first action of the New Model Army against the Redeemers. Yes?'

'He's right,' said Cale, seeing a hope of stopping her.

'The army at large doesn't need to know anything unless we succeed,' said Artemisia.

'I was talking about politics,' said IdrisPukke. 'You can

keep it from the army and the people if you're careful, but can you keep it from Bose Ikard and the High Command?'

'I'll persuade them it's a risk worth taking.'

'But politicians don't like risks, they like deals. Remember that they're so afraid of the Redeemers that they're ready to put a mad boy in charge.'

'He's talking about you,' said Vague Henri to Cale, 'just in case you didn't realize'.

'They're on the razor's edge, all of them. Then the first thing you offer them is an abject failure – they'll be begging Bosco for negotiations while the ashes are still warm on this young woman's bonfire. You can live without this victory – you might not be able to live with a defeat.'

'It's worth the risk,' said Artemisia.

'I'm not sure that it is,' said IdrisPukke.

Cale had been given his chance and he was careful not to turn it down.

'This is a new idea. We need to think about it.'

'Think about it and say no, that's what you mean,' said Artemisia.

'Not true. Talk to your river pilots. See what they have to say. Work out a plan. When you have we'll talk about it again.'

When Artemisia had left, Cale turned on Kleist.

'We haven't had a peep out of you in months but suddenly we can't shut you up!'

'You should have told us she was just along to improve the view – all we've heard from you till now is what a war genius she is.'

This was true and he couldn't think of the last word. He had it anyway. 'Bollocks!'

A few hours later Cale suffered another attack of the connip-tions – longer and more violent in its retchings than usual.

The demon, or demons, that inhabited his chest seemed to live in their own world, woke and slept on their own time, regardless of anything Cale did or did not do. They were unaware of the daily life of the boy they inhabited, indifferent to whether things went well or badly, if he was loved or hated, was kind or pitiless. The herbs worked up to a point, as he found out when he tried to stop taking them and the chest devils dry-heaved into existence two or three times a day instead of three or four times a week, which was bad enough. As for the Phedra and Morphine, he'd not had any reason to take it again and he wasn't looking for one. The horrible down after he'd used it had lasted two weeks and made him feel as if he'd had a sip from death in a bottle. He did try offering the herbs to Kleist but he irritably refused, saying there was nothing wrong with him and he didn't need Old Mother Hubbard's helper to keep him going.

Even at best Cale had to work in short bursts, resting all the time and sleeping twelve hours or more a day. However much of a disadvantage this was in some ways – he felt horrible nearly all the time – it did produce some useful effects. He could not stay in any meeting for more than a few minutes and there were plenty of them to squeeze the life out of any action that needed to be taken. Never a friendly presence to most, his attendance at any gathering was tense to the point where he seemed almost on the edge of furious violence. Because he had no choice, his already decisive character tore through complex and dangerous decisions as if he was ordering meat for the guards back in Arbell's house in Memphis. Oddly, somewhere inside his damaged mind he was sometimes at his sharpest: there was a place there cut off from the outside world he'd been building since the first moment he'd arrived at the Sanctuary. Through all those years of long use this place of retreat was as tough as the skin on an elephant's foot – and needed to be to keep out the madness that was destroying the rest of him.

Do this. Give him that. Take those. Put it there. Do it again. Release these. Hang them. None of this denied the debt he owed to his friends. He smiled when he said, 'Bring me solutions, not problems. You solve it. Every time I have to answer a stupid question think of it as hammering a nail into my coffin.'

And for the moment it worked. Each one of them could rely on the fear and dread and hope that Cale's reputation inspired. Even Vipond, a man of power if ever there was one, and who knew now even better what its nature was having lost so much of it, was amazed at what he could only describe as the magic others invested in Cale.

'I've told you,' said IdrisPukke, who relished any chance to condescend to his half-brother. 'The spirit of the times is in him. He has great abilities but that's not why, or not mostly why, he's in the ascendant. Look at Alois Huttler – you could find a thousand dunces like him giving out their half-baked opinions in any public house in the country. But Alois had the spirit of the times in him. Until he didn't.'

'When people are faced with annihilation,' observed IdrisPukke, 'it's not difficult to see why they want to believe the Left Hand of God is behind them.'

On this occasion he was sounding off about Cale in his presence. Vague Henri gurned at his friend.

'Pity all they've got is you, then.'

'Your sickness,' said IdrisPukke, 'is becoming a kind of blessing.'

'I'm glad you think so.'

'Not for you personally, of course. But didn't Bosco tell you that Thomas Cale is not a person?'

'Yes, but he's mad.'

'But not stupid. Am I right?'

'You might not be always right, but I agree you're never wrong.'

Laughter at this. IdrisPukke shrugged.

'Perhaps in his madness he recognized something we're only beginning to see ourselves. People find it easy to shine their dreadful hopes on you – the left hand of death, indeed, but on *their* side. It may be that the less you're seen to do – the less of a person who's like them – the more powerful you are.' He sighed with enormous satisfaction. 'I'm impressed by myself.' More laughter. 'We can make use of this.'

Against the weariness of being sick was the pleasure of working on the tactics of the New Model Army. The training was going better than Cale had imagined. Protected by the wagons, and using weapons based on tools they were used to working with for hours every day of their lives, the confidence of the peasant soldiers soared. The most effective of these hillbilly weapons was the threshers' flail – a pole of four or five feet long linked by a chain to another pole of eighteen inches or so. These men were used to using them for ten hours a day after harvest and the swinging heads generated such a powerful force they could badly injure a knight in full armour let alone the less protected Redeemer men at arms. But above everything they worked on finding out every weakness of the war wagons. Vague Henri had the Purgator archers shooting in massed ranks at the wagon forts to work out how to protect the occupants and came up with bamboo-covered walkways and small shelters into which anyone caught in the open during such an attack could run to protect themselves. It wouldn't take the Redeemers long to try to use something like fire arrows to set the wagons alight so he had the Swiss soldiers – who would be mostly used for attacks outside the fort and so were not being used for much during attacks –

train in teams to put out fires before they took hold, mostly using buckets filled with earth and using water only if they must. They objected to this with puzzling intensity. They were soldiers and gentlemen – it was demeaning digging dirt and so the peasants should do it. All their resentments at the bewildering changes they had been forced to endure came out in this single issue of putting out fires. Out of nothing, Vague Henri found he had a mutiny on his hands. Cale was always mocking him by saying what a nice boy he was. Up to a point this was true, but because they were used to Cale as contrast there was a general misunderstanding about Vague Henri and what he was capable of. He seemed very normal in a way that Cale was clearly not, but he had experienced the same corrosive brutality and deadliness of the Redeemer life. It was a part of him too. Realizing he was on the edge of something disastrous his first instinct was to deal with the problem the Redeemer way: kill a couple of the noisier pro-testors and leave them to rot where everyone could see their mistake. Whether he would have been ready to do this and sleep well afterwards was fortunately not put to the test. There was something of good nature but also something of calcula-tion that made him look for another way first.

Vague Henri, Cale and Kleist had talked at great length over how real they should make the practice fighting. The Redeemers took the motto 'Train hard, fight easy' to extremes. Mock Redeemer battles weren't always easy to distinguish from the real thing other than that in the former they allowed the survivors to live. All three feared the result of pushing the practice battles too hard would be to create more prob-lems than they solved and for the same reason as for the summary execution: the souls of the Swiss, peasant or gentleman, weren't accustomed by long habit to brutality. But the Swiss soldiers had to be taught respect one way or another. 'Right,' said Vague Henri to his gentlemen soldiers. 'You think you're so much better than they are. Prove it.' He followed this by going to the peasants in the New Model Army and telling them that there were doubts in Spanish Leeds they'd be up to the task of a real battle – they were, after all, peasants and would be bound to run when the going got tough. He'd avoided saying that this was the view of the Swiss soldiers because soon they were going to have to fight together. It was enough: they were incensed. But there was more at stake than just repeating the battle and the lesson of Silver Field: both sides had to be defeated this time.

Three days later, with Cale – a fascinated spectator – they watched the gloves-off attack by Swiss men at arms and mounted knights on the country bumpkins. It was nasty stuff, but the Swiss, for all their skill and determination, were at a huge disadvantage because they took ten times as many blows for each one they could land. After a bloody hour they withdrew and Vague Henri showed his final and very convincing hand. He pulled up four hundred fire-archers and got them pouring in three or four a minute each for ten minutes. By the end the peasants were driven out as the thirty wagons burnt like the seventh circle of hell.

It was a brutal and expensive point but it was well made – both sides realized they would live or die together.

'I've been to see IdrisPukke about this, twice, but he keeps pissing in my ear,' said Fanshawe. 'I want them rounded up and sent back.'

'For what reason?' said an exhausted Cale, not much in the mood for anything except sleep.

'As if you care about reasons.'

'I do now – so what are they?'

'These two hundred and fifty Helots belong to the state.'

'That would be the state that's signed a treaty with the Redeemers.'

'We're helping you in practice, aren't we?'

'I don't think we should go down the road of your good intentions. We can if you like.'

'The Helots threaten our existence as much as the Redeemers threaten yours. There are four times as many of them in Laconia as there are of us. They're here to learn from you how they can kill the state that owns them. If you don't want to be seen to be working against us let me deal with them.'

'Let's get this straight. I'm the one who *deals* with things here. You go anywhere near them and I'll have you swinging off the nearest maypole upside down and with your nose in my pocket.'

There was a silence – not very pleasant.

'Then we'll leave.'

Another silence.

'I'm not sending two hundred and fifty men back to be executed,' said Cale.

'What do you care?'

'Never mind what I care about. I'm not doing it.' Fanshawe, nevertheless, could see a concession was coming. 'I'll move them on.'

'Meaning?'

'I'll have them escorted over the mountains by some unpleasant people I know and told to get lost.'

'And if they refuse?'

'Don't be ridiculous.'

'Can I trust you on this?'

'I don't give a sack of rancid badger giblets for your trust one way or the other. I want you to stay and I promise I'll get rid of them. Take it or leave it. That's all there is.'

It made sense to Fanshawe that his instructors were much

more valuable than a couple of hundred untrained peasants so he decided to give way – though as ungraciously as possible in order to leave Cale with the impression he was deeply unhappy with the outcome. He wasn't particularly.

The next day Cale woke up from a sixteen-hour sleep still tired, and to find IdrisPukke had arrived for a short meeting.

'You should have told me about Fanshawe kicking off over the Helots,' said Cale.

'Not in my opinion,' said IdrisPukke. 'You made it clear that we, by which I mean *me*, were supposed to bring you solutions and not problems. You should have refused to see him. In fact, you should refuse to see anyone – cultivate your mystery. The more you talk to people the more human you'll seem to them and so the more comprehensible and therefore weaker. You're not the incarnation of the Wrath of God, you're a very sick boy.'

'Don't bother polishing it, will you?'

'If I must – you're a very *remarkable*, very sick boy.'

'I think we should give the Helots some help.'

'Why?'

'If we beat the Redeemers, it'll come at a price. We'll be the weaker. There's every chance the Laconics will take advantage. So, if they've got to deal with slaves, newly trained slaves, there's less chance the Laconics will be making a nuisance of themselves with us.'

'And that's all?'

'Meaning?'

'You haven't fallen for one of those generous impulses that affect you from time to time?'

'Such as?'

'You sympathize with them – you identify with them as people struggling to be free of an ugly oppressor.'

'Would that be so bad?'

'That's three questions in answer to my three questions: rude but revealing.'

'I hate to be rude.'

'You're walking a thin line, boy, we all are – you can't afford to take on a cause you don't have the power to support.'

'I'm not. But I don't see why we can't send the Helots to the east to train with the Purgators there.'

'I agree.'

A pause.

'So you'll send them?'

'I already have.'

'Great minds think alike.'

'If it pleases you to think so.'

Cale rang a small silver bell to signal he wanted his tea. He felt absurdly self-important doing something so precious but it saved the effort of going to the door and shouting. Tea arrived immediately as the butler had merely been waiting for the bell. IdrisPukke looked on with anticipation at the assortment of sandwiches laid before him, crusts removed and cut into dainty triangles: cheese, egg, and horsemeat with cucumber. There were pastries from Patisserie Valerie in Mott Street: cream selva and wild strawberry millefeuille and almond frangipane with its intoxicating whiff of sweet cyanide.

'Finding things to spend your money on?' said IdrisPukke.

Cale smiled. 'Eat thou and drink; tomorrow thou shalt die,' he said – a line spoken to him three times a day before meals at the Sanctuary.

'No arguing with that,' said IdrisPukke, taking a large bite out of a veal pie with a boiled egg in the middle. 'Koolhaus came to see me looking for a job.'

'He's already got a job,' said Cale.

'He's an able young man – very. We know him and he knows us. It's a waste. He can make himself useful.'

'I'm not going to leave Simon deaf and dumb again. Offer him more money.'

'He's ambitious. We could lose him and it would be best to keep someone who knows a great many of our secrets inside the fold. He could be a great nuisance, too.'

Cale munched absentmindedly on a red velvet cupcake.

'All right. Put him to work with Kleist or Vague Henri for a month. See how it goes. If he's got the right stuff send him to keep an eye on things in West Thirteen. But he takes Simon with him.'

'Arbell will try to stop him.'

'If Simon lets her then he's out. Send Koolhaus on his own.'

They sat in pleasant silence for a few minutes enjoying their tea.

'You should go and see Riba,' said IdrisPukke at last.

'Because?'

'We need to make more use of her.'

'I tried that already. She's learnt gratitude from her old mistress.'

To his great irritation, IdrisPukke laughed.

'You've got a very elevated expectation of other people's capacity for gratitude.'

'Not any more, I haven't.'

'I disagree; you asked her to betray her husband – and a brand new husband at that. You didn't even give her time to become disillusioned with him.'

'Well, I'm glad you think it's funny. I stopped that ungrateful cow from being disembowelled while she was still alive by that mad bastard Picarbo.'

IdrisPukke kept on eating a cake during this rant and when he'd finished eating put down his plate and said, 'You know I'd forgotten what a drip you can be.' Cale was startled but not by the refusal to grant that his resentment was entirely justified. 'You think you're so much above everyone else – don't deny it.'

'I wasn't going to,' said Cale.

'Then why are you so surprised that other people don't live up to your standards? You can't have it both ways, sonny. You need to make your mind up. Or in future stick to performing your magnanimous acts of self-sacrifice for the benefit of the heroic and exceptionally virtuous.'

IdrisPukke poured Cale a cup of tea and tinkled the bell. It was a mocking present from Cadbury for Vague Henri, bought when he discovered he ordered high tea every afternoon.

'You rang, sir,' said the butler.

'More tea, Lascelles,' said IdrisPukke.

'Very well, sir,' said Lascelles and left.

'You claim you expect nothing of others yet you clearly expect some of them to give up everything. Why?'

'Only people I risked my life to save.'

'There's a difference between what people ought to do and what they're capable of doing. You've never had a wife or a father to split your loyalties. I'm sure it cost her a great deal to turn you down which is why you should show some backbone and make use of her guilt. She'll want to help you prove she's not thankless.'

'They should have trusted me.'

'No doubt. But they were afraid.'

'I know what it means to be afraid.'

'Do you, now? You see I'm not sure that's true – or not true enough.'

Lascelles came back with the tea and after that IdrisPukke changed the subject.

29

'You're still angry with me,' said Riba, more statement than question.

'No. I've had plenty of time to cool down. I realized I asked too much from you.'

She was not convinced by his claim of forgiveness but it was equally necessary for her to act as if she were. Guilt and policy demanded it – her husband wanted to establish good relations with the newly powerful Cale.

'How are you?'

'As you can see,' said Cale, smiling.

She said later to her husband, 'He was pale the way yellow-green is pale.'

'And you?'

'Very well.' There was a pause as she struggled to decide whether to tell him. But she wanted to – and desperately.

'I'm going to have a baby.'

'Oh.'

'You're supposed to say: "How wonderful, my dear, I'm so very happy for you."'

'I am . . . I am happy for you.' He laughed. 'The thing is I can't believe, not really, that a small person can grow inside another person. It doesn't seem possible – that it could really happen.'

'It's true,' said Riba, laughing herself. 'When one of the maids let me see her tummy when she was seven months I screamed when I saw the baby turn over and her stomach bulging – it was like watching a cat in a bag.' They both smiled at each other – affection, calculation and resentment layered one on top of the other. 'Now you have to ask me when I'm due.'

'I don't know what that means.'

'When am I going to have it?'

'When are you going to have it?'

'Six months.' Another pause. 'Now you ask if I want a boy or a girl.'

'I don't really care.'

She laughed again – but nothing, of course, could be the same.

'I want your husband's help.'

'Then I'll arrange for him to come and see you.'

'I'm not being insulting, but I want actual help not what the Hanse have been offering up to now.'

'Which is?'

'You tell me. Better than that – show me.'

'I'm just his wife. I can't speak for him, let alone the Hanse.'

'No, but you can speak *to* him. You can persuade him not to beat around the bund with me. There's no time. I mean it. If he stays on the sidelines and I win I won't forget – by which I mean I'll close down the Hanse from here to the life to come.'

'What if you don't win?'

'Then he's got nothing to worry about, has he?'

She was uncertain about what to say. 'It's not just a question of what *he* believes or wants. The Hanseatic League don't have much experience of the Redeemers. They think their reputation is just scaremongering. That's what they want to believe. You mustn't say I told you this but they won't send troops, not at any price. There's nothing he can do about that – and if you ask for them the Hanse will keep you waiting for an answer for months.'

'What can I ask for?'

'Money, perhaps.'

'I don't need money – I need administrators, people who know how to order and supply, warehousing, delivery – all the stuff the Hanse knows how to do. I don't need money, five hundred good people will do.' It was a figure plucked from the air. 'With so few it doesn't have to be official. The Hanse don't have to be seen in it. But I want them and I want them now.' He looked at her, and smiled. 'I lied about the money. I want the money as well.'

As Riba got into her cab to leave she was watched from two storeys above by Vague Henri. He was remembering the time he hid behind a small hillock in the Scablands and watched her bathing naked in a pool, all gorgeously chubby curves but muscularly plump and wetly soft, and he was recalling the tingling in his chest as she unmindfully parted the folds between her legs. But that was another world.

Two minutes later, Vague Henri joined Cale for what was left of afternoon tea.

'How was it?' he asked.

'Nobody loves us,' said Cale.

'We don't care,' replied Vague Henri.

That night Cale held Artemisia in his arms for the last time. If their nakedness and embrace implied warmth there was a great cold distance between them for all the touching of their skin. Cale, inexperienced in the reasons why she never closed her eyes any more when he kissed her face, was unsure what he felt or what to do about it: he'd never liked someone and then stopped liking them before. How could something so close as being inside someone – how strange it was, how strange – turn into such a vast distance so quickly?

'I want to cross the river,' she said.

'It's complicated.'

'That's what people say when they're about to say no – to their children, I mean.'

He pulled away from her and sat up, looking for his cigars. He only had half of one left. He lit up.

'Must you smoke?'

'Worried for my health?'

'I don't like it.'

He didn't reply but he did carry on smoking.

'I want to go.' Still he didn't say anything. 'I'm going to go.' He turned to look at her. 'I'm going to go, no matter what you say.'

'You might have noticed,' he said at last, blowing a long stream of smoke into the room, 'that I'm the person who tells people what to do.'

'Oh, so what will you do, Your Enormity, have me arrested? Will you hang me up outside the Prada as an example?'

'You're raving. You need to take something.'

'I'm going.'

He looked at her.

'Go then.'

This took some of the wind out of her sails.

'Is this one of your little swindles?' she said at last.

'No.'

She stood up, quite naked, almost like a miniature woman compared to Riba.

'I understand. I see right through you to the other side. This is a good way to get rid of me.'

'So I'm the villain if I let you go and the villain if I stop you from going.'

'You're prepared to let me risk my life and the lives of hundreds because you haven't got the guts to finish with me.

Let me save you the trouble – I don't want anything more to do with you. You're a liar, and a murderer.'

The insults had let him off the hook. She had made the decision for him and a wonderful sense of relief flooded through him. 'Well?' he said, as she put on her clothes.

'I'm going.'

'You mean you're going now or you're going to cross the Mississippi?'

'Both.' She stood up, put on her shoes, walked through the door and took care not to slam it shut.

'What do you want me to do about it?' said Cale to IdrisPukke after he'd told him he'd given Artemisia permission to cross the Mississippi. 'Should I have her killed?'

'You were brought up very careless. Why does your mind always turn so quickly to murder?'

Cale laughed. 'I was, yes. But now I have you to tell me right from wrong.'

'You misunderstand me if that's what you think. It's true that sometimes, not very often, moral rules collide and you offend no matter what decision you make. But the world isn't a wicked place because people don't know the difference between right and wrong. Nine times out of ten the right course of action is clear enough but for one thing.'

'Which is?'

'That it doesn't suit people's interests or desires to do what's right. Granted they have impressive ways of dealing with the anxiety that results – by burying it deep at the back of their minds, or better still, telling themselves that the bad course of action they're about to take is really the best course of action. The moralist never lived who could tell you anything clearer than the Golden Rule.'

'There's a Golden Rule?' mocked Cale.

'There is indeed, sarcastic boy: treat others as you would want to be treated. Everything else in morality is just embroidery or lies.'

Cale didn't say anything for a while.

'How,' he said, at last, 'am I supposed to apply that to sending tens of thousands of people either to die or to kill tens of thousands of other people? In order to survive I've had to lie, cheat, murder and destroy. Now I have to do the same so that millions of others can survive with me. How does your Golden Rule help me there? Tell me, because I'd like to know.'

'But I concede there are other times when morality is very tricky. That's why we have so many moralists to tell us what to do.'

'Anyway,' said Cale, 'I have my own Golden Rule.'

'Which is?' said IdrisPukke, smiling as well as curious.

'Treat others as you would expect to be treated by them. It always works for me.' He helped himself to another cup of tea. 'So why are you against the attack over the Mississippi?'

'I wouldn't say I was against it. To be honest, I'm not sure. The thing is that if she fails . . .'

'And she might not.'

'She might not. But if she does, then her failure weakens you at the exact point you need a failure least.'

'But if she succeeds?'

'That might not be such good news as first it seems.'

'A massive blow to the Redeemers and an extra year to prepare – not good news?'

'Nobody likes you. You agree?'

'They'll like me if I'm a success.'

'Will they? They've put you in a position of such power because they're afraid . . .'

'Terrified.'

'Yes. Terrified is better. While they're scared witless they'll put up with you. But now Artemisia is one of them, not any longer one of you.'

'Is she? They didn't think so when she was the only one to crimp the Redeemers six months ago.'

'That was when the alternative was themselves – now the alternative is you.' He laughed.

'You think they'll put her in charge?'

'No. But they'll start thinking that they over-estimated you. They'd like that. Don't forget they're already thinking about what to do with you, not just if you fail but also if you succeed. If a man threatens the state, kill the man.'

'It works just as well the other way round: if the state threatens the man, kill the state.'

'Exactly . . . that's exactly what they fear . . . that you're going to kill the state if you get too powerful. So a great success by Artemisia, which gives them another year for preparation . . . they'll have the time to be a lot less terrified of the Redeemers who are now beatable by someone who isn't Thomas Cale, beatable by just a woman, in fact. You need her to succeed like you need a hole in the head.'

Cale sighed.

'You're sure you're not making this more complicated than it is?'

IdrisPukke laughed.

'No, I'm not sure at all. When I heard that Richelieu was dead – now there was a subtle mind – I didn't think: *Oh, Richelieu is dead*. What I thought was: *I wonder what he meant by that?* To be a politician is to see there might be a disadvantage to the sun coming up in the morning. Do you mind if I have the last Eccles cake?'

Cale had been looking forward to eating it himself. IdrisPukke had already had one.

'No,' he said. IdrisPukke, like all great diplomats, assumed that this meant *No, you have the last cake* and not otherwise. He took a large bite. They sat in silence for a moment.

'Kant,' said IdrisPukke.

'What?'

'Imamuel Kant. Philosopher. Now dead. He said that if you want to know whether your actions are moral you should universalize them.'

'I don't know what that means.'

'If you want to know if a course of action you're about to undertake is wrong you should ask yourself: what if everyone behaved like that?'

This seemed to intrigue Cale. IdrisPukke could see him thinking back over his past: the men killed in their sleep, the poisoned wells, the execution of prisoners, signing the death warrant of the Maid of Blackbird Leys, killing Kitty the Hare, the death of factory owners hung up outside the houses of *hoi aristoi*. It took some time.

'Well?' asked IdrisPukke at last.

'The Maid of Blackbird Leys was a good person . . . courageous, but a dope like Imamuel Kant. What if you ask the same question about your good actions? What if everyone behaved like that? What if everyone took on the Redeemers like her by putting up posters and preaching? They'd end up exactly the way she did – in a pile of ashes. If you fight cruelty with kindness it's the kindness that goes away not the cruelty. I'm sorry about the camps and what happened to the women and children of the Folk. I have bad dreams. But I didn't mean it to happen.'

'Traditionally the road to hell is paved with good intentions.'

'Well, it wasn't a good intention, exactly. If I had to do it again I'd do it differently – but I don't. I have bad dreams instead. But not every night. If you do something terrible you either throw yourself over a cliff or get on with it.'

They sat in silence for a while.

'Except for that shit-bag Solomon Solomon, I never acted out of malice. Well, him and a few other people.'

'You laughed when they killed Conn Materazzi – and you cut off a man's head for telling you to bring him a glass of water.'

Cale smiled, not needing to point out neither was true.

'It's only fair to tell you,' added IdrisPukke after a short silence, 'that Imamuel Kant also said it was always wrong to tell lies. He said that if you decided to hide a friend who'd come to your house and said a murderer was after him, and then that murderer came to your door and asked if your friend was there because he had to kill him – well, then it would be wrong to tell a lie. You'd have to do the right thing and give him up.'

'You're making fun of me.'

'No. I promise. He really said that.'

'Tell me, IdrisPukke, if you faced the extermination of you and yours at the hands of the Redeemers, who would you want standing between you and them – me or Imamuel Kant?'

Most of us experience days like this: from the moment the sun rises like a ribbon until it sets in rosy fingers everything goes wonderfully well, except for the things that go even better – money arrives unexpectedly in large amounts, beautiful women stroke your arm as if they thought nothing was more wonderful than the touch of your skin, a chance remark allows you to see that everyone who does not love you holds you still in high regard. Who is so unfortunate not to have had days like these? Cale was so fortunate that he'd been having these days for three months, pretty much, in a row – and this for someone who was held to have flocks of bad luck owls always hovering around his head. Not just funerals but disaster usually seemed to follow him everywhere. But not for the glorious ninety days in which everything he attempted nearly always worked. The Hanse administrators arrived within three weeks along with the geniuses of the order book, of freight deliveries, of incentive schemes for work of quality (backed up by threats of violence from Thomas Cale). They centralized the planning of transport so the bacon arrived maggot-free, the tack biscuits unshared with the weevils, and devised paperwork so that when wagons or weapons or blankets needed to be replaced there was something in the storehouses waiting to supply that need. The training of the peasants in their wooden forts staggered the hopes of them all as the peasants absorbed with eagerness the harshness of their instruction by the Laconics and the Purgators. No mutinous grumbles, only backbone and getting on with the job. Vague Henri and the miserable Kleist worked at every weakness the Redeemers might find in Cale's design and tactics and seemed inspired at creating solutions to the limitations that they found. The atmosphere of breaking with the past, of revolution and metamorphosis, seemed to be in the air itself. Not yet aware that Cale had lied about helping the Helots, Fanshawe, an establishment maverick of the kind that every sensible rigid society looks to find a place for, discovered he very much enjoyed destroying entrenched attitudes as long as they weren't his own.

Every decision seemed to turn out better than hoped: Koolhaus the sullen was as good as his ambition was enormous; he seemed to have the entire campaign down to the last round of cheese sorted in his brain. Within a month he was back with Cale and IdrisPukke. He either knew everything or knew how to find out about it. He seemed barely human, as if he was in possession of a magical device that could search a vast memory and provide an instant answer. Koolhaus was irritating and objectionable and had the imagination of a brick, but as a bureaucrat he was something of a genius. As for Simon Materazzi, he found war was a generous mother to those who were dismissed in more peaceful times. Anxious to be rid of his aristocratic burden, Koolhaus had spent many hours weaning Simon off the sign language and working out how he might learn to lipread. Yet again driven by self-interest, Koolhaus turned his considerable brain to the invention of an unheard-of skill. Just as anxious to be rid of Koolhaus as Koolhaus was to be rid of him, Simon worked for hours a day at perfecting this ability. The two of them had already been planning their divorce when Cale's offer arrived and led to their final weeks together. But while Koolhaus was finally able to rub the faces of others in the superiority of his skill at almost everything (barring skill with people or anything original) Simon discovered the immense pleasure and even greater usefulness of having people ignore him while he listened to everything they had to say. The Laconics were in the habit of throwing children born lame or blind into a chasm outside the capital, so someone like Simon was a novelty and they treated him as if he were an amusing monkey. Simon took his revenge by making use of the complete ease with which they talked in front of him to keep Cale informed in surprising detail about what they were up to. Interestingly, even had Simon been born a Laconic he would have lived. There was one exception to their otherwise iron rule: a child of the Laconic royal family, no matter how sickly, would never make the long fall onto the rocks of that terrible place. So it was and ever shall be. It amused the Laconics to see Simon and Koolhaus chattering silently away, hand to hand, in the beautifully fluent way they had of speaking. They would gesture Simon over to them at night and write down words for him to teach them how to sign them. They enjoyed making a condescending fuss of him and they had no idea that if they spoke while facing him he could read nearly every word they were saying – including the light-hearted abuse directed at him. When Koolhaus was recalled to Spanish Leeds, Simon made a deal with him to become his replacement, leaving an old schoolfriend of Koolhaus to stay and pretend to translate for him so that the Laconics would not become suspicious.

'Are you sure he can do the job?' said Cale, when Koolhaus returned.

'I thought you were his friend?' said Koolhaus.

'Can he do the job?'

'Yes, he can do the job.'

Koolhaus decided that Simon's skills – won with as much effort from him as from Simon – would be better kept to himself. The useful things he might, and indeed already was learning, would enhance Koolhaus' reputation for being a man with all sorts of things at his fingertips. The preparations for the crossing of the Mississippi were also going well and waited only for the weather and Cale's final say-so.

There were a few wasps in Cale's honey but the one that affected him the most directly was the introduction of rationing, a move demanded by the bureaucrats of the Hanse to prevent panic-buying, hoarding and shortages of goods that were vital for the New Model Army. Their arguments had been reviewed by Koolhaus at Cale's instruction and he'd concluded their case was unanswerable – rationing was as vital to the defeat of the Redeemers as the provision of weapons.

'It will, of course,' said Koolhaus, reporting to the OAR, 'be necessary for the sake of public morale that these restrictions apply to everyone. There can be no exceptions,' he declared piously, 'except, of course, for the Royal Family.'

As it happened, Koolhaus made his declaration while Vague Henri was in the room, having returned to Spanish Leeds briefly to discuss his preparations in the west with Cale. No sooner had the words 'Royal Family' passed his lips than Koolhaus, still inexperienced but a quick learner, realized he'd made a serious mistake. Perhaps worse than serious. 'The temperature dropped so quickly,' said a delighted IdrisPukke later to his brother, 'I thought the North Pole had stopped by for a cup of tea. God, that Koolhaus is a cocky little sod.'

Cale stared at Koolhaus, while Vague Henri drew out a dagger he had specially made for himself based on the Danzig Shank and carved, for reasons he refused to explain, with the word 'if' on either side of the handle. He raised the dagger as if he were going to cut off Koolhaus's head but only stabbed it down into the middle of the beautifully inlaid walnut table at which they were sitting. Vague Henri's hatred of the aristos of Spanish Leeds had festered from a general disdain, born of the natural resentment of the nobody for the privileged, to a particular loathing based on the way he had been treated while Cale was in the lunatic asylum at The Priory. The idea that he would have to go without his beloved cucumber sandwiches while the Royal Family carried on unaffected was more than he could bear. So he put his foot down. There was a short pause.

'So,' said IdrisPukke, 'we're agreed: rationing for all – the Royal Family and present company excepted.'

After Koolhaus and IdrisPukke left, which was almost

immediately, Cale turned to Vague Henri and nodded at the knife firmly stuck in the middle of the table.

'I'm not paying for that,' said Cale.

'Nobody asked you to,' replied Vague Henri.

There was a peevish silence.

'Why', asked Cale, 'couldn't you have just banged your fist on the table? Look at it, it's ruined.'

'I said I'd pay.'

Another silence.

'Bloody hooligan.'

30

Along the upper reaches of the icy Mississippi something stirred. Lower down the river something else stirred as well. Artemisia Halicarnassus was cursing the good weather that had been such a blessing for Cale during the training of the New Model Army. In a normal winter, as the temperature shifts back and forth between freezing and slightly above freezing, the river was hard to read, even for the experienced: the melting but still massive blocks of ice that had broken off upstream would jam together to form great dams which might stick for weeks and then, with a day of warmer temperatures, suddenly give way and flow down like a slow avalanche, some-times for miles, until they hit more dammed ice, at which it might jam again or cause a great collapse and start an even bigger flow. But the unseasonal warmth this year had made this process even more treacherous and unstable than normal.

But Artemisia had men around her who had lived on the river.for sixty years or more. There was a large field of unstable ice jammed about five miles upstream but the tem-perature had dropped to around freezing, lessening the chance of a break. The danger was from large river-bergs from upstream crashing into the groaning, cracking and unstable dam of ice. But for ten miles upstream of the block-age the skilled and experienced were sprawled along the bank, each man tied by a line of string and signalling with different kinds of tug to the next man down the size of the river-bergs as they passed them by. On the ice jam itself men were stationed to watch upstream and gauge the stability of the ice they were standing on. Once darkness had come the crossing soldiers, wrapped against the cold as thickly as an expensive present, endured an ecstasy of edgy waiting. Then the word to risk it came. Twenty boats, carrying seven hundred men armed like hedge pigs, were launched into the narrowest crossing for many miles in either direction.

But not even the sharpest river pilot with the greyest beard could see under the ice where the great bergs jutted downward towards the silty bed and created vicious eddies in the current that carved great swathes out of the bottom of the river. These turbulent and restless undertows came and went with the shifting ice above. The oak tree, water-fat, passed the berg-watchers on the shore unseen, no more breaking the surface in its massive thickness than a hunting crocodile. Then it hit the ice dam with a thud like the low bass of the deepest note in a cathedral organ. It was felt by the lookouts on the ice itself as much in the bowels as in the ear. They waited for the great crack that might split the field and loosen the dam of bergs – and kill most of them. It never came. Pushed underneath the ice by the current the oak tree began to roll – down it went like the Jesus whale, down to the bottom of the dam where a few hours before two great fangs of ice had formed. Around them the current, powerful but slow, became in a moment frenzied, unstoppable and mad, driving the great trunk, sodden and three times its former weight, faster and faster as the current was squeezed more and more between the jagged ice and the riverbed. Sideways on, the tree trunk battered between the two great crags of downward-pointing ice, sending strange but incomprehensible tremors to the blind watchers above as it boomed and bashed deep beneath them. And then it was free, the now shooting current taking the tree's super-saturated weight into a rapid but shallow climb to the surface so that it kept momentum from

337

the currents speeding from underneath the ice. At eight miles to the hour, even an ordinary runner could have kept pace with it as it headed towards the fleet of boats – but it was not the speed that mattered but its size and terrible sodden weight. Still, only so much damage might have been done had it not glanced a mid-stream rock with its snout; the great leviathan of trunky wood began to turn flat towards the slowly crossing fleet.

Despite all efforts to prevent it, the twenty boats had been bunched together by the day's strange currents and they were no small boats – thirty-five men in each. The oak did not so much smash into them as roll them up and under as if they were hardly there – barely a cry went up before each boat was at once struck beneath the water and turned over on its side. Because of the crowding, eleven boats went down in less than fifteen seconds. The tree moved on into the cold, wet dark leaving behind three hundred and eighty-four drowned men and one drowned woman.

As IdrisPukke finished telling Cale his grim news the sun came out and a warm shaft of light came through the partly stained glass windows, projecting delicate blues and reds onto the table and illuminating the bright dust in the air.

'It's certain?' said Vague Henri.

'As these things ever are. My man is reliable and said he saw her body before he left.'

'What was the cause?'

'It's thought a wall of ice that broke away from a bigger field upstream. Bad luck, that's all.'

'But you predicted it,' said Cale, softly.

'To be unfair to my prodigious powers of foresight, I always make it a point to predict more or less every possible outcome. It could have as easily succeeded as it failed.'

'Can it be kept a secret?' asked Vague Henri.

'Had they all lived or all drowned, perhaps. Not now . . . I'd say that . . .'

'She's a great loss,' interrupted Cale, awkwardly and in an odd tone of voice.

'Yes,' said IdrisPukke. 'She was a remarkable young woman.'

Nobody said anything. There was a knock on the door and Lascelles the butler crept into the room.

'A letter for you, sir,' he said to IdrisPukke, who took it and waved Lascelles away, waiting until he left the room before speaking. 'There's something iffy about that man. His eyes are too close together.' He opened the letter. 'Apparently Bose Ikard knows about the crossing and Artemisia.'

'How?' said Vague Henri.

'The same way that I knew about it, I suppose.'

'No . . . how do you know Bose Ikard knows?'

'Kitty the Hare's red books are like windows into the souls of the great and good of Spanish Leeds. Little birds everywhere sing.'

'What's he going to do?' asked Cale.

'He's got two choices, I'd say: go along with what we say until he has a chance to use it when things get really bad; or use it to arrest us now and make peace with the Redeemers.'

This startled Vague Henri, who had planned to be cock-of-the-walk for at least six months more. 'You really think he'll do that?'

'On balance? No. It's not enough to be sure of victory. He knows the consequences if he gets it wrong. He'll lay it down in the cellar till he can use it. But we have to be quick off the mark, present this as a heroic effort treacherously betrayed – noble woman, daring raid, heroic. Last words.' Cale looked at him. 'Sorry,' said IdrisPukke. 'I've lived too long and have

339

too many bad habits. But we won't honour her memory by allowing it to be seen as a total disaster. It has to be seen as a heroic failure.'

'It *was* a heroic failure.'

'Only if we present it as one. People need stories of individual daring, of courage and selfless sacrifice, of near victory and treacherous stabs in the back.'

'Let's hope we get them then,' said Vague Henri.

'Hope has nothing to do with it,' said IdrisPukke. 'I have my people writing them now. They'll be posted all over the city by tomorrow morning.' He turned to Cale, feeling himself mean-spirited and cynical. 'I'm sorry for your loss. It's a pity death took her off so soon.'

IdrisPukke left the two boys, the soft sunlight beaming through the windows as if the house were a domestic cathedral blessed by angels.

'When are you away?' Cale said at last.

'Tomorrow. Early.'

Another long silence.

'I'm sorry for your loss, too,' said Vague Henri. 'Don't know what else to say. I liked her.'

'She didn't like me. Not in the end.'

Another silence.

'Well,' said Vague Henri, 'you're easy to get wrong.' A snort of derision from Cale. Vague Henri continued trying to be comforting. 'It wasn't your fault. It's just how things are.'

'I don't know,' said Cale, after a moment. 'I don't know how I feel about her now she's dead. I don't feel the right way, that's for sure.'

PART FOUR

'Now go, attack the Amalekites, and totally destroy all that belongs to them. Do not spare them; put to death men and women, children and infants, cattle and sheep, camels and donkeys.'

1 Samuel 15:3

The Redeemers crossed the Mississippi in April, and to a landing largely unresisted. The scouts they sent out across the gently rolling plains, which extended for three hundred miles from the south bank of the river, returned with the news that almost every village, town and city was deserted and not only of people. All animals, from pigs to cows to rabbits, were gone along with the population. The fields were left unsown with wheat or barley and left to the poppies, which had come early with the unseasonably warm weather. 'It's beautiful,' said a Redeemer scout on his return. 'I doubt if the fields of heaven itself can match it: mile after mile of poppy and eyebright, hellebore and Deptford pinks, touch-me-not and fine-leaved vetch. But damn all to eat for fifteen days in any direction. Unless you're a cow or a horse.'

The scout had presumed too much on Cale's generosity. He had no intention of allowing the Redeemers to feed their animals. As soon as the ground was soft enough he'd ordered the women and children out into the fields and instead of sowing wheat and barley had them planting Crazy Charlie, Stringhat and Stinking Willy – all poisonous to ruminants. There was considerable anger at this: 'What will happen,' they cried, 'to our animals when we return?'

'I'd worry about that,' said Cale, '*if* you return.'

However, he'd carefully mapped the poisoned areas, which reassured them though that hadn't been his intention – he had just wanted to know where it was safe to feed the horses that drew the war wagons.

It was General Redeemer Princeps and his Fourth Army who'd come across the Mississippi first, veterans of the destruction of the Materazzi at Silbury Hill. Princeps knew very well what Cale was capable of, having followed carefully much of the boy's plan for the invasion of Materazzi territory when he was still at the Sanctuary. He knew that once he crossed the Mississippi there would be ugly things waiting for him and his men. He hadn't expected the landing to be unopposed, but had expected the decision not to plant. But he hadn't expected the sowing of toxic herbs to poison his horses and sheep. It took several weeks to bring in fodder and longer to find anyone who could identify the plants causing the problem. He'd expected he would have to hold a bridgehead on the south bank while the Axis tried to push them back into the Mississippi. Instead, he had three hundred miles to do with, so it appeared, as he wished. Cale had turned the prairie into a flowery wasteland. Supplying a large army in this desert of red and yellow and pink would mean a significant rethink and more time. For now, Princeps stayed close to the river and organized the means to support a new plan to advance on Switzerland. It was a week into this hiatus that a five-hundred-strong force of mounted Redeemer infantry – their horses now muzzled against the poisons waiting for them in the grass – encountered a most peculiar sight: some kind of round wooden fort, not large, containing about three acres and with a ditch dug all the way around it.

When Redeemer Partiger was brought forward by his scouts to take a look, he said a quiet prayer to St Martha of Lesbos, patron saint of those who required protection from the unexpected. She had earned her place among the list of the holy because of the strange nature of her martyrdom – she had been forced to swallow a six-sided hook on a string, with hinges on each hook so that the device could travel

344

through her digestive system without catching. Some twelve hours later, when her executioners felt the hook had travelled far enough, they hauled on the string and pulled her inside out. In Redeemer dogma, ingenuity was always portrayed as a threat and hence the need for a saint with a specific responsibility to intercede to protect the faithful from its perils.

'Send someone forward under a white flag,' said Partiger.

Several minutes later, a rider under a flag of truce approached to within about fifty yards of the war wagons.

'In . . .'

Whatever he was going to say was cut short by a crossbow bolt in the middle of his chest.

'Why has he stopped?' said Partiger – then very slowly the messenger slumped to one side of the horse and fell off.

The watching Redeemers were outraged at this breach in the rules of war, despite the fact that they never acknowledged such laws themselves. Given this, there was certainly no particular disadvantage to killing the herald but it was, in fact, an accident. The sniper who'd shot the messenger had merely taken a bead on the man as a precaution – but the wagons were cramped inside and a nervous former hoppicker had moved and jogged his arm.

'I wonder what he wanted?' called out someone and there was a nervous burst of laughter.

Partiger considered what to do next. The Redeemers were skilled enough at siege warfare but the trebuchets they used were extremely heavy and the few they'd brought were all on the other side of the Mississippi because there were no important walled towns within three hundred and fifty miles of the river. It would take several weeks to get one here. Besides, the fort wasn't very big and it was of wood not stone. Despite his understandable uneasiness at the novelty of what was in front of him, he knew he'd be expected to find out what sort of novelty it was so he couldn't just go around it. However strange, it did not look particularly formidable. He ordered an attack by three hundred. Fifty of them were armoured cavalry – an innovation by the Redeemers themselves – the rest were more lightly-protected mounted infantry.

Partiger watched as his men spread around the wagons with the intention of attacking from four directions. While they were waiting, Partiger struck up a conversation with his newly appointed second-in-command, Redeemer George Blair. He did not trust or like Blair, who was part of a new order of Sanctuarines, established by Pope Bosco himself to 'aid fidelity in all Redeemer units and ensure actions free of doctrinal or moral errors.' In other words, he was a spy whose task it was to ensure that Bosco's new religious attitudes and the martial techniques that went with them were obeyed without question.

Partiger somewhat surprised Blair by engaging in a conversation that had nothing to do with the attack on the wooden fort.

'I was thinking,' said Partiger, 'of embarking on the Seventy-four Acts of Abasement.'

'What?'

'The seventy-four acts of homage to the authority of the Pope.'

'I know what they are,' said Blair, irritably. 'I don't understand the relevance – a battle's about to start.'

Am I being tested to say the wrong thing? thought Partiger. He decided he was.

'We must keep our eyes on eternal life even in the midst of death.'

'There's a time for everything. This isn't it.'

'But surely,' continued Partiger, 'if I were to wear dried

peas in my shoes and abstain from drinking water on hot days and whip myself with nettles in an act of mortification of a kind that the saints endured, and which leaves us aghast with admiration,' he had learned the phrase about being aghast by heart from a papal letter, 'then would I not be more open to the wisdom of God and a better leader to my men?'

Finally Blair turned to look at him square on, aghast himself, but not in admiration.

'Yes, you are, of course, correct. I'd say that the more pain you inflict on yourself the better.'

'Really?'

'Yes. I understand self-flagellation with a whip made from scorpion tails is especially effective in this regard.' He turned back to the battle, leaving Partiger to consider scorpion tails. It sounded painful. Still, he remembered Padre Pio's words: *When mortifying the flesh, make sure that it hurts.*

Eight hundred yards away, the battle had begun. At first there were only feints from three groups of ten cavalry, meant to trigger a response so that they could size up the strength of the occupants. There was none. Close up, they could see the ditch around the wagon was not particularly deep but was full of sharpened sticks. One of them rammed their heaviest lance into one of the wagons to see how stable and well-built it was. Nothing to write home about, he said, when he returned. So it was decided to rush in from all four sides, the signal being a volley of forty or so arrows into the centre of the fort. The arrows went up, the men rushed the wagons and Cale's New Model Army and its way of making war came to its first great test.

The trouble for the Redeemers was that they lacked any of the basic tools – no ladders, no battering rams and only a few ropes. Once they got into the ditch they dropped down only a few feet, but with the sides of the wagon walls at six foot tall they were nine feet away from their wooden-wall-protected opponents. As soon as the Redeemers attacked, the slot windows were partly opened and Vague Henri's light crossbows went into action. They were shot at a distance of only a few feet – they were so close to their opponents it didn't matter they were so much less powerful. In the restricted space bows were useless but the crossbows were devastating, particularly now they could be reloaded so quickly. The roof of the wagon was double-hinged so that it could be pushed up and over to either side depending on circumstances. This time they flew off with the roofs crashing backwards to the inside of the fort. Immediately half a dozen peasants and one Purgators stood up and, with most of their bodies protected by the wall of the wagon, started to stab and swing down into the mass of Redeemers standing in the ditch. The flails with lead balls and spikes did huge damage crushing the flesh under the Redeemers' light armour, though it could penetrate too. Excitable in their success and inexperience, some of the polemen leant out and exposed too much of their upper bodies, and a couple went down to archers.

'Keep under guard! Stay in! Stay in!'

The Purgators in each wagon had to keep pulling back the over-eager peasants as they enjoyed the thrill of hurting an opponent without them being able to hit back. The Redeemers, ten times the soldiers of the men who were wounding them with every blow, were impotent. They were four feet further away from their enemy than they could reach. They couldn't get under the wagons either, and the wheels were covered with earth to stop rope from being tied around the spokes. Their position was hopeless. After five minutes they withdrew – but not without being picked off by the crossbow men, now able to stand up and take good aim at the retreating priests, many of them moving slowly because of the blows to their upper thighs and knees.

The peasants stood and cheered. The Purgators told them to shut up.

'They're going to get better every day at taking us on. Can you say the same?'

This quietened them down but they were delighted with their first mouthful of killing.

The Redeemers withdrew back to Partiger, who was bemused as well as angry. He berated the men while Blair walked around and examined the wounded.

'Didn't you inflict any damage?'

'We think we got a handful,' said one of the centenars.

'A handful? We have thirty dead. And for what? Anyway, that was the archers, not you. How many did you kill?'

'You can't kill someone if you can't reach them.'

'Don't answer back!' shouted Partiger.

'What about the grappling hook?' asked Blair. There was only one in the whole unit. No one saw the need for more.

'I only got it on the side for thirty seconds before they cut it,' said the sergeant who'd used it. 'But I got a good pull on it from my horse. More might do it – but the wagon was tethered down far in. We'll have to pull them apart not just topple 'em. Stronger horses, bigger hooks and chains not ropes might do it. But they can pick off the horses real easy.'

'What about fire? They're just made of wood, yes?'

'Might work, sir, but wood won't burn 'less you can get a lot of fire going.'

'Arrows?'

'Real easy to put out. I've seen some used at Salerno had oil and packing to set a fire. Never done it myself.'

'A word,' said Blair to Partiger. They walked to one side. 'Any ideas?'

'A siege, perhaps?'

'They've probably got more food than we have. Besides – why are they here? There's nothing worth protecting.'

'Look, Redeemer,' said Partiger. 'We're not really equipped, as you say. We should withdraw and report this. This is for siege troops not mounted infantry.'

This was a fair point. 'Did you notice anything about the wounded?' said Blair, knowing that he had not.

'The wounded?'

'Yes. Their wounds – they're mostly crushing wounds: head, hands, elbows.'

'Yes?'

'They're not going to heal quickly – or at all – most of them.'

'Your point, Redeemer?'

'What if it's deliberate?'

They didn't get time to continue the discussion. Fifty Swiss cavalry emerged from the fort and swept through the unprepared Redeemer camp, killing a hundred and scattering the rest. Within fifteen minutes they were back inside the protective ring of wagons just as the sun went down.

The traumatized Redeemers pulled out from their position during the night but within an hour of dawn the Swiss were back as they tried to retreat. They were badly hampered in their efforts to withdraw by the numerous wounded from the attack on the bastion, which had delivered much more in the way of broken arms and smashed knees than the fatalities of the unexpected Swiss attack just before dark. The dead could just be left behind. The Swiss kept up a continuous long distance sniping from the dozen heavy-duty crossbows Vague Henri had assigned to each wagon fort. Every few minutes there were skirmishes from the more expert Swiss cavalry, who would race in and pick off stragglers then run away before the able-bodied Redeemer guards could respond. By the time they left off and returned to the bastion, Redeemer numbers were half what they had been when they first set eyes on the fort three days earlier. The New Model Army had lost ten dead and eleven wounded.

Blair, though not Partiger, survived to give a report and to urge a swift response. But it was an odd story and entirely isolated so no one in the lower levels of authority Blair could reach took him seriously. But over the next few weeks the general headquarters of the Redeemer Fourth Army were forced to change their opinion. The bastions started turning up in increasing numbers and causing terrible casualties. Now aware of the danger, they sent out heavily armed counter forces equipped with ladders, siege hooks and siege torches but by the time they arrived the bastions were long gone. Once he was made aware of the problem, Princeps, furious at the delay, doubled the number of his patrols in order to identify bastion sites quickly and bring larger forces to bear on them. But it was here that Artemisia's scouts came into play: operating mostly on their own, they were able to provide constant information about Redeemer movements. In effect, each wagon fort operated at the centre of a web of information up to fifty miles in all directions. Any small Redeemer force they could ignore, anything somewhat larger they could resist and anything larger than that they could move with half an hour's notice and have vanished by the time a major force had arrived. There was no catching them either – Michael Nevin's wagons could move much faster than any Redeemer army. The Redeemers were caught in a trap: small, light units could catch up with the bastions but were not strong enough to break in; heavy units that might have succeeded were too slow.

There was a month of this fighting before the Redeemers managed to delay a bastion long enough to catch them with a thousand heavy infantry armed with siege weapons. It took four days to break into the camp and annihilate the occupants. This was a blow to the New Model Army, puffed up by a month of easy victories and despite the warnings of the Purgators and Laconics who trained them that a defeat was inevitable. There was much corresponding joy in victory from Princeps when he heard the news – but it didn't last once he heard the details: the lives of two hundred Swiss peasants had come at the price of nearly four hundred Redeemers, and another hundred with the crushing wounds that took so long to heal and used up so much in the way of resources. As worrying was the report of one of Princeps' personal centenars, who he'd ordered to take part in the siege to give him a proper sense of the battle and the soldiers who fought it.

'It was murderous getting in, Redeemer, as hard as any fighting I've ever done. They'd arranged it so that we were easy to hit but to strike back was almost impossible. But once we got inside, that was the shock – they had a few soldiers, maybe fifty, who knew what they were doing and were hard work but the ones who'd been killing us for three days – once we were inside and it was hand to hand – it was like cutting down big children.'

From then on the problem facing Princeps was how to break the shell to get at the soft insides. The problem for Cale was that the creation of the war wagons had been far too successful for its own good. Their successes had been so easy and so comprehensive that the New Model Army was dead drunk on its triumphs. The defeats, when they started to come, winded them badly – there were, after all, no survivors. From euphoric arrogance to demoralized failure was such a short step and so great a fall that an emergency (one might almost have said a panic) meeting was held halfway between the Mississippi plains and Spanish Leeds. Cale was sicker than usual, it had been a bad few weeks, but he was forced into a war wagon filled with mattresses and, along with IdrisPukke and Vipond, tried to sleep his way to Potsdam where the meeting had been arranged with Fanshawe, Vague Henri and the Committee of Ten Antagonist Churches. On the way into Potsdam, he'd decided to get out and ride. For all its padding the converted war wagon was uncomfortable when he couldn't sleep, and today all his old wounds – finger, head and shoulder – were throbbing and grinding out their claims on his attention (*Me, too!* they screamed, *What about us!*) To add to his misery his right ear was aching. He put on a coat and pulled up the hood against the cold and to keep the wind away from his sore ear. This was not something he would normally do because only the Redeemer Lords of Discipline wore hoods and they were not a memory he wanted to revisit. Cale was now, of course, more experienced in the strangeness of the world than many practised hands three times his age, but he was astonished at the electric effect even a word of his presence had on the soldiers camped on his way into the city. The mysterious force that moves rumour with astonishing speed through even the largest and most dispersed military force brought the New Model Army out in droves wherever he went. At first sight he was greeted with adoring silence that quickly burst into ecstatic cheers, as if he were the Hanged Redeemer entering into Salem. Cale was amazed that so many could draw such power from so sickly a hand-hurting, ear-aching, shoulder-groaning weakling such as him. Uncertain how to respond, he thought perhaps he should speak to them; but when he tried the retching, an hour earlier than it was due, silenced him, and it was all he could do to keep it under some sort of control. So he sat, dog-sick, on his horse and looked about at the men, in their hundreds and then thousands, inspired by his mere presence. To them his pale and cadaverous silence was far more powerful than anything he could say, even though he had learnt a dozen inspirational speeches from the writer whose plays he'd found in the Sanctuary library that seemed to cover the entire range of ways in which to manipulate a crowd: *Friends, comrades, countrymen, lend me your ears*; or: *Once more into the breach, dear chums*; and the ever dependable: *We few, we happy few, we band of brothers.*

But not even a tongue touched with the lighted coals of God himself could have done better than his enforced silence. They did not want anything so fallible as a human being who could talk to them man to man – they wanted to be led by an exterminating angel, not by some bloke. He may have felt like death but he now looked the part. And that was what mattered: he was something fatal from another world, something and not someone, who had made them powerful and all-conquering in the past and now was here to do the same again. They needed him to be inhuman, the essence of death and plague, to be wasted, pale and skeletal because he *was* those things and was on their side. The cry went up – one or two voices at first then tens, then hundreds and then a roar.

'ANGEL! ANGEL! ANGEL! ANGEL! ANGEL!'

Vipond and IdrisPukke, following just behind, no beginners in the seen-it-all-before and surprised-by-nothing stakes, were left amazed and even shaken by what they were seeing and hearing and, above all, what they were feeling: even they were carried along, like it or not, by the power of the crowd. But the preachers and padres and moderators of the Committee of Ten Churches heard it too and recognized it for the devil worship that it was.

*

354

'I expected loss heavier than this – and from the start – getting worse as the Redeemers worked out how to deal with us. These deaths. They can be replaced. I've planned for this.'

A tired and irritated Cale was in a furtive meeting set up before the official one with the Committee of Ten Churches was due to begin – it was thought necessary to get their story straight to minimize any religious contributions.

'But Thomas, darling,' said Fanshawe, 'what did you expect? Killing and being killed is a profession. These people are peasants, salt of the earth, of course – no doubt – but fashioned by a lifetime shovelling shit and gleaning turnips – whatever *they* are . . . it's no preparation when it comes to the big red one. You can't expect it.'

'We need,' said Cale, 'to plan on losing one wagon train in three. I always expected losses like that.'

'You can expect what you like. It can't be done,' said Fanshawe. 'It's not in their souls to die in those numbers – any more than it's in yours to reap cabbages and have carnal knowledge of your more fetching sheep.'

When Fanshawe was gone he left behind a miserable inner circle.

'Is he right, do you think?' said IdrisPukke to Vague Henri.

'Underneath the piss-take? Pretty much. In the fight at Finnsburgh the Redeemers almost broke through. I was shitting myself if you want to know. Now they know what's coming if the Redeemers win a brawl. Nobody gets used to that.'

'Any ideas?'

'No'

There was a depressed silence.

'I have a suggestion.' It was Vipond.

'Thank God someone has,' said Vague Henri.

'I'd wait,' said IdrisPukke, 'until you heard it before you get your hopes up.'

'In spite of my brother's sneers,' continued Vipond, 'I think we saw something remarkable today. The conventional view of people like myself is that a leader must be either loved or feared to be effective in a time of crisis – and given that love is a tricky thing and fear is not so tricky – then fear it is.'

'You want me to make them more terrified of me than they are of the Redeemers?'

'In other circumstances I don't see that you'd have any choice.'

'I can do that.'

'I'm sure you can. But there may be another way, less damaging to your soul.'

'My lugholes,' said Cale, 'are open as wide as a church door.'

'Good. You saw your effect today on the very kind of man Fanshawe said was about to break?'

'Yes, I saw it.'

'Whatever seized them, it wasn't love or fear.'

'What then?'

'I don't know. It doesn't matter what it is but you could feel it between your thumb and forefinger – I don't know . . . belief, perhaps. It doesn't matter of what kind, in their eyes wherever you are the gates of hell are on their side.'

'Thanks.'

'That's why the noses of the Holy Joes were out of joint. They knew what power was moving through their flock. But seeing is believing, Cale – you need to be out and about, among them every day and everywhere. They need the Exterminating Angel where they can see him. Watching over them, working through them.'

Cale looked at him.

'You might just as well ask me to fly. As far as what was going on today, I felt it all right, but what it was about you can read in the stars. They saw a bad angel watching over them, I agree – but it was all I could do not to fall off my horse or throw up all over them.' He smiled, one of the not so pleasant ones. 'I couldn't do it if my life and the life of everyone around me depended on it.'

At this point – and in a way that in other circumstances might be regarded as theatrical – Cale threw up on the floor.

In fact, he felt a little better once the vomiting had stopped but the meeting was at an end and so, dish-rag weak, Cale left the Cecilienhoft where it had been held and headed for a night's sleep at the No-Worries Palace. As everyone knew where he was, a vast crowd had collected outside and at the sight of him great shouts went up.

Despite Bosco's rare enthusiasm for information, and his desire to improve its quality amongst those who served his cause, it was not easy for Redeemers to pass themselves off as anything other than what they were. They had paid but unreliable informers and also fellow travellers, unofficial converts to the One True Faith whose desire to become Redeemers was as intense as their reasons were vague. They tended to be the despised, the failed, the hurt, the slightly mad, the deeply resentful – and often for good reason. But their limitations were plain enough: they were not disciplined or very competent, however zealous they might be. Had they been capable and rooted, it's unlikely they would have been such fertile ground for insurrection. But it was one of the more level-headed and skilled of these converts who'd made his way to the Cecilienhoft where everyone knew Cale was planning the destruction of the Pope. There were guards there certainly, but no one had expected or planned for the crush of the soldiers of the New Model Army desperate to see him, along with the people of the city packed together with the mass of refugees evacuated from the Mississippi plain. Indeed, the confusion almost saved Cale from his attack – there was no planned route and so no way of being somewhere he could be expected to pass by. So crushed was he by the crowd that the assassin too was flotsam and jetsam, compelled to follow the flow and swirl of the river of people as it moved forward and back. Sometimes Cale moved away from him, sometimes back towards him. At one point, as the crowd grasped for a touch of his clothes or called for a blessing, an old woman who must have been stronger than she looked forced a small jar into his hand: 'The ashes of St Deidre of the Sorrows – bless them, please!' In the general racket he couldn't properly hear what she was saying; he thought the ashes were a gift and didn't want to be unkind. Given the state of him she would probably have had the strength to grab it back but the crowd decided and swept her away as she cried out for her dreadful loss.

With Vague Henri and IdrisPukke a good ten yards behind, the exhausted Cale was spilled into a break in the crowd made by the few guards who had been able to stay with him but where his murderer could finally get to him, too. The would-be assassin was no skilled killer and it's hard to hide the look of someone with slaughter on his mind. It was within a second or less that Cale saw him coming at him and it was his eyes that gave him away. Kitten-weak and weary as he was, millions of nerves came to his aid like angels and, as the man brought the knife down to his chest, Cale took the lid off the jar of Deidre's ashes and threw it in his face. As anyone will know who has looked closely at the ashes of the dead they are not like ashes much at all, more gravel than anything fine enough to easily blind a man. But Cale was lucky that these relics were fakes and consisted of the clinker from the forger's fire. The effect was instant: in terrible pain the murderer cried out and dropped the knife to try to clear the spiky cinders from his eyes. The few guards around were quick enough to grab the assassin and they'd already stabbed him three times in the heat of their panic before they realized Cale was shouting at them to stop. Any chance of getting something useful out of the man was gone. Cale stood and watched as Vague Henri and IdrisPukke joined him. Perhaps it was the mixture of sudden fright and exhaustion, but he thought he had never seen blood so red or ashes so white. The murderer muttered something before his eyes rolled into the back of his head.

'What did he say?' asked Cale.

The guard who'd been closest to the dead man looked at Cale, shocked and confused by what had happened.

'I'm not . . . I'm not sure, sir. It sounded like "Do you have it?"'

'You look gruesome,' said Vague Henri. 'The Angel of Death warmed up.'

Cale had come back into the room from boaking up in the jakes of his apartment at the No-Worries Palace, a newly built refuge with all the most recent innovations in plumbing. Fortunately he had held off vomiting in front of the crowd; his slow and fragile departure was interpreted by all who witnessed it – and even more strongly by those who didn't – as a sign of his ethereal detachment from even the most terrifying events. He lay down on the bed and looked so dreadful that Vague Henri repented of his lack of sympathy. He was, in truth, angry with Cale for nearly having died.

'Can I get you anything?'

'A cup of tea,' said Cale. 'With sugar lumps.'

With Vague Henri gone, Cale was left alone with IdrisPukke.

'I thought you were feeling better?'

'Me too . . . but I made the mistake of trying to *do* something.'

IdrisPukke walked over to the window and stared out over the newly installed lavender maze.

'The thing is,' he said, 'Vipond is right. Without you to fire them up I can only see it going one way, to be frank.' Cale didn't reply. 'I suppose taking that stuff your witch-doctor gave you wouldn't help?'

'Into a hole, six by two.'

'Pity.'

A thought struck Cale, tired as he was.

'That woman who gave me St somebody or other's ashes. I didn't think the Antagonists believed in relics – or saints.'

'Antagonism is a pretty broad church, which is to say they have an expansive number of ways of loathing each other. She must have been a Piscopalian – they're pretty much just like Redeemers in what they believe except they don't accept the authority of the Pope. The others can't abide them because of all the ritual and saint worship but mostly because they believe in the Verglass Apocalypse – they think the world was once nearly destroyed by ice as a punishment from God and that in ice it will end.'

'So?'

'The others insist that God uses water to discipline mankind – ice is a blasphemous invention from the mind of heretics.'

'I need to sleep.'

A few seconds later he heard the door close and in seconds he was out.

He was in a valley surrounded by high and craggy mountains swept by wind and lightning. He was tied to a post, arms and legs bound, and a small cat was eating his toes. All he could do was spit at it to drive it off. At first the cat retreated but as he ran out of slobber the cat slowly made its way back to his feet and began eating them again. He looked up and in the distance he could see an enormous puppet Poll laughing and holding out a naked foot, twiddling her toes to show that she still had them and shouting, 'Eat up, kitty, kitty!' Next to her, on each of the other mountain ridges that surrounded the valley he saw three versions of himself striking a theatrical pose. In one he was holding his sword pointing at the ground, in another he was kneeling on a high rock with a massively ornate sword held across his chest. The final version of Cale was on the highest of all the ridges, legs akimbo, back arched as if he was about to soar into the air, with his cloak flailing behind him like a ragged wing. But what struck him most was that he was hooded in all of them, his face completely obscured in shadow. *I never wear a hood,* he thought to himself, and then the cat started eating his toes again and he woke up.

'I had a dream,' he said to IdrisPukke and Vague Henri a few hours later.

'What would it take,' said IdrisPukke, 'for you not to tell it to me?'

'There was three of you?' said Vague Henri when Cale had finished. 'I'd call that a nightmare.'

'You can smirk all you like,' said Cale, and then smiled himself. 'I never saw the hand of God so clear in anything.'

'I can't say I feel the same,' said IdrisPukke. 'Perhaps you'd like to explain it for those of us without a direct line to God Almighty.'

'Imagine there were thirty of me – spare me the jokes.'

'All right.'

'You saw what happened today. I didn't *do* anything – I was just *there*. They did it all; I did nothing. They needed someone to save them.'

'There's nothing much to that,' said Vague Henri. 'You

already *have* saved them. They want you to do it again, that's all. There's nothing magic about it.'

'You're wrong,' said IdrisPukke. 'I've seen generals worshipped by the crowds for some great victory. But they don't want a man now, they want a god, because only the unearthly can save them.'

Vague Henri looked at Cale.

'Isn't that what Bosco wanted you to be?'

'Well, if you can come up with anything better, you gobshite, be my guest.'

'Children!' said IdrisPukke. 'Play nicely together.' He turned to Cale. 'Go on.'

'They don't need me – they need the Left Hand of God. So we give it to them. That's what the dream was telling me – all that standing on a mountain in a cloak and waving a sword. *Be seen!* it was saying – but where you can't be touched, show them you're watching over them. Wherever they fight, there I'll be; wherever they die, there I'll be. Lose – there I'll be. Win – there I'll be. In the darkest night – or in the brightest day.'

'But you won't, though, will you?' said Vague Henri.

'All right, it's a lie. So what? It's for their own good.'

IdrisPukke laughed.

'Vague Henri is quite wrong,' he said. 'Don't think of it as a lie, think of it as the truth under imaginary circumstances.'

'What about the cat eating your toes?' asked Vague Henri. 'What does that mean?'

'It was just a stupid dream.'

Cale should have rested for a week but there was no time and in three days he was back in Spanish Leeds, having worked out the details of his forgeries.

'Numbers.'

'Twenty.'

'Too many.'

'They don't have to do anything – they're not impersonating me. They just have to be good at striking poses. A pantomime is all we need. The theatres are shut so we'll have our pick.'

'And if they talk?'

'We put the fear of God into them. And pay them decent money. And keep them isolated and watched – four people at all times.'

When they arrived back it was to some upsetting news for Cale.

'We heard you were dead.'

The unusual thing was that, despite the fact it was untrue, the issue of a formal confirmation that Cale was indeed alive didn't do much to stop the rumour that he was dead from gaining ground. More strongly worded official denials were issued. 'Never believe anything,' said IdrisPukke, 'until there's an official denial. You've been invited to an engagement at the Palace – with the King. He thinks it might be true.'

'He *wishes* it were true,' said Cale.

'I'm in two minds about what's at the root of all this – the attempt to kill you at Potsdam, obviously. But I don't think they want you dead – not yet. No doubt in the fullness of time if you were to fall off a cliff it would be very acceptable. But not now. For the present they're more worried about the Redeemers than they are about you.'

'Should I go?'

'I think so. This is one lie that won't be doing any good – best to strangle it now. If we can.'

'But I'm not dead,' said an exasperated Cale. 'It's ridiculous.'

'But proving that isn't so easy.'

'But I'll be there. They'll be able to see me.'

'What if you're an imposter?'

One person who had no mixed feelings at all about the possibility of Cale being dead was Bose Ikard. He arranged for priority in invitations to be given to those who had met Cale in the past. But Cale kept his inner circle pretty close – and they weren't vulnerable to Ikard's promises or threats.

He decided to pursue another tack: sex. It was not subtle but Bose was too old and experienced to believe there was any particular virtue in subtlety. The walls of his apartments were, so to speak, cluttered with the mounted heads of sophisticated opponents who had looked down on his powers of discrimination as rather crude and had done so right up to the moment he'd had them killed. He'd once had IdrisPukke sentenced to death – a mistake, he now conceded; he'd swapped him for someone whose death, at the time, seemed more pressing. The truth was that Bose was afraid of IdrisPukke because he was an artful man with a penetrating grasp of complex matters, able to put the boot in when it was called for. It was this respectful loathing that fuelled his belief in the rumours about Cale being dead. It was the kind of thing he feared IdrisPukke could pull off. This was why he was talking to Dorothy Rothschild. Dorothy was certainly not a whore but she was something like one: reassuringly expensive, though no fee as such was ever negotiated. Her reward came in the shape of access to power, introductions concerning expensive contracts for this and that – she went on her back cushioned by the expensive silken sheets of enormous influence.

In truth, Dorothy was a deeply interesting woman but she didn't look like one: she looked like sex. If two frustrated young men with a little artistic flair had thought up the woman of their desires and drawn her on paper she might have looked like Dorothy: hair long and blonde to the point of being white, of medium height, a waist tinier than that of a young boy, breasts bigger than was really plausible on such a tiny frame, legs improbably long for someone under six foot tall. She shouldn't have been possible but there she was.

She had a corrosive wit, kept mostly under control, born out of her sensitivity, which was considerable. Her intelligence and emotional insight had been set on the wrong path by a dreadful event when she was nine years old. Her older sister, beloved by all, had gone on a picnic to a nearby lake with family friends, where she had drowned when a boat capsized. On hearing the news the dead child's mother, not realizing her youngest was standing behind her, called out: 'Why couldn't it have been Dorothy?'

Even an emotional clod would have been marked for life by this and Dorothy was very far from that. But the wittiness she developed to deflect the world often outraged it and she was constantly having to apologize for this or that wounding remark. She had married young but within two years her husband had been killed in a war vital to the survival of the nation for reasons that no one could now remember. As a person from a family of minor importance she had naturally been visited by minor royalty, a matriarch set aside for state condolences. She'd been asked by her regal visitor if there was anything she could do for her – the proper answer being no.

'Get me another husband.' It was out before she knew it. It resulted in the appalled matriarch giving her an angry telling off for making light of her late husband's tragic sacrifice.

'In that case,' said an unrepentant Dorothy, 'how about going and getting me a pork pie from the shop on the corner?'

It was this outrage that led to Dorothy being ostracized

from all but the margins of society and ending up, after many adventures on the wilder shores of love, as the greatest and least perpendicular of all the great horizontals of the four quarters. It was this reputation that brought her to the chair opposite Bose Ikard.

'So I want you to charm the little monster.'

'Won't it be too obvious?'

'That's really your problem. I can have you introduced innocently enough, then it's up to you.' He passed a file over to her. 'Read this.' He began offering his opinions but she was more concerned with finding room in her vanity bag for the file, slowly emptying its contents onto the desk in front of her in order to create room. Eventually the file was squeezed into place and she began refilling the bag with the objects she had put on the table. Last among them was an extremely old, dried-up apple that had been lurking unseen at the bottom of the bag for over a week. Bose Ikard was staring at the apple with disapproval: it hardly spoke of her reputation for sophisticated entrapment. 'Don't mind that,' she said, seizing the ancient apple with mock delight. 'It was given to me by my nanny when I was a little girl and I can't bear to part with it.'

Cale's visit to Potsdam had produced an upsurge in morale among the troops and a renewed determination to fight that diminished in power in proportion to the distance from Potsdam. It gave IdrisPukke time to create his troupe of imposters but that was all. Getting actors wasn't difficult but getting ones that could be relied on to keep their mouths shut was more of a problem, as were the costumes. After the first day of try-outs it was clear that they had a major difficulty: the actors were too small, which is to say they were normal height, but Cale's dream of a powerful cloaked figure standing on a lonely mountain crag to encourage the faint-hearted came up against a practical snag: once the costumed actors were at any kind of distance – a precaution necessary not to give the game away – no detail about them could be recognized: not the grand gestures, the menacing hood or even whether they were kneeling or standing. They were just black specks and, worse, black specks against a black background.

'We have to make everything big,' said IdrisPukke. 'Big costume, big gestures, big everything. A pantomime larger than life.'

Within a week he'd hired every theatrical fabricator in Spanish Leeds and for two hundred miles around and built several giant costumes with stilts and extended arms and huge shoulders and enormous heads.

'The head's about right,' said Vague Henri to Kleist, when they were shown it. 'Not sure about the rest of it.'

'Kiss my ears,' replied Cale.

'It's got to be like this or we'll have to think again.'

In fact, IdrisPukke did both. The puppet Cale could be made to work in the right place, with fires behind it to create enough light to see it and with puppeteers to wave his ten-foot-tall cassock about so it looked as if he were braving great winds. But they also had to go back to a version of their first model, with padded shoulders and false arms, made by a man who usually built the mannequins for the magician's trick of sawing the woman in half using imitation legs. 'In pantomime,' he said, 'everything has to be big, it's true, but it's got to be the right kind of big.'

This second version had to be viewed from a much closer proximity but in the twilight where it couldn't be seen so clearly. Best of all for showing it off was the magic hour, the time before evening falls when the light allows even the crudest shape to take on the glow and power of another world.

'Why,' said Cale, 'is everything always more difficult than you think? Why is stuff never less difficult?'

Feeling ill and irritated he arrived at that evening's festivities in a very bad mood. That the entire evening had been set up to try to discover whether or not he was dead made him even more snaky. 'If they're looking for an excuse to take me on, let them try.' He had taken recently to muttering to himself. This time it was loud enough to attract Vague Henri, who was in the next room writing a letter about boots.

Vague Henri put his head round the door.

'Did you say something?'

'No.'

'I heard you talking.'

'I might have been singing. So what?'

'It wasn't singing, it was talking. You were talking to yourself again. First sign of madness, mate.'

That night Bose Ikard made a point of re-introducing Cale to the comparatively few people who had spoken directly to him, all of whom had been instructed to ask him as many complicated questions as possible. His success in drawing Cale out reached its height when he was introduced to the King – his longest response to the supreme head of state was, 'Your Majesty.' For the rest it was a single word or a shrug. In desperation, Bose Ikard brought in Dorothy. She entered the room and it was no exaggeration to say that there was something like a gasp at her appearance. She was wearing a red velvet dress cut shamefully low and red velvet gloves that covered her arms a good deal more than the dress covered her breasts. Her waist was cinched skinny-boy-thin, the skirt of the dress was decorous enough when she was still, but when she moved it revealed her left leg almost to her hip. With her crimson lips and white-blonde hair she should have looked like an expensive tart – but she could carry it off in a way that simply caught you in the chest, whimpering with desire. And this was an effect by no means limited to the men. She stopped and talked to a few of the most important people in the room, her lovely smile revealing teeth like little pearls, all except one of them that was a little snagged, an odd proportion, which only made her seem more beautiful. She stopped for a little while to talk to Bose Ikard and positioned herself so that Cale could see and appreciate her gorgeousness. Then, when she noticed he had observed her two or three times while pretending to look indifferently around the room, she walked directly up to him. She'd decided that bold would work best with him, bold and beautiful.

'You're Thomas Cale. Chancellor Bose Ikard has bet me fifty dollars that I won't get more than two words out of you.'

There was, of course, no such bet and she did not expect him to believe her. Cale looked at Dorothy thoughtfully for a moment.

'You lose.'

32

Perhaps one day a great mind will discover the exact point in any given situation when the person who has to make the decision ought to stop listening. Until that day it's no wonder that prayer, divination, or the disembowelling of cats are as useful strategies as any. Stupid advice sometimes works; intelligent advice sometimes fails. The appearance of Cale's puppets had been a surprising success. Everyone agreed that the will of the New Model Army to fight had improved beyond measure – a will as important, perhaps, as weapons, food or numbers. It was so successful that it was decided the troops needed even more of it. The problem was that the Redeemers also had a will to fight that was founded on more than clever illusions: death for them was merely a door to a better life. So it was argued – not unreasonably – that if fake Cales could do so much good, how much more would the troops benefit from the presence of the real one. Mysteriously, morale amongst the New Model Army had increased as much in areas where the puppets hadn't been seen as where they had. Clearly then just a few short appearances by Cale himself might tip the balance.

Vague Henri was begged and cajoled and nagged until news arrived of another hideous victory by the Redeemers at Maldon. Everyone was shaken by this defeat, even Vague Henri, so he agreed to approach Cale. Had he known all the facts of the loss at Maldon he wouldn't have done so. A few weeks later it became clear that the rout had not been the result of Redeemer superiority but was entirely due to the stupidity of the New Model Army commander, who had allowed the Redeemers to escape to high ground and ensured defeat from a position where victory would have been inevitable.

In fact, if anything, the flow of victories was moving slightly in favour of the New Model Army, except nobody knew it. So it was that, based on a false proposition reasonably arrived at in the face of compelling evidence that was completely mistaken, Vague Henri persuaded Cale to tour the battlefield in person. Cale was deeply reluctant but Vague Henri said it wouldn't be for long and they'd travel in a wagon-train much bigger than the standard one. Cale had been feeling a little better and his personal carriage had been fitted with springs so that it was much easier for him to rest on the move. Things were critical, apparently. It was a crisis. Something Must Be Done. What choice did he have?

The first five days of the seven-day tour went well. Cale's presence – away from anywhere dangerous – was a tonic for the troops far beyond expectations. It continued to be a great success right up until the moment when it turned into an appalling disaster – one that was set to deliver absolute victory into the hands of the Redeemers by means of the deaths of Cale and Vague Henri on the same day.

To avoid an unseasonably heavy storm coming down from the north, Vague Henri had halted the train. Unfortunately the same storm had also threatened a large expeditionary column of Redeemers, who had decided to avoid it by turning for the safety of their own lines. It was this coincidence of circumstances that brought a force of some fifteen hundred Redeemers, chosen to go this far because of their skill and experience, to blunder into Vague Henri's unready wagon-train which, big as it was, had only some six hundred soldiers. Worse than that, many of them were not so skilled and experienced: Vague Henri had made the mistake, pressed as he always was for time, of handing the choice of soldiers over to someone too easily bribed to allow persons of rank and influence (already the New Model Army was falling into bad habits) to buy the great status offered by being able to boast they had served with the Exterminating Angel himself.

Vague Henri immediately ordered the wagons circled. As soon as Cale emerged to investigate the noise he spent five minutes looking over the Redeemers, who were putting themselves in order about eight hundred yards away, and told Vague Henri to stop.

'Why?'

'That small lake there.' It was a tarn about three hundred yards away. 'Form a semi-circle against the lake shore, same size as here – then with the wagons left over form another semi-circle inside.'

Vague Henri was able to catch the wagons still on the move so there was no delay putting the horses back in harness or digging up the pegs used to fasten the wheels firmly to the ground. The Redeemer in charge realized that now was a good time to attack but he was a cautious man and delayed too long, wary of being drawn into a mysteriously cunning trap. By the time he decided to move, the New Model Army formation was in place, the horses being uncoupled and the wheels hammered.

The central question for both sides was the same and neither knew the answer. Was help on the way? Vague Henri had sent out four riders for help as soon as he saw the Redeemers. For the Redeemers the question was whether they'd caught all of them. Without help or extraordinary luck it was only a question of time before they overran the stockade – unless they'd failed to catch all of the New Model Army riders. If so, help might be on the way eventually. Even then they were in a good position, with odds of better than two to one in their favour. They were also in a better position than they knew, given that half the soldiers in the wagon-train were made up of inexperienced administrators of one kind or another. Cale, more than anyone, believed in the importance of good administrators but not here and not now. It took about twenty minutes for Cale and Vague Henri to realize that they were not being protected by the engine of violence they'd worked so hard to create.

'This is your fault,' said Cale.

'Put me on trial when it's over.'

'You're only saying that because you know you're going to die here.'

'And you're not?'

'*Now* you're worrying about me? It's a bit late.'

'Stop whining.'

There was a bad-tempered silence – then they got on with it.

'We need height,' said Cale.

'What?'

'We need a platform in the middle of that,' he said, pointing at the small semi-circle of wagons. 'It doesn't need to be more than about six feet up – but we'll need room for twenty crossbowmen and as many loaders as you can. The Redeemers are going to break through the first wall so we've got to turn the space between the two into a slaughterhouse – that's all I can think of to keep them back.'

Vague Henri looked around, working out what he would use to build the tower and protect it. It would succeed up to a point. It wouldn't make much difference if all his riders had been stopped.

'You look terrible,' he said to Cale.

In fact he could barely stand. 'I need to sleep.'

'What about that stuff Sister Wray gave you?'

'She said it could kill me.'

'What? And they're not going to?'

Cale laughed. 'Not if they know it's me. I'm probably all right.'

'But they don't know it's you.'

'It might buy us time if they did.'

'Too clever.'

'Probably. I'll sleep on it. Sort out the experienced men and divide them into the good and the better. Of the best I'll need seven groups of ten. Put the weakest in the first group of wagons and wake me an hour before you think the Redeemers are going to break in. Now walk me slowly to my carriage so they don't see their Exterminating Angel fall over on his face.'

On the way, a terrified-looking quartermaster walked over to them and reported there had been a mistake with the boxes of villainous saltpetre used to charge the handguns. Three-quarters of their supply turned out to be bacon, which was packed in identical crates. The quartermaster was surprised to be calmly dismissed. There was a reason.

'This is your fault,' said Vague Henri to Cale.

It was true, it *was* Cale's fault – months before he'd realized they were spending a fortune and huge amounts of time making crates of every different size and shape for their supplies, so he'd standardized them. A simple but clever idea promised to destroy them all.

Cale had expected he might, if he was lucky, get two or three hours. Vague Henri woke him after seven. It always took him a couple of minutes to become wakeful in any way but he could see immediately that there was something different about Vague Henri. More than Kleist, and very much more than Cale, he'd always retained something of the boy about him. Not now, though. There was no point in delaying so he took the tiny packet of Phedra and Morphine out of his drawer and poured the dose straight into his mouth. Sister Wray's dire warnings whispered in his ear. But she'd given it to him because she knew there would be days like this.

Cale followed Vague Henri outside. In the hours he'd been asleep hell had arrived. All the wagons in the first wall were in a terrible state – walls broken, wheels smashed; half were pulled to the ground by Redeemer ropes and six of them were on fire. In the inner semi-circle the dead and the wounded lay in ragged lines of around two hundred – and though there were screams, mostly it was the horrible silence of those in the kind of pain that was going to kill. And yet Cale could see Vague Henri had preserved the line without using two hundred of the most skilled and experienced. Cale looked directly at him and Vague Henri stared back: something, something had changed.

'What you've managed here,' said Cale, 'not even *I* could have done it.' If they ever praised each other, which was rare, it was always with an edge of mockery. But not this time. Vague Henri felt the effect of this praise as deeply as it was possible to be affected by the deep admiration of someone you love. A short silence. 'A pity,' said Cale, 'you let it happen in the first place.'

'Well, it's a pity,' replied Vague Henri, 'that because of your stupid boxes we're all going to die.'

The first wall of wagons was still holding, if not for much longer – already the Redeemers were pulling at the burning wrecks. Cale thought he had about ten minutes. He shouted the fresh troops forward and gathered them in their pre-arranged groups of seven.

He gave them, of course, the speech he'd stolen from the library in the Sanctuary.

'What's the name of this place?' he asked.

'Saint Crispin's Tarn,' said one of the soldiers.

'Well, he that outlives this day, and comes safe home, will strip his sleeves and show his scars and say "These wounds I had at Crispin's Tarn." And then he'll tell what feats he did that day. Then shall our names be as familiar in the mouths of everyone as household words from this day to the ending of the world. We few, we happy few, we band of brothers; for he today that sheds his blood with me shall be my brother.'

Cale did not make the usual offer to let any man go who did not wish to fight – no one that day was going anywhere. One day his trick speech would fail to work but not today. 'Each one of you,' he shouted, and the drug was beginning to do its work, his voice was strong and carried above the noise behind, 'belongs to a group of seven named after the days of the week because I've not had the time and the privilege to know you better. But each one of you is now responsible for whether the future lives or dies. Keep your shields touching. I want you close enough to smell each other's breath. Don't lag behind, don't charge ahead – that's the style I want and the spirit. You know the calls – listen as well as I know you can fight and you'll do well.'

He stood forward and pointed to either side of the semi-circle.

'Monday there. Sunday at the far end. Everyone in order in between.' He waved at them to go.

Vague Henri meanwhile had gathered up the remaining weakest fighters and now led them forward to reinforce the wagons not on fire.

A few minutes more of the tug-of-war with the burning wagons and then they collapsed; the Redeemers pulled what was hooked to their chains back and away to leave what now looked like gaps in a row of broken teeth. Vague Henri had just enough time to return and enter the small semi-circle in front of the tarn and organize his crossbowmen on the stumpy ragged tower of earth and stones and wood.

Five minutes and then the first Redeemers entered through the largest gap to Cale's left. Now he could feel the poison pumping in his veins – not real strength or courage but jumpy, edgy and overstrung. But it would have to do. He realized his judgement was twitchy too; part of him wanted to rush the Redeemers in the breach and fight. Vague Henri had been instructed to save what remained of their failing supply of crossbow bolts and only try to hit the centenars. The centenars dressed exactly like other Redeemers for precisely this reason but Vague Henri could tell them even through the smoke. One went down, hit in the stomach, and then another.

'Wednesday!' called out Cale. 'Walk on!' They moved forward in a line – the Redeemers waited – clear now for them what attitude to take.

'That'll do!' called out Cale and the Wednesdays stopped, leaving the Redeemers confused – they'd expected to defend the breach but they were being encouraged in. This wasn't right. Cale raised his left hand to Vague Henri and five bolts from his overstrungs encouraged the Redeemers to do the right thing – or the wrong one – and advance.

However bad things looked for the wagon-train, the Redeemers were worried too. It had taken them too long to get this far. With such odds they'd expected to overrun the wagons and be on their way before reinforcements came. They knew that if they'd got all the New Model Army outriders they had all the time in the world. But they couldn't be sure. So, fearing they were pressed for time, they moved past the wagons and into the half circle.

'Tuesdays!' shouted Cale. 'Come by! Come by! Quickly. Quickly.' The Tuesdays moved forward, the left edge slightly faster, taking the group in an anti-clockwise move to seal the space to the Redeemer right. 'Thursdays! Away to me! Quickly!' The Thursdays moved anti-clockwise and blocked the moving Redeemers from spreading to their right. The replacement centenars would have withdrawn at this to the breach but they'd been told to push on.

'Alleluia! Alleluia!' they screamed and hit the New Model Army lines of shields with their own – here it was mostly cut and shove and the crash of sword and mallet against shield with everyone trying to get in a blow without being caught themselves. But the problem was that the Redeemers were by far the better soldiers in an open fight and it was telling much quicker than Cale had hoped. But he'd planned for it – hoping to stall them here to get time for reinforcements to arrive – if they were on their way. But too soon his men were beginning to fall back. Cale, in his fifteen-year-old pomp, would have used the rest of the days of the week to support the retreat back to the semi-circle around the tarn. He would have seen that he'd got it wrong and backed away in as good order as was possible. The only reason he was able to take to the fight was because of Sister Wray's drugs – but she would have seen almost immediately that he was reacting badly: his face was flushed, his pulse racing and his eyes like pin-holes. Seeing the three days of the week were being pushed back and about to collapse he raced forward, picked up a hideous looking poleaxe from a wounded soldier and grabbed a short mallet abandoned in the ground then burst through the line of the Wednesdays and launched himself into the astonished Redeemers.

> *Wide-mouthed the dogfish loves to swim*
> *The fishes go in fear of him*

Filled with rage and drug-powered to insanity, Cale lashed at the Redeemers around him with the blunt-toothed poleaxe – a thug's weapon wielded by a thug with savage handiness and utmost craziness: brutal the crushing insults to teeth and to faces, blunt the breaking of scalps and of fingers, the splintering of knees and elbows. His hammer to their chests caused their hearts to stop as they stood, shattered spines and cheekbones; he hammered ribcages, fractured bones, legs tore, noses burst. Even Redeemers were stunned at the violence – and then the discouraged of the New Model Army, seeing the madman who'd come to their rescue, rushed to his aid and startled their betters as if they were taunted by Cale's delirious poison, unhinged by the blood and the shit smells and the horror.

Now more Redeemers poured in from behind but made things worse as their panicking comrades tried to escape the mad-infected counter-attack. Cale was stepping on the wounded living to get in his blows on the retreating enemy. He was in such a mania that he'd have been a terror holding a baby's rattle in either hand. The drug released in a flood the pent-up anger against the men falling back in front of him – the whining and begging of men who were dying and the crowing and gloating of his men at his shoulders – these are the signals and the sounds of a battle, the terror and pain and the singular rapture.

The Redeemer advance collapsed and but for one centenar, who kept his head and pulled away men who were standing like stumps to be slaughtered, they might have had a blow hard enough to make them leave. As they retreated Cale had to be held back from following – lucky for him, as once in the open beyond the outer rim of wagons he'd have been killed. No drug would have helped him there. The leader of the Fridays managed to hold Cale in the kind of grip possessed only by a six and a half foot tall former blacksmith. He held him back long enough for Vague Henri to arrive and talk him back to the semi-circle in front of the tarn. Now it was dark and as Vague Henri gave Cale over to a field doctor, with whispered advice about a medicine that had gone wrong, he tried to work out how to cover the breach.

Had the Redeemers attacked the same point again they would have been through in a few minutes but they were, understandably, amazed at what had happened and, believing the New Model Army had found some berserk mercenaries, decided that they should try a different approach. For the next two hours they attempted an attack on the outer perimeter with the intention of setting all the wagons on fire and then pulling the burnt remainder out of the way to give them a clear line of assault to the semi-circle backed onto the lake. Vague Henri held them off until two hours past midnight and then ordered the survivors to retreat to the tarn and watch the Redeemer engineers pull the outer perimeter apart. At four in the morning the last attack began.

The Redeemers gathered on the inside of the perimeter and sang: *Alleeeeluuuueeeeaaaa!*

Alleeeeluuuueeeeaaaa! Lit from behind by the red embers of the burnt-out wagons they looked like some monstrously armed choir from hell. To the left, other Redeemer soldiers began to sing.

> *Death and judgement, heaven and hell.*
> *The last four things on which we dwell.*

To the right:

> *Faith of our fathers, living still we will be true to thee*
> *till death.*

In a harrowing way it was beautiful – though that thought never crossed the fearful minds of those watching and listening.

Brought back to the wagons in front of the tarn, Cale had been taken to the tent for the wounded behind the stumpy tower built by Vague Henri. His mind seemed a little clearer but his body below the waist was shaking uncontrollably in a way that looked faintly ridiculous. Vague Henri told the doctor what he'd taken.

'Give him something to calm him down.'

'It's not that easy,' said the surgeon. 'You shouldn't be mixing these drugs – it's not safe. As you can see, you can't tell what'll happen.'

'Well,' said Vague Henri, 'I can tell you what'll happen if you don't get him into a condition to fight.'

It was hard to argue with this so the surgeon gave him Valerian and Poppy in a dose large enough to put down the former blacksmith who was now standing over Cale in case he made a run for it.

'How long to see if it works?'

'If I told you I'd be a liar,' said the surgeon.

Vague Henri squatted down in front of Cale, who was shaking all over and breathing in and out in short bursts.

'Only fight when you're ready. Understood?'

Cale nodded between shakes and breaths and Vague Henri walked out of the tent knowing this was likely to be his last night on earth and feeling all of two years old. He climbed up the makeshift hump in the middle of the semi-circle – tower was too grand a word for it – and exchanged a few words with the fifteen crossbowmen and their loaders. Then he turned to the rest of the men – his men – at the barricades. He thought that at this time of all times they deserved the truth.

'First,' he lied, 'I've heard that reinforcements are on their way. All we have to do is hold out till mid-morning then we'll make them sing a different tune.' There was a loud cheer, which made an odd clash with the music of the Redeemers.

Did they believe him? What other choice was there? Everything for Vague Henri was now about the art of delay. He decided to offer the Redeemers talks about surrender, not really thinking it worth the risk. When the messenger failed to return he was furious with himself for wasting a man's life when he knew, really, what the answer would be. *You're weak and useless*, he said to himself. He turned to the immediate problem: the shortage of bolts. He'd been setting the loaders to making the new ones all day so there was a good supply but keeping the Redeemers back for long enough would probably need more by far than he'd stockpiled. If reinforcements arrived at all it had better be by nine in the morning. After that no one would need to worry any more.

The plan he'd put together was simple enough: the raised platform gave them a line of sight everywhere to the front except for an arrow's shadow about six feet in front of the wagons. Any Redeemers who made it to the shadow would be able to fight the defenders without being picked off by the crossbows on the tower. Vague Henri's job was to keep the Redeemers back from the wagons so that only a comparatively small number in the protective shadow could fight hand-to-hand with the defenders. But this plan, he was sure, depended more on Cale than on him: the defenders on the wagons needed an exterminating angel on their side if they were to make it through the night.

Still singing, on came the first line of Redeemers, slamming their shields with their swords in slow accompaniment to the dirges Vague Henri had been forced to listen to as a boy morning, noon and night. Through a stroke of luck he'd discovered a second case of overstrungs when there should only have been three for an entire camp: close-quarter fighting didn't require such long distance power so they were only used for sniping, and then hardly ever. On another occasion this mistake might have been a disaster but today incompetence had been a glorious gift. With ten of these crossbows against them the Redeemers would be getting a nasty shock on their way to the wagon barricade.

So it proved. The Redeemers were expecting to come under fire from the much weaker crossbows Vague Henri had designed for close in-fighting, and against which their shields were a pretty good defence. They hadn't even started to advance when bolts from the overstrungs took out four centenars, four others and wounded a further two. Worse was to come. Almost immediately another volley of five from the other overstrungs, handed to the crossbowmen by their loaders, again struck the dense Redeemer ranks with the same result. Taken by surprise, there was enormous confusion about what to do and for a moment Vague Henri thought they were going to retreat out of range. He was almost right but then one of the centenars, lashing to the left and right and screaming bloody murder, blocked the way and drove them forward.

'Run! Run! Run! Get under the safety of the wagons!'

As the eight hundred or so Redeemers made a chaotic dash for the shadow of the wagons where the bolts couldn't reach them they took heavy losses from the crossbows on the mound and as they got closer the less powerful crossbows in the wagons had greater effect. Worse still for the Redeemers, too many had come to attack the wagons – there wasn't enough room in the shadow for all the priests who made it there. More than two hundred were left directly in the line of fire from the mound. After a short period of carnage in which more than fifty Redeemers were killed, the centenars managed to work out their mistake and drove back only three-quarters of the number of men that just a few minutes before they had driven forward.

The Redeemers at the wagons fought on, protected from Vague Henri but not from the defenders inside the wagons, now under intense and deadly pressure. Still, the defenders were well protected and died only at a rate of one of them to six Redeemers. It was Vague Henri who held the balance. As Redeemers slowly died in front of the wagons they had to be resupplied by Redeemers now hiding in the dark back, beyond the old perimeter. Once enough Redeemers had died the centenars raced forward from the dark in groups of thirty or so to replace them. Life and death for the defenders depended on the rate of fire from the stumpy hillock and how many Redeemers the crossbowmen could kill as they made their dash from the dark across the open space to the relative safety of the wagons.

A murderous rhythm was being beaten out by Vague Henri and the defenders and they'd survive only as long as that rhythm stayed the same. If they ran out of bolts or the wagons were breached the fight was over. Vague Henri now believed it was over anyway. *If only Cale was here*, he kept thinking to himself. *He'd know what to do.*

By now the exterminating angel was snoring away in his carriage, being watched over by the former blacksmith, Under-sergeant Demsky. Briefly visited by the surgeon a few hours into this second fight, Demsky was told that Cale would be unconscious for hours and that Demsky would be of much more use in the field.

'I should watch over him,' said Demsky.

'If those Papist scum get over the wagons,' said the surgeon, 'all you'll be watching over is his death and then your own.' Cale snored on. The surgeon's point was impossible to disagree with and after a brief check they left Cale to the dark.

Half an hour later Cale woke up, the Valerian and Poppy mixture having worn off. The same could not be said of the Phedra and Morphine that Sister Wray had so fearfully given him. Even more demented than before he'd fallen into his herb-induced sleep, he picked up a poleaxe and rushed outside. His carriage had been moved to the safest place on the far side of the small hillock and about thirty feet from the water of the tarn. Under normal circumstances he would have been seen within a few steps, even in the dark – but it was two hours into the battle and everyone was wrapped up in the fight for survival going on in front of them. This was why only Cale saw the line of Redeemers in the lake, wading their way towards the completely exposed rear of the camp along some kind of raised shallow that they'd discovered, the width of two men. The water was still waist-high and their progress was slow but there were enough of them to turn the fight in a matter of minutes. Roaring for help, which went unheeded due to the great noise of the battle, a naked Cale – the surgeon had stripped off his blood-glazed clothes – ran into the lake and waded towards the startled Redeemers – a lone boy, completely naked and screaming at them.

Not even the gentlest and most loving dove of peace could fail to thrill at the majesty of his angelic violence – no hero had ever fought with such strength and graceful skill, such divine rage and cruel magnificence. As each Redeemer came on he dealt out such savagery to arms and legs and heads that soon the shallows of the lake were awash in severed limbs and fingers and heels and toes – all the frigid lake incarnadined with Redeemer blood as they came on at him relentlessly to be martyr-fodder in the cold black water.

If anyone in the battle behind him had found the time to look back into the lake they would certainly have seen something not soon forgotten. For an hour, lashing around him in the water, the hallucinating Cale fought madly against an endless line of Redeemers who did not exist, deadly foes magnificently vanquished who were entirely figments of his drug-drenched imagination. After an hour of deluded heroism all his mind-enemies were dead. And so, exhausted but triumphant, he made his way back to his carriage while the real battle continued, touch and go, and fell into a peaceful sleep.

On the mound, Vague Henri could feel the sweat dripping down his back as if, realizing he was going to die, fear beetles had hatched from his spine and were making their escape. On and on it went and the pile of bolts that were keeping them from a horrible death diminished like sand in a timer that would never be reversed. Then, at first unnoticed, the sky began to lighten and the pale red of dawn began to bathe the wagons below in a delicate pink and then the sun moved up above the horizon and a breeze blew up, dispersing somewhat the smoke that hung over the fight. Then the fight stopped and a peculiar silence fell on the men, Redeemer and New Model Army alike. Surrounding them on the low rise that overlooked the tarn, at a distance of a mile or so, were perhaps five thousand soldiers who had marched through the night to save their exterminating angel.

The Angel of Death himself was fast asleep and he was still asleep half an hour later when Vague Henri came to check on him, along with the surgeon and Under-sergeant Demsky. They looked down on him for a minute or two.

'Why is he so wet?' asked Vague Henri.

'All the herbs, probably,' said the surgeon. 'The body's way of trying to get rid of all the poison inside. He is our saviour – what can be said in praise of him that's good enough?'

It would be hard to say whether Cale's supernatural reputation inflated more from his (as it was now believed) single-handed destruction of the Redeemers just as they were about to claim victory, or the fact that having completed this extraordinary feat he'd retired to sleep through the remainder of the fight, as if he knew, indeed had in some way guaranteed by his single intervention in the battle, that victory was certain whatever the Redeemers then did or did not do.

It was a mark of Vague Henri's maturity and the strength of his moral fibre that he was able to find a sufficiently strong chamber in his heart to lock away for ever his incandescent fury that all the credit for the success of that most crucial night went to Cale. Mostly, at any rate.

'*I* won the battle of Crispin's Tarn.'

'If you say so,' replied Cale whenever Vague Henri brought it up in private, which was quite often. 'I can't remember much about it.'

'You said that not even you could have kept the Redeemers out.'

'Really? Doesn't sound like me.'

Of the real attack Cale had launched against the Redeemers he could only recall the odd fleeting image. For some time afterwards, all that remained of his heroic attack on the non-existent Redeemers in the tarn itself was the occasional strange dream. But soon even that faded. Vague Henri had his revenge for being robbed of the credit in a manner that would have been applauded by all fifteen-year-olds at all times and in all places. So impressed and grateful were the people of Spanish Leeds that a public subscription was filled ten times over to provide a fitting reminder of the heroic victory at Crispin's Tarn. At the site of the battle a stone statue was erected, in which an eight-foot Cale stood on the bodies of dead Redeemers while those about to be hideously slaughtered cowered before his unearthly mightiness. Vague Henri had bribed the stonemason to alter the inscription at the foot of the statue by one letter so that it now read:

In eternal memory of the heroic deeds of Thomas Cake

33

In the two weeks after the battle of the tarn Cale felt horrible and slept on and off almost continuously. When he was awake he either had a vicious headache or felt he was about to throw up and often did. One of the ways he found to take his mind off his misery was to lie in a dark room and remember all the wonderful meals he'd eaten with IdrisPukke: sweet and sour pork, angel's hair noodles with seven meats, blackberry crumble with the berries just picked and served with double-thick cream. Then, a double-edged pleasure, he'd think about the two naked girls and what it was like to touch them and be inside them (still a notion that astonished him whenever he thought about it – what an idea!). As long as he could avoid the hatred he felt for Arbell and the guilt – and such a complicated guilt – over Artemisia, then it seemed to help him vanish to a place where pain was dulled, including those. Often he would remember specific days and nights and fall asleep while thinking about them. After two weeks he woke up one morning and felt much better. This happened from time to time, the sudden arrival of several days of feeling almost normal – as long as he didn't do much. A few hours into this oasis he began to feel very strange; an intense desire would not leave him alone. It was so strong that he felt it was impossible to resist. Probably, he thought, it was caused by nearly dying at Crispin's Tarn. Whatever the reason it was driving him mad and it was not going to be resisted.

*

'Do you have hanging gimbals?'

'No.'

'Any history of thrads?'

'No.'

'Do you have a history of the drizzles?'

'No.'

'Would you like a pigeon? That would be extra, of course.'

'No.'

'A Huguenot?'

'No.'

'A gob lolly?'

Like all obnoxious boys of his age, Cale was wary of being made a fool of.

'Are you making this up?'

The sex-barker was indignant.

'We are *celebrated*, sir, for our gob lollies.'

'I just want . . .' Cale paused, irritated and awkward, '. . . the usual.'

'Ah,' said the sex-barker, 'at Ruby's House of Comforts we supply the *un*usual. We are notable for the unconventional most of all.'

'Well, I don't want it.'

'I understand,' said the disdainful barker. 'Sir requires the *mode ordinaire*.'

'If you say so.'

'Would sir want to avail himself of our kissing service?'

'What?'

'Kissing is an extra.'

'Why?' Cale was more bemused than indignant.

'The *fille de joie* at Ruby's are women of quality and hold kissing to be of all acts the most intimate. They are therefore obliged to ask for extra.'

'How much?'

'Forty dollars, sir.'

'For a kiss? No thanks.'

In a sex-barker's working life awkward customers were the rule but the pale young man with the dark circles around his eyes (though pale and dark didn't do his unhealthy colours justice) was now really and truly getting on his nerves.

'All that remains is for the young sir to provide proof of age.'

'What?'

'At Ruby's House of Comforts we are strict on such matters. It's the law.'

'Is this a joke?'

'Indeed not, sir. There can be no exceptions.'

'How am I supposed to prove how old I am?'

'A passport would be acceptable.'

'I forgot to bring it with me.'

'Then I'm afraid my hands are tied, sir.'

'Is that extra too?'

'Very droll, sir. Now piss off!'

There was laughter at this from the waiting customers and the tarts arriving to take them away for their rented ecstasy. Cale was used to being denounced, he was used to being beaten, but he was not used to being laughed at. Nobody smirked at the Angel of Death, the incarnation of God's wrath. But now he was just a sick little boy and how he burned for his former power as they sniggered. If he had not been so weak it's hard to see how he could have controlled himself under such provocation – they would have seen the terrors of the earth to shut their gobs. But watching him from the other side of the room was a very large man with a hard look in his eyes. Despite the scorn-acid eating into his soul he was obliged to walk away, already working out a plan to do something hideous to spite Ruby's House of Comforts in due course. So it was lucky for Ruby herself that, hearing the raised voice of her barker, she had come down to see what was up. She was even luckier that she recognized Thomas Cale.

'Please!' she called out, as Cale went to open the door. 'I'm dreadfully sorry. My person here,' she signalled towards the barker as if he were something that had waited too long to be thrown into the bins, 'is an idiot. His stupidity will cost him a week's wages. I'm most dreadfully sorry.' Cale turned around, enjoying the look of aggrieved injustice on the barker's face.

'Two weeks' wages,' said Cale.

'Let's agree on three,' said Ruby, smiling. 'Please come through to the privatorium. Only our most honoured guests are taken there. And everything tonight, of course, comes with our compliments.'

'Even the kissing?'

She laughed. The boy, it seemed, was willing to be smarmed.

'We'll find places you didn't even realize *could* be kissed.'

Although the barker was no wiser as to the identity of the boy, he'd never seen Ruby treat anyone with such deference. But it was more than deference, she was afraid. At any rate, he realized three weeks' wages were the least of his troubles.

In the privatorium was a sight to bulge the eyes of any boy, no matter how wicked. There were women everywhere, cocooned on banquettes of goya kidskin, on sofas of yellow velvet and day-beds covered in bittersweet vicuna from the Amerigos. Tall women, short women, tiny women, large women – brown and white and yellow and black women, one of them covered from head to foot except for one breast with the nipple painted poppy red. Another dressed like the innocent daughter of a Puritan was modestly clothed in white linen and a black dress – except that she wept tears of sorrow and held up a sign: *I have been kidnapped. Help me, please!*

Others were naked and seemed to sleep. One young girl, her feet and hands bound inside a wooden frame, was being tormented by a woman tickling between her outstretched legs with a swan's feather.

'Dutch champagne!' called out Ruby to a pageboy wearing leather blinkers. She turned to Cale. 'It's the best vintage in a hundred years.'

She gestured for him to choose one of the women in the room, trying to give Cale the impression she was at ease, but something terrified her about the white-faced boy and she hoped he would decide quickly. She was astonished at what he said next.

'I want *you.*'

Ruby was in her early fifties and had retired from whoring more than twenty years before. During that time such requests had been made but delicately or firmly rejected as the case might be.

'But these are some of the most beautiful women in the country.'

'I'm not interested. Only in you.'

Ruby knew how to make the best of herself, it was true. She had considerable skill in paint – enough, not too much – and she could afford the best efforts of the dressmakers of the city. She had by no means let herself go but she loved her food and was pleasantly lazy. And the truth was that she had never been beautiful. She had made her way to the top of a craft that took a dreadful toll on most through her warmth and wit. Her neck was too long for most tastes, she had a small nose but of an unusual shape and lips so full they verged on the peculiar. 'When I'm tired,' she used to joke, 'I look like a tortoise.'

But Cale thought she was gorgeous.

She was a woman of strong mind, and harsh if she needed to be, but what could she do? This white-faced boy could not be refused. Faced, then, with the inevitable, she put on the smile she had contrived over thirty years on her back to come easily and gestured him towards the door, watched by the open-mouthed and excited tarts.

'Who on earth was that funny-looking kiddiewink?' said the Puritan maiden who could now stop weeping.

'You're such a stupid slut!' said the girl who'd now stopped tormenting her partner with the swan's feather. 'That was Thomas Cale.'

The Puritan's eyes widened in delighted horror. 'I hear he came back from the dead and keeps his soul trapped in a coal-scuttle.'

Ruby Eversoll might not have believed in revenants or imprisoned souls but she knew enough hard facts about Cale to be afraid. She had once been owned by Kitty the Hare and while she was delighted by the news of his death, and how long and horrible his dying, she was aware of what kind of creature you would have to be to be capable of murdering Kitty in his own home. The fact that he was just a sick-looking boy only made him more unsettling. As she unlocked the door to her apartment she realized she was trembling. Ruby Eversoll had not shaken with fear in a very long time.

Cale would have been astonished if he'd known what Ruby was feeling. If he was not, perhaps, as apprehensive as most boys of fifteen or sixteen would have been in the same circumstances, he was still nervous – slightly out of his depth, slightly ashamed at paying someone to have sex with him, but also agitated at the unfamiliar pleasures of a woman so very different from Arbell or Artemisia. At the thought of his late lover he felt a stab of something – something like loss, something like remorse. But that was all too confusing so he put it away and concentrated on the statuesque Ruby.

'Shall I undress?' asked Ruby.

'Um . . . yes, please.' It certainly didn't sound very commanding but Ruby was too agitated to notice.

Ruby was a professional; Ruby knew her job. Very slowly she began to unclip the hooks and eyelets at the front of her dress from the top down. As she opened each of them Cale became transfixed by her breasts. Held in and forced upwards by the engineering talents of her dressmaker, with each unclasping the soft roundness, held up by the dress, seemed to swell as if they were desperate to be free at last. He did not notice he'd stopped breathing. She dropped the corset to the floor, undid her skirt and stepped out of it. Now all she wore was a white silk shift. Oddly, and to Ruby, incomprehensibly, she felt deeply awkward as she undid the ties down the front of the tissue-thin shift and then shrugged it to the floor and stepped away. Cale's lungs, if not Cale himself, decided it was time to breathe – and it was the gasps from Cale that began to tell Ruby that perhaps she had misunderstood something.

Above the waist she was naked now. Even as a slim young woman she had been proud of her breasts. She was no longer slim, or anything like it, but whatever her pleasure in butter and eggs and wine had added, and it had added a great deal, her breasts had retained something of their youthful lift. They were, to put it simply, very large, the pink nipples enormous. Cale, used only to the sight of the lithe Arbell and the tiny Artemisia, for whom the word delicate was gross, stared as if he was seeing a naked woman for the first time again. How was it possible, he thought (though thought was nearly paralysed), for the same creature to be so different? He had not, of course, shared Vague Henri's gawping epiphany while spying on the abundant Riba when she was bathing in the Scablands. Reaching to one side, Ruby undid the drawstrings at the side of her pale blue pantalettes and let them drop to the floor. It was as well that Cale had been undergoing a period of feeling stronger that week or else he might have dropped dead on the spot and the future of the world taken a very different turn.

There was an intense stillness in the room as Cale, utterly struck, looked at Ruby. Ruby began to feel her dread of the boy recede and the almost forgotten pleasure of intoxicating someone with the power of her body reassert itself. Slowly, enjoying each step more, she walked towards him and, holding out her arms, there was no other world, folded Cale into her body. That moment, the sense of being wrapped in a paradise you could smell and touch, would stay with him until the day he died, to be turned over in his mind whenever he was at his lowest point, a refuge against despair.

But now he was burning with greed. He dragged her onto the bed and began as if he wanted to eat her up. His mouth and hands were everywhere, fascinated by everything about her. Her belly was fat, nothing like the boy-flat tummies of Arbell and Artemisia. Ruby's stomach was round and pillow-soft and shimmered when he touched it like one of the curds in the banquets of the Materazzi. She was all curves and folds and he touched her everywhere, his delight so great that she began to laugh. 'Patience,' she said, and got to her knees. He knelt behind her, lips devouring her neck and experienced, according to the Hunterians, one of the seven great pleasures the world has to offer – holding a pair of weighty breasts in the palms of both hands.

As if desperate to discover the other six, he pushed Ruby back onto the bed and began kissing her nipples with such unrestrained hunger that he went too far.

'Ow!' she squealed.

He sat up – shocked and alarmed. 'I'm sorry. I'm sorry. I didn't mean to hurt you.'

The nip had been really painful but he was so remorseful

and she so taken aback by the intensity of his desire for her that she could do nothing but reach for his cheek and smile.

'It's all right,' she said, and fanned her face with her other hand. 'Just slow down a little.'

'Tell me what to do,' he said sweetly. Now she felt how hysterical she'd been to project such dread around such engaging regret and such innocence.

'Well, I don't want to dampen your enthusiasm but just try to draw the line at eating me up.'

In the hours that followed, Cale experienced another three of the remaining six great pleasures (about two of them it is, quite rightly, against the law of the land to be anything other than silent).

Kleist's observation that wherever Cale went a funeral was sure to follow had become a commonplace. Certainly the general view of the hideous events that took place in Ruby's House of Comforts later that night was that it proved that truisms get that way by being true. It was, of course, unfair to suggest that Cale was responsible for what happened, and preposterous to state that it was clear evidence of his super-natural status as some kind of earthly surrogate of death himself. But, as Vipond was later to observe to his brother, if Cale hadn't insisted on getting into an argument with the sex-barker that evening it would have ended with only a slight bruise to his sense of his own importance.

'So it was *his* fault,' said IdrisPukke, 'that some dog-shit gatherer cut the throat of a high-class tart because he thought she was laughing at the size of his penis?'

'Of course not. But it's not coincidence either – he may not be the Angel of Death but there are some people born to cause trouble in the world. And he's one of them.'

*

Shortly before ten o'clock that evening, as Cale lay pleasantly exhausted on Ruby's bed (blankets of Linton cashmere, sheets of Eri spider silk), a man in his early thirties arrived downstairs at the House of Comforts for a once-in-a-lifetime experience of beauty. He was a purist – which is to say that he spent his days collecting pure from the streets of Spanish Leeds. Pure was what the local tanners, who required its noxious substances to soften leather, called dog-shit. If the sex-barker had realized his profession the man would not have been let through the door, but the purist had known better than to present himself at such a special place in the clothes of the lowest of the low. He'd hired a suit and had a wash at the municipal bathhouse and a shave at the barbers. He was so nervous about being rejected he'd also drunk more than he'd intended. But had it not been for his row with Cale earlier that evening, the barker would probably have decided that the purist didn't look quite right and was just a little too much the worse for drink. It was a question of tone: Ruby's was a high-class place and the purist didn't pass the test. But on this night he did. The barker was peeved; more, he was miffed. He'd been humiliated because of Cale and so that night he decided to take it out on his fat slut of a boss and let the purist in.

The shriek that reached them as Cale lay with his head on Ruby's left breast was one he knew horribly well: the terror of someone who realized they were going to die.

'My God!' Ruby started to her feet and began to dress but Cale was at the door and trying to lock it shut when it burst open, knocking him backwards. Having killed one of the whores, the purist had panicked and headed the wrong way into the dead end of Ruby's apartment. Already the shouts of the bodyguards – Ruby had four – made it clear he could not retreat. He stepped into the room, locked the door behind him and grabbed Ruby around the neck, pulling her towards the window. Terrified as he was, he saw that three floors up there was no escape here.

Cale, who had taken a hefty blow to his forehead, slowly stood up.

'That hurt,' he said to the purist.

'Get me out of here or I'll cut this bitch's throat as well.'

The evidence of death was all over the man – it covered his face and the hired suit and the oddly small knife he was holding at Ruby's neck.

'Can I put my trousers on?'

'You'll stay where you are. Move and she's dead.'

'How am I supposed to get you out of here if I can't move?'

Cale could hear talking outside. Then one of the body-guards called out.

'The Badiels are on their way! You can't get out. Let the woman go and we won't hurt you.'

The purist pushed Ruby (who was impressively calm under the circumstances, thought Cale) towards the door.

'Tell the Badiels to let me go. If they try to come in I'll cut her throat. Then I'll cut the boy's throat as well.'

'Can I talk to them?' Cale asked.

'You shut the fuck up or I'll cut her throat.'

'I don't think you will.'

'Just watch me.'

'Why waste a hostage when if I talk to them I could help you out?'

'How could a scrawny chit like you be of any use?'

'Let me talk to them and find out. What have you got to lose?'

The purist thought for a moment but thought wasn't coming easily. The bleakness of his situation was closing in.

'All right. But watch what you say or I'll cut her throat.'

Cale walked to the door.

'That's far enough,' said the purist.

'Who's in charge out there?' called out Cale.

A short silence.

'I am.'

'Can you tell me your name?'

Another silence.

'Albert Frey.'

'All right, Mr Frey, I'd like you to tell this gentleman who I am.'

'I don't give a fuck who you are,' said the purist.

Frey had a problem. An intelligent man, he'd decided not to refer at all to Cale on the grounds that he'd be handing the killer a hostage who would give him even more power. Was this really what Cale wanted?

'It's all right, Mr Frey,' said Cale. 'You can tell him.'

Another pause. 'The young man in the room with you is Thomas Cale.'

The purist looked at the pale and skinny naked boy in front of him and compared the sight with whatever legends he'd heard. The mismatch was simply revealed.

'Bollocks!' said the purist.

'It isn't bollocks,' said Cale.

'Prove it then.'

'I don't see how I can.'

He nodded at Cale's groin. 'P'raps you can piss poison all over me. Can you?'

'Unfortunately I had a slash just before you came in. It might take a while.'

'I hear Thomas Cale keeps his soul in a coal-scuttle. Is that right?'

'I don't even know what a coal-scuttle is.'

There was a thunderous bang on the door. The purist,

startled, dragged Ruby back and pressed the knife harder to her throat.

'Mr Cale!' boomed a voice.

'Yes!'

'You shut up!' shouted the purist.

'Are you all right?'

Cale raised his left hand, palm outward to ask the purist's permission. Too scared to speak, the man nodded his agreement.

'I'm Over-Badiel Ganz,' said the man. 'Tell that evil-doer that if he comes out he'll get a fair trial.'

The purist gave a frightened gasp of derision. 'And then be taken straight to Topping Bob to cut my head off.'

'Do you hear me!' shouted Ganz. 'Come out of there and no one will harm you.'

Cale raised his voice.

'Over-Badiel Ganz, this is Thomas Cale.'

There was a silence – a nervous one.

'Yes, sir.'

'If you say another word until I tell you to you're going to be very sorry. Do you understand?'

Another pause.

'Yes, sir.' This time he was barely audible.

Cale stared at the purist. 'You're completely wrong, y' know, about them cutting your head off.'

'What d'you mean?'

'About eight months ago, give or take, I signed a warrant on a young girl, sixteen or seventeen years old, and the next day she was taken into the Square of Martyrs in Chartres and they hanged her, then took her down and revived her, then the executioner cut her open and while she was still conscious cooked her bowels in front of her. You see, the thing is I liked her. I liked her a lot.' He called out to Ganz. 'Did you hear that, Over-Badiel? That's how this man is to die, you understand?'

'Yes, sir.'

Cale looked back at the purist.

'Now, even though I don't like you I'm going to make a deal with you.'

'I'll cut her throat – that's the deal.'

'Go ahead,' said Cale. 'I'm sick to death of hearing you tell me what you're going to do. She's just a whore.'

'When I cut her throat I'll do the same for you.'

'No, you won't.' He smiled. 'All right, you probably won't. Me being naked and all that is a disadvantage, true. But I'm not a helpless girl. I know what I'm doing.' He was bluffing. He might have felt well enough for once to experience four of the seven pleasures with Ruby but without the Phedra and Morphine anything more arduous was well beyond him.

'I'm the one with the knife.'

'All right, so you kill me. They're still going to slice your tonk off and cook it in front of you.'

With all the talk, and what talk it was, the purist had time for the horrible events and the horrible predicament they'd put him in to take effect. He was visibly shaking.

'What's the deal?' he said, voice catching.

'The deal is you let the tart go and I'll kill you.'

Ruby had been impressively calm until then and, to be fair, her eyes bulged only a little.

'Are you taking the piss? I'll cut her throat.'

'So you keep saying. You know as well as I do you were over and done with the moment you killed that girl. You can't take that back. You either let me deal with you now and it will be quick and painless or you wait a few days and become a legend for suffering. Fifty years from now people will still be saying, "I was there."'

Now the purist began to cry. Then he stopped and terror became anger and he tightened his grip on Ruby. Then he began weeping again.

'It'll be quick,' said Cale. 'I'll be the best friend you ever had.'

There was more weeping and more panic but then he loosened his hold on Ruby and she eased herself away. The purist, now crying uncontrollably, stood with his arms down by his side. Cale went over to him and slowly took the knife from his hands.

'Kneel down,' he said softly.

'Please,' said the purist, though it was not clear why. 'Please.' Cale was remembering that Kitty the Hare had said that too before he died.

Cale put his hand on the man's shoulder and eased him downward.

'Say a prayer.'

'I don't know any.'

'Repeat after me: Into my hands, O Lord, I commend my spirit.'

'Into my hands, O Lor . . .'

A sudden stab from Cale under his left ear. The purist fell forward and lay absolutely still. Then he began to jerk. Then stop. Then jerk, then stop.

'For God's sake, finish him,' called out Ruby.

'He's dead,' said Cale. 'His body's just getting used to it.'

An hour later, just before Cale left the House of Comforts, and while they were finishing a drink alone, Ruby said to him, 'I felt there was something dreadful about you earlier on. Then I thought you were lovely. Now I don't know what to think.'

She was tired, of course, and though she'd seen more than a few bad things this was the worst night of her life. Still, it wasn't what Cale wanted to hear and he left without saying anything more.

PART FIVE

The Angel of Death has been abroad throughout the land; you may almost hear the beating of his wings.

John Bright

34

There have been six battles fought at Blothim Gor. No one remembers any of these fights except in the name: 'Blot' is ancient Pittan for blood, as is 'him' in the language of the Galts, who wiped them out and stole their land. 'Gor' means the same in old Swiss. Blood, blood, blood – a fitting place for the first use of Robert Hooke's hand-shooters. The war on the Mississippi plains had lasted six months by the time he got the balance of metals, powder and ease of use. Until then the fighting could have gone either way. The butcher's bill was hideous, the Redeemers' willingness to die in their thousands was beginning to edge out the advantage of the war wagons and the fraying soldiers inside them, born to cut wood, milk cows and dig potatoes. What kept them fighting was the sight, and rumours of the sight, of Thomas Cale. In the dying light of dusk he would appear on buttes and on cragged ridges and rocky wolds, still, except when the wind blew his cloak behind him like a wing, watching over them: pathfinder, dreadful guardian steward with his legs akimbo or kneeling, watching with his sword across his knees, shadowy predator, dark custodian. And then the stories began to make their way through bastion after bastion of a mysterious pale young man, no more than a boy, who would turn up wherever the fight was almost lost and battle side by side with the wounded and the lost, his presence calming their fear and radiating it back into the hearts of their almost triumphant enemy. And when it was over, and impossibly they had won, he would bind the wounds of the living and pray, tears in his eyes, for the dead. But when they looked for him again he would be gone. Scouts returned with stories of being trapped by the Redeemers when all hope was lost and they had surrendered themselves to a dreadful fate when an ashen young man emerged from nowhere, hooded and thin, and fought beside them against impossible odds only to prevail. Yet when the fight was over he was gone, sometimes to be seen watching from a nearby hill.

Ballads were written and spread within the week to every wagon on the Mississippi plains. Many had been written by IdrisPukke himself, after these stories had filtered back to Spanish Leeds. He hired dozens of travelling singers to go around the wagons singing his folk songs. But they also picked up the ones written by the men of the New Model Army themselves, clumsier, more sentimental than those written by IdrisPukke but mostly more powerful, so much so that when the returning singers played them to him he could feel the thrill along his neck and arms, finding himself moved and shaken even though he knew they were just propagation.

'What *is* truth?' said Cale, when IdrisPukke told him, shamefaced, about how the songs made him feel.

Cale, for whatever reason, perhaps shame or a cooler head even than IdrisPukke's, claimed that while the circus, as he referred to the twenty puppet Cales, had its effect in keeping the New Model Army from disintegrating through the spring and summer campaign, their resilience owed as much, or more, to his ability to keep the wagons supplied with decent food and weapons and new men with good boots and warm clothes – all delivered through the lightweight carts that Nevin had made for him and which could move so fast even over bad terrain that the Redeemers were rarely able to interdict them. No one, he said to IdrisPukke, wants to sing a heroic song about a decent pair of boots and lightweight supply wagons.

Even so, it was a damned close-run thing. It was Hooke's killing machines that brought the Redeemers to their knees on the Mississippi plains. Until then, they were using new tactics against the wagons, Greek fire and a lighter battering ram under a hood of bamboo to protect them from the blows and arrows of the bastions. They also had an advantage because of their belief that death was merely the door to a better life and, of course, that the life they left behind was a desert. But Hooke's guns offered not only more slaughter than even the Redeemers could deal with but also horrible injuries, each blast wounding as many as six men at a time with ragged cuts that could not be stitched or easily cleaned so that the wounds became septic and refused to heal. And Hooke's was not the only inventive mind concerned with dealing out pain and injury: it had occurred to the peasants that if they mixed a little dog-shit with the contents of the handguns they could ensure that the hideous wounds inflicted by them would fester most painfully.

Within three months the New Model Army was back over the Mississippi and with a bridgehead at Halicarnassus they were able to defend, despite the murderous counter-attacks of the Redeemers, for the same reason it had been the last place to fall.

Up until Bex the war against the Redeemers brought only defeat; after Hooke's handguns it was only victory. But there was not an easy triumph in any battle, from the clash at Finnsburgh between barely enough men to fill a public house (and where the only member of the Swiss royal family died during an unlucky visit to bring a tonic to the troops) to the five hundred thousand who drew up to face one another in the battle for Chartres.

Who remembers the individual battles in any war, more than the occasional name, let alone what happened there or why it was important – or even the war itself? Which of you has forgotten the battles that led Thomas Cale to the walls of the Sanctuary itself? Where are the cenotaphs remembering Dessau Bridge or the battle at Dogger Bank? Where are the memorials to the First Fitna, the siege of Belgrade, the Hvar Rebellion or the War of the Oranges? Who can tell you about the Strellus and their matchless defence of the grain silo at Tannenberg, or the slaughter at Winnebago, or the defeat at Kadesh where twenty thousand men froze to death in a single night? Where are the henges at Pearl Harbour or Ladysmith? Where are the shrines, the headstones as far as the eye can see, for Dunkirk or the fall of Hatusha, for Ain Jalut and Syracuse or the massacre at Tutosburg? And why remember the first day of the Somme with so many tears when more died more horribly at Towton in an afternoon? After a three-month siege of the Holy City, the total deaths were how many? No one was counting any more.

Later the same day, after the city fell, Cale and Vague Henri stood in the Sistine Chapel under its glorious ceiling depicting God creating man – hands outstretched to one another in eternal love.

'Beautiful, isn't it?' said Vague Henri.

'Yes, it is,' said Cale, and meant it. 'Have it painted white.'

There was a knock on Gil's door that immediately seemed to say 'I am a timid and guilty person.'

'Come in.'

It *was* a timid and guilty person: Strickland, Bosco's body servant, a man whose sense of his own miserable inadequacy and innate worthlessness hung about him like a personal fog.

'There was no one in the ante-room,' said Strickland. 'So I knocked.'

What Gil wanted to say was: *So what? Get on with it.* What he actually said was: 'How may I help you, Redeemer?' In fact, he was extremely curious. Not even Strickland would have acted so guiltily if he'd been instructed to come. Something must be up. He hedged and ummed and then came out with it.

'His Holiness has been in his room for six days and nights without food and only a cup of water once a day, which he's instructed me to leave outside his locked door.'

While the denial of pleasure was more or less a permanent state of affairs for the Redeemers, fasting for more than a day was regarded with suspicion. Fasting for six days was forbidden: such extremes brought about strange results. Most of the Redeemer heresies, including Antagonism, had begun with mad visions brought on by starvation. But Gil wasn't surprised, exactly. The gaps between audiences with Bosco had become ever longer – three weeks was not uncommon. The more victories won by Cale, and these days there were only victories, the more meetings were cancelled because the more incomprehensible was God's plan to bring about the remaking of the human soul. For Bosco, Cale was not the executioner of the plan but rather the plan's incarnation on earth. Now that incarnation was at the outskirts of Chartres and certain to take it, Bosco and ten thousand Redeemers had withdrawn to the Sanctuary. 'God means something by this,' Bosco had said. ' He's telling me but I can't hear.'

Gil's decision to leave had come up against the problem of all such decisions: it was easier said than done. Where would he go? What would he do? How would he live? The withdrawal to the Sanctuary had helped. Not even Cale could break into this place – not a thousand like him. Two thousand men, let alone ten thousand, could keep this place for ever – and the army wasn't made that could stay outside it for more than a few months. So Gil decided to wait and see and put one or two devices into operation. Perhaps Bosco would starve himself to death but he doubted it. Something told him that there was trouble in this. He stood up.

'Let's go to his rooms.'

Taking several men with him he made his way to Bosco, trying to work out what he was going to do – but when he arrived at the tiny corridor leading up to Bosco's apartments the Pope was standing in the doorway and smiling.

'Gil, my dear!' he said. 'When I tell you what all this means you'll laugh at me for failing to see something so very obvious. I couldn't see for looking. Come in, my dear fellow. Come in.' And in this mood of jubilation an alarmed Gil was hurried into Bosco's most private rooms.

So now the armies of the Axis turned south towards the great barbican and buttress of the Redeemer faith, to the fountain and the origin of it all: the great catastrophe itself. There was not much of a sense of triumph as the siege army camped outside the hulking mass of the tabletop mountain on which the Sanctuary was constructed. Chartres was not built to be held against an army and yet it had needed three months of blood and suffering before the New Model Army were able to get inside its defences. The Sanctuary was a problem of a different order. No one had come close to taking it in six hundred years. It was hard to see how anyone could: it was vast enough to feed itself on the miraculously fertile soil transported from the Voynich oasis and there were vats to store water for two years or more. But on the arid scrub that surrounded it even dog grass and arse-wipe struggled to survive. In summer the heat was unbearable even though the nights were freezing, and in the winter, only four months away, it could get so cold it was claimed birds fell out of the sky frozen solid. This was an exaggeration, of course, not least because there wasn't anything much for birds to live on. It was also the case, for reasons no one understood, that winters were sometimes almost mild. Mild or not, the scrublands before the Sanctuary were not suitable for men to live in and particularly not men in such large numbers. But there were many more difficulties than merely feeding twenty thousand soldiers in hostile circumstances miles from anywhere in a landscape which, for two hundred miles in every direction, had been scoured of every source of food, every well poisoned and every building burnt.

Cale was nicely looked after, it had to be said, in comfortably outfitted wagons with leaf springs and a decent mattress to keep him comfortable on long journeys, and another larger wagon in which to work and meet the great and the good. For all their success, the forces gathered around the Sanctuary represented, in part, those as hostile to Cale as the Redeemers gawping down at him from the walls of the Sanctuary. Once they realized the Redeemers must lose, the Laconics had changed sides and had contributed an army of three thousand to the Axis, which was now camped alongside the New Model Army. The Laconic general notionally in charge, David Ormsby-Gore, was in fact answerable to Fanshawe, whose central problem was whether to move against Cale now, when there would be many opportunities, or wait until the Sanctuary fell and then get rid of him. The trouble with waiting was that it was now clear that conquering the Sanctuary might take a long time, easily long enough for the Redeemer Fifth, Seventh and Eighth armies, who'd retreated to their vast territories in the west to regroup after their mauling at Chartres, to counterattack. The Laconic Ephors wanted Cale dead out of a desire for revenge for the defeat at the Golan, but Fanshawe was more concerned for the future. It was a long time since he'd learned that Cale had not only declined to expel the Helots but had made sure they had been trained to create an insurgency against the Laconics. Once Cale had defeated the Redeemers, or at least forced them back beyond the Pale, he feared he would have enough power and sympathy for the Helots to train and supply them. He might even intervene directly to support a rebellion. In fact, looking for a cause of any kind, other than that of his own survival, was very far from Cale's mind.

'When it's all over, we could buy a nice house,' said Vague Henri. 'What about that Treetops place you're always going on about?'

Cale thought about this pleasant notion. 'Hard to defend. Treetops. It's a bit too close to a lot of people with ungenerous thoughts. We need to go over the sea.'

'What about the Hanse? I bet with all that money they've got nice houses. One with a lake or a river.'

'Best to go where we're not known. I hear good things about Caracas.'

'We could bring the girls with us.' The girls in the Sanctuary were a difficult subject between them.

'They might already be dead.'

'But they might not.'

'All right. I agree: a nice house with lots of girls in Caracas then.'

'Do they have cakes in Caracas?'

'Caracas is famous for its cakes.'

There was no more time to work on the future because IdrisPukke arrived unexpectedly with bad news from Spanish Leeds.

'They're planning to impeach you,' he said.

'I suppose,' said Cale, '*impeach* isn't a good thing – not medals and a parade an' that?'

'No. More like put you on trial in secret in the Star Chamber followed by a private meeting with Topping Bob.'

'What's he supposed to have done?' asked Vague Henri.

'Does it matter?'

'It does to me,' said Cale.

'Set fire to the bridge after Bex.'

'They can't prove I did it.'

'They don't need to. Besides you did set fire to it. Also perjury is a capital case.'

'They told me to lie.'

'But you still did it. The summary execution of Swiss citizens.'

He did not say anything in reply to this accusation because it was also true.

'The illegal raising of taxes.'

'They agreed to that.'

'You have it in writing?'

'No. What else?'

'Isn't that enough? Just setting fire to the bridge would have the entire population of Switzerland fighting to get their hands on the rope.'

'What choice did I have?'

'Don't ask me, ask them. An impeachment before the Star Chamber doesn't at all require that the accusations are true in order for a guilty verdict – but it doesn't help that you actually did all these things.'

'You could march on Spanish Leeds yourself.' This from Vague Henri.

'Not without taking the Sanctuary first.'

Cale turned to IdrisPukke. 'Why aren't they waiting to get me until after it falls?'

413

'They're worried it will take too long – or that if it doesn't the New Model Army will do exactly what Vague Henri says.'

'But the New Model Army is still Swiss – and the King rules by the will of God. The same God they believe in.'

'They're peasants, not Swiss citizens – and they're not peasants any more. Wars change people.'

'It's asking a lot,' said Cale.

'Try asking it.'

'Not till we've taken the Sanctuary. Then we'll see.'

'And your invitation to Leeds?'

'I'm pretty sure you can find the right words. Besides, it may not be as long as the whingers think – taking down the Sanctuary. Hooke will be here tomorrow with a new engine.'

'And if it works, what then?'

'I'll worry about that when it happens.'

'To be honest, I don't think you can afford to do that. You need to start making plans now.'

'We were thinking,' said Vague Henri, 'of going to Caracas.'

'I'm afraid this isn't the time for stupid jokes. I'd say the chances of you being allowed to retire to a peaceful retreat are approximately none.'

'No rest for the wicked?'

'Something like that. You have many talents, Thomas, and making enemies is one of them.'

'Nobody likes us,' said Vague Henri. 'We don't care.'

IdrisPukke looked at him. 'You're being more than usually trying, Henri. I wonder if perhaps you might like to stop.' He turned his attention back to Cale. 'You've shown yourself to be a great tactician, but the time for tactics is coming to an end. Where are you going? That's the question for you now.'

But Cale was only a boy when all was said and done and he had no idea where he was going and never had known.

*

The next day Hooke arrived with three of his new howitzers: big fat barrels of steel, in principle the same as his all-conquering hand-shooters but so strongly built that they could fire a ball of iron the size of a small melon. It took several hours to set up the howitzers in their ugly wooden cradles and work out their elevations for the first assault on the walls of the Sanctuary, which were uniquely strong because the stones had been mortared together with a mixture made from rice flour, which set like the hob of hell.

Confident of success, Hooke had arranged for all three to be set off by men in specially padded armour. The army who gathered to watch pressed in so closely that the firing had to be delayed while they were pushed back, a process so laborious that Cale decided to let them stay. A wiser head prevailed in Hooke and eventually the watching soldiers were far enough back to satisfy him that the firing could go ahead. The three men in their special armour lumbered with their torches towards the howitzers and lit the fuses. There was a short fizz of powder and then a massive and almost simultaneous explosion, which burst two of the howitzers into a dozen pieces, cutting down all three of the armoured men and shooting back into the crowd of soldiers and killing a further eight. The third gun fired as it was meant to and sent the massive cannon ball smashing into the wall of the Sanctuary, where it simply bounced off, leaving behind a small dent. There would be no quick end to the siege of the Sanctuary.

But if it were not to be quick or even reasonably so then it was hard to see how he could avoid it collapsing. With winter coming on Cale would have to disperse the army before it fell apart through lack of food, water and the momentum needed to keep such disparate groups – predictably the New Model Army and the Laconics already hated each other – in the field in such hostile conditions. Even Cale was surprised to realize how little safety his great successes of the last few months had brought. In many ways, he wasn't much safer than, say, the day after Deidre had slaughtered the Two Trevors. He'd expected to reach a position of power that offered a respite, a defence, an asylum, but he could see that while he really did have power, great power, it wasn't made of the solid stuff he'd thought it would be. He'd thought it would be like a wall, but it wasn't: it was like something else he couldn't put his finger on.

But however elusive the question of how powerful power really was, he clearly had a great deal of it and that was why he was able to do something very foolish. He'd become obsessed with knowledge and feared never having enough of it. It was to him like the soother he saw in the mouths of infants. He saw very early on that information was odd stuff: you could easily end up with too much, or most of it was wrong or, even worse, correct but in a half-baked or misleading way. Still, he fancied himself, with some reason, as a good sifter of the stuff and had learned never to trust one source, not even the source he valued most in the world: IdrisPukke. It was true he felt a certain shame about this but not enough to stop him. The most important of these alternatives was Koolhaus, who had grown ever more disdainful and obnoxious the more he was able to demonstrate his superior intellectual gifts to the world. It was never enough for Koolhaus to be right, someone else had to be wrong as well – and he wanted them to know it. This was a weakness, perhaps a crippling one, as was the fact that his emotional grasp of the world was rather crude. Nevertheless, as a source of information and an evaluator of it he was invaluable. There was also Kleist. Intelligencing was the kind of work he was good at and which kept him busy: it was enough to distract to a certain extent from the fact that he was dangerously close to the sharp knife or the expensive narcotic from which he would never wake up. Kleist was not ready yet but he thought about it often. He made it through many bitter nights comforting himself with the thought that he could bring things to an end. Then there was Simon Materazzi. Cale had given Simon the freedom to go wherever he wanted. Simon could tell him what was happening in the camps and the streets. It was Simon who was the first to let him know that the puppet Cales were working to raise spirits and the first to let him know when the endless defeats and the slaughter that followed had demoralized the troops to such an extent that they couldn't go on working any more. But by then Hooke had perfected and made hundreds of the shooters that were to change everything and give the men the one thing that made manipulation of their trust unnecessary: success. It was from both Koolhaus and Kleist that Cale received the same information at almost the same time, and from IdrisPukke shortly after: Arbell Materazzi had been given permission to leave for the protection of the Hanse. It revolted and shocked him how much it hurt to read that she was leaving. Even he realized the stupidity of feeling as if she had betrayed him all over again. He never stopped, not really, thinking about her. He realized, and this proved it, that she never thought about him at all, unless as someone to be avoided. No amount of anger with himself at the grossness of his stupidity could stop his useless and childish heart from crying out above his fury: *How could she? How* could *she?*

If you despise him or find his weakness detestable or even merely irritating it was no more than he found himself. She was an infection in his soul and that was that.

The idiocy of what he did next was obvious to him even as he did it: he wrote to Kleist and told him to take however many troops of the Spanish Leeds garrison of the New Model Army he needed to arrest her and bring her to the Sanctuary.

'Fucking idiot!' said Kleist, on reading his order. But at least it gave him something interesting to do.

'Windsor has the crab.'

'Really? Bad luck,' said Fanshawe. 'He's sure?'

'Had one of the quacks look him over. He's a dead man.'

'It's an ill wind, I suppose,' said Fanshawe.

'Possibly Windsor would take a different view,' said Ormsby-Gore. Ormsby-Gore did not care for Fanshawe. He talked too much and he had a diplomatic way of telling him what to do that he suspected was not as diplomatic as it sounded. What were really orders were dressed up with 'I wonder if it wouldn't be a good idea if . . .' or 'I could be mistaken but it might be worth trying . . .' and so on. The Laconic way was to say what you had to say with the fewest words possible, a habit Ormsby-Gore took to extremes. For Fanshawe to be so roundabout in his orders felt like he was taking the piss.

'Still, you have to admit,' said Fanshawe, 'it's convenient and he *has* volunteered.'

The crab, a tumour that grew in the neck and was said to look like one, was a disease that afflicted Laconic males. About one in every fifty developed this condition, which was held by their enemies to be caused by everything from their hideous soup – made from blood and vinegar – to engaging in too much buggery with young boys. Given that it was invariably fatal and that long illnesses in Laconic society were notable by their absence it was the tradition that anyone so afflicted would offer themselves for a suicide mission as a means of making themselves useful.

'How bad is it?'

'Bad.'

'But we have some time?'

'Suppose.'

'It might not be necessary to wait too long.' He paused, hoping that Ormsby-Gore would be forced to speak. Fanshawe recognized this was childish but it gave him considerable pleasure. 'What do you think?'

A pause. 'Your patch.'

'Still, I'd be very interested in your opinion.'

'Act,' said Ormsby-Gore, not because he believed they should murder Cale immediately but because it offered him the chance to use the fewest number of words.

'You know, Ormsby-Gore, you could be on to something. Those howitzer thingies of his were the most appalling bloody shambles. What a *cauchemar*! Don't you think?'

'Don't speak French,' said Ormsby-Gore.

'I know what you mean,' agreed Fanshawe. 'I've often regretted that I do.'

He didn't have the slightest interest in Ormsby-Gore's opinion but the question of when to kill Thomas Cale was still a problem. Hearing rumours about Hooke's arrival he'd been pretty sure something like the howitzers was on the cards. If they had worked and the Sanctuary fell quickly then in the confusion it might have been possible, even probable, that an arrow in the back from a Redeemer would be taken at face value. The Swiss wouldn't go looking for an explanation and with Cale dead they'd go back to holding the whip hand in the Axis again. There was only the New Model Army to worry about – they hated the Laconics and if there were a sniff of their involvement in Cale's death there'd be trouble, particularly if they were stirred up by IdrisPukke and that rather engagingly yummy

Henri boy. But, handled with care, the circumstances might mean there'd be no suspicion at all. Bad luck and handkerchiefs all round. The thing about sieges was that, once you were stuck into one like this, what mostly happened was nothing. Killing him and trying to make it look like something else was almost impossible to get away with when nothing much was happening. Windsor and his crab turning up was an unexpected benefit because he wouldn't expect to survive the event – but it was more risk than Fanshawe was willing to take. An opportunity might come but he decided to wait.

35

'You're under arrest.'

Kleist was rather pleased with the way he'd used the bridge over the River Chess to cut Arbell Materazzi's escort in two. Not that it would have made much difference if they'd taken them armed only with wet towels. They were kids. The Materazzi rump had mostly died at Bex. The few that were left had been dumped by Cale and sent to guard Redeemers in the prison camp at Tewkesbury in order to avoid any chance of one of them distinguishing himself in combat. Whatever he owed Vipond, helping to ensure a Materazzi revival was not going to be part of the repayment.

'On whose authority?' Arbell was with a young man, softly spoken. 'It's Mr Kleist, isn't it?'

'You are?'

'Henry Lubeck – Consul to the Hanse.'

'You're free to go, Lubeck.'

'I'm sorry, Mr Kleist, but you haven't answered my question.'

'Be a good boy and fuck off out of it.'

'It's all right, Mr Lubeck,' said Arbell. 'This person is a creature of Thomas Cale's. You've a lawful warrant, of course?'

Kleist took out a piece of paper and a lead pencil – these days he was always having to write things down – wrote 'You're under arrest' and signed it. He was about to hand it to her but stopped. 'There should be a charge.' He thought for a moment and wrote 'For tax evasion'.

'What about my escort? What will happen to them?'

'They'll be disarmed and come with us. We'll let them go in a couple of days.'

'Where are you taking me?'

'It's a surprise. But don't worry, you'll find it interesting. You might learn something. Tell your people not to do anything stupid. Five minutes and we're on our way.'

A coincidence is a peculiar thing. We all know that every time we happen on someone we know in an unexpected place there must have been a hundred such meetings in our lives that never quite came about – that long-lost love was eighty feet away instead of five; or they were five feet away but we happened to be looking in the opposite direction. And so on. Each coincidence implies hundreds of near-coincidences almost happening but not quite. There's something unpleasing about the loss of all those chances for something wonderful that might have changed our lives but for a few feet or an undistracted glance.

Kleist's near wonderful event that day was that his wife Daisy and their child were in Arbell's column, where they would now have to stay for at least three days. It wasn't, though, altogether an amazing chance that she was there. Daisy had recently been dismissed as kitchen char to a merchant family for stealing vegetables – not one or two carrots and the odd potato, but sacks of the things. Once she'd left they discovered that her larceny extended to small but valuable items of jewellery. As a result the Hermandad came looking for Daisy and she realized it was time to be gone. The problem was that she had no useful skills – she was a useless charwoman – and she had a baby and no one was leaving Spanish Leeds; with the front line of the war moving ever westward they were only coming back. After several anxious days, unwilling to risk the Hermandads on the city gates, she had been forced to bribe the cook in Arbell's train to take her on as a washerwoman for no pay. This at least got them out of the city and once she was out it made sense to stay with the protection of the column. There were entirely untrue rumours of Redeemer fifth columns. Fed up with hard work for no pay she had been planning to disappear from Arbell's entourage in the middle of the night along with whatever was valuable she could lay her hands on, but the arrival of the New Model Army had put an end to that. It was now too dangerous to run for it. It might be thought inevitable that in a column of only two hundred-odd people, most of them soldiers, that a meeting with what she thought was her dead husband was bound to take place. But she made a point of staying out of sight (just in case) and even when she was obliged to come out of the washing wagon it was placed at the end of the line so that no one had to look at the more menial servants going about their manky tasks. Lay down your bet, then, for the great game always playing behind our backs – for Daisy a life of grim uncertainty, for Kleist a solitary death. Roll the dice, spin the wheel, shuffle the pack. Play.

Kleist had spent the first day riding at the front, quite comfortably numb, the weather warm, the constantly changing scenery a narcotic to his cancerous distress. Despair with its fifty shades of grey can give the soul wounded days like this. He only went back down the line once, when Arbell was finishing her evening meal. He missed Daisy clearing up the dirty plates by nearly two minutes.

The next day there was a shout to halt and he rode back down the line to see what was causing the delay – a broken spoke on an ancient wagon wheel. Daisy had been sent to bring up water to the nobs and she arrived just as Kleist, seeing he would just have to wait until the wheel was fixed, turned back to the front. She caught a brief but clear enough sight of him. But he had changed; he was gaunt where he had once been jaunty and vigorous in his own cool way. And of course he was long dead in the gullies and barancas of the Quantock Hills. How could he be this big kahuna on a horse with the power to make even the aristos shut up for once?

On the third and last day Arbell's followers were told they could clear off. Kleist, after a bad night, went down the column to check that no one was hanging on to Arbell who might be a nuisance. She was attempting to take five of her entourage with her, including two men who were clearly used to handling themselves.

'You can have two maids. That'll be enough.'

'And who's to protect me?'

'Oh, we'll do that, Your Highness. You're as safe as Memphis with us.'

'You think that's funny?'

'Not really – but it's hot and it's the best I can do at the moment. Two maids.'

'Three.'

'How about one?'

To make the point that this was the end of the conversation he turned his horse away and stepped it down the line as if he wanted to check that his orders were being carried out. Daisy was about fifty feet away, sideways on and bending down to pick up their daughter, who kept trying to run away under the wheels of the turning wagons. This time he saw her face clearly enough, but a year can be a long time for someone her age and she had filled out, no longer a lanky girl but a young woman. Something in the way she moved stirred now unpleasant memories and had she laughed rather than just smiled to herself at the little girl's desperate efforts to get free of her protective embrace he would have recognized the sound anywhere. And then she had the child firmly embedded on her hip as it reached out with pudgy hands to pull Daisy's now much longer hair and she moved on past a covered wagon and out of sight. There was no numbness now but a terrible surge of loss and grief. He wanted to get away and spurred the horse back towards the front of the column and signalled the horsemaster to move the convoy on.

It was the moment of the final entry for Kleist into the black place where the doors are shut and the windows are barred. Except for one thing. As he rode ever farther away from the millions of joys he had so nearly stumbled upon, he could not entirely forget the image of the young woman which had given him such dreadful pain: the easy to dismiss familiarity of the way she moved. It made sense to get away from the cause of such agony. Going back to look at her would only make things worse.

But all the same he turned around. Then he stopped. It was foolish. Pointless. Ridiculous. He turned around again and rode away from the woman for several minutes, making it impossible to go back to wound himself further for no reason. Too far now. Then some pointless hope of something, of at least seeing an echo of everything he'd lost, made him turn again. He wanted to rush and not rush. But a certain composure returned to him, a sense that he was headed for a last, thin ghost of a reminder of her presence. You could not call it hope, because she was dead, but it was movement away from the black room. Impatient, he drove on, now he had made the decision, anxious to see it through. *Look at her, get it out of your system and stop this idiocy.* He raced past the end of his own column and then towards the meandering remainder of Arbell's former followers. As he arrived they looked at him warily – what new thunder here? He ignored them and slowly began to search among the untidy line. Then he saw her just ahead. With hips that Daisy had never had, he almost said nothing – she was not even a distant simulacrum of the girl he'd lost. Something terrible collapsed in his heart. He turned the horse away at the pointlessness – but the horse, having been pulled about more than it thought fit, jibbed at another clumsy pull and snorted in irritation. Daisy looked round at the unexpected intensity of the sound, wary of harm to the little girl. Kleist stared at her. Still ignorant, she stared back, leery of the peculiar-looking young man, then alarmed as she saw his already pale face go white. He let out a dreadful cry as if he were dying.

Then it came to her. She drew in a breath as deep as if it had to last for the rest of her life. He was off his horse and tried to get to her so quickly he slipped and fell in the mud, then up and slipped again, utterly ridiculous. 'Daisy! Daisy! Daisy!' he shouted, then grabbed her and the child in a mad embrace. But she couldn't speak, she could only stare. Watched by the astonished onlookers, they knelt in the mud, unable to weep, and simply groaned. The toddler found a new toy in playing with her father's hair, casually accepting of the joyous agony wrapping her in its arms. 'Honour!' shouted the baby – although it could not have been what she really said, that was what it sounded like to the watching servants. 'Honour! Honour!'

Imagine then the jumbled brew of mixed and bruised emotions that arrived at the siege camp in front of the Sanctuary a few days later, the traumatized joy of Kleist and Daisy and the seething fear and anger of Arbell Materazzi.

Cale had already prepared a fenced-off compound for Arbell, well-guarded and away from the nosy in the walled tent city that had grown up near the walls of the Sanctuary. He'd considered carefully whether to wallow in the pettiness of ensuring the compound was as uncomfortable as possible or to show Arbell that he was somebody to be reckoned with through his ability to provide luxury even in a shithole like the scrubland in front of the Sanctuary. Fortunately for Arbell, he chose the latter. He was also regretting in a half-baked way his decision to bring her here at all – it's not given to many people to do whatever they want and he was discovering another facet of such immense clout: absolute power tends to confuse absolutely.

Arbell and her two maids were met by her new guards several miles from the camp and removed to her comfortable prison so that no one would see her. Kleist barely noticed; he could barely contain himself as he took his wife and child to see Cale and Vague Henri.

As soon as he came into their command post, where they were failing to come up with a solution to the impregnability of the Sanctuary, they could see a miraculous change in his manner, not just because he was happy where he'd been for so long miserable, but that he had about him an intensity that made him seem almost mad. With him came the wide-eyed Daisy, holding her baby on her hip. In garbled bursts of rapturous speech the story flowed out of him, disjointed and hard to follow. But the basics were clear enough: this was the wife and child come back from the dead. For the three of them one thing united them – astonishment that life could ever be so madly kind. They were beside themselves; surprised, no, shocked by joy. They hugged Daisy, hugged the baby, then hugged Daisy again and demanded a repeat of the whole story, full of questions about where she'd been and who with. And though she was mortified when Kleist told them why she'd been on the run from Leeds, they were delighted, particularly Vague Henri, whose loathing of the ruling class of the city had only increased with his absence. They ordered food and drink and gave her an official pardon for all crimes in the past, and, as they were so happy, in the future as well. And then Daisy noticed that Kleist had gone completely white. As she reached for him he fell off his chair, hit his head – an appalling blow on the leg of the table – and threw up. The quacks were called and he was taken up carefully by the guards and put in Cale's luxurious wagon.

'He's just overwrought,' said the doctor. 'Not surprising, really – I'd have a stroke if it had happened to me. He just needs some peace and quiet with his wife and child. He'll be all right.'

'I'll leave my steward with you,' said Cale to Daisy. 'Anything at all you want, just tell him. We'll come back later.'

'Make it tomorrow,' interrupted the doctor.

'. . . we'll come back tomorrow. Anything at all.'

They went back to the command centre and had several drinks and a smoke.

'He has a baby. Amazing,' said Vague Henri.

'Do you think he'll be all right?'

'Yeah. It all got a bit too much, that's all.'

But he was not all right. Certainly he recovered in a manner of speaking, but he was shook, as the Irish say. And over the next few days he remained shook, always a slight trembling and the stance of someone who'd just taken a blow, an overwhelmed look, a dazed look. During a brief visit the next day the two of them, puzzled because it didn't seem to make sense that he might be worse, began to realize that they might be wrong: their experience of suffering in their lives (brutality, death, violence) might have been unusually intense but it was not necessarily broad. On the way to talk to the doctor, the other unfortunate subject surrounding Kleist's return involved them in a bitter discussion: Vague Henri, until Kleist mentioned it in passing, had no idea that he'd come to the Sanctuary dragging Arbell Materazzi with him.

428

'You're a bloody idiot.'

'Yes.'

'And now?'

Cale didn't say anything.

'This could stir up a lot of those snakes you're always going on about.'

'I don't think so. Nobody loves us – but nobody loves her either. The Materazzi are nothing – just a nuisance.'

They walked on in silence for a while.

'What does IdrisPukke say about it?'

'IdrisPukke doesn't know and he doesn't want to know.'

'And you're sure of this because . . . ?'

'He told me.'

'So what are you going to do with her?'

'Let her poach delicately in her own juices.'

In fact, he discovered that keeping Arbell interned nearby but not having to see her gave him a certain ease. He had control of a kind he'd lost: he knew exactly where she was. That was something else about power he'd noticed, something good this time: it was like drinking – it made the world glow. At dinner with Vague Henri that night he was unusually silent. After half an hour without speaking he looked at Vague Henri and asked casually, 'Do you think I'm mad?'

'Yes,' said Vague Henri. But it was an odd question oddly asked and he was spooked.

With every day that the Axis stood outside the Sanctuary gawping at the walls Cale's power was slipping away. Increasingly, the only option was to disperse the army, leaving a rump to keep the Redeemers from getting out. But then all the Redeemers had to do was wait for the forces in the west to counter-attack and lift the siege the following year, or even the next. Then it could be resupplied and used as a base to move against the Axis. The Hanse were already complaining about the cost of their mostly Hessian mercenaries, the Laconics couldn't be trusted and now new religious squabbles had broken out on all sides. Cale knew that the Redeemers had the resources to regroup and that Bosco would be putting all his energy into buying the means to copy Hooke's handguns. If he succeeded, Cale's greatest advantage would be lost. To make things worse, the poisonous but incomprehensible religious differences that had caused the ten churches of Switzerland to split from one another were re-emerging now that the threat from the Redeemers was fading. Preventing these religious schisms from infecting the unity of the New Model Army was an increasing headache. Cale needed to kill the war quickly and that meant taking the Sanctuary. But the Sanctuary didn't want to be taken.

He was sure there must be a way because there was always a way. Under Bosco's brutal discipline he'd been forced to stand for hours in front of maps and a flat board littered with bits of wood to signify troops and towns and rivers and impossible odds and made to work a way out of intractable problems. If he didn't, he took a beating. If he took too long he took a beating. Sometimes he even took a beating when he got it right. 'To teach you the most important lesson of all,' said Bosco. When he asked what it was, Bosco beat him again. 'Perhaps if I hit you a couple of times?' offered Vague Henri. Cale decided instead that they should walk around the problem. These days his safety meant having people around him all the time, something he hated, so taking a hefty guard with them they went for a ride around the walls of the Sanctuary, making sure to stay well back. He'd stop and look, stop and look. There was a solution. There was always a solution. He found it in the Little Brother.

'Now you point it out,' said Vague Henri, 'it's obvious.'

And it was. It was so obvious that it was clear the Sanctuary must fall. Nothing could stop it. In two months they'd be inside the walls.

The next day he gathered the considerable number of interested parties, their mutual hostility growing ever more irksome, and took them through his plan. First, not with any great skill, he drew the outline of the flat-topped mountain on which the Sanctuary was built. His drawing didn't have to be up to much for the assembly to recognize what it was: its shape haunted their dreams.

'Something's missing' said Cale. 'Any offers?'

'The Sanctuary.'

'Yes. But not that. Something else.'

Silence. Cale went back to the drawing and added an outcrop of rock about fifty feet higher than the table-top mountain and with a slope on its far side, but with a gap of about eighty yards between the outcrop and the mountain proper. 'This ridge is called the Little Brother. This gap between it and the walls of the Sanctuary – we're going to fill it in.' He drew a line between the two, ending at the very top of the Sanctuary wall.

Do rooms gasp? This one did. As Vague Henri had said, once it was pointed out it was obvious.

'The gap's enormous. It'll take years,' said someone.

'It'll take a month,' said Cale. 'I've had Mr Hooke do the calculations.'

'That would be the Mr Hooke who killed eight of my men with his exploding pile of crap?'

'Without Hooke,' said Cale, 'most of the people in this room would be rotting quietly in the Mississippi mud. So shut your gob.' He then went into detail about Hooke's calculation – the volume of barrows of earth and the number of men they had to deliver them.

'Their archers'll pick us off by the hundred.'

'We'll build defensive roofs for them to work under.'

'They'll be heaving rocks over the walls too – they'll have to be bloody strong roofs.'

'If you're telling me soldiers will die, yes, they will. But we can work from the top of the Little Brother as well if we need to. In the end it's just filling a hole. When it's done, they're finished.'

Later Ormsby-Gore and Fanshawe discussed the day's events.

'My men are soldiers, not bloody navvies.'

'Don't be such a bore, darling,' said Fanshawe. 'I feel as if all my birthdays have come together. He really is a clever old thing. Pity he's got to go.'

The trouble with nay-saying doom-mongers is that they're bound to be right eventually. No matter what great enterprise you set out on, things will always go wrong. So it was with the attempt to fill in the gap between the Little Brother and the Sanctuary. The predicted rain of arrows could be protected against with covered walkways but these could be easily smashed with rocks that were much heavier than expected because the Redeemers, once they saw what was intended, had come up with a sling device, based on the trebuchet, that could heave rocks weighing several tons two hundred feet from the walls. Nothing the Axis could build would sustain that kind of weight falling from such a height. No one, of course, was foolish enough to say 'I told you so' to Cale's face but if words were fog it would have been difficult to find your way around the camp.

The problem was solved in a few days and merely involved more effort. Barrels of rocks and stones were hauled to the top of the Little Brother and heaved over the edge. It was a sweaty, arm-bending, sinew-stretching curse but it worked. By the time Hooke devised a rail on which wagons could be pulled up the hill using counterweights it didn't even speed them up much. Day by day, day by day, the gap was filled. Even if it was slow, every member of the fractious Axis could see progress and also the inevitable result of where that progress was leading. The promise of success brought harmony of a sort. The Swiss became more patient and put their plans for impeachment and a quick evacuation back until after the Sanctuary had fallen. Even the Laconics started pretending to treat their allies as equals: Fanshawe wanted the Sanctuary taken and with it the opportunity to paste Cale with no questions asked.

Every night Cale would walk over to the compound where he was keeping Arbell. At times the temptation to go in was almost unbearable but his dreams about her kept him out. They took place in any number of different places he didn't recognize (*Why?* he thought. *Why not places that I know?*) but it was always him hanging about, skulking like the lunatic draper in the mad ward at the Priory, who'd been left standing at the altar by the woman he adored and who spent the days weeping and asking everyone if they'd seen her. But the one constant in Cale's dreams was the look on her face when, heart full of dreadful hope, he walked up to her. The look she gave him was bad enough in his dreams without seeing it in reality. So he watched the warm light inside the tent and the shadows lengthening and contracting as she moved about – though he knew it might just be the maids seeing to the boy or combing her hair. He tried to stop himself going to watch, of course, and sometimes succeeded but pathetically rarely.

He had become very used indeed to the comfort and solitude of his comfortable wagon, now occupied by Kleist and his family, and to replace it had put several dozen expert carpenters and former upholsterers turned soldiers, who would have been better employed on the siege, to create something even more sumptuous.

Kleist was a cause for worry. He was at once happy beyond words at the return to life of his wife and child and also shattered by the cruelties that preceded it. The sway of the one could not affect the weight of the other.

'What's wrong with him?'

The doctor shrugged, as if to indicate that it was obvious. 'He was brought up in this awful place.'

'So were the two of us,' said Vague Henri.

'Give it time,' said the doctor. There was a difficult silence. 'I'm sorry, I misspoke. I didn't mean . . . um . . . to be unduly alarmist.' But he very nearly did mean it, he just didn't mean to express himself so bluntly. 'Out of the crooked timber of humanity no straight thing was ever made' was his philosophy; if you bent a sapling out of shape while it was young it was obvious it would grow up even more deformed. Pleased as he was with his woody metaphors he was wise enough to prune this one back. 'What I was . . . driving at was that obviously people are affected by their past but it's just as important to recognize that even the same physical diseases affect different people differently – so how much more so with mental diseases.' The two boys just stared at him. 'I mean, even the strongest people mentally can only take so many shocks – Mr Kleist had the shock of being brought up in this place, then the delightful shock, but still a shock, of falling in love and marrying and becoming a father. Then the shock of discovering them murdered and burnt to ashes. Then the torture you told me about and being taken to the edge of death itself in the most painful and revolting way.'

'But now he has them back,' said Vague Henri, desperate for Kleist to be well.

'But it was just another shock – do you see?'

'No, I don't see,' said Vague Henri. 'I was brought up here as well. I was in the cells with him at Kitty the Hare's place. All right, I didn't lose a wife and child but . . .' But what? He couldn't think of an objection – look at what had happened, even to Cale.

The doctor was going to suggest that Vague Henri tried in future to live a more tranquil life, just in case; but he had the sense to keep it to himself this time.

'What should we do about Kleist?' asked Cale.

'He needs calm. Get him away from here for one thing and to somewhere free from any strain or disharmony.'

Cale smiled. 'If I knew somewhere like that, I'd go myself.'

'That would probably be a good idea,' said the doctor, unable to help himself.

'That shit-bag Bose Ikard and his pals are out to get us,' said Cale to Kleist and Daisy. 'It's time that some of us weren't here.'

Neither of them, wary, said anything.

'People are always out to get you, aren't they?' said Daisy.

'Oh, indeed they are, Mrs Kleist. But the Swiss are sitting on all our money. We want Kleist to take as much as he can carry and put it beyond reach – set up somewhere we can retire to when the balloon goes up.' The balloon, or *balon*, was a red flag used by the Redeemers to signal that an attack was imminent.

'Where?' said Kleist.

'We were thinking somewhere over the sea. The Hanse is pretty welcoming to the wealthy. And Riba owes us.'

'Does *she* know that?' asked Daisy. 'My husband told me when you were in the desert he suggested you should leave her there.'

'She's right, he did,' said Vague Henri.

'But we never told her that,' said Cale. 'Besides, Riba was the cause of everything. She knows she let us down about Kitty so this is her chance to make it up.'

'Why not send Vague Henri?' said Kleist. 'She won't mind helping him.'

'I've got to stay here.'

'Yes?' said Kleist. 'Why?'

There wasn't the slightest hesitation.

'The night before we make the assault on the Sanctuary I'm going to go in heavy-handed to take the quarters where the girls are being held. So you're really the only person who can do it. Besides, you're the only one of us with a wife and family.'

So it was settled. Kleist would return to Spanish Leeds and with Cadbury's help – Cadbury was very keen also to get some of his money out of harm's way – he'd get out of Switzerland with all their money and as much as they could sell off in the meantime.

'You were a bit harsh on Riba,' said Vague Henri, when Kleist and Daisy had left.

'I'll squeeze Riba dry if I have to – and it still wouldn't be enough.'

There was a bad-tempered silence. It was Cale who decided to make things up. 'That was pretty quick thinking when he asked why you weren't going.'

'No, it wasn't.'

'What?'

'No, it wasn't quick thinking,' said Vague Henri. 'That's what I'm going to do.'

'Don't be bloody stupid. He probably killed them months ago, years even.'

'I don't think so.'

'Based on?'

436

'Based on I don't think so.'

'No.'

'What do you mean?'

'*No* isn't clear enough?'

'I'm not asking your permission.'

'Look, I may have gone along with some half-wit notion of yours that we're equals – nobody else thinks that. You'll do as you're bloody well told.'

'No, I won't.'

'Yes, you will.'

'No, I won't.'

This bickering went on for some time. There were threats from Cale to have him arrested until the siege was over and invitations from Vague Henri to shove his threats up his arse. But what broke the deadlock was an appeal to Cale's heart, peculiar object that it was.

'Annunziata, the girl I told you about – I love her.' This was not true. He cared deeply about her, more than the other girls although he cared deeply about them too. Why the desire to save them was so intense he could not say. But there it was. He had better insight into Cale's soul than his own. Everyone has a sentimental spot for something, even, or especially, the wicked. It was said that Alois Huttler found it hard not to weep when he saw a puppy and that he kept a painting in his bedroom of a little girl feeding a lamb milk through a horn. At any rate, Cale could hardly deny the power of love, given its hold on his own soul. It was, after all, the source of much of his self-pity that he had risked his life so madly to save Arbell.

Two days later Kleist and Daisy were lined up in their heavily guarded train, with Cale and Vague Henri there to see them off.

'What's to stop me lepping off with the money?' said Kleist, hands shaking like an old man.

'Because,' said Cale, 'you can trust us.'

'Trust you?' said Kleist, 'Oh, right. Trust you.'

'What are you talking about?' said Daisy. 'I don't understand.'

'Tell you later.'

'I've written to Riba,' said Vague Henri. 'She'll be all right.'

'And if she isn't?'

'Mrs Kleist seems to have her head screwed on. You've got money – you'll work something out.'

'Thanks,' said Kleist, and seemed to mean something particular by it, but Cale wasn't sure what.

He shrugged, awkward.

Holding the little girl, Daisy kissed both of them on the cheek but said nothing. Then Cale and Vague Henri watched them leave, a strangely desolate experience for them both.

36

Over the next two weeks the man-made ridge from the Little Brother loomed towards the top of the Sanctuary walls while Vague Henri practised climbing in the dark with his hundred volunteers. One man died on the first night, screaming as he fell, a noisy accident that would have had the lot of them killed if it had been the real thing. A climb of this type would only be possible with the right kind of half-moon – if they could see too easily then they could be seen too easily. Luckily the right phase was expected at the same time as completion of the ramp. It was decided to climb in small groups of ten further around the side of the Sanctuary where the climbers would be mostly obscured from any watching guards. They'd collect on the mountain just below the walls and then move up as it became dark; one of Artemisia's alpine climbers could take a line to the top and pull up a rope ladder designed by Hooke.

'It's the stupidest bloody thing I've ever seen,' said Cale.

'Mind your own beeswax,' replied Vague Henri.

As the ramp came closer the builders became more vulnerable once again to the arrows, bolts, rocks and boulders thrown at them by the Redeemers – an assault as hideous as it was desperate. They slowed the progress but it was not enough, as the Redeemers must have known. Then, twenty feet from the walls, construction stopped. To complete it would have allowed the Redeemers to attack across it themselves. Hooke had provided a wooden bridge affair, covered in on the roof and at the sides and about forty feet long.

When Cale decided to attack, the bridge would be pushed along the ramp to close the gap, like a plank going over a river. It was wide enough to take eight soldiers shoulder to shoulder. Hooke had also provided an unpleasant way of clearing away anyone in front of the bridge, a variation on Greek fire. He had built several great pumps to spray a large area in front of the emerging soldiers, which would cover every Redeemer within fifty yards in a liquid fire.

'God forgive me,' said Hooke.

'Just remember they'd happily do the same to you – they would've done it already if I hadn't saved your skin.'

'That's supposed to make me feel better, that I'm no worse than they are?'

'Suit yourself. I don't really care.'

The last few days before the attack over the ridge passed at a feverish speed, an unpleasant sensation for Cale and Vague Henri, as if they were rushing towards something out of their control. Now that it was coming, what they were doing seemed unbelievable to them. They were going back to the place they hated most in all the world and yet which had made them; and they were going to clean it out. Two days away and they were pin-eyed with agitation – but also self-possessed and still.

IdrisPukke, who had returned to witness the taking of the Sanctuary, was made uneasy by the two boys, though tense enough himself. 'They were like the old adage,' he said later to Vipond. 'Those houses that are haunted are most still – till the devil be up.'

If there'd been any moisture in the air you would have said there was a storm coming. At night the grasshoppers stopped their usual throbbing racket. There seemed to be fewer sand-flies trying to get at the moisture in the soldiers' mouths.

People with the luxury of living quiet lives look down on melodrama, on sensational action, on exaggerated events intended to appeal to coarser emotions than their own. The life they lead, they think, is real: the day-to-day ordinary is how things truly are. But it's plain to anyone with any sense that for most of us, life, if it's like anything at all, is like a pantomime where the blood and suffering is real, an opera where the singers sing out of tune, wailing about pain and love and death while the audience throw stones instead of rotten fruit. Delicacy and subtlety are the fantastical great escape.

It was late afternoon when Vague Henri came to see Cale before he started the climb up to the Sanctuary walls.

'Can't believe,' he said, 'I'm trying to break back into that shithole.' Cale looked at him.

'I wanted to run your funeral arrangements by you.'

'Oh, yeah?'

'I thought we'd wrap you up in a dog blanket and dump you out of the crapper in the West Wall. If I can get a band together we'll play "I've Got a Luverly Bunch of Coconuts". You'll like that.'

'You're not,' said Vague Henri, 'a very nice person.'

'I'm telling you not to go on with this bloody bollocking bollocks, aren't I? Those girls are dead and if you go up there you'll be as dead as them.'

'I'm touched that you care.'

'I don't care. Don't think it. I just feel sorry for you, that's why I've put up with you all this time.'

'If I don't go I won't be able to sleep at night. That's the honest truth. I'm afraid not to go.'

'You'll get used to it. You can get used to anything. And there are worse things than not being able to sleep.'

'Can't stop now – it'd look bad.'

'I'll have you arrested.' It wasn't a threat but a plea.

'No. Don't do that. If I found out they were alive I'd hate you.'

'*Why?*'

'I just would.' Vague Henri smiled. 'Give us a kiss.'

'No.'

'Your hand then.'

'What if it's catching, what you've got?'

'Not you. You'll be all right.'

'But you won't.' He was angry now that he could see persuasion wouldn't work. 'You're still a Redeemer, that's it.'

'What?'

'Oh, you're not a fucking swine, not you, but you can't wait to sacrifice yourself for something. It all went into your head, all that camel-shit about . . .' He stopped, unable to find the words. 'You're just another martyr – and don't worry I've got a martyr's funeral ready for you – we'll sing "Faith of Our Fathers" . . . *We will be true to thee 'til death* . . . Remember that bollocks? Do you want it before or after the coconut song?'

'You have been practising that, haven't you?'

'Just go – I can't be bothered with you any more.'

'I'll be all right. I can feel it.'

'Yes? Fine. Go away.'

'I think you'd come with me if you could.'

'No, I wouldn't.'

'You say it because you have to say it, being you.'

'That isn't it. All things being equal, and if it didn't involve a terrible risk to my own life, then yes, I'd help you. I like to see good deeds done, I do, but your price is too high. I can see I'm a disappointment to you – but the honest truth is that I'd rather live than see justice done.'

442

Vague Henri shrugged and went off to climb back into the Sanctuary.

Cale had felt exhausted before Vague Henri came to say whatever it was he'd come to say. Now he felt as if he'd been wrung out. After he'd taken the Phedra and Morphine to deal with Kitty the Hare he took Sister Wray's advice not to use it much more seriously. He felt sometimes as if he was so weak that he might just stop breathing. When they were younger, Vague Henri had heard from one of the Redeemers that a sudden loud noise could kill a locust. They tried, dozens of times, but it never worked. Now he felt as if a sudden loud noise could see him off quite easily. All the more reason, then, to stay away from the Phedra and Morphine. But he knew he couldn't get through the next twenty-four hours without it. *Just once more*, he thought. *Wipe the Sanctuary clean and then off to the Hanse with all the swag and then it's cucumber sandwiches and cake for ever and ever.*

He had a couple of hours' sleep, though his guard had to wake him, and then took exactly the dose of the drug that Sister Wray had instructed. By now he realized she hadn't been exaggerating about its poisons building up – every week now, sometimes for half an hour at a time, he had the sense that someone was frying something in his head.

Half an hour later he was standing on top of the Little Brother as Hooke finished preparing his huge wooden tunnel for its final move onto the walls of the Sanctuary. The peak of the Little Brother had been built up by forty feet, so that the tunnel could be pushed downhill to the gap between the infill and the walls that the tunnel would bridge, allowing New Model Army troops to spread out quickly and in large numbers. There was no hiding the plan from the Redeemers

443

so no guesswork was needed to see that they would do everything to stop the attack where it began. Establishing that bridgehead was going to be a murderous business. It was the attackers' only weak point – something that wouldn't be lost on Bosco.

The assault began as soon as it became light in order to give them all the daylight possible. Cale expected a disaster of some kind but, though there were a thousand decisions to be made, there were no earthquakes or sudden plagues, no mysterious parhelions to disturb the superstitious. There was only mounting dread at what was coming.

At just before five, Hooke came to tell him they were ready. Cale walked up the last few feet to the top of the Little Brother and looked across to the Sanctuary. His heart beat faster, his head felt as if it were bursting as he looked out over his former home, seeing the still shadowy places where he had spent so many thousands of days in fear and dread and misery. So much cold, so much hunger, so much loneliness. He stared for a long time. Such a shattering moment called for a great shout. But something caught his eye inside the Sanctuary, to the right. It was the quarter where the girls were kept. From its furthest edge a spidery line of smoke wafted gently into the air. He gave the slightest of nods to Hooke and it began.

'Ready!' called out one of the centenars.

'Set!'

'Go!' A huge cry of HEAVE! went up. The enormous structure shook but didn't move. HEAVE! Again it shook but again nothing. HEAVE! This time it shifted a few inches. HEAVE! Now a foot. HEAVE! Now two. Now properly onto the reinforced slope the tunnel went with the pull of the earth. But the worry was about stability not speed. Men rushed back and forth between the front and sides of the tunnel, calling to each other and to Hooke, looking for the rubble to give way and let the tunnel dig in or some other disaster they hadn't thought of. A couple of times they had to stop and levers, thirty-foot long and by the dozen, were brought to lift the structure where it had cut into the still loose soil. But there was no attack from the walls. Cale would have been pouring everything he could onto the heads of the attackers. And all the time, one after the other, fires were started along the edges of the ghetto where the girls were kept.

'Where are the Redeemers?' asked Fanshawe as they headed into the hut where they kept the maps of the Sanctuary. Inside were half a dozen officers from the New Model Army and three Laconics, led by Ormsby-Gore. IdrisPukke was also there.

'I don't know, but they won't be doing anything pleasant, I'm sure of that.' He decided to change his plan. 'I want five hundred of your men to go in right after the first rush.'

Fanshawe looked over at Ormsby-Gore. 'All right with you?'

'That isn't what was agreed,' said Ormsby-Gore.

In a formal sense there were no soldiers less cowardly than the Laconics. But in practical terms it was as if they were rather chinless. The problem was that it took so much effort and time and money to engineer one of these hideous killing machines, and there were so few of them, that though they were happy to die, they weren't all that willing to fight. Each one of these monsters was as valuable as a rare vase.

Cale, made even more bad-tempered than usual by the drugs and what might be happening to Vague Henri, looked Ormsby-Gore directly in the eyes, not a wise thing to do under the best of circumstances. 'There are no agreements here,' said Cale. 'You do as I say or else I'll cut your bloody head off and kick it down the mountain.'

There are people you can say this kind of thing to and people you can't. Laconics in general, and Ormsby-Gore in particular, belonged to the category of people you can't. The last syllable of the last word was barely out of Cale's mouth when Ormsby-Gore, exalted among an already exalted society of homicidal freaks of nature, pulled a knife and stabbed Cale in the heart.

37

Or would have done if it had been anyone other than Thomas Cale who was made wildly hyperactive by a drug that had a fair chance of killing him at some time in the next twenty-four hours. The speed and power of the blow was Ormsby-Gore's undoing. Missing his chest by a fraction, Cale spun his attacker round, pulled him in close and had his own knife at his throat. The onlookers might have been astonished by the speed of what had just happened but what held them in absolute silence was the barking mad expression in the boy's eyes.

Even IdrisPukke remained silent, fearing that any movement or sound would set Cale off. From outside there was silence for the first time in hours. How long a second is when life or death is in the room. Then came an enormous SNAP! from outside, followed by a crash and the cry of a furious engineer.

'The fucking fuckers fucking fucked!'

No one in the tent said anything and no one moved. Except Cale. Unable to contain himself at the heart-rending exasperation of the engineer he started laughing – not the mad hysterical giggle of the frenzied lunatic but the ordinary laughter of someone struck by the absurdity of what was happening. Fanshawe took his chance.

'I'm just going to take away Ormsby-Gore's knife,' he said softly, holding up both of his hands. 'You understand that, my dear fellow, don't you?' Ormsby-Gore stared at Fanshawe in a manner that indicated he did not understand in any way whatsoever. *The trouble with people who are not afraid of death,* thought Fanshawe, *is that they're not afraid of death*. So he must find something else.

'The thing is, darling' he said, 'if you don't drop the knife I will, with Thomas Cale's permission, take out my own and then I'll cut your bloody head off and kick it down the mountain myself.'

For Ormsby-Gore this was quite a different matter: to be executed on the field of battle for disobeying an order would mean unforgivable disgrace and unending infamy for him and his family. He dropped the knife almost as quickly as he'd drawn it.

'May I?' asked Fanshawe, taking both Ormsby-Gore's hands in his own to reassure Cale that he had him under control. Cale let him go and Fanshawe eased Ormsby-Gore to a steady position, moved him outside and quietly had him arrested and taken away by four of his own men. He went back into the tent.

'Might I suggest that he be dealt with in whatever way you choose after the Sanctuary has fallen? It would be a pity to distract the troops, don't you think?' Fanshawe didn't like to think how the Laconic soldiers or the Ephors at home would react to the execution of Ormsby-Gore but he cheerfully expected that Cale would be dead before it became an issue.

Cale didn't say anything, giving barely a nod to signal his agreement, then went outside to find out what had caused the snapping sound and the engineer's lament. A large container full of gelatinous Greek fire had been brought up to be loaded into the tunnel for the final push to the Sanctuary walls. It was volatile stuff and didn't take to too much shaking about. Unfortunately it had fallen off a rail on the top of the embankment. They had tried to ease the container back onto the rail using an oak lever. The snap was the sound of the lever breaking. The container rolling down the hill and smashing against a pile of rocks was what occasioned the heartbroken oath from the engineer.

Hooke, now used to the difference between a battlefield and a chemical workshop, had already called up a replacement, which needed only a few minutes' work before it was moving quickly towards the tunnel.

'Are you well?' said Idris Pukke, who had followed him out.

'It won't happen again,' Cale replied. 'Probably. You might want to let people know it might be best not to disagree with me for a few days.'

'I'm not sure that will be necessary.'

It wasn't clear Cale had heard.

'I've missed something – I've missed something important.'

'What do you mean?' IdrisPukke was alarmed – like everyone else he saw the fall of the Sanctuary as inevitable however costly.

'Why aren't they attacking? They should be attacking now. Bosco knows something that I don't.'

'Then stop.'

'No.'

'Why?' But it was a question to which IdrisPukke knew the answer. 'You told Vague Henri not to go. I told him not to go myself, for what it's worth.'

Cale looked at him. 'If we don't go soon they'll take him prisoner. Do you know what they'll do to him?'

'I can guess.'

'I'm sure you can. But I don't have to because I've seen it. Except this will be worse. They'll burn him. *In minimus via.*'

A sergeant interrupted them.

'Sir, Mr Hooke says the tunnel is ready to load.'

'Wait a moment, Sergeant.' He turned back to IdrisPukke. 'You're an educated man – know what it means?'

'It's not familiar, no.'

'It means "In the smallest way" – it means they'll burn him on a pile of sticks not big enough to boil a can of water. I've never seen it myself. Bosco told me about it. He said it took twelve hours. So no, I can't stop.'

'You don't know for certain that's what he'll do.'

'I don't know for certain that Bosco knows something I don't. Nobody *knows* anything.'

'If Vague Henri were here with us, you'd stop.'

'But he isn't.'

'You know that if we don't take the Sanctuary before winter then they'll have reinforcements before we can come back. There are members of the Axis already at each other's throats. The Swiss want your head to bounce down the street. God knows what will happen if you fail here.'

'Who says I'll fail?'

'You do.'

'I said I don't know what's going on.'

'Then wait.'

'And if I do? Suppose *now* is the right time. Suppose if I wait I've given them the chance to . . . I don't know what . . . something I haven't thought of. What if Bosco's ill and this is my best chance? Nobody *knows* anything.'

'You know what you'd do if Henri was here and not there.'

'Do I?'

'Yes.'

'I thought you were going to tell people not to argue with me?'

'I didn't think I was included.'

'Well, you're wrong.' He called to the sergeant, 'Give Mr Hooke the signal to load.'

With a few shouts it began.

38

'I want a favour,' said Cale.

Fanshawe brought up the five hundred Laconics Cale had asked for and was told they'd be sent in immediately after the first wave of the New Model Army. Not many were expected to survive.

'A favour? Of course. Probably.'

'I want a hundred of your men to relieve Vague Henri as soon as it's clear what's going on.'

'That's a big favour – it's a hefty risk.'

'Yes.'

Fanshawe looked down at the map of the Sanctuary and its inner buildings.

'It's a bit of a maze there, old boy. Getting lost would be easy and costly. But if you were there to take them in and guide them . . .'

Cale was fairly sure that Fanshawe had been thinking hard about what he was going to do about him. He didn't need to think very carefully about the chances of either him or Vague Henri emerging alive from the fog of battle.

'Unfortunately I'm needed here – but I've arranged for three of my Purgators who know the ghetto better than I do to take you to it.'

Fanshawe considered declining, not that he'd expected Cale to be stupid enough to agree, but it would look bad to refuse. If there were to be any questions about who was responsible for Cale's tragic death at some time during the next twenty-four hours it would do no harm to have demonstrated to the

New Model Army that the Laconics had been right behind their leader in a risky enterprise to save his closest friend.

Fanshawe went off to make the arrangements and Cale, collecting IdrisPukke on the way, went back to the summit of the Little Brother and a small tower that had been erected on top to give him as clear a view as was possible. Then it began. The ropes holding up the front of the tunnel were lowered slowly and it transformed into a massive bridge to cover the thirty-foot gap to the top of the Sanctuary walls.

Still there was nothing. There was a pause of a minute or so, a series of indistinguishable shouts and then the hand pumps, manned by twenty soldiers to build the pressure, were primed to bursting for two minutes. More shouts. A pause. Then the pumps were let loose by Hooke and the liquid in the containers burst out of a set of eight barrels like the spray from the world's greatest fountain. Hooke lit the eight torches underneath and there was an explosive roar like the crack of doom and the spray ignited in a vast arc of flames, covering the walls in front and a hundred yards to either side. For twenty seconds this hideous device deafened everyone behind it – then Hooke, frightened it would explode, turned it off. For a minute longer the liquid burned like the lake of fire at the centre of hell and then, almost as if it had been blown out, it vanished. There was no delay – the New Model Army, lower legs protected against the heat – were through the tunnel and onto the bridge as quickly as they could to take advantage of the devastation before the Redeemers could respond.

'YOU'LL BE FINE! IT'S ALL GRAVY FROM HERE!'

'GET YOUR EYES ON! GET YOUR EYES ON!'

'VALLON TO THE EDGE! VALLON . . . YESSSS! TO THE EDGE, YOU SHITHEAD!'

'OVER THERE! OVER THERE! LOOK WHERE YOU'RE FUCKING STEPPING!'

'MURDER HOLE! MURDER HOLE!'

'HERE, BUDDY! HERE!'

But there were no bodies horribly burned. There were no survivors of the fire ready to beat them back. The shouts stopped. Then there was nothing but a terrible noiseless solitude on every side. This only raised the horrible tension, the soldier's terrible fear of the unexpected worst: when and in what way would the blow come? They moved on packed together against the hideous fight to come. 'SLOWLY! SLOWLY! EYES ON! WATCH FOR IT! WATCH FOR IT!'

Adding to their fear was the black smoke from the Greek fire, which covered everything in front of them in a thick smog. As they moved forward, every ordinary thing assumed the shadowy obscurity of some hideous threat, only to be revealed as a pile of barrels or a holy statue offering blessings to the saved. So a halt was called. Two thousand men, shoulder to shoulder, even the Laconics waiting behind them spooked and shaken at the terrible uncertainty of something hideous to come.

Very slowly – it was an almost windless day – the smoke began to patch and smudge, each clearing spot seeming to reveal a menace that never came. Then a small gust and then a harder one whirled and revolved the smoke into beautiful spins and rolls. The wind blew through clearly and what they saw was the defining vision of the lives most of them expected to lose that day. Everywhere, from every post, every batten in every one of the roofed walkways, from wooden frames driven into the courtyards in their hundreds, everywhere they looked were thousands of Redeemers hanging by the neck.

39

The New Model Army was well used to slaughter by now and the Laconics were, of course, a society given up entirely to its requirements. But this was not death as they knew it and so, despite the fact that what they were seeing meant that they would survive the day and that this multitude of hanged men were their most bitter enemies, a mood of creepy uneasiness settled on them all as they moved slowly through the Sanctuary. Each new prospect, each square, each court-yard, each covered pathway, each prayer garden contained only row after row of the hanging dead. The only sound was of creaking ropes, the only thing moving the slight drift and swing of bodies stirred by the light winds.

Slowly they moved inside the buildings of the Sanctuary; they could not do otherwise. In every corridor, at intervals three foot broad and long, Redeemers hung by their necks from the roof into which single hooks had been set in con-crete. In every room. In every office. Every alcove. Every chapel. In the six great churches there must have been a thou-sand each on a dozen different levels, as silent as the decorations suspended from the tree of mortality on the Day of the Dead. The order came to halt and the Laconics and their Penitent guide headed into the recesses of the Sanctuary, hampered at every step by the bodies they set swinging back and forth as they made their way to the ghetto and Vague Henri.

Against the strongest advice to stay out of the Sanctuary until it had been thoroughly searched ('It's obvious, sir, they'll hide and wait for you to come.') Cale arrived, wide-eyed with bleak astonishment. They were right but he could not bear to wait and, closely surrounded by Purgators (what were *they* thinking?), he moved into the old spaces now bizarrely transformed into a priestly abattoir. How oddly his soul reacted to being back again. It was not like returning to a former home because he realized that something about what Sister Wray had said was right: he had been here in the past, he was here now, he would always be here.

The Purgators kept him in an ambulacrum where they'd cleared a space of hanged Redeemers and where he was out of everyone's line of sight. Within a few minutes they brought him a boy that one of the New Model Army had found hiding in a box.

'He means a confessional, sir,' said a Purgator.

'What are you?' asked Cale.

'An acolyte, sir.'

'So was I. You're all right, don't worry. No one's going to hurt you. What happened here?'

It was understandably garbled stuff but simple enough. Bosco had addressed five hundred of his closest followers and announced that, because of Thomas Cale's treachery, he had decided to remove the faithful from the earth and never to think of mankind again. As a reward for their fidelity they were to be permitted to join God in eternal bliss by the same means as the Redeemer himself.

'All of them went along with this?'

'Not all, sir. But the Pope created a group of counsellors to assist all those who needed spiritual support.'

'But not you.'

'I was afraid.'

'You'll be safe now.' Cale turned to one of the staff sergeants of the New Model Army. 'Get him away from here. Get him some new clothes and get my cook to feed him.

Make sure he's safe. Why, for God's sake, isn't there any news about Henri?' He sent two more of his Purgators. Five minutes later, when he had decided to go himself, dangerous as it was, Fanshawe turned up looking uneasy.

'What's up?' said Cale.

'I've had some news back but it's the usual mess of stuff.'

'But you've heard something?'

'You know as well as I do the first news is always horse-shit.'

'I understand. What is it? Tell me what you've heard.'

'Have it your own way. The news is that your friend is dead. I spoke to someone who said they saw him.'

'Did they know him? How well?'

'He'd seen him around and about. Who hasn't? The place is an inferno apparently – you know what it's like: nothing makes any sense at first. He's probably heard the same thing about you.'

Cale called out to his Purgators and was heading to the ghetto when, from an entrance blowing light grey smoke into the courtyard, a figure walked out. Even though the smoke obscured him and his face was black, the way he moved gave him away immediately. Then Vague Henri recognized Cale – and also that he was staring at him in a peculiar way.

'What?' he said, defensive.

Cale looked him over for a while.

'There was a rumour you were dead.'

Taken aback by this, Henri gave the impression he was considering how reliable it was.

'No,' he said, at last.

Cale kept looking at him.

'What happened?'

Vague Henri smiled.

'Nothing much. We got in real neat. We only took out half a dozen on the way to the girls. Now I can see why.'

'They didn't attack?'

'No.'

'What about the fires?'

'We scared the shit out of the nuns. One of them spilt a pan of hot fat – the place went up like a hay-rack – spread under the floorboards and everything. That's why the fires kept breaking out all over. Got a bit scary.'

'Are the girls all right?'

'Fine. All of them.' He laughed. 'Bosco put them on half an acolyte's rations – thin as a hair now.'

'A hare?'

'Yeah – on your head.'

'Oh, I thought you meant, you know, a rabbit kind of hare. Doesn't make sense, a rabbit, does it?'

'No.'

'I wonder why he didn't kill them?'

'I suppose,' said Vague Henri, 'there's good in everyone.'

They both smiled. Cale nodded at the bodies hanging all around the courtyard.

'What do you make of this?'

'I don't make anything of it,' he said, suddenly angry. 'Fucking good fucking riddance.' Then he laughed; humour certainly but horror also. 'Didn't see it coming, though.'

'Bosco told them this was how they'd get to heaven.'

Vague Henri nodded.

'Find him yet?' Cale asked.

'No. Want to?'

'One way or the other. He'll be in his room, maybe.'

'Not,' said Vague Henri 'a good idea to go wandering around without being firm-handed.'

'I'm impatient. Really, I can't wait.'

Windsor, the cancer-infected Laconic tasked with killing Thomas Cale that day, was feeling particularly unwell. He was not long for the world one way or the other. He'd seen Cale talking to Vague Henri and tried to get to a high vantage point where he could get a decent shot. He put on a cassock he'd stripped off one of the Redeemers. He'd hoped for a good deal more confusion and days of fighting to give him an opportunity but now everything was static and soldiers were milling about in their thousands, gloomy and depressed by the hanging dead; having been wound up so tight and then it all being over there was nowhere for their horrible mix of feelings to go but inside.

Unfamiliar with the Sanctuary and its twists, Windsor got lost on his way to a walled ledge he'd spotted, and by the time he arrived it was only to see Cale and Vague Henri leaving the square on a reconnoitre which could only be considered seriously ill-advised. Though, of course, if they'd done the wise thing and stayed where they were, Cale would have had only a few seconds to live.

Windsor got rid of the cassock – there were plenty spare where that came from – and headed off in pursuit of the two boys, though not with any great optimism that he'd find them in the vast confusion of the place. On the other hand, there were now Laconics wandering all over the Sanctuary so there would be no problem stalking them. He paused only to vomit, something he now did three times a day.

It was no easy progress for Cale and Vague Henri – although the floors were clear, everything above two feet was packed with hanging priests and their headway was slow and singular as they pushed their way through the packed mass of dangling bodies. Just as he expected, Windsor was quickly lost, but while staring out of a window he noticed that though he couldn't see the two boys themselves they gave away their trail by the movement of bodies swinging back and forth in their wake. He decided that it would be quicker, even with brief stops to check their progress, to crawl under the priests rather than push through them. The thought had also occurred to Cale and Vague Henri but not only did they find the idea of crawling under their former masters objectionable, the truth was that they were enjoying themselves. The general soldiers might have been cowed by the Redeemers' grim willingness to embrace death in such a terrible and determined fashion but Cale and Vague Henri were made of sterner stuff – this hideous end struck them as entirely deserved and better than anything they could have thought up for themselves. It was no exaggeration to say that once they'd got over the initial shock they were thrilled by what had happened, an ecstasy of satisfaction that all their pain had been in some measure reimbursed. These deaths were very sweet to both of them, a sweetness that required to be made complete by a confrontation, dead or alive, with Bosco himself.

At one point Windsor came within forty yards of them but the darkness and the maziness of the place defeated him again: he took a wrong turn and crawled off under the vault of pointy feet ever further into the inner snarl of the Sanctuary.

As Cale and Vague Henri came to the end of the largest of the corridors they heard a sound. At first it was hard to make out, stopping and starting – it was a scratching sound and a scrabbling sound like a trapped animal, a small one, trying to escape. It was a desperate sound: scratch and scrape, silence, scratch and scrape. In the increasing darkness and silence it tightened the skin on the back of their skulls. *Scratch and scrape, silence, scratch and scrape.* Then an odd scuffing fluttery sound. Slowly they moved to the end of the corridor, where it turned right and also opened up into a space the size of a large room. Twitchy, they lowered themselves to the ground and saw what was causing the sound: manic, sandalled feet, flapping and scrabbling at the floor and wretchedly trying to get contact with something solid to support the weight of its body. The knot must have slipped or the rope stretched. As the corner of the corridor turned there was enough space for them to sit back against the wall without the lines of turned down feet in their faces.

'Getting too dark to see,' said Vague Henri.

Scrabble, scrabble, scrape.

'It's pretty close – just the other side of this latitude here.'

Scrape, scrape, scrabble.

'That sound – it's giving me the shrinks.'

'Then let's get away from it.'

Keeping close to the stone, they eased along the wall of the Latitude. *Scrabble, scrape, scrabble, scrape.* Then suddenly a wild and desperate scratching and rasps as the choking man, raging to breathe, lashed out for purchase on the floor.

'Oh, for God's sake!' said Vague Henri and pushed through the hanging dead and grabbed the choking Redeemer by the waist to ease his weight and cut him down with his knife.

The dying Redeemer, almost gone, took in a breath of air and regained consciousness – but only of a sort. An overseer of the hanging itself, he had been among the last to hang. The rope had seemed all right but it turned out to be inferior stuff and had stretched to allow the tips of his toes to take enough of his weight to keep him alive for hours. When Vague Henri took him by the waist he was able to breathe and started to wake up from the death nightmare he'd been trying to run away from: a devil was coming for him, bug-eyed and fat with gappy teeth, all pink and white with a slimy, drippy, red erection and laughing madly, like a pig might laugh.

It was not Vague Henri but this horrible demon holding him in his arms – reaching for anything to save himself he pulled out a sharpened pencil he'd been using to count off his list of those he was to hang and, with the strength of the utterly terrified, he stabbed at the creature holding him who cried out and fell away, dropping the Redeemer and finally breaking his neck.

'Ow! Ow!'

'What's the matter?'

'Bastard stabbed me.'

Cale started pushing his way through the hanging bodies that mocked him by banging into him and each other. There was a little more space around the now dead Redeemer – when he'd come to hang himself there was room left over. Vague Henri was feeling around under his arm and towards his back.

'He stabbed me,' he said, indignant. 'He stabbed me with a fucking pencil.'

The Redeemer, soul now in everlasting bliss, or not, did indeed have a pencil grasped in his right hand.

'Lucky that's all it was. Bloody stupid bloody thing to do.'

'Shut up – have a look.'

He held up his left arm and turned his back. It took a while to find the hole in the wool – Cale had to cut his way in to get a proper look.

There was indeed a pencil-shaped hole – but not much blood, though it was pumping a bit.

'What's it like?'

'Well, I wouldn't want one – it'll sting a bit.'

'It does.'

'It's not too bad. Let's go back, get it seen to.'

'It's all right. We've come this far. Give me a couple of minutes.'

He took a few deep breaths and then began to recover.

'How far?'

'Just down the corridor a bit.'

'Do you think he'll still be alive? He might be waiting to take you with him.'

'He probably won't even be there.'

'Bet you a dollar.'

'No.'

'Why not?'

'What would be the point?'

'I feel a bit wobbly,' said Vague Henri. He looked it, too. Beads of sweat, small ones, had begun to cover his face and he was looking pale. He sat down, using the wall to support his weight. Cale didn't like the look of him.

'Let me see the wound again.'

Vague Henri turned to his right. Now it was pumping blood slightly, so not too bad, but there was more than he expected. It must have gone in a bit deeper than he thought. But even as Cale looked the blood stopped flowing. He eased Vague Henri back to rest against the wall but by now he was already dead.

40

IdrisPukke was standing in the main square of the Sanctuary talking to Fanshawe, whose mind was elsewhere, wondering if Windsor had managed to kill Thomas Cale. He was so preoccupied that he didn't notice at first that IdrisPukke had stopped talking. Then everyone around them went silent as well. Across the large square Cale was walking slowly towards them, carrying Vague Henri piggyback, as if he were a small child who'd fallen asleep after a too-exciting day. For a moment no one moved, unable to grasp what they were seeing. Were they fooling about? They often did. Cale stopped and then hitched the boy further up his back as if he were about to slip off. Then a dozen men ran towards them and he allowed them to take Vague Henri into their arms. IdrisPukke and Fanshawe walked slowly up to him. Vague Henri was dead – they had too much experience not to recognize the terrible absence.

'What happened?' asked IdrisPukke.

Cale didn't seem to hear. 'He's not going back into a room in this place. Get one of the tables out of the refectory over there. They're big – you'll need a dozen men.'

It was clear he didn't want to talk so they stood for five minutes with Cale as he looked around the Sanctuary as if he was trying to remember where he'd left something, with Vague Henri being held carefully in the arms of four of his own people. Then the table, clearly as hefty as Cale had said and some thirty-foot long, was hauled into the middle of the square. Cale took Vague Henri from the men and laid him carefully in the middle and then arranged the body at first with his hands by his side and then folded on his chest. Death had already drawn his top lip back over his front teeth, mocking him with the rabbity smile of the dead. It was with some difficulty that Cale pulled it back into shape. Then his eyelids started to open and Cale couldn't get them to stay shut. He signalled one of the sergeants to give him a white scarf he was wearing; he folded it several times and then put it over Vague Henri's eyes like a blindfold. Still no one said anything until one of the soldiers gasped: 'Good God!'

Everyone looked up except for Cale, who was lost in a world of his own, staring down at his friend. Around him there was silence so intense that it finally pierced the fog of his disbelief that Vague Henri was gone for good. He looked up. At the far end of the square, barefoot, dressed in white linen and with the penitent's noose around his neck, Pope Bosco XVI was walking towards them with a gentle smile on his face. He was much thinner than when Cale had last seen him and the linen tunic was much too large which, along with the gaping of his mouth as he made the effort to walk, gave his face the look of a chick not quite ready to leave the nest. It took the old man almost a minute to make it over to the group standing next to the huge table and whose eyes moved silently back and forward between Cale and the old man shambling towards them. Cale did not move nor blink but watched Bosco entirely transfixed. It seemed to those watching that the old man and Cale had become the only people who existed in the square. Bosco stopped, still smiling lovingly at the boy.

'I've been waiting patiently for you – to explain everything and to ask your forgiveness for the terrible suffering I caused you.'

Still Cale did not move or say anything. He looked as if he would never speak again.

'I could not understand how God was speaking to me through all your many victories over us. Waterless and without food I prayed for day after day. I could see but I could not perceive, hear but not understand. Then in his mercy for my stupidity he cut away the skin from my eyes. When you came here as a boy I saw at once what you were but I thought that you needed me to teach you how to wipe away his great mistake. Every night I wept at the pain and suffering I must inflict on you so that you would have the strength of soul and body to do such unspeakable work. All of the things I did to make you strong only built hatred where there should have been love. The death of the world was an act of holy tenderness to mankind and not a punishment – it was to be done as a gift so that he could begin again. I thought you were the incarnation of God's wrath but you were his love made flesh, not his anger. In my incompetence I maddened you and made you hateful when all I should have done was treat you with the kindness that you were to show the world by helping all its souls into the next life to start again. My fault, my fault, my most grievous fault.'

Bosco knelt down in front of Cale.

'Forgive me, Thomas. God was telling me through all your victories against us that the damage done to your soul had to be undone by the man who caused that damage. I thought that I and my fellow priests would be the last to join God for the great renewal of souls, but now it's necessary for us to be first, so that you can go about God's work with a spirit at peace. Only by our poor sacrifice can your soul-hatred be wiped away.'

Bosco, tears of gratitude pouring from his eyes, held out both of his arms and began to pray.

'Purge me with hyssop, Lord, and I shall be clean: wash me, and I shall be whiter than snow. Deliver me from my guilt so that the spirit and the heart of Thomas Cale, which I have broken, may rejoice.'

As Bosco prayed, Cale began to look around as if for a key he had absentmindedly misplaced. Everyone else stared at him, horribly thrilled at what was happening. Fanshawe spoke softly to IdrisPukke as Cale walked over to the far end of the table on which Vague Henri's body was lying and started pulling at a small piece of two by four that had been nailed to the refectory wall and the table to keep it from moving.

'Think of the information we can get from Bosco,' said Fanshawe. 'We need him alive.'

'I agree. Be my guest.' Fanshawe did not move.

Cale's attempt to pull away the block of wood, no more than nine inches long, was unsuccessful, the nails still being in too deep. Then he gave the block an almighty wrench and it came free. As he walked back to Bosco the old man was still praying.

'With this sacrifice of your priests wipe away all tears from his eyes so that there shall be no more sorrow, nor shall there be any more pain.'

Slowly Cale began to circle behind him – a weighing up of something clearly going on in his mind.

'Just as the Hanged Redeemer offered his broken neck for our salvation, with the sacrificial chokings of Your Redeemers wipe clean the needless insults to his soul, so that he will be free at last to do his terrible kindness to the world. Free at la –'

Cale took two steps forward and brought the block of wood down on the top of the old man's head. But it was not an especially hard blow and it was not an especially heavy piece of wood. Bosco's head jerked forward slightly, not much, and a thin line of blood dripped down his face. He opened his mouth as if to continue but not a sound emerged. He tried to speak again but immediately there was another blow and again his head jerked forward but again the blow was much less heavy than it could have been. The men watching were not at all strangers to the hideous but already some of them were looking away. Then another blow. Another trickle of blood.

Bosco was waving his head about and his hands had fallen halfway to his sides. He gasped.

'Into . . . thy . . . ha – '

Another blow stopped his mouth but still he was too strong to fall or the blows deliberately not heavy enough. Then another crack of wood against skull and another. This time he almost fell on his face but something drew him nearly upright again. Another blow and this time a cry from Bosco as half a dozen lines of blood flowed down his shaved skull and covered his face.

'For God's sake, Thomas, enough,' said IdrisPukke. Cale looked directly at him like a fox smelling a slight sniff of something in the wind: Important? Not at all. Then the interruption was entirely dismissed as if it had never happened. He turned to concentrate on Bosco again. He dropped the stained block of wood and then, with great care, took hold of the penitents' rope around Bosco's neck and started to sway him gently from side to side, supporting his neck so he would do no harm, the way a mother holds the head of a baby she's about to bathe.

'Thomas!' called out IdrisPukke.

But it was no use: he was somewhere very far beyond the reaches of pity. Cale pulled Bosco up to his face and slapped him with one hand to bring him round. Slowly, Bosco woke up. As he recognized Cale he started to smile lovingly at the boy.

'I want . . .'

But what Bosco wanted was cut short in a second as Cale, hyena-souled, whipped the rope upwards and then down with a snap so furious it broke the old man's neck with a loud crack.

There was a sound from the men around, an intake of breath. Cale pulled Bosco's face back to his own until they were almost touching, fixing his death in his mind so that he would not forget – then, very carefully, he laid the dead man on the ground and walked away. The witnesses were shaking, every one of them, even Fanshawe. They had all seen hard deaths before, and anger, but nothing like this, not from someone who was still, really, a boy.

41

The fire that had nearly suffocated Vague Henri the day before had still not been put out completely and after a few hours it regained its hold, though only in the ghetto where the girls had been held. Still it was enough to give off an orange glow that lit the undersides of the grey clouds that had settled low over the Sanctuary and enabled IdrisPukke to find Cale, about half a mile from the gate, about four hours after he'd killed Bosco.

'I'm very sorry about Vague Henri,' said IdrisPukke.

There was no reply at first.

'How did you know I'd be here?'

'I didn't. I sent people out but I thought that somewhere here would be a possibility.'

Cale was sitting on a rock about a hundred yards from the isolated compound where Arbell Materazzi was being kept. 'Were you thinking of going in?'

'I was mulling it over, yes.'

'Would you mind if I asked you not to?'

Again there was no reply for a time.

'I was thinking of burying Vague Henri at the Voynich oasis,' he said eventually.

'I don't know it.'

'Not far from here. A lake. Nice trees, birds singing and stuff. He'd like that.'

'He would, yes.'

'I want the girls to go. They'll cry, I suppose. He'd like that as well. Stupid really. What difference does it make?'

'I've been to a fair number of funerals. They make a difference sometimes.'

'Not to him.'

'No, not to him.'

A few minutes' more silence. Then Cale laughed.

'Did I ever tell you about Vague Henri and the upside down prayer book?'

'I don't believe you did.' In fact he'd told IdrisPukke the story when they were at Treetops.

'Don't know where he got the idea but he tore the cover off the missal we were supposed to read for an hour a day and glued it on upside down. He'd take it out whenever he came across a pig who didn't know him and start reading. It drove them crazy when they saw it – pretending to read the Holy Missal . . . blasphemy! They'd come racing over and rip it out of his hands and clip him on the ear. But he didn't mind. Then he'd show them the cover had been stuck on upside down and tell them he was waiting for a new one. Even piggy Redeemers had to do a grovel at that. Some of them even said they were sorry. He made a fortune betting the acolytes he could get a Redeemer to ask for forgiveness.'

Another silence.

'I hate her.'

'Yes.'

'I never hated her before. I pretended I did, but I didn't. I was ashamed that she stopped loving me and sold me up but I didn't stop loving her, not for a moment.' Another silence. 'Do you know about mortification?'

'No.'

'Bosco said it meant that you could die of shame – you know, shame for your sins. I felt mortification by loving her. So weak – weak and ashamed.' For the first time he looked over at IdrisPukke. 'Do you know why Henri died?'

'No.'

'Because of her.'

'I don't understand.'

'See, I came back here because of her. I brought her here to show her. I mean I didn't plan it or anything, not in my head. But I can see it now. Now he's dead.'

'See what?'

'I wanted her to see the Sanctuary – so she'd understand why I was so odd and then she'd love me again. And then I wanted to show her that I could destroy it – that she didn't have to give me away to Bosco because I could have beaten them. I would have done. I have done. I wanted her to see what a dreadful thing she did for no good reason. But all I did was bring Vague Henri back so that he could die in this shithole. Here of all places. To die here.'

He began putting his fists to his head, grinding his temples with his knuckles as if to drill a hole to let something out.

'Don't go down there,' IdrisPukke said.

'Think I might.' Cale stood up. 'Bosco was right, you either kill the past or it kills you.'

'Don't go. You're in a state of mind where something grim might happen.'

'You're right, it's true – unspeakable things are on my mind.'

'What would Vague Henri say?' He was getting desperate trying this one.

'Vague Henri's dead. No votes for him.'

'I don't know how bad or good she is. I barely know the girl. What I do know is that she's a blight on you. You can only make things worse if you go anywhere near her. The two of you share a madness that will cut you both in two. Get her away from you.'

471

Another short silence.

'When I murdered Kitty the Hare there was something I didn't tell you about. It was the look in his eyes – I suppose he was terrified as well but it wasn't his fear that stuck in my mind, it was the shock. *This can't be happening to me*, he was thinking while I beat the life out of him, *not me*. Day after day Kitty was guilty of every kind of cruelty and violence yet when that violence came to him in his own home he was dumbfounded. Couldn't get that look of amazement out of my mind.' He turned again to IdrisPukke. 'Know why?'

'No.'

'I've just realized myself. I want to see that look again, really I do. I want to see it in the eyes of that shit-bag Zog, and Bose Ikard, and Robert Fanshawe and his Ephors and everyone like them everywhere in the world. I want to see that shock in their eyes: *Me? Not me. This can't be happening.* The world is full of people who need to die like that.'

'So, the Left Hand of God after all.'

Cale laughed.

'Who said anything about God?'

'What about all the people you're going to have to kill to get to them?'

'I'll give everyone the chance to budge out of the way.'

'And if they don't agree to budge?'

'Then they'll get what's coming to them.'

'And so will the thousands upon thousands who won't be able to get out of the way even if they wanted to. Bosco thought you could rule the world – but he was mad. What's your excuse?'

'What choice do I have?'

'We always have a choice.'

'You know, I've never heard you say anything stupid before. Are you really telling me I can stop? Not even if I wanted to. No one's going to let me be, no one's going to let me take myself off somewhere and eat cake with girls in peace and quiet. I tried that. I wouldn't last six months if I walked away now.' He looked at IdrisPukke. 'Tell me I'm wrong.'

'Your joy is all in laying waste to things – blight and desolation is what makes your soul glad.'

'What?' For some reason Cale was furious.

'Wasn't that what that puppet said to you?'

'Oh, that thing. Yes.'

'I don't agree, for what it's worth.'

'Thanks – I'm touched.'

'But if you go down there and kill Arbell Materazzi, that's the first step. You can't come back from something like that.'

'You know what I learnt from killing Bosco? There's nothing like an itch that you can finally scratch. Enough talk now. We'll talk again tomorrow.'

'You can't kill someone just because they don't love you any more.'

'Why not?'

'Suppose everyone behaved like that?'

'Then people would be a lot more careful.'

'Will you come with me?' said IdrisPukke. 'Sleep on it?'

'No.'

What was IdrisPukke to do? Nothing.

He made his way back to the main compound, tripping on stones and matted webs of arse-wipe as he went.

All that night priests were falling through the air. Flocks, doles, bevies, parliaments and trains of the lately hanged were being hauled in their hundreds to the West Wall of the Sanctuary and heaved over the side to freefall the three hundred feet onto Ginky's Field, where for six hundred years the

473

bodies of the Redeemers had been set aside. What did they fall like? Like nothing you've ever seen.

Some three hours into this grim rite – known as the First Defenestration of the Hanged because the gap in the wall through which the bodies were pitched resembled a window – Windsor finally escaped from the recesses of the Sanctuary and made his sick and exhausted way to Fanshawe. 'It's too late now, darling,' he said. 'You'd better get some sleep and you can try again tomorrow.'

But there wasn't to be another chance for Windsor. By the time the sun came up Thomas Cale was miles away, sitting in the back of a wagon on its way to the materials depot at Snow Hill.

IdrisPukke had men out searching for months but there wasn't a trace of the boy. He didn't give up, of course: he paid a good deal of money to intelligencers who knew how to keep their mouths shut to report on rumours about even the most tenuous sightings of Thomas Cale. There were plenty of those. It was not difficult to discount the story that he'd been seen in the prow of a great ship setting out across the Wooden Sea, accompanied by eight maidens in white silk, bound for the Isle of Avalon from where he would return after a long sleep to save the world when it was next threatened with destruction. Then it was reported he was making his living as a juggler in Berlin, or selling hats in the markets in Syracuse. Alarmingly plausible was the news, more than a year later, that he'd been killed trying to interrupt the marriage in Lebanon of Arbell Materazzi to the Aga Khan, Duke of Malfi, a man so extravagant he was known as the Emperor of Ice Cream because his fortune was melting away. But IdrisPukke quickly confirmed from a guest who'd been at the ceremony that the celebrations had passed off impeccably. Later still there was the rumour that he had drowned, along with Wat Tyler, in the Great Fiasco on the Isle of Dogs; then that he had been crucified next to Buffel-low Bill during the religious wars at Troy.

But though the sightings were as numerous as they were unreliable a pattern of sorts emerged from a few reports, very small in number, that he hoped were true. There were a number of claims he had been seen down in Emmaeus in one-horse towns buying nails, saws and olive oil. The ordinariness of this reassured IdrisPukke: it was warm there, even in winter, and the countryside was covered by mile upon mile of forests of elm and ash, as well as hundreds of small lakes where it would be very hard to find someone who didn't want to be found. He liked to think of Cale keeping occupied hammering and sawing things and eating well – though he could discover nothing very solid to these reports even after he'd sent reliable people down there to make inquiries. But he hoped he was somewhere around there at any rate and keeping safe.

APPENDIX i

Statement on behalf of the Unified Nations
Archaeological Survey (UNAS)

As the legal judgment by Moderator Breffni Waltz so elegantly
details the origins of the discovery of the Rubbish Tips of Paradise and the 'creation' of the so-called Left Hand of God trilogy,
I will not rehearse them here. Neither do I intend to detail the
legal challenges to the entirely improper claims of ownership by
either Dr Fahrenheit or the Habiru people, rights which clearly
belong to the entire world and not to an individual or a tribal
group who have shown scant respect for this most precious of
archaeological sites.

No one is denying the contribution of Dr Fahrenheit in discovering the tips and had he immediately called in the Unified
Nations Archaeological Survey, as he should have done, this
would be a very different story: he would now be admired as one
of archaeology's greatest sons instead of being reviled as its greatest villain. Early on Fahrenheit came up with the working
hypothesis that the origin of the pages in the Field of Books was
not a library or anything equally carefully structured but a rubbish
tip consisting largely of discarded papers, somewhat similar to
those uncovered in the early years of the last century at Oxyrinchus (though those remains are no more than eighteen hundred
years old – proof that even a great city can vanish very quickly

476

from the memory of history). It turns out that he was right. What he was not able to do was discover the location of the rubbish tip itself. However, while he was looking for what one might term the mother lode, he kept discovering individual scraps of paper and it was from these, matched by his quick grasp of the Habiru language, that he was able to find the very few words these two civilizations had in common and so unravel the meaning of many of these documents, some of which may be up to fifty thousand years old, or even older. What he had in his possession were many higgledy-piggledy scraps of paper – bits of old letters, accounts, legal documents – but only one book. It was never found in its complete form but the papers continued to turn up in large quantities and in approximately the same place – there were so many fragments that once he had mastered the language of these texts he was able to recreate almost in their entirety the series of what turned out to be three books.

But what did that tell him, or us, about their status among the people for whom they were intended? Were they to be found in such numbers because the Left Hand of God trilogy (as he called it – none of the title pages have so far been discovered) was considered one of the great artistic treasures of this lost civilization? In short, was the author the equivalent of our own giants – a Bramley or Ginsmeyer – or was he an Allin Harwood or Jinna Lorenzo, widely read and as widely derided? Or was he a deluded self-publisher whose books went straight from the printing press into his attic and from there directly to the rubbish tip en masse without selling a copy to anyone other than a luckless friend or relative?

As such, completely shorn of any context, either historical or aesthetic, these books set us an interesting challenge. For now we must make something of them, good or bad, only through a simple and direct reading unmediated by accumulated layers of cultural status. If we fail to be moved and stimulated, are we rejecting a work once considered by its readers to be of sublime quality? And if we *are* stirred, are we being stimulated by a book so worthless its contemporaries thought it only fit to be thrown away? Other central questions remain, of the sort we can usually take for granted in order to tell us what to think about what we are about to read. Is it some kind of historical fiction? Is it a contemporary work describing recent events? Is it entirely imaginary? Did the Redeemers exist in fact, or are they merely the product of an unhealthy imagination, or is their presentation merely propaganda written by someone belonging to an opposing cult? Are the characters based on real individuals and as such would have been known to their audience or are they entirely inventions of the writer? Are the many differences in style to be explained by the erratic nature of the writing or are these references to known works that the reader would have recognized, or are they just thefts? Was it written by more than one person? Or none of the above? Only one of these questions, concerning the Materazzi and the Redeemers, has already been partly answered (see below 1#). We must accept we may never know how to read these texts accurately.

Mr Fahrenheit attempted to solve these problems by the simple expedient of ignoring them. He published the first two books in the series as if they were contemporary examples of the genre usually described as 'fantasy' – though lacking as they do any dwarfs, fairies, monsters or elves it's not easy to understand why. Be that as it may, the books published under the family name of Fahrenheit's mother were reasonably successful in commercial terms, if found odd by many and distinctly disliked by others. The translation, though racy and free, cannot be said to be inaccurate.

The Unified Nations have now legally taken control of the site called by the Habiru the Field of Books but popularly known as the Rubbish Tips of Paradise after a newspaper headline more concerned with a memorable phrase than any degree of accuracy (the rubbish tips are *east* of the fabled Eden by some two hundred miles). The 'ownership' of the text of the Left Hand of God trilogy is subject to legal appeal between UNAS and Fahrenheit and the Habiru. Following Mr Fahrenheit's committal under the Mental Health Act to a care facility in Cambria, an agreement has been reached to publish the third volume, *The Beating of His Wings*, in a translation by Fahrenheit where the profits are paid directly to the Habiru. In due course, and in the light of the extensive research on the documents being uncovered by UNAS, a proper academic translation will be published to include footnotes and a detailed analysis of the historical context as well as a professional commentary.

We can hardly fail to hope that, as more material is uncovered in the Rubbish Tips of Paradise (as we are now more or less obliged to call them), we will discover many great masterpieces of our hidden past. Who can say what shocks and delights are to come?

Doctor Professeur Ajax Plowman
42nd of Brumaire AD 143. 812

1# Since it details an event mentioned frequently in the trilogy, I refer those interested to the first proper academic paper by UNAS based on translated documents from the Rubbish Tips of Paradise: 'The Praxis of Aggression: Historical Verification for the Battle of Silbury Hill and the Decline of the Materazzi Hegemony', *History Today*, vol 277, pp. 62–120.

APPENDIX ii

Some of the following statement by Paul Fahrenheit has been redacted under the laws of criminal libel and several statutes of Unified Nations Hate Crime legislation.

Concerning the self-serving propaganda of the Unified Nations Archaeological Survey (UNARSE), the ▮▮▮ obscurantist mediocrities who make up the cultural commentariat and academia, the ▮▮▮ who is now Chair of the Arts Council, and the ▮▮▮ hacks of the mass media, all of you can ▮▮▮ in a ▮▮▮.

Furthermore, ▮▮▮▮▮▮▮▮▮▮▮▮▮▮▮▮▮▮▮▮▮▮▮▮▮
▮▮▮▮▮▮▮▮▮▮▮▮▮▮▮▮▮▮▮▮▮▮▮▮▮▮▮▮▮
▮▮▮▮▮▮▮▮▮▮▮▮▮▮▮▮▮▮▮▮▮▮▮▮▮▮▮▮▮
▮▮▮▮▮▮▮▮▮▮▮▮▮▮▮▮▮▮▮▮▮▮▮▮▮▮▮▮▮
▮▮▮▮▮▮▮▮▮▮▮▮▮▮▮▮▮▮▮▮▮▮▮▮▮▮▮▮▮
▮▮▮▮▮▮▮▮▮▮▮▮▮▮▮▮▮▮▮▮▮▮▮▮▮▮▮▮▮
▮▮▮▮▮▮▮▮▮▮▮▮▮▮▮▮▮▮▮▮▮▮▮▮▮▮▮▮▮
▮▮▮▮▮▮▮▮▮▮▮▮▮▮▮▮▮▮▮▮▮▮▮▮▮▮▮▮▮

What could be drearier once you have learned the basics of thinking and reading than to carry on living in an intellectual nursery with someone telling you what toys to choose and why. 'This is a nice toy, little boy or little girl, but not that one – it does not meet with our view of toyness.' And what could be more foolish than to see the world through the eyes of most of the commentariat: the teacher, the academic, the cultural commentator, the critic, the massed ranks of opinion-formers who clog up our world like

███████ in a midden. But death above all to the Dooey Decimal System which places the world in order down to the eighteenth point. The best picture of the human mind is never the library, with its convenient and deadly order, but the rubbish tip: life in its fundamental nature is haphazard, random, full of the rotten and the beautiful, the wrongly discarded, full of the profound truth of chaos. It cannot be packaged neatly for your discovery. You must be an outdragger, a tinker in life's journey looking for the surprising, the unexpected, the object that comes to hand to be made use of in a different way from the one intended. As for ████████ ████ ████ ████ to all of them.

The traveller who goes exploring with an official guide, even a counter-cultural one, and a carefully worked out itinerary is no explorer, merely a high-minded tourist. The next time you enter a library do so with a blindfold! The Rubbish Tips of Paradise are more interesting than paradise itself.

As Vague Henri would say: Death to the barn owl!

Paul Fahrenheit.
The Priory
Cambria
18th of Germinal AD 143.799

Acknowledgements

I'd like to thank my agent, Anthony Goff, and my editor at Penguin, Alex Clarke; Alexandra, Victoria and Thomas Hoffman, and Lorraine Hedger who types up my handwritten manuscripts with miraculous accuracy. Thanks also to the Penguin Rights department: Kate Burton, Sarah Hunt-Cooke, Rachel Mills and Chantal Noel. Also Nick Lowndes and my copy editor, Debbie Hatfield.

The description of King Zog and his habits is based on *The Court and Character of King James 1*, probably by Sir Anthony Weldon.

Bose Ikard's speech claiming he has reached agreement with the Redeemers is substantially that of Neville Chamberlain's speech in 1938 on returning from a meeting with Adolf Hitler, claiming that he had secured 'peace for our time'.

The German philosopher Arthur Schopenhauer makes his usual extensive contribution to the observations of IdrisPukke. Sister Wray's comments on the sun are from William Blake. The popular tune sung by Riba in the carriage has a line based on the title of W. H. Auden's 'O Tell Me The Truth About Love'. The line, 'Love has no ending' comes from Auden's 'As I Walked Out One Evening'. The words 'under' and 'umbrella' are borrowed from Rihanna Fenty. The trial of Conn Materazzi is partly based on the transcript of 'The Trial of Sir Walter Raleigh' in Cobbett's *Complete Collection of State Trials*. Cale's comments about being seen to watch over his men echo the letter by Sullivan Ballou to his wife shortly before his death, and first quoted in *The Left Hand of God*. In some foreign editions this acknowledgement was inadvertently omitted. The exchange between Dorothy Rothschild and Cale that ends Chapter 31 is from a line by the underrated American President Calvin Coolidge. There are many half quotes or ones so buried and rewritten that I can no longer recognize or trace them. If the reader suspects other sources from Homer to Homer Simpson they can, of course, resort to Google cut and paste – the greatest sneak in the history of knowledge.

Artemisia

The character of Artemisia in *The Beating of His Wings* is inspired by, but not based on, Artemisia of Halicarnassus, the admiral who fought for the Persians against the Greeks at Salamis in 480BC. Against prevailing opinion she strongly advised Xerxes not to attack the Greek fleet in the narrow straits where they would have too great an advantage. Fortunately for the subsequent development of the Greek Golden Age, the growth of democracy and, very possibly, Western civilization itself, Xerxes went along with the advice of the majority and as a result lost heavily. Although alternative history is a bit of a mug's game, who knows if Artemisia had been listened to more carefully whether the Americans might have had to weed Saddam Hussein out of London or Paris rather than Baghdad. Perhaps there wouldn't be an American democracy at all.

Contemporary feminist historians are deeply suspicious of the traditional account of her death, which claims she threw herself off a cliff because she had fallen in love with a younger man who did not return her affections. For them, perhaps rightly, it smacks of the sexism of the classical world. Such a tough-minded woman, they argue, would not have been so psychologically fragile. But perhaps not – the classical world also has similar tales of great soldiers confused by love – take Antony and Cleopatra. In our own time the militarily-much-admired former general David Petraeus, who stabilized the collapsing American occupation of Iraq in 2008, and had a reputation as a subtle and sophisticated thinker, was forced to resign his job as Director of the Central Intelligence Agency over his affair with his biographer. As Thomas Cale would have to accept, there's nothing that unusual about having nerves of steel and a heart of glass.

Jan Ziska

The origin of the tactics and practices of Cale's New Model Army lies with the Hussite general Jan Ziska, military leader of what was, as Luther later acknowledged, the first Protestant Christian sect in early fifteenth-century Europe (based around the modern Czech Republic). Alexander the Great inherited an army whose skill and tactical superiority had been established by his father, but Ziska is very close to being unique in military history, in that he developed a way of fighting professional armoured soldiers in huge numbers using peasants armed with weapons based on agricultural implements and farm wagons. He also pioneered the development of lightweight gunpowder weapons. This problem-solving, tactically brilliant, completely original genius is barely known outside the Czech Republic. For further reading, try *Warrior of God: Jan Zizka and the Hussite Revolution* by Victor Vernay or *The Hussite Wars, 1420–34* by Stephen Turnbull and Angus McBride.

Bex

The battle at Bex is sometimes but not always based on the Battle of Towton in 1461. Again oddly, despite probably having the highest death rate in English history (including the first day of the Somme) at around 28,000, Towton has faded from popular memory in favour of less important and less bloody conflicts. For further reading, try *Blood Red Roses: The Archaeology of a Mass Grave from the Battle of Towton AD1461* Veronica Fiorato (author, editor), Anthea Boylston (editor), Christopher Knusel (editor) and *Towton: The Battle of Palm Sunday Field* by John Sadler.

Some readers have been critical of the way in which the names of 'real' places turn up jumbled together without rhyme or reason in the geography of the world of The Left Hand of God trilogy. I'd ask them to consider the following: Riga Sweden Egypt Belfast Greece Norfolk Manchester Hamburg Kent Warsaw Cambridge London Peterborough Syracuse Rome Amsterdam Potsdam Batavia Dunkirk Reading (not far from Lebanon) Dover (not far from Smyrna) Mansfield Stamford Norwich Hyde Park Troy Bangor (next to Nazareth not far from Bethlehem) Sunbury Palmyra Westminster Emmaeus Mt Carmel Delhi Berlin Peru. The list could go on. What do these disparate places have in common? They are all towns, villages and small cities within 250 miles of New York (formerly New Amsterdam).

Find out more about The Left Hand of God trilogy by visiting:
www.redopera.co.uk

Making the World Strange

An Essay by Paul Hoffman

Consider the following first draft synopsis of an epic fantasy novel set on a planet far, far away called Gondwana.

Eight years after the end of the Great War, in which the vile Alois Hutler, tyrant and genocidal murderer, was finally defeated in the shadow of the Brandenburg, his most powerful enemy, Elector Joseb Jugasvili of Eurazia, the greatest mass murderer in history, dies. But not before he has stolen, by means of grand treachery, the secret weapon created by the Oceanic Empire, his undefeated enemy – a weapon so powerful it can destroy the world. The power struggle between the Oceanic and Eurazian empires continues as, wary of annihilating each other, they probe each other's weaknesses in the proxy wars of the Khmer and the Bukhan and other disputed territories. When a new young emperor, John of Boston, comes to power in Oceania the Eurazians see their chance to test his inexperience and place one of their stolen weapons on an island near Oceania. They wait to see what John of Boston will do. He orders them to remove the weapons or he will use his own device and bring about the end of the world. Millions lie awake at night in terror as the transmitters bring news of the imminent death of the world. But then the Eurazians back down and the world is saved – for now at least. A few months later, John of Boston is assassinated by a returned defector from Eurazia – the world's greatest hope for peace and freedom seems to have died along with the saintly young emperor. What is Oceania to do now about its restive Black Untouchables –

descendents of slaves brought to Oceania during the previous centuries?

Oceania gets to the moon but is traumatized by an appalling war in the disputed Khmer territories. Then Eurazia collapses without warning. Oceania, now the only great power on Gondwana, is attacked by religious extremists and is dragged into more unwinnable wars, known as 'the quagmires'. Meanwhile, a powerful new empire springs into life in the Far East. But then a Black Untouchable is elected president of Oceania. And now the temperature of Gondwana is rising with incalculable consequences for the entire globe. Religious tensions increase alongside the rise of consumerism and the cult of celebrity, and equal rights are demanded by groups whose values threaten established moral values.

So far so instantly recognizable. But this serves to highlight the problem of writing about the world we live in. These are huge-scale events and therefore almost impossible to write about, even in the one form – the novel – that has any chance of tackling them. The central problem is that because we experience life as individuals we are much more caught up with everyday living: How will I earn my keep? How will I get this man or woman to love me? How do I get a decent job? The result is that the forces gathering strength around us can easily seem remote, even tedious. In my first novel, *The Wisdom of Crocodiles*, published in 1999, one section is devoted to dramatizing how and why the world's financial system was bound to collapse sooner or later. One American publisher offered to buy the book on condition that I removed this section. It's not as if I didn't stoop to every trick in the book to make it entertaining, including the presence of a lawyer with a flick knife and a judge with a rubber nose and a terror of giant fruit bats.

When it came to *The Left Hand of God*, I wanted to find a

new way of telling stories, one that began with a single individual's life, in this case the life of Thomas Cale. His life would begin slowly to merge with and to affect great events happening in an outside world of which he knew practically nothing at the start of the book. By the end he was often the reluctant agent of history. But this involved using a narrative that was very far from new (something indignantly pointed out by the book's critics): a young man of obscure origin but with great qualities escapes his oppressive upbringing and, by means of heroic swashbuckling, makes his fortune and ends up winning the heart of a beautiful princess. Surely this is indefensibly trite and unoriginal? Or worse, a cynical attempt to pander to the laziest desires of a mass audience in a genre more or less inherently despicable (fantasy, for the avoidance of doubt).

It depends. Firstly, I'd argue that the story of an apparently obscure young man (from Oedipus to Luke Skywalker) setting out to make his way in the world of great events goes far deeper than cliché ever could. This is the story of every human life – to a greater or lesser extent it's the truest of truisms. And it was in this inescapable narrative that I found one way of wrapping the personal and the larger-scale world together. I asked myself what was the story I knew best. My own, of course. I found that having made it to my early fifties I was, for some reason, now compulsively drawn back to my early life (whereas my first two novels had been set in the modern world of work and technology). But the thing is I wasn't born, so to speak, in the modern world at all. I was born in 1953 in a house without electricity or running water, by the light of a paraffin lamp. We even got our drinking water from, as it turned out, a poisoned well in the garden. My first memory of my father was of him falling out of the sky. This wasn't a false memory caused by the hallucinogenic effects of poisoned water, but one from just after my father had taken up freefall parachuting. His obsession with the sport radically altered my life: I saw my first violent death at the age of six after a friend of my father's fell to his death when his parachute malfunctioned due in part to his over-confidence (what was this but a replay of the death of Icarus?).

Over the next ten years I must have seen my father come close to being killed on nearly a dozen occasions. In those days parachuting was a military sport and I saw the Cold War (the one feebly disguised in the above synopsis) being fought out repeatedly between the American and Russian teams at world championships. The Americans won this sporting war through the same method that ultimately caused the collapse of the Soviet Union – putting so much money and energy into new technology that the Russians were unable to keep up. As with the war between Thomas Cale and the Redeemers, technical ingenuity ensured victory. It was a wonderful lesson to a novelist that even the biggest historical and polit-ical event could be seen played out in miniature, where the nuances were much easier to capture in human terms.

By now my father was the British Parachute Champion, and because he was a soldier he was sent to Kenya to start up the Kenyan Army First Parachute Regiment, expressly to fight bandits in the lawless Northern Frontier District. He went off to a peculiar world where most of the fighting was done with spears and AK47s. Aged ten, I went off to a very much weirder one: a Catholic boarding school in Cowley, an industrial suburb of Oxford. This is the basis for The Sanc-tuary. The only major difference between the imagined and the real place was that in the real place they weren't allowed to kill you. This was 1964, and while the modern world as we know it was in the process of exploding into the future, I was on my way back into the past. And a brutal one at that. Readers have often pointed out, not usually approvingly, that the world of the trilogy is an odd fusion of the Middle Ages and the nineteenth century, along with flashes of modernity. The reason for this is straightforward: that was the peculiar world we lived in at the school. Mostly we were subjected to a harsh religious philosophy of sin and damnation that would have been entirely recognizable to someone born in the thirteenth century – and on Thursdays we were allowed to watch *Top of the Pops*. Violence from the priests was not continuous but it was ever-present and arbitrary. One of my eleven-year-old friends once popped a blown-up paper bag in the dining hall. The priest in charge took him out of sight, punched him to the ground and gave him a good kicking. This kind of brutality was not a daily occurrence as it was in so many Catholic schools, but it could happen at any time and came from priests who would treat you in a reasonably civilized manner for months at a time and then, without warning, beat you savagely for a trivial infraction. Add to this the constant psychological harassment, the revolting food, the cold, the total lack of privacy (I spent years sleeping in a dormitory with seventy other people), the grinding boredom and the idiotic stories of heaven and hell and you can, perhaps, imagine how deadly this place was to any kind of joy or pleasure.

Inevitably the violence and harsh treatment took a real toll on the pupils, several hundred boys from the age of ten to eighteen, most of whom came from tough working-class or underclass backgrounds. The threat of serious violence from each other was a constant. I was attacked within hours of arriving at school, and when I slipped, my attacker stamped on my head. This was a place where fighting was something you had to be prepared to do at any moment. One psychologist who specialized in dealing with the casualties of such places called them God's concentration camps. The shameful thing is that the school I attended for seven years was probably no more than halfway up the pyramid of abuse in Catholic boarding schools – many others were much worse. The litany of cruelty in the Irish government's 2009 Ryan Commission report on historical maltreatment in Catholic schools beggars belief. The *Irish Times* called it 'a map of hell'. But it can't be emphasized too much that this medieval world existed alongside the gilded paradise of Oxford University less than two miles down the road, and swinging Carnaby Street an hour away by car.

So far, so grim. Even so, while I was writing about The Sanctuary I often found myself laughing. What I remembered was that the only real weapon we had against the priests was to mock them. Granted the jokes were mixed with hatred and contempt but we were also kept at least partly sane by realizing the sheer witless absurdity of these men and the things they expected us to believe (though there were a fair number of pupils who were absorbed into the deranged belief system that was destroying them). So we developed our impersonations of individual priests giving sermons full of lurid descriptions of small children being roasted and dismembered eternally in hell for coveting their neighbour's ass.

When I decided to write *The Left Hand of God* it seemed to me that the story lay in trying to answer a question: how do people brought up in such extreme and enclosed circumstances make their way in an outside world so different in almost every way? I could have written something straightforwardly autobiographical, but I wanted to write a novel that traded on my experience but also went much further, exploring my growing sense that there was no normal world out there, just numerous alternatives, some odder than others. This idea was intensified by what happened to me in 1971.

When the local government wanted Catholic girls admitted into the day school, the priests found the suggestion so repellent they simply shut it down. This meant that I suddenly found myself in a state school surrounded by teachers who were reasonably normal people. One of them, the sculptor Faith Tolkien (daughter-in-law of J. R. R.), had become a teacher to support herself after her divorce, and arrived at her new school to be faced with an extremely unpleasant teenage boy without any academic qualifications (the education I had received was as bad as everything else at the school). I gave her a particularly hard time, I must guiltily admit, but after six months I finally admitted I'd stumbled upon a woman of unique kindness and intelligence. An already implausible life was about to become even stranger.

Once she realized I was not just a sociopath, she went about transforming my life. Because my academic record was so dismal no university would even interview me, so Faith decided to enter me for Oxford, where at the time they offered places based on open competition. She spent a year giving me extra lessons and, despite the dire warnings from her fellow teachers that what she was doing was bound to end badly, I duly took the entrance exam and was accepted. As far as I'm aware I'm the only Oxford graduate ever to have failed all his O-levels. I used to make Faith laugh by telling her that I only went to Oxford because I couldn't get in anywhere else. But having spent so many years in a place utterly removed from the modern world I was now heading into another. Where once I'd slept in the same room as seventy people, surrounded by priests who believed there were real devils flying above them in the night air, I now had a room of my own the size of a small cathedral and a college servant to make my bed, and was surrounded by some of the finest minds anywhere in the world. It was like going from

Mordor to Narnia. What these experiences confirmed for me was that there is no one 'modern world', there are numerous worlds – some of them very large, admittedly – endless alternative realities distinguished from the ones in fantasy and science fiction only by the fact that they actually exist. If you doubt this, consider how unbelievable the world described in the Gondwana synopsis above appears. As those who have read the first two books in The Left Hand of God trilogy will now have realized, The Sanctuary is rooted in a real place. Unsurprisingly enough I clashed with the world of Oxford in pretty much the same way as Cale clashes with the world of Memphis.

By now it was impossible for me to believe in what is called realism in fiction, because my life proved that realism didn't exist; realism didn't have what it takes to explain what's real, just as modernism couldn't explain what was modern. To go back to the fantasy synopsis at the beginning, and to labour the point of what I'm driving at in terms of the sheer melodrama and strangeness of the world we inhabit, I was born in the same year that Stalin, the greatest mass murderer in human history, died. Mao died in the year I graduated from Oxford. In the decade between, while I was relentlessly warned I was going to a spiritual hell, I can remember lying awake in October 1962 worrying, with good reason, about whether the Cuban Missile Crisis was going to bring the world to an end. Within fourteen years of my leaving Oxford, the Soviet Union had collapsed. Within a decade the Chinese empire began its electrifying rise. So if I've strained the point, it's for a good reason. Huge events like this can seem to swamp the individual and their personal story, and so fiction turns its back in the face of a hopeless task and either descends into garish simple-mindedness (though I've also been accused of that) or stylistic narcissism (I've been accused of that, too). But fiction exists in part to dramatize these changes and point out something inescapably true: Mao and Stalin were individuals, not forces. Individuals helped and opposed them, or just watched. The Cuban Missile Crisis emerged out of great ideological clashes, but it was averted, just about, by people not so different from you and me blundering about trying to guess what was going on in the minds of other people trying to do the same thing on the other side of the world. You may notice that Henry Kissinger's comment on this process of powerful individuals blindly trying to direct great matters is quoted twice in *The Beating of His Wings*. The repetition is because I think it's an observation about confusion and its place in all our lives, one that's of central importance to what I'm trying to convey in these books. I hope we can accept as a fictional licence that one person – and a deeply disturbed boy, at that – could be tied in with the kind of rise and fall of empires and ideologies outlined in *The Left Hand of God*; it's the best way I can think of to get a grip on the way individuals and the forces of history, politics and ideology clash in our many and various real worlds.

It would be impossible in a conventional 'realistic' novel to write about this diversity and complexity because there's too much of it. Each section would take years of careful research (I've tried this: *The Wisdom of Crocodiles* took thirteen years to write). By inventing a hypothetical world like that of *The Left Hand of God* (and combining it with the notion of The Rubbish Tips of Paradise as outlined at the start of this novel) it becomes possible to take elements from history – for example, the most romanticized and most hideous of all societies, the Spartans, and mix them with elements of the first true trading bloc, the Hanse. There's nothing impossibly anachronistic about this any more than the fact that the US is now engaged in a war in Afghanistan, a society that is fundamentally early medieval. In an obvious sense we all live in an overblown fantasy novel. But it also enabled me to mix writing about worlds and ideologies of which I had personal experience (Catholicism, the rural poverty I was born into, and the world of Oxford privilege I stumbled into), with worlds and ideologies I had only read about. In this way, I tried to mix and match, copy and re-imagine something of the strangeness of the world we all inhabit – but in a manageable and coherent way. In the year that I first watched my father competing against the Americans and the Russians in his Cold War of Sports, Mao Tse Tung was setting out idealistic policies that were to starve to death as many as thirty-five million people; while I was sitting in my room at Oxford eating crumpets in 1975, Pol Pot was slaughtering more than a quarter of the Cambodian population in order to create year zero for the perfect state. The Catholic world in which I was brought up relentlessly pressed on us one motto in particular: Death rather than sin.

In The Left Hand of God trilogy I've tried to condense the monstrous ideology that human beings must be changed for the better at any cost, an ideology that has so plagued human history, into one person. Redeemer Bosco's plan to remake the human soul by destroying the world is my avatar for this kind of murderous idealism. The trilogy is my way of trying to blend together, in a world of infinite complexity, the relationship between my own life and the extraordinary world into which we've all been born.